\*\*\*\*\*\*\*\*\*\*

**Into the Battle**

Rise of the Republic – Book Two

**By**
**James Rosone**

\*\*\*\*\*\*\*\*\*\*

Illustration © Tom Edwards
Tom EdwardsDesign.com

Published in conjunction with Front Line Publishing, Inc.

ISBN: 978-1-957634-05-0
Sun City Center, Florida, USA
Library of Congress Control Number: 2022902558

# Table of Contents

# Chapter One
## Invasion

**The Rhea System**
**RNS *Rook***

"Captain! We're getting our first signal returns," Commander Fran McKee suddenly announced, concern in her voice. "It appears there are two Zodark ships in the system. One is breaking orbit from New Eden, and another was in orbit around one of her moons, but they're both heading toward us now."

The Earth fleet had only been in the system for sixty-eight minutes before the Zodarks had detected them. "Very well. Let the war begin," Captain Hunt said as he clenched his fists.

He turned to his weapons officer, Lieutenant LaFine. "How long until they're in weapons range at current speed and intercept course?" Hunt asked.

"They're close to eight million kilometers out. I'm estimating at least two and a half hours until they're roughly the same distance as the last time we fought each other."

*God, those ships are moving fast*, Hunt thought, marveling at how quickly they were going to intercept their fleet. If they were at a standstill, it'd take his ship almost ten hours to reach them.

Hunt ordered the ship to general quarters to signal the crew to prepare for battle. They had been speeding ahead of the rest of the assault fleet now for thirty minutes, so they had built up a bit of distance between them and the orbital assaulter ships carrying the Republic Army soldiers and the Deltas that would be carrying out the ground assault.

When the enemy ships were within three million kilometers, they tried to acquire the Earther ships, just like the last time humans had fought the Zodarks.

Twenty minutes later, Commander McKee announced, "They've got a lock on us." The two ships blinked red on the tactical display. A yellow circle was flashing over the top of the *Rook*, indicating lock acquired.

"Lieutenant Commander Robinson," Hunt called out to his electronic warfare officer.

"I'm on it, sir. Commencing jamming now," replied Robinson.

Moments later, the weapons lock on the RNS *Rook* disappeared.

The weapons officer, Lieutenant LaFine, announced, "Captain, the Zodark ships are increasing speed again. They're now one million kilometers out and closing fast. Do you want me to engage them with our Havoc missiles?"

The Havoc was their newest ship-to-ship missile they'd been outfitted with before they left for this mission. The four-stage missiles gave them a lot of controllable range and speed.

"Weapons, hold fire until they reach three hundred thousand kilometers," Hunt commanded. "Then fire a spread of five Havocs at each Zodark ship. Next, fire a single nuke at each ship. Repeat the sequence two more times. Let's test their reaction to our missiles. When they pass two hundred and fifty thousand kilometers, fire the magrails. Send a screen of slugs their way." The magrail slugs were penetrators, designed to punch through a ship's armor and then explode their five-thousand-pound warheads inside the guts of a ship. The warheads also had the capability of detonating via a time delay, proximity to an object, or any other setting the gunners were told to incorporate.

"Yes, sir, we're on it," Lieutenant LaFine replied. His fingers danced across the keys at his console as he relayed the orders to the various weapon sections.

*This battle's unfolding a lot faster than the last one*, Hunt thought apprehensively. During their previous foray into the system, it had taken the *Rook* and the Zodark ship more than five hours to get in range of each other's weapons.

Half an hour later, LaFine announced, "Firing missiles."

Everyone watched the missiles streak away from the *Rook* on the main screen. They looked like little blue arrow icons as they raced toward their targets. Over the next ten minutes, the blue arrows grew to three distinct barrages of missiles. Now it was just a matter of time until they closed in on their targets.

The icon denoting the lead Zodark ship started to blink yellow. The missiles' targeting sensors were burning through the Zodarks' jamming. The icon continued to blink yellow for close to thirty seconds before it became a solid red icon, meaning they had acquired a lock on their Zodark targets.

"The lead Zodark ship is attacking our missiles," LaFine called out as they watched several of their missiles wink out of existence. At first, it was only the lead wave of missiles, then the Zodark ship went after the second wave. The targeting AI responded to the Zodark threat, and the second wave of missiles took evasive maneuvers. Next, the third wave of missiles did the same. Moments later, the Zodark ship fired its pulse beam at the *Rook*.

"They're firing on us," called out one of the officers. "Deploying countermeasures."

The supposedly new and improved sand and water or SW missiles flew out a few megameters in front of the *Rook*, then detonated their sand-water mixture to create a barrier to defray the enemy lasers. It dispersed only part of the Zodark laser before its powerful beam hit them head-on.

"Brace for impact!" yelled Commander McKee as she gripped the edge of her workstation.

"Evasive maneuvers!" shouted Captain Hunt as the helmsman applied power to their forward maneuvering thrusters. The ship veered to the right as they sought to move away from the pulse beam trying to cut through their armor.

The ship shook violently, like it had just hit a wall while moving at full speed, and everyone grabbed for something to steady themselves.

"Try to roll the ship, helmsman!" barked Captain Hunt, hoping they could prevent the laser beam from cutting through their armor like it almost had in the last battle.

"We've got a hull breach on deck four, section two," shouted one of the engineering petty officers. Alarm klaxons blared as red and yellow lights illuminated the damage control board.

The ship turned hard to one side as the Zodark laser lost its position on the hull.

"Damage control teams to deck four, get that breach sealed!" Commander McKee ordered the engineering section on the bridge.

Seconds later, LaFine called out, "Fire main weapons," sending the firing orders to the gun crews.

The outer cameras on the ship showed the magrail turrets moving to face the closest Zodark ship. Seconds later, the guns collectively fired. They kept firing rapidly, sending slug after slug of their new smart munitions at the charging alien ships. The continuous volley of twelve thirty-six-inch shells raced out magnetically charged barrels at twenty-five megameters per hour. The initial spread was crossing the distance between them rapidly as the two warships continued to race toward each other.

"Whoa, what the hell is that?" called out Commander McKee in surprise. "That second ship is launching fighters. I'm showing ten—no, twenty new contacts. Scratch that, it's now fifty new enemy contacts, Captain."

*Damn, now they've got fighters, too?* Captain Hunt bemoaned.

During their last engagement with the Zodarks, the enemy ship hadn't launched any fighters. Then again, neither of these two ships matched the specs of the previous two Zodark vessels they had encountered.

"Alert the point defense systems we have inbound fighters," Captain Hunt ordered. "Fire the main guns at that lead ship. LaFine, we need to take that one out before we engage the other one."

Just then, all but one of the first volley of projectiles missed the Zodark ship as it made a sharp turn. That one projectile made a last-second maneuver that enabled it to hit the rear half of the ship. It sliced right through the armor before its five thousand pounds of high explosives detonated inside the guts of the ship.

The next volley of nine slugs sailed right past the Zodark ship as it made a radical maneuver at the last second. The smart munitions couldn't adjust swiftly enough to score a hit.

When the enemy ship made its last maneuver, the third volley of shells made a rapid adjustment to match the new direction the ship was sailing. Seven of the nine slugs scored direct hits across the midsection and forward section. When the warheads penetrated the Zodarks' armor, the warheads exploded, causing a series of secondary explosions that rippled throughout the enemy ship.

Several small bursts of greenish light flickered from the Zodarks' pulse beam batteries as it targeted the incoming waves of magrail slugs fired from the *Rook*.

"Crap! They're going after our magrails!" shouted Lieutenant LaFine, in shock that they could actually do that.

The *Rook*'s magrail weapons crew watched in horror as several waves of their slugs were zapped out of existence.

The *Rook* shuddered again when the next volley of five Havoc missiles launched. The initial boosters lit up the darkness like a flare as the Havoc missiles raced toward the damaged Zodark ship.

Half of the third wave of Havoc missiles had now closed the gap on the enemy warship. Two of them got zapped out of existence at the last second, but the third, fourth, and fifth missiles managed to score direct hits. Those missiles plowed through several meters of armor before their warheads detonated, ripping a huge gashes in the Zodark vessel.

"They zapped all of our nukes, the bastards," called out one of the targeting officers in disbelief.

As the next volley of missiles took over their independent flight, five additional magrail shells slammed into the top aft section of the Zodark vessel near its engines. Several new explosions rippled throughout the rear part of the warship before the propulsion system flamed out.

"They're dead in space!" Commander McKee shouted excitedly.

"Missiles impacting in ten seconds," called out LaFine as they anxiously watched them track closer and closer. "Three...two...one...impact!" They watched three of their six new missiles explode against the side of the Zodark ship.

"Damn, they got our other nuke," LaFine called out in frustration.

Eight more magrail projectiles slammed into the Zodark ship near the forward section of the vessel. A massive explosion took place, whiting out the screens on the *Rook* for just a moment. Once the sensors adjusted to the flash, the bridge crew saw an incredible sight—the front section of the Zodark ship had been ripped in half. The two chunks continued to separate from the momentum of the blast. Meanwhile, the remaining fires on the two sections slowly died out as the atmosphere that was feeding them bled away.

Before they could celebrate, Commander McKee urgently called out, "Enemy fighters are inbound and engaging us now with a missile...uh, we have another problem. I'm showing one hundred more fighters heading toward us."

The image on the main screen shifted from the broken-apart warship to the second ship that was traveling behind them. This ship appeared twice as large. It was some sort of carrier ship they hadn't encountered before.

The *Voyager*, which had been trailing behind the *Rook*, sent wave after wave of Havoc missiles at the Zodark carrier ship. Strings of magrail slugs from their main guns joined the fray, adding their own volume of fire to the battle.

As the enemy fighters angled in for an attack on the *Rook*, Lieutenant LaFine announced, "Activating point defenses."

Fractions of a second later, the AI took control of the *Rook*'s close-in weapon system or CIWS. The darkness of space around the *Rook* erupted in a spectacular display of fireworks. The ship's forty-two seven-barreled 20mm autocannons spewed out thousands of rounds a second at the Zodark fighters, their missiles, and their torpedoes.

Captain Hunt watched the battle taking place through the video feed of one of their tactical drones. He saw numerous waves of missiles or torpedoes heading right for the *Rook*, with several groups of smaller fighters flying in various formations followed closely behind. Then, the *Rook*'s AI defensive system activated the point defense systems, and the entire space around the *Rook* lit up like a Christmas tree. Red streaks of light from the tracer rounds spewed forth as a veritable wall of lead, shielding the *Rook* from the Zodark missiles.

As the *Rook*'s projectiles eviscerated most of the enemy missiles, the Zodark fighters flew into the maelstrom. Nearly half the fighters were wiped out in the first few seconds before they had time to react.

Several of the enemy missiles, which had been extremely maneuverable, suddenly transformed, becoming what looked like a blazing orange comet and losing some of their maneuverability at the same time. The helmsman of the *Rook* made several hard, radical course corrections, causing some of these mystery weapons to miss the *Rook*, but several more were about to hammer them.

"Brace for impact!" warned Commander McKee as half a dozen missiles that got through their defensive screen streaked through the wall of lead.

*Bam, bam, boom...*

The *Rook* shook violently from each of the impacts. Warning alarms blared and red and yellow lights flashed over different sections of the ship's damage control board.

*Hull breach in deck one, section five.*

*Hull breach in deck one, section twelve.*

*Hull breach in deck six, section two.*

The automated computer alarm called out the severe threats to the ship that demanded immediate attention.

"Firing main guns at the carrier now," LaFine yelled to be heard over the alarms going off around them.

"What the hell hit us?" barked Captain Hunt to no one in particular.

Commander McKee turned to look at him from her console. "I don't know how, but those missiles transformed—they weren't like lasers. They cut a deep gouge in the ship, like one of our magrail slugs would have done."

Captain Hunt shook his head in frustration. *Great, a whole new weapon system to worry about.*

The ship shuddered several times as the main magrail guns turned their attention to the remaining Zodark vessel. The weapons crew fired more Havoc missiles in between volleys from the magrails.

As he continued watching the battle taking place, Captain Hunt saw the remaining enemy fighters repositioning for another assault. He could also see from the drone footage that atmosphere was bleeding from several of the hits his ship had taken. Flames emanated from parts of the *Rook*, while other parts looked blackened and scorched.

"Enemy fighters are coming in for another attack run…missiles inbound…count is rising…forty-two missiles!" Commander McKee called out.

Lieutenant Molly Branson, their coms officer, shouted, "Incoming message from the *Ottawa*. They're moving forward to engage the enemy carrier now."

The view on the large monitor at the front of the bridge shifted from a single image of the fighters closing in on them to a widescreen overview of the battle happening around them. This was the view Captain Hunt had been looking at a few minutes ago. It now showed the *Rook* in the center, surrounded by a small swarm of around forty remaining Zodark fighters. A little further out was the Zodark carrier, fifty thousand kilometers away.

The *Voyager* was now seventy megameters away, speeding forward to get in position to help. The overview also showed the *Ottawa*, one of the newer destroyers, racing ahead of the *Rook* toward the enemy carrier. Its own CIWS point defense weapons were blazing away at the Zodark fighters and missiles as they flew right into the melee. Trailing behind the *Ottawa* were the three other destroyers, looking to get in the fight.

Another monitor on the side of the main bridge screen had a camera following the massive Zodark vessel. It was a real beast of a ship, although Captain Hunt could see multiple spots where their magrails had hit. He watched as the ship conducted a series of radical course corrections every few minutes—whoever was in command of that ship had clearly learned from the first battle that if they wanted to survive, they had to find a way to avoid being pummeled by the *Rook*'s magrail guns.

Just coming into view on the main screen, the *Ottawa* closed the distance between itself and the Zodark carrier. While the *Ottawa* was significantly larger than the Zodark fighters, it was incredibly small in comparison to the Zodark carrier.

When the *Ottawa* got within twenty-five thousand kilometers of the enemy ship, the carrier fired several pulse beams at it. The *Ottawa*, a smaller destroyer with more maneuverability, made a bold series of moves to get away from the beam. When it looked like the strategy had worked, Captain Hunt breathed a sigh of relief.

Moments later, his eyes widened in shock as a third beam sliced right through the *Ottawa*, cutting it in half. The rear half of the destroyer blew apart seconds later.

"Holy crap! They just blew up the *Ottawa* before they could even fire a shot!" one of the officers on the bridge exclaimed. Captain Hunt didn't know who had spoken, but he was thinking the exact same thing.

"Brace for impact!" Commander McKee yelled out again as another pair of Zodark missiles made it through the barrage of point defense shells and then transformed into a comet-like slug.

*Bam, bam!*

More alarm bells went off; a couple of new sections of the ship were flashing yellow. One was flashing red, which meant they had either a severe fire underway or a hull breach in that vicinity.

"Got 'em! That was the last of those little bastards," Lieutenant LaFine announced with satisfaction as the last group of Zodark fighters was finally destroyed.

Returning his gaze to the enemy warship, Captain Hunt watched a string of shells from the *Rook*'s main gun hit the Zodark carrier. He'd counted at least twelve hits against the carrier so far. He relaxed his clenched fists a bit when he saw the Zodark carrier's failed attempts to outmaneuver the magrail shells.

Flames poured out of the Zodark vessel in several sections. It was clear more and more of the *Rook*'s magrail slugs were punching through their armor and causing serious damage to the guts of the ship. One hit blew out a massive jet of flames before it extinguished itself.

Captain Hunt hated relying on their magrails and missiles to destroy the Zodark ship. Magrails took time to cross the vast distance, giving the enemy vessel time for defensive maneuvers, and causing many of their magrail slugs to miss the mark. Sadly, the Republic Navy starships' pulse beam lasers weren't strong enough to cut through the enemy's armor like kinetic weapons could.

In contrast, each time the Zodark carrier fired one of its pulse beams at the *Rook*, it slammed into his ship seconds later. The *Rook* was taking so many hits that Captain Hunt wasn't sure they were going to make it. Looking at the damage control board, he saw yellow lights across dozens of areas of the ship intermixed with flashing red sections. He was losing people, a lot of people. He needed to end this fight promptly or his ship was doomed. But his only strategy was to keep firing missiles and hoping their slugs eventually blew something critical up.

It felt like forever, but the *Voyager* was finally within range to join the fray. Volley after volley of their magrail slugs slammed into the Zodark ship. The *Voyager* steadily moved into a blocking position between the *Rook* and the enemy vessel to act as a shield.

As Captain Hunt watched the *Voyager* block for them, the Zodark warship appeared to pick up speed to make a run for it.

Two of the three remaining RNS destroyers finally caught up to the *Rook* and were in range to fire their own weapons. They initiated a series of magrail volleys and missiles at the retreating Zodark ship as they joined the fray on the flanks of the *Voyager*.

When the RNS destroyers got within twenty thousand meters of the enemy vessel, the Zodarks fired several pulse beams at the smaller Republic warships. One of the beams hit the lead destroyer, and like the *Ottawa*, the ship was cut right in half. A second later, another beam sliced off the front section of a third destroyer, crippling it. The last destroyer broke away, trying to escape the Zodark ship's pulse beam. It was becoming abundantly clear the new RNS destroyer armor spec was no match for the Zodark pulse beams at close range.

"Take that ship out before it can get away!" Captain Hunt roared angrily, growing frustrated that the Zodark vessel was successfully opening up some distance between them. If the enemy ship kept gaining speed, they were going to escape.

A few minutes later, a stream of thirty-six-inch magrail shells finally landed all along the rear section of the Zodark carrier. Seconds later, a massive explosion ripped two of the six engine ports right off the main body of the ship. Then another volley of slugs pounded the wounded carrier further.

On the bridge of the *Rook*, the computer monitors briefly whited out again from another massive flash of an explosion. When the resolution came back in focus, they saw a chunk of the rear section of the Zodark carrier blown wide open. Without engines, it was adrift, only moving from its initial forward momentum.

Hunt watched the ship slide sideways a little bit; it was clearly not able to stabilize itself. With the engines and main reactor offline, the remaining weapon systems appeared nonfunctional. A few lights indicated a functioning power source, but the ship was no longer firing at them.

A wild thought entered Captain Hunt's mind. He turned to his XO. "Commander McKee, send a message to the rest of the fleet to cease fire. Next, send a message to the Delta commander—tell him to board that vessel if possible and capture it. Take prisoners if they'll give themselves up, but let's take that ship."

She smiled at the idea, even though she looked like it was probably the craziest thing she'd ever heard. McKee reached for her communicator and passed the order along to their ground detachment.

The Deltas were the shock troops for both space and ground combat. They had trained to conduct hostile boardings of spacecraft, assault orbital stations, or attack ground facilities from orbit. Having undergone a year of physical enhancements and augmentations, they were a cut above their regular army counterparts, the Republic Army soldiers. They were far and above the most feared soldiers in Sol.

"Captain, Admiral Halsey is sending you a message," his coms officer relayed.

Captain Hunt nodded in acknowledgment. "I'll take it at my station."

He moved back to his captain's chair and opened the channel. He saw her tense face, strained by stress. "Captain Hunt, is your ship OK? It looks like you sustained some serious damage."

Glancing over at the damage report readout, he did a quick scan. "Nothing we can't fix, Admiral. We have a couple of hull breaches, but they didn't punch too deep. Four meters of armor is clearly not enough when going up against these bastards, that's for sure."

"Well, in any case, good shooting," Halsey replied. "What's with calling a cease-fire? We were just about to finish that ship off."

Captain Hunt paused for a moment. "If you agree, I plan on ordering my Special Forces to board it and capture it," he explained.

A smile crept across Admiral Halsey's face. "Really? What makes you think you can capture it?"

"I think if the enemy was going to abandon ship, they would have already done it," Hunt pointed out. "That leads me to believe they're going to make repairs to regain control. Right now, the ship doesn't appear to have power to its weapons or propulsion systems, which gives us a unique opportunity. If we can get a boarding party on the ship and take control of it, it'll be an enormous intelligence boon. Admiral, I think it's worth the risk."

Instead of overriding him, Admiral Halsey nodded as if praising his initiative. "Good call, Hunt. Do you want us to assist you?"

Captain Hunt looked at the drifting enemy ship for a moment and thought about how to respond. He hadn't really considered how *many* Zodarks might be on board. He had a company of Deltas led by Captain Hopper that could do a lot on their own, but having more soldiers on hand couldn't hurt either.

"I think Captain Hopper would appreciate the help, Admiral," Hunt finally said with a nod. "Once my Deltas depart the ship, I'd like to continue toward New Eden while we repair the ship. Then we can conduct a more thorough scan of the moons and the planet before the rest of the fleet gets much closer."

She wrinkled her brow like she was about to disagree with his assessment, but then she consented. "OK, Captain, you can continue toward the planet, but only if you think your ship is still able to carry the fight to the enemy. Right now, you look pretty beat up. I don't want to risk losing the *Rook* because we didn't take the time to get her fully repaired. In the meantime, I'll take operational control of the Deltas once they leave your vessel. Oh, and Captain, when you do get near the planet and those moons, deploy your satellites and surveillance drones. I want to know what's down there and what we're facing."

"We're on it, Admiral," Hunt replied with a smile. "If my engineers tell me we need some time or even a day or two to get things fully repaired, we'll wait. I won't risk the ship like that." With that, he cut the feed and got in touch with his Delta commander. He wanted to personally brief him on the new mission he was giving them.

## Chapter Two
## Hostile Boarding

**RNS** *Rook*

The Synth drones had attached close to three dozen small thrusters to the front of the vessel to slow it down. That was a bit of a test, to see if the Zodarks had any defensive capability to stop them. When the enemy didn't interfere in their operation, the Deltas figured they probably wouldn't encounter any resistance in attaching their own ship to the vessel once they found a soft spot to breach.

Captain Hopper cleared his throat. "Listen up, Deltas! This is going to be a combat breach of a massive Zodark vessel. The only intelligence we have on this thing is it appears to be some sort of carrier. It was deploying fighters to attack our ship when its engines were sheared off, leaving it adrift and out of power. This ship isn't going anywhere, and our admiral wants it.

"As the captain said earlier, chances are this ship has enormous intelligence value, so it's worth the risk for us to board and seize it. We will attach ourselves to one of the many holes in the ship created by our magrails. Because we have no idea if the ship has lost its atmosphere, or what kind of atmosphere the Zodarks actually maintain on their ships, I want everyone to keep your combat suits sealed up."

The briefing went on for another ten minutes. They went over what squads would handle each part of the breach and then how the platoons would handle clearing the ship. Their primary goal was securing a couple of additional sections so the rest of their Delta battalion on the *Voyager* could join them. Then they'd systematically work on clearing the ship of enemy combatants.
*******

Master Sergeant Brian Royce made his rounds as the soldiers prepared to leave, checking on his platoon to make sure they were packing extra fragmentation grenades and flashbangs. He wanted his platoon armed and ready for a close-quarter fight, which meant bringing some additional tools of the trade.

Twenty minutes later, Master Sergeant Royce's platoon climbed into their Osprey and prepared to embark upon a historic mission for the Special Forces community: the first-ever seizing of an alien space vessel.

As the soldiers strapped themselves into their harnesses and attached their rifles to the locking port next to their seats, the two crew chiefs walked down each side of the craft, doing a quick double-check of their passengers and equipment. When their shuttle was hurled down the magnetic launch tube, the last thing they wanted was a piece of equipment not being properly locked down, flying around and injuring people or vital ship systems.

Lieutenant Aaron Crocker was seated near the flight engineer and the pilot; he'd help them find a spot to insert the platoon. Royce, meanwhile, was positioned near the rear troop hatch.

Some of the soldiers were whispering quiet prayers, some rubbing a rosary while saying a few Hail Mary's. Others were playing whatever workout or fight song they'd selected to get them pumped up and ready for the mission. Each soldier, man or woman, had their own private ritual before the start of a mission. Royce had his own routine; he'd usually listen to a hard-hitting rock band. Now, as the platoon sergeant, it was his responsibility to make sure his soldiers were ready for combat.

"Everyone's ready, all equipment is locked down," called out one of the crew chiefs to the pilots and the flight engineer.

Moments later, the Osprey moved forward until it was safely in the magnetic launch tube, ready to be shot down into the blackness of space. Another minute went by, and then they felt the Osprey being hurled forward. In seconds, they were weightless in their straps, on their way to make history.

The pilots banked their shuttle towards the alien craft and chased after it. The closer they got to it, the more imposing it seemed. They knew how big it was because they'd been briefed, but nothing could prepare them for seeing how enormous it was close up. The Zodark carrier ship was still moving at a good clip while the temporary thrusters steadily slowed the beast down.

As Master Sergeant Royce looked forward to the cockpit of the shuttle, his eyes went a little wide as he saw how big the Zodark ship was.

He chuckled to himself as he thought, *That's what she said...*

"What's so funny, Sergeant?" Lieutenant Crocker inquired. The lieutenant had a slight grin on his face like he almost knew what he had thought. The two of them had become pretty good friends over the last year.

Royce blushed briefly. Not wanting to share this private thought aloud or over the NL, he coughed and replied, "Oh, um, I'll tell you after we get back on the ship, sir. Time to put our war faces on."

He refocused his mind, then barked out, "This is it, Deltas! We've trained to assault a hostile ship in space. We've trained on how to clear a warship in zero g. Now it's time to earn our pay and put that training to good use. I want weapons set on blasters—no magrails unless I order it."

The Osprey sped over toward the Zodark ship, zipping past blown-out chunks and holes in the armor from the engagement with the *Rook*. Captain Hopper pointed at something, and the pilots steered in its direction. A few minutes later, they descended over a section of the ship with a massive blast hole. The Osprey was more than large enough to cover the entire hole.

When the Osprey settled on the outer hull of the Zodark vessel, one of the crew chiefs released his harness and floated for a moment in the troop compartment until his magnetic boots attached to the floor. With a metallic clunking noise with each step, he then made his way over to look at one of the computer panels. He hit a few buttons, and everyone felt the shuttle latch itself to the Zodark vessel as the ship created an artificial seal between the two ships. A few seconds later, they heard a hissing noise as the compartment below them pressurized just a bit. They weren't filling it with oxygen, but they were making sure there wasn't a vacuum building up beneath them or a pressure buildup that might break the ship's seal.

The crew chief then gave the pilot and Captain Hopper an all clear. They could begin their operations.

Nodding, the captain turned to Royce and gave him a thumbs-up to get things going.

Master Sergeant Royce made sure his boot magnets were activated before unstrapping himself. Standing up, he barked, "Breaching team, on me."

Royce made his way over to the floor hatch in the center of the shuttle. A moment later, the crew chief told him they were ready. Royce brought his rifle up and flicked the safety off. So did the rest of his breaching team. The crew chief then unsealed the hatch and opened it, revealing to everyone on the Osprey a real honest-to-goodness alien ship.

Royce aimed his rifle with its powerful light down into the dark hole. *Nothing. All clear.*

He turned to his team. "Follow me," he ordered as he disconnected his magnetic boots from the floor and dropped down into the blown-out cavern below.

Royce floated down fifteen meters to the bottom before his magnetic boots attached to the ship, leveling him out. The two flashlights attached to the shoulders of his suit flicked on, providing him with enough light to see around him. The rest of his five-man breaching team landed moments later and joined him. The team did a quick check of the hole, looking for a bulkhead or compartment door they could breach and gain entry into the ship. It wasn't easy, since they had no idea where they were on the alien ship, or what lay on the opposite side of the sealed bulkheads.

Royce reasoned that if a Zodark ship was anything like a human ship, they had corridors and bulkheads—compartments they could seal up in case of a hull breach. After a few minutes of searching through the torn and twisted metal, one of his Deltas found a hatched door about ten feet in height, about the same size as a Zodark.

One of the Deltas walked up to the door and pulled out a small cutting laser. He activated it and used it almost like a pen as he cut a hole into the door.

Meanwhile, Royce sent a message through his NL, telling the rest of the platoon on the Osprey to join them.

Once a hole in the bulkhead had been cut open, the first several Deltas moved in, rifles at the ready. Royce was the third guy in the bulkhead. Soon he found that his instincts were correct—the Zodark ship was laid out like a human vessel, with sealed hatches separating long hallways to prevent a massive depressurization in case of a hull breach.

Royce immediately noticed as soon as they entered the hull that the artificial gravity had returned. He wasn't sure how or why, but as soon as he had gained entry into the hull, he was back to operating in a typical gravity environment.

*That's going to make our job of securing the ship a lot easier*, he thought.

The Deltas advanced thirty meters into the hallway before they came across the next sealed door. The guy who had cut through the first door moved forward and proceeded to cut a hole in the next hatch. He'd barely started cutting when the locking latch suddenly lifted and the door was pulled inwards, away from the Deltas.

Master Sergeant Royce saw a Zodark standing in the doorway. The blue four-armed alien with vicious looking talons had a look of shock on his face when he realized who had been cutting through the door.

"Charge!" Royce yelled as he ran forward. He lowered his shoulder and rammed into the Zodark's stomach, knocking the enormous ten-foot-tall creature down.

Three or four Deltas ran and jumped past Royce and the Zodark he had tackled to the ground as they searched for more targets further down the hallway.

When the Zodark recovered from his initial shock, he grabbed Royce. Seemingly without effort, the ferocious creature threw Royce across the hallway into a wall. Before he could respond, one of his Deltas fired his blaster at the Zodark, killing him.

After Royce had a few seconds to shake off the shock of being thrown, he nodded his thanks at the Delta who'd covered for him and took off at a trot to catch up to the rest of his team. As he ran, he heard a lot of shouting ahead from the Zodarks and some of his own soldiers. Blasters were being fired. Then the heavier M90 squad automatic weapon tore into something. After that, he heard the unfamiliar sound of some unknown weapon firing.

Royce brought his rifle to his shoulder as he joined his team.

"Frag out!" shouted one of the Deltas. A few seconds later, an explosion ripped through the air.

Shouts and screams of agony, presumably from a Zodark, echoed throughout the corridor. It sounded horrible to Royce's ears. It was a shrill and dissonant noise he'd never heard, and it really unsettled him.

As Royce rounded the corner, he saw the hallway open into a large flight deck. There were a couple of shuttlecraft and what looked like a starfighter. He also observed numerous piles of containers or large boxes positioned along the walls in neat looking rows.

Royce spotted three of his soldiers propped up against some container boxes, using them for cover. A dozen enemy soldiers on the opposite side of the hangar were firing at them. Royce picked a container for his own cover and started shooting at the hostiles.

Then a second group of Zodarks appeared from another corridor further down the hangar. That group fanned out and added a volume of fire to the melee.

*This is turning into a hot mess.*

Royce pivoted his rifle toward this new threat and fired several of his 20mm smart munitions at them. The AI targeting computer built into his M85 configured the rounds to explode at just the right position to inflict the most damage possible. Royce wanted the enemy to keep their heads down while more of his team filtered into the hangar. If he took a few of them out in the process, that was a bonus.

"Keep that SAW going on that group at two o'clock! Gregory, I want that freaking HB firing yesterday!" roared one of Royce's squad leaders.

Private Gregory, their M91 heavy blaster soldier, changed positions to aim at the cluster of enemy soldiers Royce had fired on a few seconds earlier. In seconds, the soldier had a near-constant stream of blaster bolts firing at the Zodarks, who were trying to move around their flank.

Flashes of light flew in Royce's direction and toward his soldiers. It was definitely a chaotic mess. Royce ducked just as an energy burst impacted the containers he and Private Gregory were hiding against. The energy bolts blew the containers apart and the overpressure of the explosion threw the two of them backward. Their bodies skidded across the metal floor of the hangar until they thudded against the wall.

Private Gregory didn't miss a beat; the young soldier rolled into a kneeling position with his M91 tucked in his shoulder and cut loose a solid three-second burst at three Zodarks who had charged toward them.

"Frag out!" yelled another soldier further away from Royce as he threw a pair of grenades at the Zodarks.

Royce caught a glint of something heading right for him. He rolled instinctively to his left just as two blaster bolts hit the floor of the hangar where his body had just been. He leaped to his feet and ran toward the starfighter, fifteen meters in front of him. With his rifle tucked in his shoulder, he squeezed the trigger, hitting one Zodark in the chest, another in the left shoulder, and a third one center mass in the face. All three of them went down, either dead or writhing in pain.

"Someone needs to cover that right flank!" yelled Sergeant Wagner, the leader of the second squad.

*'Bout time they got up here*, Royce said to himself as he took a knee behind the starfighter's nose gear.

"Covering fire!" yelled one of the soldiers to Royce's left.

Two of Royce's soldiers jumped up and ran forward toward another object to hide behind, while a handful of his guys laid down a steady barrage of blaster fire.

Royce watched one of those balls of light fly out from the Zodark weapon and hit one of his soldiers in midstride. The soldier staggered forward, convulsing as if he'd been struck by lightning. Then his lifeless body slid across the floor from his forward momentum until it hit a container and stopped moving.

Several blaster shots hit the starfighter Royce was hiding behind, forcing him to roll and duck behind another piece of equipment, one that they likely used to service the craft. As Royce moved to the new position, he shifted his rifle, aiming it in the direction of the enemy fire. The AI targeting tool helped him zero in on two Zodarks near his position, and he squeezed the trigger. The first few blaster bolts hit the first Zodark several times in the chest; more slammed into his comrade, ripping two of his four arms right off. Then a third shot ripped open part of the second Zodark's neck, spraying bluish liquid everywhere.

"They're charging up the middle!" roared Sergeant Wagman as his squad rushed forward to fill in the gap.

The sound of battle was growing louder as more human soldiers filtered into the hangar. Two of Royce's Deltas lobbed a couple of fragmentation grenades in the direction of the enemy while another three Deltas laid down covering fire, screaming and shouting as they did.

*Crump, crump!*

When the grenades went off, they tore into the remaining Zodarks, who appeared surprised by the power of these little devices. The charging soldiers managed to finish off the last of the enemy in the hangar.

As the shooting came to a halt, Royce jumped out from behind his covered position and moved forward with his other soldiers to make sure the enemy soldiers were dead. Approaching the dead, dismembered, and wounded Zodarks, Royce observed some of his soldiers double-tapping the bodies as they neared them. Royce did the same to the Zodark bodies near him as well. They weren't about to let some of them play possum, and frankly, they had no idea if they were legitimately dead or just knocked unconscious.

Using the NL, Royce sent a quick update to Captain Hopper and urged him to get the rest of the company up to the hangar. This was a big place for him to hold on to with a little more than a squad.

*Master Sergeant, how large is that hangar? Can you hold it with the soldiers you have while we work on securing another section closer to the Osprey's breaching point?* Captain Hopper inquired.

Royce shook his head in frustration. He'd already looked at the platoon's blue force tracker, and he knew they needed help. *Negative, sir, this place is too big for a single squad to hold. I've got six KIAs and three wounded. There are several corridors that appear to lead further into the ship—we'll probably see some pockets of enemy soldiers moving to engage us from there.*

A few tense seconds passed before Royce received a reply. *That's a good copy. I'm heading your way with the rest of the platoon. I've got the other three Ospreys swapping positions with ours to disembark the rest of the company. We'll have more troops there shortly. Just hang tight.*

Royce sighed as he took the pause in the battle to catch his breath. He watched the other soldiers double-check their powerpacks on their M85s and magazines on their grenade launcher. No one knew for sure when more Zodarks would show up again, so they were using the short reprieve to get ready.

Moments later, a new sound echoed throughout the hangar deck—a weird alarm similar to the general quarters alarm they'd heard on the *Voyager* and *Rook*. Then a Zodark voice spoke loudly and urgently over a PA system.

"This doesn't sound good, Sarge. What's the plan?" asked Sergeant Peckman, one of his other squad leaders.

Royce shook his head in frustration. It was taking too long for the rest of their unit to catch up. "Screw it, follow me!" he bellowed. "Let's keep killing these animals. Hopper and the rest of them can catch up with us. We can't stay here with our thumbs up our rears while we allow the enemy to regroup and attack us again.

"Wagman, stay here with the remainder of your squad," Royce continued. "Guard the wounded and make sure no other Zodarks pop out of those entrances down there."

With the decision made, Royce raised his rifle to his shoulder and moved forward down the corridor out of the hangar, taking the rest of the squad deeper into the bowels of the ship, with Sergeant Peckman taking up the rear.

The AI targeting system built into their heads-up displays sent out small radio pulses ahead of them. The HUDs acted like sonar as the radio waves traveled down the corridor and into any open spaces, mapping out potential threats and giving him a good view of what lay ahead.

What the HUD was telling Royce now was that a large group of Zodarks were forming up a few bulkheads in front of them. If he maintained their current direction, he'd lead his squad right into them.

He passed the word along to the rest of his team and shared the view he was seeing with them. After brainstorming a few options, they opted to form a firing line. Royce ordered them to flick their M85s from blaster to magrail as they readied their rifles.

The six of them stood there, rifles pointed at the next sealed-off bulkhead, ready for the Zodarks to enter the compartment on the other side. As soon as they did, they'd all cut loose with their magrails. Unlike the blasters, the magnetic railguns would send projectiles right through several inches of armor or steel. They'd punch right through the bulkhead, eviscerating everyone on the other side.

A voice chirped in Royce's head through the neurolink. *Master Sergeant, hold your position,* Captain Hopper ordered. *We've just entered the hangar. I'm sending another squad to back you guys up. The rest of the unit is going to fan out down the other parts of the corridor. We have Fourth Platoon swapping places with our shuttle right now. We got held up resealing some of the bulkheads so they could disconnect and the new shuttle could deliver our reinforcements.*

Shaking his head in frustration, Royce replied, *Good copy. We've got about thirty tangos heading toward us. When they enter the next corridor, we're going to light them up with the magrails.*

*That's a good copy. Just don't go crazy with the magrails inside the ship. We don't need any more hull breaches to contend with.*

Royce noted that Hopper didn't tell him he *couldn't* proceed with his current plan. That was permission enough. Otherwise, his eight soldiers didn't stand a chance.

"They're moving into the next corridor now," called out one of the soldiers nervously.

That was the cue. Royce nodded, then shouted, "Let 'em have it!"

In the next ten seconds, the six of them unloaded more than five hundred 5.56mm projectiles right through the sealed bulkhead in front of them and into the corridor behind it. The rounds sliced through the Zodarks, who had tightly grouped themselves together as they prepared to charge out of the hallway to attack them.

One of Royce's soldiers fired his 20mm explosive penetrator into the torn-apart bulkhead door, and it exploded in the middle of the wounded Zodarks. Their screaming and wailing was utterly horrific. It was terrifying in its own right, but they couldn't dwell on that. They had to push through and finish them off and then continue clearing the ship.

Just as Royce's soldiers were about to move forward, one of the Zodarks flipped the body of one of his comrades off himself and fired his blaster at them. One of Royce's soldiers took two shots to the upper chest and face. The man was flung backward from the blast, dead before his brain could register what had just happened. Another soldier charged forward, firing his rifle, but was hit multiple times in the chest before he could take the attacker out.

Chris, one of Royce's soldiers and friends, ducked to the left, just in front of him. He was suddenly hit by two rounds that would have hit Royce but claimed Chris instead.

Master Sergeant Brian Royce watched the look of surprise cover Chris's face, then he saw intense pain right before the light in his eyes faded out entirely. It all happened so fast, yet each second played out like a movie, with Royce in the audience, unable to stop it from happening.

Royce screamed with a primordial rage from the depths of his soul as he pushed past his now-dead friend. He charged into the piles of corpses and dying Zodarks toward the one beast that had played possum and killed two members of his platoon. He fired his magrail relentlessly into the enemy soldier, watching one of the projectiles rip a chunk of the monster's face off as two more hit him in the upper chest. A third and fourth round struck him in the neck, practically severing his head. He fell backward from the blows onto a pile of bodies. Bluish liquid and gore splashed everywhere and pooled on the floor.

As Royce jumped into the middle of the melee, he struck one wounded Zodark in the side of the head with the butt of his rifle, fired a point-blank shot into the face of another, and then butt-stroked a third across the face as he brought his blaster to bear on him.

Three more Zodarks jumped into the bloody melee from the next corridor as they sought to stop these human soldiers from taking their ship. One of the Zodarks' hands grabbed the back of Royce's exoskeleton combat suit and threw him across the confined space until he hit a wall.

Royce's rifle clattered to the ground from the hard hit just as a clenched fist connected with his abdominal armor plate. The punch practically knocked the wind out of him. If he hadn't been in his combat suit, he was certain it would have killed him. Royce looked for his rifle, but it was out of reach. One of the Zodark's other arms grabbed at Royce's helmet and bashed his head against the wall, causing him to see stars.

Using his free arm, Royce's right hand unsheathed his six-inch combat blade and jabbed it into the side of the Zodark's throat. He twisted it briefly and then, using the added mechanical strength of his combat suit, yanked it hard, practically severing the beast's head in the process. The Zodark dropped limply before him.

Another Zodark had drawn two shortswords in place of his blaster and was hacking one of Royce's soldiers to pieces. Royce reared his hand back and threw his knife for all its worth at the back of the Zodark. The blade sailed through the air and dug deep into the creature's back. The beast let out a guttural scream as he reached around to try and pull the blade out of his back.

Reaching down to his right thigh, Royce grabbed for his M72 Sig Sauer pistol and fired the hand cannon at the wounded Zodark. He then turned and fired several more rounds into the lone surviving Zodark, who had been rolling on the ground in a hand-to-hand fight with two of his guys.

At this point, Royce and the three remaining soldiers collapsed to the floor or sat against the wall, exhausted and shell-shocked from what they had just lived through. This had been worse than any of their previous battles with the Zodarks.

As Royce looked around them, all he saw was dead bodies. He turned around to where they had just come from and saw the bodies of five comrades killed in the confrontation.

A couple of seconds later, thirteen more Deltas from the second squad walked up to them, clearly appalled to see Royce sitting there, pistol in hand in the center of the corridor, completely surrounded by dead enemy soldiers.

Master Sergeant Royce looked down. Bluish blood and gore covered his body armor. The carnage that lay before them was surreal.

"Master Sergeant, are you OK?" asked the newly arrived squad leader in a tone of deep concern. The man was a staff sergeant, and one of Royce's friends.

Royce only now fully realized that they had caught up to them. He nodded slowly, not saying anything as the alien blood continued to drip off his armor and pistol.

He shook himself free of the daze he'd been in, walked over to one of the dead Zodarks and pulled his knife out of the beast's back. After wiping the blood off the blade, he placed it back in his chest rig. Then he holstered his pistol and reached for his rifle.

Royce paused for a second. When he saw everyone still looking at him, he was spent emotionally. But they still had a job to do. So, he turned away and called out loudly, "Come on! We have more of them to kill if we're going to capture this ship."

He then raised his rifle to his shoulder and pressed forward, deeper into the Zodark carrier, his soldiers following him.
*******

For the next two days, three companies of Deltas fought to clear and capture the massive Zodark vessel. The Zodarks put up a hell of a fight as they battled the Deltas at every turn. Ultimately, the Deltas' superior tactics and the use of their magrail guns in certain instances subdued the remaining Zodarks. Eventually, the Deltas were able to hack into the ship's onboard PA system. They started broadcasting an offer to accept surrender in the Zodarks' language.

"There is no more need to die or waste your lives," the announcement began.

At first, the message seemed to have no effect whatsoever, but they stayed patient and kept trying. In the meantime, they stopped trying to seize the ship in hopes that their offer might be accepted. After several hours of playing their message, eventually, a Zodark called out to them.

"I'd like to speak with whoever is in charge," he shouted. The translators in their helmets spoke the Zodark words to them in English almost simultaneously.

Major Cornelius stepped forward. "I'm the man in charge," he announced, his translator spitting his words out in Zodark. Cornelius was the battalion commander for the 2nd Battalion, 1st Special Forces Group. He was the lead Special Forces officer in charge of this expedition. He'd flown over to the Zodark vessel a few hours ago, once they'd offered some terms of surrender.

The Zodark puffed his chest out a bit as he stood as erect as his body would allow. He stood a little over three meters tall and looked like a towering giant compared to the humans who'd boarded his ship.

"I am NOS Grakus. I am the commander of this ship," the Zodark began, studying Cornelius's body armor and helmet as he spoke. "Are you the commander of the starship that fought me? Who are you? Where have you come from?"

The major nodded and waved his arm to signal that the two of them should walk to the side of the hangar to talk. The beast didn't move at first, but then he followed the lead of the soldier who had boarded his ship.

"Royce, keep the guys ready, I'm going to accompany the major," Lieutenant Crocker said in a hushed tone so only the two of them could hear.

"Copy that, sir. Stay frosty, head on a swivel with these animals," Royce said calmly in reply.

Lieutenant Crocker, along with several soldiers, stood not too far from the Zodark and their commander as they watched the interplay take place.

Cornelius unfastened his helmet and took it off. The Zodark let out a curse word and uttered the term the Sumerians had told them meant "slaves." It must be how the Zodarks viewed their human pets.

"Thank you for agreeing to talk with me," Cornelius said, speaking first. "I was hoping we could find some way to end this fighting."

The NOS let out a guttural laugh before he looked down at the Delta commander. "We are Zodarks; we do not surrender. You—you are our cattle, our slaves. Wherever your people came from, we will find you, and you will pay tribute to us like every other human colony, or your entire planet will be wiped out."

Before Cornelius could respond, the big creature swiped at the major's face and head with his talon-like fingernails, practically ripping the Delta commander's face clean off. Then, one of his four hands reached down to grab at something on his utility belt and hit a button. Fractions of a second later, an explosion ripped through the hangar deck.

Lieutenant Crocker and several of the soldiers standing guard with him were vaporized in the blast, along with half a dozen other soldiers further away. Then guttural yells emanated from several parts of the ship as the remaining defenders did their best to fight and liberate their vessel from the humans who had boarded it.

Over the next several hours, hand-to-hand combat determined their fate as they engaged in the most brutal fighting since they had first boarded the ship. Red and blue blood painted the halls, and dead bodies were stacked throughout the ship. Eventually, the remaining defenders were wiped out, due in large part to the advantage that the magrails and hand grenades had provided to the Earthers. A total of twenty-six Zodarks surrendered. When they finished counting the bodies, they found that almost two thousand Zodarks had been killed in this brutal combat.

With the ship now in their control, the Republic set about the task of towing it back to New Eden while their scientists and engineers continued to examine it. Several of their Sumerian allies came aboard to help them understand the Zodark technology. It was going to take them some time to learn and understand what they had captured. Of paramount importance, though, was learning as much as they could about the enemy vessel's offensive and defensive capabilities so they could develop a counterplan to deal with them.
*******

**New Eden**
**RNS *Voyager***

As Admiral Abigail Halsey looked at the casualty reports from the capture of the Zodark ship, her stomach tightened. She felt ill, knowing how many of her Special Forces soldiers she'd lost. If these enhanced super-soldiers had this tough of a fight against the enemy on a ship, how much tougher were the Zodarks going to be on the surface of a planet, where it would be easier to hide and avoid detection?

Placing the casualty report down, she looked at the latest damage report assessment from Captain Hunt. The *Rook* had somehow survived battle with not one but two Zodark ships. But it had sustained some serious damage during the clash. Captain Hunt had initially thought the ship was in better shape; however, after further examination of the hits they'd taken, it was clear they were going to need more than a few days to get everything repaired. Ultimately, what they needed was a shipyard.

One of the three main magrail turrets had been damaged, and it looked like it was going to take them several more days to get just one of the three barrels operational again. Two of the ordnance fabricators on the decks below the main turrets had been thoroughly destroyed— that meant they only had one functional fabricator.

Hunt's crew had also suffered badly. He tried to play off the injuries, insisting that many of them were, in fact, walking wounded. But when Halsey talked privately with the *Rook*'s lead medical officer, the commander told her a different story. Of the six hundred and twenty-eight sailors assigned to the *Rook*, two hundred and thirty-four had been killed during the battle or died shortly after it had ended. Another three hundred and fifty-six sailors had been injured. While many of the crew were functionally wounded and still able to perform their duties, they were nowhere near ready for another fight.

Suddenly a chime at the door to Halsey's office sounded, letting her know someone was outside. "Enter," she commanded.

She smiled when Admiral Zheng Lee walked in. He was the Tri-Parte Alliance or TPA commander, and technically, her second-in-command. He commanded the eight heavy transports and two warships their alliance had sent to be a part of this joint fleet.

"Admiral Halsey, it's good to see you," he responded with a smile. "I felt this meeting might be better held in person than over the holograph. May we take a seat?" asked Admiral Zheng as he motioned for them to move to a pair of couches she had set up in her office.

"Of course, Admiral Zheng. Thank you for reaching out," replied Halsey. "Yes, let's take a seat and talk."

She walked over to a small table nearby and proceeded to prepare a tea for the admiral and a black cup of joe for herself. She then carried the two drinks over to the couch, handing the Chinese commander his favorite brand of tea, while she sat down opposite him with her coffee. They each took a minute to take a couple of sips before they got down to business.

Admiral Zheng began. "Admiral Halsey, I wanted to congratulate your forces on successfully capturing the enemy warship. I know it wasn't easy, and your people suffered some terrible losses in the process. I also feel for the loss of your other ships in this, our first real battle with the enemy. I must say, it was a terrifying battle to watch unfold from afar.

"For a moment, we thought the *Rook* was lost. The ship was being pounded so hard by the enemy lasers and those new comet-weapons. We'd never seen anything like it. By chance, were your forces able to capture any of them on the enemy carrier?"

Halsey nodded. "As a matter of fact, Admiral, we captured a lot of them. The Sumerians tell us they're plasma torpedoes. We also seized more than a dozen of those fighters they attacked us with and a couple of different types of shuttlecraft. When we get the ship towed back closer to New Eden and we offload your heavy transports, I'd like to load up as much of the Zodark equipment as possible. I'll send it back to Sol so our scientists can start studying it.

"I'm also having our engineers cut off some portions of the enemy ship's armor and dismantling some of their pulse beam weapons as best we can so we can bring it back to be studied. The more we can research their technology, the more we can integrate that knowledge into the new warships we're building back home."

Admiral Zheng smiled at the news. "This is most reassuring, Admiral. I'm glad our two nations are finding ways to work together and share technology like this. I believe our joint efforts are going to give our people a fighting chance against these hideous beasts." He paused to take a sip of tea. "So, what would you like my force to do now that the main battle is over?" he asked. "What are your thoughts on how you'd like my ships and transports to deploy?"

Admiral Halsey paused for a moment as she thought about that. Finally, she leveled her gaze at him. "First, we need to scan the surface of New Eden and start looking for signs of any Zodark forces. They may have established some military outposts or reinforced some of their mining camps. In either case, we need to neutralize them quickly and then secure the mines. We've got to start mining as much of the Trimar and Morean minerals as we can and get them transported back to Earth. Those are the only resources our shipyards need to get the rest of our new fleet built. We've got to turn this system into a fortress before the enemy can reinforce it on us."

"I agree with you, Admiral," Zheng replied. "If you do not oppose, I'd like to offer our two warships, the *Han* and the *Xi*, to move into orbit of New Eden and start working on identifying what possible enemy encampments are down there. Do I have your permission to issue the order?" the Chinese admiral asked. He clearly didn't want his forces to miss out on all the action.

Admiral Halsey leaned back in her chair. "That sounds good—thank you for offering. Once we've found their locations, I'll order the orbital assault ships into position. We'll proceed with eliminating any threats to the transports before we allow them to enter the planet's orbit. It's imperative that we get the planet secured so we can start work on the space elevator. We need to get that thing built so we can start our mining operations."

The two of them chatted for a while about the finer points of how to carry out their plans. An hour later, the TPA admiral left to return to his ship and get his people ready for the next phase of the operation. Both leaders were under a lot of pressure by their home governments to secure the planet and get the resources needed to build a fleet strong enough to defend Sol.

## Chapter Three
## More Surprises

**New Eden – High Orbit**
**RNS *Rook***

It frustrated Captain Hunt to watch the *Xi* settle into orbit over New Eden. His ship was supposed to lead the way for the orbital assault, not one of the less powerful TPA warships. However, until his crews repaired the main guns and the munition fabricators, his combat power was significantly reduced.

He still had more than a dozen hull breaches needing to be sealed on the outer hull of the ship. His lead engineer, Commander Jacob Lyons, had a small group of repair Synths crawling over the exterior of the vessel sealing the ship, using their newly invented nanite paste. It wasn't a long-term solution, but it would work until they could get back to a shipyard.

Hunt hated to admit it, but his ship had taken a beating in this last fight. *No, scratch that, a butt-whooping*, he thought. The fact that they hadn't been blown apart was more due to luck than anything else. It was probably the three destroyers that had attempted to attack the enemy carrier that had ultimately saved his ship—that, and the fact that the *Voyager* had moved into position as a shield between them and the enemy ship.

Had the Zodark carrier been able to keep its weapons focused on them instead of the destroyers and the *Voyager*, then chances were the *Rook* would have been blown apart. He'd have to make sure he wrote up a recommendation for some gallantry awards for the sailors and commanders on those ships. They had earned them.

Hunt looked down at the tablet on his desk. He had been reviewing the after-action review or AAR reports from Captain Hopper and some of the other NCOs from the assault on the Zodark carrier. They were impressive to read. Short video segments highlighted some of the key points mentioned in the report. Two videos had been specially marked from Captain Hopper for him to view. They were brief, so Hunt figured he'd take a moment to watch them.

The first was a scene of Master Sergeant Brian Royce. His breaching team of seven Deltas had not only found a way into the enemy ship, but they had also led the initial charge. Hunt watched the short video of the gunfight in the hangar and how the seven-man team had dealt with an overwhelming number of enemy soldiers attempting to rally a defense. It was impressive to watch how fast and agile the Delta team was.

The second video was time-stamped not too long after the first. Hunt clicked play, and what he saw was truly incredible. He saw a lone figure clad in his exoskeleton combat suit, charging headlong into a multitude of both dead and wounded Zodarks. The soldier thrashed about with his rifle, using it as a club in certain circumstances and shooting the enemy at point-blank range when required. The surreal fight lasted only a minute or two, but at the end of it, the man stood there, triumphant. Hunt noted it was the same man, Master Sergeant Brian Royce.

At the end of the AAR report, Captain Hopper recommended Royce be immediately awarded the Distinguished Service Cross for his actions. He also recommended meritoriously promoting him to lieutenant to take the place of Lieutenant Aaron Crocker, who had been killed in the suicide blast by the Zodark NOS. Hunt initially agreed with the recommendations, but on further reflection, he decided he'd try to upgrade Royce's award to the Medal of Honor. He'd never seen something so crazy or heroic in his life. Hunt had a feeling he'd be seeing this video again—things like this tended to go viral.

Hunt continued reading the report and sighed. The battalion of Deltas had been mauled in the process of seizing the Zodark vessel. They had started this mission with five hundred and forty Deltas. They were now down to four hundred and thirteen. The officer and senior NCO ranks had been devastated during the assault, so they needed to make some battlefield promotions to keep things running.

A knock at the door broke Captain Hunt's concentration. Looking up, he saw Commander Fran McKee standing there. He smiled and waved her in.

"You look about as tired as I feel, Fran," he said with a chuckle. "How go the repairs?"

She made her way over to the set of chairs in front of his desk and sat down in one of them. She sighed briefly before she replied, "Oh, they're going fine—just taking longer than I'd like."

Hunt grunted. Everything in space either took time to accomplish or killed you in fractions of a second—seldom was there an in-between.

"How's that nanite paste working out?" he inquired. The technology was something new they were trying out, and he still wasn't completely sold on it.

She shot him the stink eye. "I'm no engineer, Captain, but I have a hard time believing that slapping a bunch of sticky nanite paste over a hole in the hull is going to seal it up properly. I think it should be used to help fill in the gouges cut into the hull, but not to seal it. I'd much rather trust a proper weld than some nanite crap the R&D boys cooked up."

Hunt snickered. "I'm sure Commander Lyons has thought about that, or he wouldn't have recommended we use it. My understanding, Fran, is that he's only using it to seal up the patches. I hear the paste is made of that same type of material they'll be using for the new space elevators. It's supposed to be a 'molecularly perfect' material," Hunt explained, using air quotes.

He leaned forward in his chair. "Changing subjects, Commander— what's the status of New Eden? Do we know what's down there on the ground yet?"

She sat up a bit straighter in her chair. "As a matter of fact, that was one of the reasons I was coming to see you," she replied, her tone of voice much softer, as if she were afraid someone would overhear. "One of the satellites did find something on the ground. The *Xi* and *Voyager* have just entered the planet's orbit. They're going to conduct a more thorough scan of the planet before they deploy the ground forces. However, they already found Zodark activity at one of the mining colonies we previously attacked."

His left eyebrow rose in surprise. "Really? I'm actually shocked. The planet doesn't seem to have any planetary defenses—"

"Sorry to interrupt, Captain, but you're receiving a flash message from Admiral Halsey," announced Lieutenant Branson, his coms officer. "I'm patching her through to your station now."

A moment later, an image of Admiral Halsey on the bridge of the *Voyager* appeared. A warning klaxon blared in the background. "Captain Hunt, it would appear the Zodarks kept a surprise waiting for us on the surface—we're taking pretty accurate ground fire. They're launching some of those smaller fighter aircraft like the ones that attacked you from that carrier we captured.

"I'm going to pull the *Voyager* and the *Xi* into a higher orbit. I want your ship to move into a blocking position between us and the planetary defenses below. Between our two ships, we'll have more point defense systems to handle the enemy fighters and any of those plasma torpedoes they may fire at us."

*Crap, this isn't good*, Hunt thought. *What else do they have waiting for us on the surface?*

"That's a good copy, Admiral. We'll start moving to your position now," Hunt replied. "I'll have my tactical officer coordinate with yours, and we'll start lobbing some slugs down on those enemy pulse batteries on the surface."

"Just do it, Captain. Halsey out," she said. Then her holographic image disappeared into the chaos of her bridge.

Hunt turned to McKee. "XO, move us into a blocking position as the admiral ordered," he ordered. The two of them stood and headed toward the bridge, while Hunt continued issuing orders. "Tell Commander Lyons he needs to pull his repair crews in from outside the ship. Our people or repair Synths can't be outside if we have to make sudden maneuvers."

As he entered the bridge, Hunt immediately saw the image of the orbital battle taking place around the *Xi* and the *Voyager*.

"What's going on, people?" Hunt called out to the officers on deck as XO McKee made her way back over to the tactical station. She'd need a few minutes to get caught back up.

"Sir, the *Xi* and *Voyager* are taking ground fire from at least four known positions," Lieutenant Cory LaFine explained. "The weapons appear to be pulse beam batteries. Sensors are also showing several large swarms of fighters forming up around one of the ground bases."

"Is that formation of fighters still close to the surface, or are they heading up to orbit to attack our ships?" Hunt asked as he took his seat in the captain's chair.

LaFine furrowed his brow as he examined his screen. "They're still forming up near the surface, a few thousand meters above the ground. They haven't advanced toward our ships yet."

Hunt smiled; an idea had just popped in his head. "OK, here's what I want to do. Weps, use our working magrail turret to send a couple dozen slugs into the formation of fighters near the surface. I suspect they are circling in a tight pattern while they figure out how and when they're going to attack us. Let's see if we can't take a few of them out before they become a threat.

"Next, I want some firing solutions on those enemy pulse batteries. Let's spin up some of our Havoc missiles and give 'em a try. Use the conventional warheads and see if we can get lucky and take out a good chunk of the ground force they have defending the area."

The next ten minutes went by in a blur. The *Rook* entered the planet's orbit as they maneuvered to get in position between the two other ships. Even wounded, the *Rook* still had more armor and weapons than the other ships in the fleet.

Once they had settled in orbit, the two working forward turrets fired their thirty-six-inch shells down into the formation of the enemy fighters.

"Firing main weapons now," called out Lieutenant LaFine.

The ship shuddered a bit as the large magrails started firing through their magazines.

"Missiles are firing now," LaFine announced.

Captain Hunt heard a low rumble as the first stage of the Havoc missiles ignited and were ejected out of their launch tubes. The missiles streaked out through space, accelerating as they headed toward their targets. The empty missile tubes were reloaded and made ready for another orbital strike should they need to fire another round.

Hunt and the rest of the crew watched and waited as the slugs traveled toward the swarms of enemy aircraft. At first, the enemy fighters didn't seem to detect them—they didn't respond as if something dangerous were headed their way. Then the first couple of five-thousand-pound high explosives detonated, throwing shrapnel in every direction. Nearly forty of the enemy aircraft blew up instantly. The remaining Zodark fighters immediately kicked their thrusters into overdrive to escape the exploding projectiles.

Captain Hunt and the rest of the bridge crew watched as the missiles streaked toward their intended targets. They had fired twelve missiles at each of the four known pulse batteries in hopes that a few might get through and do some damage.

Hunt counted. *One, two, three, four...* Several of the missiles winked out of existence as the Zodarks engaged them. The captain's heart pounded and he gripped the armrests of his chair, nervously hoping. Seconds later, the weapons officer announced that two of the missiles had gotten through to one of the laser cannons and burst into balls of flame. The site was obliterated.

"Sir, we've got several more explosions," Lieutenant LaFine continued. "We've successfully taken out a layer of their planetary defenses."

"Good job, Lieutenant," said Hunt joyfully. "Fire another wave of missiles at the remaining defenses. Engage our magrails to join the fray now that we've dispersed those fighters. We need to take those pulse beams out before we can land the ground pounders."

"Brace for impact!" called out Commander McKee as she white-knuckled her chair.

Moments later, the *Rook* shook violently. Just as Hunt thought the jarring was over, the ship shook a second and third time from two more pulse beam hits.

"Making evasive maneuvers, sir!" called out the helmsman.

The defensive system continued to fire out countermeasures seeking to change their position and throw the targeting systems of the enemy weapons off. The slightest change in a direction across thousands of kilometers would cause the next shots to miss while the tracking laser worked to reacquire them.

"Commander Robinson! Where the hell is my jamming?" shouted Hunt angrily as he turned to his electronic warfare officer or EWO.

"I'm working on it!" Robinson growled. His fingers tapped away feverishly on the screen before him.

"Captain, we've got a hull breach on deck one," declared Commander McKee. She immediately turned to relay a new order to the damage control parties. Deck one, the troop deck, had a lot more open areas—it was the least compartmentalized section of the ship, and fortunately, at the moment it was completely empty of their normal troop complement.

"Damn it! Where's my jamming? We can't take another hit like that," barked Hunt at Robinson again.

"Enemy lasers have lost lock; they're down for the moment," announced Robinson, clearly relieved that he had gotten the enemy fire off them.

"Those fighters are heading toward us," Lieutenant LaFine said urgently. "They'll be in the range of our point defense systems in ten minutes."

"LaFine, now that those pulse batteries are jammed, start laying some magrail slugs into them," Hunt ordered. "I want those guns offline before they're able to burn through our jamming again."

He turned to his XO. "Commander McKee, see if the *Xi* and the *Voyager* can set their magrails to use proximity fuses and start shooting at those incoming fighters. If I had to guess, they'll be packing more of those nasty plasma torpedoes."

McKee grimaced at the thought of more of those little bastards hitting them—those weapons had nearly destroyed them last time. "On it, Captain."

Suddenly the ship shuddered hard as the thud of an explosion rippled throughout the ship.

Commander Lyons from Engineering called through to Hunt's communicator. "Captain, I need you to bring the ship into a higher orbit so we can get the breach on deck one sealed up. We're just on the edge of the atmosphere right now. We're getting thin layers of air rushing in, and it's fueling the fires. The Synths can't get the flames under control as long as they have a fuel source." It sounded like utter chaos in the background behind Commander Lyons.

Captain Hunt tapped the sensor on his communicator. "Copy that, Jake. What the hell was that last explosion?" Hunt asked, hoping it wasn't anything too serious. They were already in trouble, and those inbound fighters were still getting closer.

More shouting could be heard as Commander Lyons replied, "Some of the ordnance for the ground pounders cooked off. It blew out a couple of areas we had just sealed up. We've now got another breach on deck five because of it. My people are on it, and we'll get it taken care of, sir."

Hunt nodded in satisfaction, more to himself than to his friend, who couldn't see him. "That's a good copy, Jake. Just so you're aware, we have more fighters inbound. I imagine we'll be dodging plasma torpedoes in a few minutes."

"Captain, we can't take any more plasma torpedo hits, sir," Lyons asserted. "We still have multiple hull breaches that are being sealed up with duct tape and superglue right now. I can't guarantee we'll hold together if we take a couple hard hits like that again."

*Crap, that's not what I wanted to hear*, Hunt thought nervously. He watched a swarm of fighters closing in on them. "Gotta go, Jake. Just get your people ready for some more action."

A couple of minutes went by, and then the ship's point defense weapons opened fire. The roar from the dozens of 20mm Phalanx CIWS guns could be heard even on the bridge. The point defense weapons used regular good old-fashioned propellent: no magnetic railguns, just liquid propellant. The cyclic rate of the older-style guns was nearly triple that of a magrail system. It made more sense to use the older technology for last-minute defensive actions like this.

The CIWS spewed out a wall of lead in the direction of the enemy fighters. Several groups of fighters broke out of their formations. The Zodarks were trying to separate and give each other the best possible chance of getting in range to launch their plasma torpedoes before they cut and run.

Hunt was transfixed on the screen in front of him, where scores of fighters were getting wiped out by the CIWS as the AI computer coordinated which guns to use on which groups of fighters and then shifted the guns around when a single fighter or group of them was taken out. The AI running on the ship's quantum computer could calculate how to best fight the ship and what targets to engage far faster and more efficiently than a human operator could. It didn't mean a human was taken entirely out of the loop, but the AI was usually leveraged more for close-in-defensive actions like this, where milliseconds made the difference between life and death.

Then Hunt felt his stomach drop. A group of four fighters the CIWS hadn't been able to take out yet fired off two plasma torpedoes each. From their previous battle, he knew that they only had a few seconds to get the *Rook* out of the way while the missiles were converting to plasma torpedoes and lost their guidance system.

"Eight torpedoes inbound," called out Commander McKee, her voice rising an octave.

"Helm, evasive maneuvers now!" Hunt shouted to be heard over the warning alarms blaring on the bridge and the continued roar of the CIWS and other gun systems.

The ship veered hard to starboard and picked up speed as more power was channeled to their main thrusters.

Two more sets of plasma torpedoes appeared, but they were heading toward the *Xi* and the *Voyager*, not the *Rook*. All three ships were now making radical maneuvers as they did their best to avoid the incoming torpedoes. Their point defensive systems continued to fire rapidly at the incoming threats. One of the satellites caught an incredible view of the battle—the three starships spewed tens of thousands of red tracers into the darkness of space and the atmosphere below in a wild defensive act.

"Enemy gun batteries are down! Our last barrage from the main guns took the last of the planetary defensive systems out," exclaimed Lieutenant LaFine, excited that they had succeeded.

"They missed! Four of the torpedoes missed!" exclaimed one of the officers on the bridge.

*Now there's just four*, thought Hunt.

"Oh God! Two of these are going to hit," said Lieutenant Hightower, his navigations officer, as he desperately turned the ship hard into another radical turn that caused nearly everyone to grab hold of something, anything.

"Brace for impact!" yelled Commander McKee as she grabbed the sides of her chair, a tight grimace on her face.

*BOOM...BOOM!*

Everyone was rattled hard as the *Rook* shook violently. Suddenly, the entire bridge blacked out. The computer screens went black, and so did their tactical view of what was happening around them. They couldn't even hear the roar of the CIWS or any of their other gun systems—the ship's power had been knocked out.

Seconds later, the emergency lights flickered on. The computers rebooted as the backup power units came online. While the systems were rebooting, Hunt felt something he wasn't expecting: a drop in not just their speed but what he perceived was their altitude. He didn't have any instruments to look at just yet, but he had a sickening feeling that they were starting to fall deeper into the planet's orbit. If that happened, they could end up literally crashing into New Eden. These ships weren't made to fly through the atmosphere, and there was nothing aerodynamic about them.

"Helm, what's going on? Are we falling into the planet?" demanded Hunt.

The lieutenant didn't answer right away. He was clearly doing his best to get his terminal back up and running, as was everyone else on the bridge.

Tapping the sensor on his communicator, Hunt called down to his engineering department. "Jake, what's going on? I need the main power back online like yesterday!" Hunt exclaimed.

A few seconds went by, and nothing. Hunt tried to hail his chief engineer on his communicator a second time. He needed to know what the hell was happening back there.

"Fran, why can't we get through to Engineering?" Hunt barked. He immediately realized he probably shouldn't have yelled at her like he had, but he needed answers.

She turned to look at him, her face backlit by her computer monitor, which was now online. She hesitated momentarily before she replied, "Sir, it looks like most of the engineering section is gone. Both of those torpedoes hit the rear half of the ship. I think it might have been sliced right off. I'm not getting any response from our damage control parties anywhere in the entire rear half of the ship."

"Can you patch us through to the *Voyager*?" Hunt implored his coms officer. "We need to know what happened before I give the order to abandon ship."

Branson nodded as her fingers tapped a couple of keys. A second later, he got an audio connection with their flagship.

The *Voyager* confirmed the unthinkable: the plasma torpedoes *had* sheared off the rear half of his ship. They were now in a downward descent into the gravity of the planet. Hunt only had one decision left—he needed to save as many of his crew as possible before it was too late.

In that instant, everyone stopped what they were doing and looked at him. They all realized the ship was doomed, but they waited for him to give the final order.

Looking up at the people who had fought so valiantly with him, Captain Hunt knew they had done their best. Now it was time to save his crew. He then uttered the words no ship captain ever wants to say, but every leader must be willing to say, "Abandon ship!"

In the next few minutes, a flurry of activity took place across the ship as everyone headed to the escape pods, some helping to carry the wounded with them. The ship designers had had the forethought to position several very large escape pods near the medical bay, which made evacuating the wounded quickly possible. The designers had realized that in most cases, if you had to abandon a starship, there wasn't very much time before it was game over.

The ship started to shake and rattle a lot as it entered the upper atmosphere, the lower portion of the hull superheating as it raced across the sky like a shooting star. Hunt saw from the readout on his tablet that everyone was either in an escape pod or had ejected from the ship in one. It was time for him to join his crew.

He sprinted over to one of the last pods, stepped inside and powered up the unit. He closed the door and strapped himself in, mentally preparing for what he knew was going to be a bumpy ride. He then hit the eject button, and the little tube he was standing in shot out of the ship like a bullet.

Through the small window of the escape pod, Hunt saw his ship streaking through the sky below him. The rear half of the *Rook* was torn apart and missing. Other sections of the ship looked scorched and mauled from the battle. The bow of the ship turned bright red as the hull heated up from the friction of the atmosphere and its uncontrolled descent to the surface below.

Hunt watched scores of little escape pods descending to the ground all around him. He was sure some of the crew members who had gotten out while the ship was still in orbit would be picked up by the *Xi* or the *Voyager*. Many others, like him, had ejected inside the planet's atmosphere, so they were on a one-way trip to the surface, whether they wanted to be or not.

As the pod buffeted from the air moving around him, it heated up. Then the little heat shield at the bottom of the escape pod deployed to protect the pod from burning up in the atmosphere and deflect some of the growing heat that would otherwise have cooked him.

Once the pod descended to fifteen thousand feet, it opened a guidable parachute above. Hunt used a small joystick to guide the pod's landing. The vessel had a very rudimentary navigation system, which basically consisted of a couple of compressed air canisters to help with maneuvering. The system was, after all, designed for use in space.

As his escape pod drifted down to the ground, Hunt looked for where best to land it. The whole place seemed so strange and alien to him—he now understood what the Deltas meant about not getting distracted by all the new stuff on the planet's surface. He was finding it hard not to just look all around, but he knew he needed to stay focused on finding a safe place to land.

A couple groups of escape pods were clustering together a bit as their occupants angled for what looked like a fairly open field not too far from a more densely forested area. Hunt figured he'd try to steer his chute in their direction.

A few minutes later, his escape pod thudded on the ground and fell over. Luckily, the pods were balanced in a way that ensured that when they fell over, the door would always face up, so the passengers would be able to get out. The pod dragged a little as the chute was still getting caught by the wind. It pulled Hunt along a few feet before he was able to disconnect the chute and stop the pod from moving.

Captain Hunt lay in the pod for a moment; he couldn't see much just yet. However, knowing he needed to get out and start looking for his people, he hit the unlock button on the door to open it. The air inside immediately escaped with a slight hissing sound, replaced with the fresh air of the planet. He took a deep breath in and had to admit, the atmosphere was freeing after being stuck breathing recycled air on a starship for the last month.

# Chapter Four
## The Zodarks

**Space Command Headquarters**
**Earth – Sol**

"Who the hell leaked the video, Admiral?!" President Alice Luca demanded angrily as she stared daggers at him.

Trying to deflect some of her rage, Admiral Chester Bailey opened his palms as he replied, "It would appear someone within the TPA smuggled a copy of the video off their secured server. It then ended up on a transport to the Gaelic Outpost, where it was uploaded to a server and beamed to Mars, Lunar, and then Earth. It was propagating throughout the public domain faster than we or the TPA could squash it."

The President's face turned a darker shade of red as she did her best to control the rage building up within her.

"Madam President, if I may," Bailey offered, "this might actually work to our benefit."

Luca tilted her head slightly to one side. "How do you figure, Admiral?" she asked icily. "The entire world is in a frenzy. The TPA is publicly saying we brought this new threat upon the world by deviating from the planned expedition to Alpha Centauri. I wasn't even president when the decision was made to scrap that mission in place of New Eden."

Bailey nodded as he let her vent. Then he took a deep breath. "The video leaking like it did wasn't right," he admitted. "But we can use that, Madam President. Fear can be a powerful motivator. Right now, the world is terrified of the Zodarks—let's use that to our advantage."

With her anger starting to subside, the President leaned in. "What do you suggest, Chester?"

Admiral Chester Bailey turned around in his chair and walked over to the wall.

*President Luca rarely ever uses my first name*, he thought. She was obviously really overwhelmed. Then again, who wouldn't be? She'd hardly been president for a year when the Zodarks were discovered. Now she had to deal with the political and military mess her predecessor had left behind.

As Admiral Bailey moved his hand across a blank spot on the wall, a small keypad suddenly illuminated. He typed in a code, then placed his thumb on a biometric scanner and looked at a small camera. There was a slight hiss as the safe unsealed itself and opened up, revealing a well-hidden spot in the middle section of the wall.

Bailey pulled an old-fashioned paper folder out of the safe and walked back to his chair. Sitting down, he handed it hesitantly to the President.

"I propose we move forward with this," he said as she took the folder with yellow and red stripes on it marked "Presidential Eyes Only." Only a couple of people in the entire world had clearance to see what was in that folder or work on any of its contents. It was so secretive that no electronic copies had been made, so there would be no way for the information to be copied or stolen.

She smiled as she accepted the file. "I was told by President Roberts that the Director of Space Command kept a secret paper folder known only to a handful of people. I thought it was kind of a joke, but now I see he was serious. What's in this thing that's so secret it can't be on our servers?"

"You'll see, Madam President," Bailey replied enigmatically.

As President Luca read, a slight smile crept across her face. She nodded a couple of times as she flipped through a couple more pages. Eventually, when she had read through the bulk of the document, she suddenly closed it, placing it down on the table next to them.

"I see your point, Chester," she began. "While I agree with the contents of this report, and it's clearly been thought through extremely well, I'm not sure how we convince the TPA to go along. As you know, their economy is nearly twice ours. Their population is also four times as large as ours. How do you propose we get them to agree to this?"

"Madam President, as large as the TPA is, their military ability to defend Earth or Sol is sorely lacking," Bailey said, crossing his arms. "Half of their space fleet is now deployed to the Centaurus system. They've left the bulk of the defense of Sol and handling this new threat to us.

"I think we can make the case that their forces and economy should be folded into ours. The key to all of this is making sure an equitable governing board or senate is established. That way, they won't feel like they're being cut out of the political process. Then I think we can make this work."

President Luca steepled her fingers. "You believe they'll go for this...form a new republic with us?"

Bailey nodded. "If we choreograph it right, yes. In a few weeks, we'll get our first com probes back from New Eden. If we've achieved a great victory, then it'll add fuel to our movement. If we suffer a defeat or loss, it'll add to the fear we can use to drive home the need for this to happen. In either case, Madam President, it'll be a win-win situation for us and Sol."

She lifted her chin as she thought about the proposal. There was a significant pause as she worked through the risks. Admiral Bailey realized she was probably considering what would happen to her own position of power—there was certainly no guarantee that she would be chosen to head up this new government.

*They'd probably make me the head of the entire military force*, he thought as he considered his own fate.

Slowly, a smile spread across Luca's face. *I wonder if she's planning to become the de facto Minister of Defense*, he thought. If the two of them teamed up, they would run the most critical facets of the government; she could always secure the prime minister position down the road.

"OK, Chester, let's see if we can put some of this into motion and test the waters," she directed.
*******

**Ten Days Later**

*Admiral, we've just received the first com drone from New Eden*, announced Bailey's staff officer over his neurolink.

Admiral Bailey perked up at the news. *Transfer the file to my terminal and schedule a meeting for later in the day to discuss the information*, he ordered.

Once the administrative tasks had been taken care of, Bailey clicked on the packet of information the drone had brought back. He then entered his pass code to unlock the encrypted data package. For security purposes, only a select few people had the pass code needed to open the com drone's files—this was a deliberate effort by Space Command to ensure they controlled the flow of information. If, God forbid, the Earth fleet got wiped out, they didn't want everyone knowing about it before they figured out how to respond.

After opening the first set of files, Bailey read a collection of summary reports to get a quick idea of what had happened. The BLUF or bottom line up front statements said the fleet had arrived safely in the system. It also contained a packet of information on what appeared to be two completely different types of Zodark ships from what they'd previously encountered.

Before Bailey read the additional information, he clicked on some closeup images of the two ships.

*Interesting*, he thought. *No...huge and terrifying is more like it.* These were warships, straight-up frontline combat ships.

Admiral Bailey then looked below the images at the next BLUF section, which encapsulated the synopsis of the battle. Since the com drone had a BLUF statement of the battle, Bailey knew Admiral Halsey's fleet had won, or at least survived. Now he just needed the details.

The more Chester read about the battle, the more his stomach churned. Admiral Halsey's fleet had succeeded in destroying what they had classified as a Zodark battleship, but they had lost three of the four destroyer escorts in the process. They had also engaged a Zodark carrier. His heart skipped a beat when he read that they had boarded and captured the crippled ship. The last part of the message said they were going to try to get the captured ship repaired so it could be brought back to Sol, or taken apart so key components, as identified by their Sumerian allies, could be brought to Earth for further study.

The file on the first day of the battle also had more than two thousand hours of videos attached for further analysis. Admiral Halsey had included over a thousand hours alone of just the Deltas boarding the Zodark carrier.

Bailey took a couple of minutes to watch a few of the clips. Seeing how these beasts fought scared him to death. *They're savage animals*, he thought. He figured he'd seen the worst of it when he'd watched one of them break out of the brig on the *Voyager* on the last mission, but the close-quarter combat that took place on the Zodark ship was surreal.

The Deltas were the Republic's most ferocious fighters. They were physically enhanced, augmented combat soldiers. Aside from the exoskeleton combat suits they fought in, their bodies had been considerably improved to make them even stronger, smarter, and tougher soldiers. If these super-soldiers were having a tough time fighting the Zodarks, how would the regular nonenhanced soldier fare?

*We're going to need to train more of these enhanced soldiers or move entirely to combat Synths,* he realized.

Next, Bailey read the damage report from the *Rook.* The ship had been badly mauled during the battle. More than thirty percent of the crew had been either killed or wounded in action. The vessel was combat ineffective at this point, at least until it could get to a shipyard for a complex overhaul.

An hour went by as Bailey finished skimming through the remainder of the report. He'd seen enough to know what needed to happen. They had fought a courageous battle against the Zodarks and achieved a great victory, but it had been costly. Now his staff would need to work on crafting a plan to disseminate this information to the rest of the public in coordination with the TPA.

*******

"Admiral Bailey, this is incredible news. Did Admiral Halsey or Admiral Zheng say when the ground assault would begin?" asked Admiral Hong through his holographic display.

Admiral Hong Jinping was Bailey's Tri-Parte Alliance counterpart. Now that the TPA military was fully involved in the capture of this new world, the two militaries were working closer than ever before.

Bailey shook his head. "No, they didn't," he replied. "Knowing Admiral Halsey, I believe she will probably want to conduct a thorough sweep of the planet's two moons and make sure there are no other threats before she begins operations to secure the planet. Since we received the first com drone today, we should receive a new one each day for the next fourteen days. I'm sure we'll receive a lot more information in tomorrow's drone."

Admiral Hong nodded. "Then I suggest we wait until we receive tomorrow's com drone before we make any public announcement, Admiral," he replied, speaking in a tone that implied this was not a suggestion at all but more of an order. "We should make sure nothing unfortunate has happened to our fleet. We have to assume the Zodarks sent a distress message of their own once our fleet arrived in the system."

Bailey opened his mouth to say something but stopped. He had to admit, Admiral Hong was right. They couldn't assume the Zodarks hadn't sent a message out once the Earth fleet had arrived in the system. They should wait for at least one, maybe two more days before they announced to the world what had happened in the Rhea system.

Bailey suddenly remembered the video images of that Delta sergeant fighting the Zodarks, which was attached to a recommendation to award the man the Medal of Honor. That inspired an idea of how they'd roll out the release of this information in a couple of days.

Looking at the holographic image of Admiral Hong, Bailey replied, "You are right, Hong. I agree with you. Let's wait and collect a few more days' worth of com drones as we build a bigger picture of the situation in the system."

Admiral Hong's ego seemed to puff up at the words "I agree with you," and the rest of the conversation was rather cheerful.

Once the meeting had ended, Admiral Bailey, his executive officer, and a handful of advisors followed him back to his office. When the door was closed, the group took their seats.

Bailey cleared his throat. "In the packet of information Admiral Halsey sent us was a series of videos," he began. "Two, in particular, were from the breaching team that had stormed the Zodark carrier. I believe the sergeant that led that assault was named Master Sergeant Brian Royce. Captain Hunt, his company commander, had a note attached to the video, recommending the soldier be awarded the Medal of Honor. After watching the video, which I highly encourage all of you to do as well, I agree. I'm going to ask the President's approval."

There was some slight murmuring from the group, as if they all wanted to stop what they were doing and watch the video so they could see what all the fuss was about.

"I'd like us to use that video and the images of Master Sergeant Royce—let's turn him into the poster child of human victory in the face of this terrible evil. We can craft these videos into media campaigns to sow fear in the hearts of every person in Sol about the Zodarks, and end with a message of hope that they can be defeated just as this sergeant demonstrated. Let's get our best people on this."
*******

**John Glenn Orbital Station**

## Musk Industries Headquarters

Andrew Barry, the CEO of Musk Industries, had his swivel chair facing out to the floor-to-ceiling windows of his office, overlooking the massive shipyard his company ran. In the last six months, his shipyard had grown from twelve construction bays to twenty. Space Command had another fifty bays under construction on a massive new shipyard just beyond the moon. Even the shipyard facility in orbit above Mars had grown from six construction bays to twelve, with another eight in the works.

His company and his lead competitor, BlueOrigin, were experiencing an enormous economic explosion. The two Republic shipbuilders couldn't hire enough workers or buy enough synthetic humanoids to keep up with the demand for ships being ordered by Space Command. Barry knew it was a race against time to get these powerful new fleets completed.

Right now, he was in the midst of a perfect storm. While he had more construction orders than he could possibly fill, he was also short critical resource elements to fill these orders. The mining fleets in the Belt had nearly tripled in size over the last six months—so had mining operations on Mars and elsewhere around Sol. But none of it could keep up with the sheer demand from the shipyards of Earth.

Staring outside the window, Barry watched as the two *Ark*-class transport ships finally pushed away from the station with the help of a couple of tugs. The two ships would be transporting some sixty-two thousand people to the Alpha Centauri colony. It would take the *Arks* eight days to travel there, and another week to offload its human passengers and their cargo. Then the *Arks* would return to Earth and start the process all over again.

Between the Republic's two *Ark*-class transports, the myriad of smaller ships the TPA had, and vessels owned by other private shipping companies, Earth was transplanting half a million people a month to Alpha Centauri. The exodus would probably speed up if the shipyards were allowed to produce more civilian ships. However, right now, the only nonmilitary ships they could build were mining barges for the Belt. All other construction efforts had been directed at building up a new fleet to defend Sol and establish a military outpost in the Rhea system.

A knock at the door returned Barry's attention to the here and now. He swiveled his chair around and saw Admiral Chester Bailey standing at the door, two of his aides in tow.

*This must be important if the fleet admiral is visiting me in person without an appointment*, he realized.

Standing up, Barry waved them in. "Admiral, it's good to see you. I trust everything is OK?"

The admiral grimaced, which meant he probably wasn't here to share good news.

"I've had better days, but thank you for asking. We need to talk, Andrew." Bailey said as the four of them took a seat at the conference room table on the far side of his office.

"Sure thing, Admiral. What can I do for you?" inquired Barry. His curiosity was piqued now.

"What I'm about to show you is classified, so I'll need you to sign this nondisclosure affidavit before we proceed."

Andrew Barry already had the highest security clearance one could obtain in the military. Being the CEO of the largest shipbuilder in space meant he was privy to a lot of classified ship programs and weapon systems. It felt odd having to sign another NDA.

Keeping those thoughts to himself, Barry nodded and placed his finger on the biometric signature block of the NDA. The admiral pulled a small holographic display out of a secured briefcase one of his aides had handed him and turned the device on. An image of a battle appeared.

"This is a time-compressed video of the conflict that took place in the Rhea system. As you can see, our forces encountered two new types of Zodark ships," Admiral Bailey explained as they watched the battle unfold. "The first one appears to be a battleship or large warship. Our real concern is this other one that kind of hung back from the main battle. As you can see, it's huge. It's roughly three kilometers long."

*Three kilometers…that's enormous*, Barry thought.

He watched the fight between the warships unfold, impressed with the high volume of fire the *Rook* was able to throw at the Zodark vessel. The gunners on those ships really knew how to maximize their weapons. What Barry found really interesting was how rapidly the enemy commander reacted to the *Rook*'s weapons once the battle started.

The enemy ship took some hits from the *Rook*'s magrails, which appeared to catch them off guard at first. But then the Zodark vessel took evasive maneuvers. The commander probably realized their armor wasn't going to hold up to the onslaught being thrown at them. Despite the size of the enemy warship, its ability to maneuver seemed unhindered.

*Dang*, thought Barry, impressed by the alien tech.

Admiral Bailey sped the video up a bit to get to the battle between the *Rook* and the carrier. To Barry's surprise, the *Rook* tore through the enemy battleship far faster than he would have thought possible. Clearly, their upgrade to the larger magrail turrets and the integration of the new Havoc missiles had paid off.

Then the Zodark carrier engaged. Wave after wave of fighters spilled out of hangars built into the side of the Zodark carrier ship. The enemy fighters raced toward the *Rook* at incredible rates of speed. The *Rook* engaged them with their magrails and then later their CIWS point defense weapons. The red tracers whipped through space at an incredible rate—it was nothing short of amazing to see.

Something suddenly caught Barry's eye. "What the hell is that?" he grilled the admiral, pointing at the objects being fired by those tiny little fighters.

With a look of concern on his face, Admiral Bailey explained, "*That* is why you signed a new NDA. The after-action report from the battle by Admiral Halsey says they're plasma torpedoes. They're unlike anything we've seen before—"

"Plasma torpedoes? How exactly do they work?" Barry interrupted. The thought of a plasma torpedo had never even occurred to him; plasma would melt any guidance system, engine or fuel source that he knew of.

Admiral Bailey sighed. "I'm honestly not sure about all the technical specifics. I believe the folks at DARPA are trying to decipher it. What I want you to see is this."

Moments later, the image zoomed in so they could see the torpedo with much more clarity. On the surface, it looked like a standard missile, something they were used to seeing and understood—a rocket motor on the back, a guidance system in the nose, and high explosives packed near the head of the body—but this was different.

Barry creased his eyebrows as he watched the guidable missile transform itself into a plasma weapon. The *Rook* did its best to evade the enemy torpedoes. Many of them missed, which Barry noted was mainly due to the enhanced maneuvering thrusters they'd added during the

*Rook*'s refit. He made a mental note that this was not only a feature they should include in all future warship designs but one that should be improved to allow the ship even greater maneuverability in situations like this.

When the plasma torpedo hit the *Rook*, it tore right through the ship's armor. It didn't appear that there was any high-explosive warhead, at least not after the torpedo converted from a steerable offensive weapon into an unguided plasma weapon. But when it hit, it did an enormous amount of damage.

Turning to look at the admiral, Barry asked, "You have video, pictures, and damage assessments for my engineers to review?"

Bailey nodded. "We do. Fortunately, the *Rook* didn't sustain many hits from these plasma weapons." He paused the video. "We succeeded in crippling that enemy carrier after that. We sent a boarding party over, and after a two-day intense battle, we captured it."

Holding his right hand up to stop the admiral from saying anything further, Barry exclaimed, "Whoa, you're saying we have a captured Zodark carrier? Is there any way we can get it back to our shipyards for study?"

Bailey shook his head. "Not right now. The ship was severely damaged in the battle. Maybe in time, once we're able to rebuild its engineering section and figure out how to use their FTL system, we might be able to get it back to Earth. Admiral Halsey's message said they're going to send a few dozen captured plasma torpedoes, some enemy fighters, and a plethora of other captured equipment on the next transport back to Earth. But before we talk about that, I have one more video I need to show you."

The admiral changed to a different video file, time-stamped a few days later. The footage showed several of the allied warships in orbit over New Eden. A new battle took place as the fleet battled planetary defensive weapons. Barry noted how powerful the Zodark ground-based lasers were. Despite being fired from the ground, they kept most of their potency through the atmosphere and still hit the ships hard enough to cause considerable damage. They were also extremely effective at targeting the fleet's Havoc missiles.

Then he saw more of those little fighters entering orbit, heading toward the fleet. The human forces engaged them the best they could with their weapons, but eventually, several of those plasma torpedoes emerged. Barry watched as three of those torpedoes plowed into the TPA ship, the *Xi*, tearing the heavy cruiser apart. A slew of escape pods emerged around the wreck as the ship fell into the atmosphere of the planet. The *Voyager* succeeded in dodging the plasma torpedoes, but the *Rook* took two more hits and the rear half of the ship was completely sheared off.

Admiral Bailey chimed in at this point in the video. "We lost the *Rook*," he announced matter-of-factly. "A lot of the crew was able to abandon ship, but casualties were pretty high. The *Xi* was also a total loss, as you can see."

"Damn…that leaves us with only the *Voyager*, a destroyer and the other TPA cruiser in the system? Are we going to send the *Bishop*? It's the only other major warship we have left," Barry asked in a hushed tone.

The RNS *Bishop* was the *Rook*'s sister ship. It had just completed construction a year ago and for the time being, was anchoring First Fleet protecting Sol.

Bailey shook his head. "No, we can't send the *Bishop*. That would leave Sol defenseless. The *Voyager* and what's left will have to make do."

Barry shook his head in disbelief. These two warships plus the three other destroyers represented the bulk of the fleet's firepower. He wasn't sure they'd be enough.

"We're going to need a lot more ships and *soon*," Barry urged.

Admiral Bailey nodded at the frank assessment. "That's putting it mildly. Admiral Halsey said she was ordering the ground forces to begin their operation and get the space elevator constructed. They're going to start mining operations immediately. She's under orders that as soon as she has enough minerals mined to construct two of our new battleships, she's to send those resources back on one of her transports. Before she left with the fleet, I told her she needed to send a transport back to Sol every five to seven days with whatever they had mined up to that point."

Bailey paused. "As we get these resources brought back to Sol, I need everything done to get some of these warships completed as rapidly as possible. We have no idea how long it'll take the Zodarks to send another fleet. If they send more ships soon, then I'm not sure the *Voyager* and a handful of cruisers are going to cut it. When these resources arrive, how long will it take you to have at least one of these new battleships ready to go?"

Barry sat back in his seat, thinking for a moment. He honestly wasn't sure. He had been hoping they'd have more time to gather resources, but it was clear that time was something they were going to be short on.

"We've already started construction on a lot of the ships," Barry replied. "We just haven't pieced them together yet. If I know the resources are on the way, then we can start putting the ships together. By the time we get the Trimar and the Morean we need to build the reactors and fuel them, we'll be ready to close the ships up. Once that happens, most of the construction can move along briskly.

"If we *had* to, we could deploy the ships with only the basic essentials needed to fight and finish the ships while traveling to New Eden. I don't like the idea of doing that, but clearly, the situation is dire. It warrants us doing something drastic like this to make it happen."

Leaning forward, Admiral Bailey fixed Barry with a hard stare. "Then I suggest you get to it. We may not have much time, Andrew. The fate of our entire people may be relying on the ability of five shipyards to produce the needed tools of war. We mustn't fail, Andrew—we may not get another chance."

# Chapter Five
## The Rescue

**New Eden**
**Planetside**

Before he left the escape pod, Captain Hunt had made sure to grab the small backpack with emergency supplies in it. *Who knows how long we'll be out here?* he'd wondered.

As he advanced toward one of the other escape pods in the field, he saw some survivors climbing out and went to check on them. His head of security from the ship, Victor Dubois, was with that group, along with a couple of the masters at arms.

Dubois immediately took charge of the situation and began organizing search parties to look for more survivors, while Hunt used the radio from their pod to contact the fleet above. Their first priority, aside from organizing a rescue mission, was locating the rest of the survivors.

No one knew for certain if there were any Zodarks in the area. What they did know was that hundreds of escape pods streaking through the sky like a meteor shower would certainly have given their positions away.

Three hours after they had made planetfall, they had managed to round up several hundred survivors. Hunt was starting to feel disheartened by just how few crewmembers they'd found, until he remembered that many of the crew had probably managed to escape while the ship was still in higher orbit, before it had fallen into the atmosphere. They would have been picked up by the *Voyager* or the *Xi*.

"Captain Hunt," said Dubois, "I think we should start breaking the survivors down into smaller groups and begin positioning them at certain intervals along our perimeter. We don't know how many Zodarks are in the area and if they are, we should look to organize some sort of defense."

Hunt nodded. He was grateful Dubois was there since he wasn't exactly the expert on ground combat. "That's a good idea, Commander. Figure out how many weapons we have and make sure those who know how to use them best are the ones to get equipped first. Then use your discretion to dispense the rest of the arms."

For the next twelve hours, survivors continued to trickle in, but otherwise, all was quiet. *Maybe the Zodarks were too far away and didn't even realize we'd landed*, thought Hunt.

Around midnight, Hunt awoke suddenly to the sound of screams of agony. "What the hell is that?" he yelled. It was the most horrifying and gut-wrenching noise he'd ever heard, and it grew louder and louder until it suddenly stopped. Just as he was about to go grab Dubois, one of his crew members ran toward the center of camp, and then summarily threw up.

"Sir...I don't think you want to see that," the man said, after he'd finished emptying his stomach.

Captain Hunt and Dubois had to investigate after that. What they found was truly gruesome. A Zodark had captured one of the guards along the perimeter, tortured him, and then thrown the dismembered body parts toward the center of the camp. Hunt felt sick.

Outside the camp, Hunt suddenly heard the Zodarks hooting and hollering. It sounded like they were doing some kind of war dance.

Hours later, they were still keeping up their ritual, keeping all of the Earthers awake and on edge. The Zodarks managed to pick off a few more guards, subjecting Hunt and his crew to the horrifying noise of one of their comrades being dismembered and slowly killed.

A few times, the Earthers had managed to catch a few of the Zodarks before they succeeded and picked off a few of their numbers, but as the evening went on, tensions continued to rise.

"Why don't' they just attack us already?" Fran McKee bemoaned to Hunt when it was just the two of them.

"They will. Soon. Right now, they just want to wear us down, terrorize us a bit before they move in for the kill," Hunt replied, speaking softly so only she could hear him. "They are toying with us is what they're doing."

Dubois suddenly appeared. "Captain, I think we should have everyone collapse in close," he suggested. "Let's tighten up our perimeter for the time being. It's too hard to cover this much ground in the dark."

"Make it happen, Dubois," Hunt replied.

The masters at arms not only had the M85 rifles, they also had night vision goggles, which allowed them to see at night. The problem was they didn't have enough of them for everyone. They were also short on weapons. They had a total of forty-two M85 rifles and forty-eight pistols—not exactly a lot of weapons to protect and defend a few hundred crewmen on a hostile planet.

Roughly an hour before dawn, the Zodarks launched their first assault, swarming toward their right flank. The MAs who had night vision goggles were able to see them coming and opened fire from a distance. They cut down a number of the vicious beasts with the magrails before they were able to breach their perimeter. However, once the Zodarks made it inside their lines, the enemy used shortswords and their talon-like fingernails to slash and cut the Earthers apart.

The attack was swift, violent and short-lived. It wasn't until daylight rolled around that they knew the true horror of what had transpired that evening. Fifty-two of Hunt's crew members had been killed in the attack and another thirty-eight were injured. The captain himself couldn't help but vomit when he saw his fellow spacers' ripped and torn apart bodies.

They also got a good look at the Zodarks themselves. For many, this was the first time they'd seen one up close and in person. They were truly hideous beasts—something about their torsos having four arms just seemed so unnatural. Their bluish skin matched the blue blood that pooled around their enormous ten-foot carcasses. They were a monstruous enemy to contend with.
*******


Captain Miles Hunt heard that horrible primordial scream the Zodarks were known to make, and it sent a shiver down his spine. The initial attack had ended hours ago, but since then, the enemy had continued waging a campaign of psychological warfare.

"Where the hell is that rescue party?" demanded Commander Fran McKee, his XO. Her face had streaks of dirt and dust on it, her hair was matted with sweat and grit, and her uniform was covered in grime from a day of hard work and fighting.

The MAs along the perimeter were checking their M85s and the handful of Zodark weapons they'd captured, making sure they were ready for the next Zodark attack. They'd already expended their supply of 20mm smart grenades, so they were down to just a few magazines of magrail rounds and a powerpack for the blasters.

Holding just a pistol in his hand, Hunt yelled, "Listen up, people! Admiral Halsey said our rescuers have already disembarked the

*Voyager*. They should be landing within the next twenty minutes. We need to hold it together for a little while longer."

Another guttural yell rang out in the distance, and Hunt felt the hairs on the back of his neck stick out straight. The remaining crew members were on edge. It had been a rough twenty-four hours.

Commander McKee messaged Hunt through the neurolink. *Sir, I'm not sure we'll survive another Zodark attack. They nearly wiped us out during the last one.*

*I know, Commander*, he replied. *But we're in charge, and we need to stay strong for everyone. If we freak out, they freak out. I need you to help me hold it together, OK?*

Without saying anything, she nodded, then looked down at the sidearm she was holding and walked over to the perimeter line. If the Zodarks attacked in the next twenty minutes, they were going to need everyone with a weapon on the fighting line.

Hunt looked to the sky above them. He hoped like hell those forces arrived soon, or they were dead.

*******

The air suddenly snapped, like a lightning bolt had shot through the air. One of Hunt's fleeters was hit by a single blaster shot fired from the tree line a few hundred meters away. A guttural yell emanated from the same position seconds later.

"Here they come!" shouted one of Hunt's security officers.

"Let 'em have it!" barked another one of his security members.

The fleeters who had the M85 rifles tore into the ranks of the charging Zodarks. Their magrails sent slug after slug at the charging horde.

Blue blaster fire from the Zodarks raced across the distance between the two groups as small clusters of Zodarks charged forward. Each time they attacked, they let out a hideous scream, which definitely had a psychological impact. Due to their size, the Zodarks covered a lot of ground very rapidly.

The fleeters did their best to shoot at the charging Zodarks, trying to keep the enemy as far away from them as possible. Once the Zodarks got within knife range, they easily slaughtered the fleeters. Unlike the RA soldiers or the Deltas, the stranded fleeters weren't equipped with body armor or exoskeleton combat suits.

"Watch the right flank! They're trying to get around us on that side!" shouted Commander McKee, doing her best to help manage the fight.

Dubois had unfortunately been killed during the previous attack. The next two officers in line had either been killed or injured as well. Hunt and his remaining officers were trying their best, but they weren't trained for ground combat. They fought starships, not soldiers.

*Something isn't right. Everyone's moving over to the right.* Sensing something was wrong, Hunt turned and trotted over to the left flank. A couple of laser blaster shots whipped over his head as he crouched and moved from one covered position to another. Hunt saw six of his people hunkered down against clumps of dirt, tree stumps, or whatever else they could find to take cover behind while the Zodarks fired at them.

One of the fleeters popped up and fired several rounds from his M85 rifle in the general direction of the Zodarks. When they dropped below cover again, several blue lights pierced the sky right where they had just been. Another one of his people jumped up and fired several shots— before they could duck back down, their head was ripped clean off by one of the Zodark blasters. The headless corpse fell to the ground, to the horror of one of the female enlisted members sitting nearby. She screamed as blood squirted from the decapitated body.

Hunt wanted to join her and scream in terror himself. Instead, he choked down his horror, ran up to the corpse and grabbed the M85 from the man's dead hands.

"Look out!" someone nearby shouted. Hunt turned just in time to see a Zodark soldier jump into their position.

The Zodark howled, its talon-like fingernails clawing at the closest humans, slashing through their flesh.

One of the security personnel fired his M85 into the back of the Zodark, punching several holes through it. Its lifeless body collapsed on the two humans it had just mauled.

Turning to where the Zodark had emerged from, Hunt pointed the rifle in that direction, ready in case another one of those hideous beasts appeared.

"I need you up here with the rifle, sir," one of the fleeters thundered as she pointed to a position not far from her.

Hunt saw where she had pointed and nodded; she was right. If he was going to handle one of the rifles, then he needed to be up on the firing line, helping them hold the enemy back.

Looking over the lip of his new covered position, Hunt saw close to three dozen Zodarks charging the right flank. Another two dozen were charging their center position, and so far, no one was charging directly in front of him, the left flank.

Looking to the fleeter with a rifle not far from him, Hunt asked, "Should we shoot at the Zodarks attacking the center of our lines?"

She turned briefly to look at him. Hunt saw she was a lieutenant from one of the weapon departments. "We can," she replied. "Just make sure you don't stick your head up too long. I think they have some snipers in that tree line further back. That's how they got Bill over there." She pointed to her dead companion, the man Hunt had taken the rifle from.

Suddenly, a sonic boom ripped through the air. Hunt looked up to the sky, hoping it was their rescue transporters. Two all-black Ospreys descended from the clouds. They approached from the northeast, probably a thousand feet in the air. Hunt thought it was strange that they didn't appear to be slowing down.

*If this is a rescue operation, then why aren't they preparing to land?* he asked himself.

As the Ospreys got closer, a twin-barreled chin-mounted magrail gun opened fire on the charging Zodark soldiers, cutting many of them down. Excited cheers rang out among the stranded fleeters. Hunt realized these were Special Forces Ospreys when he saw a side gunner behind the pilot tear into the Zodarks with a high-firing multibarreled gun. The damn thing sounded like it was ripping fabric in the air from their vantage point.

The Zodarks appeared to be caught off guard at the appearance of a spacecraft out of nowhere. Many of them stopped charging their positions and fired at the aircraft overhead.

When one of the Ospreys turned away from them, Hunt saw the rear hatch was open.

*Oh my God, that's insane*, he thought. Soldier after soldier jumped right out the rear ramp. They were a hundred meters in the air with no parachutes or ropes to manage the descent. They just ran right off the back of the aircraft in a scattering pattern throughout his lines.

Hunt watched a falling soldier point his rifle down at the Zodarks; the Delta fired his rifle at the enemy with critical accuracy. The whole thing was so surreal.

As the free-falling soldiers got closer to the ground, a small rocket or oxygen unit expelled something near their feet, and their falling bodies suddenly slowed down. When they landed, they looked as if they had only jumped a few feet in the air, not out of the back of an aircraft. It was the most amazing tactical stunt Hunt had ever seen.

When the Deltas landed on the ground near his fleeters, they immediately went into action. With their rifles tucked in their shoulders, they ran at full speed right for the Zodarks. No fear, no hesitation, they just charged forward, their rifles firing.

Turning to look at the enemy line, Hunt watched the Zodark attack starting to falter. Several Zodarks were hit by the charging Delta soldiers. The two groups were now locked in steady combat, firing at each other as the distance between them continued to close.

As five Delta soldiers ran toward his position, Hunt wasn't sure if he should try to flag one of them to stop and talk with him or just stay out of their way.

Three of them ran ahead toward the Zodarks. One of the super-soldiers knelt down near one of Hunt's wounded fleeters and treated his injuries while another Delta walked toward him.

Hunt couldn't tell who it was right away because of their helmets and visors. As the lone figure got closer, he saw the name stenciled on the man's armor and smiled.

"Captain Hopper, it's damn good to see you," Hunt said, remaining crouched down and out of the line of enemy fire.

Zodark blaster bolts were still whipping overhead and around the area. Oddly, it didn't seem to faze the Delta commander in the least; he just walked up to Hunt like it was no big deal.

"Captain Hunt, it's good to see you're still alive. Admiral Halsey sends her regards," Hopper said. He walked past Hunt and fired a few shots with his rifle before ducking down behind some cover. He turned to look at Hunt. "I'm sorry for the delay in getting to you and your crew, sir. We had to assault another Zodark orbital defensive position before we could come to your rescue. The orbital assault ships are entering low orbit now. They'll begin dropping the RASs shortly."

Hunt had been a little ticked off at the wait. They'd had no idea there were Zodarks in the area when they'd crash-landed. He had lost a lot of good people because they had to wait until it was their turn to be collected.

Hunt sighed. "It's water under the bridge at this point, Captain. Thanks again for arriving when you did, though; I think we would have been in some serious trouble if you hadn't. Is there a Zodark base nearby we didn't know about?"

Hopper shrugged. "Not that we're aware of, but there's a lot about this new world we don't know or understand—like a magnetic anomaly that screws up our sensors from the air."

Gunfire and shouting continued around them as the Deltas pushed well past the fleeters' positions. They were pursuing the Zodarks into the woods, something Hunt had no intention of joining.

Looking up at his Delta commander, Hunt asked, "Am I keeping you from managing your unit?"

A short pause ensued, and then Hopper looked down at Hunt. "No, sir, I'm managing the battle from my suit, coordinating between my AI, the neurolinks, and our drones deployed all over the place. I have complete situational awareness of what's happening around us right now and where my soldiers are advancing. Besides, Master Sergeant Royce is leading the assault for me, and the man's a freaking beast of an operator. He'll hunt those Zodarks down and finish them off.

"Oh, before I leave to go catch up to them, Admiral Halsey said my orders are to recover you and protect the rest of your crew. I've held a dozen of my guys back to pull security while the rest of the company pursues the Zodarks and either captures or kills 'em."

Hunt let out a stressed laugh. "Twelve soldiers? That's all you need?" he countered.

Hopper chuckled. "It may not seem like much, Captain, but my Deltas are substantially better soldiers than these Zodarks. We're quickly learning that our rifles are far better than theirs in a fight—especially if we have any sort of distance or an open area to fight in, like what we have here and in those trees."

"When's our crew being brought back to the *Voyager*, or where are they going to send us?" Hunt asked.

Hopper pointed his right hand up, and Hunt saw several shuttlecraft descending. They looked like they'd land close to where the bulk of Hunt's people were.

Once the shuttlecraft had settled on the ground, the spacers advanced toward them. The wounded were the first to board, then everyone else. It would take a few trips to get them all brought back to space, but soon they'd be back in a familiar environment, a starship.

Before Captain Hunt headed over to the last set of shuttlecraft, he extended his hand to Captain Hopper. "Thank you, Captain, for coming to our aid. Please convey my thanks to the rest of your men."

Hopper nodded. "I'll see you back on the *Voyager* in a few days," he replied. "In the meantime, my unit is going to hunt down the remaining Zodarks in the area before we move to another hard spot that needs capturing."

*******

**RNS *America***
**1st Orbital Assault Battalion**
**"Big Red One"**

"Listen up, RASs! This is it—the big drop, the mission we've been training for," barked the lieutenant. "In a few minutes, we're going to board the dropships. Fasten yourself in and get ready. Once we land, I want each squad leader to hit their objectives and expand the perimeter rapidly. More waves of troops are landing after us to get that perimeter expanded. Squad leaders, make sure your squads are loaded up with extra ammo, grenades, medpacks and water. Now, move out!" As he finished his speech, the NCOs swiftly took charge of things.

The hangar bay of the RNS *America* was abuzz with activity. NCOs and officers pushed their soldiers through the last-minute checks and opportunities to load up on as much extra ammo and supplies as possible before they boarded the dropships. No one knew for certain how long they'd be on the surface or when they'd get a supply drop, so they were stocking up on the most important supplies they'd need in a fight: ammo and medpacks.

"This is it, Big Red One! Time to load up and get this show on the road. I'll see each of you down on the surface," shouted their battalion commander, Major Ernie Coons.

Sergeants and officers yelled at the soldiers to pile into the dropships. Months and months of training had led them to this very moment. Now it was time to execute what everyone in the military knew was perhaps the most dangerous job in the Army—an orbital assault. A platoon of fifty-two soldiers packed in like sardines, unable to do anything other than hope and pray the pilots were able to deliver them to the surface in one piece.

Private First Class Paul "Pauli" Smith was nervous as heck. His stomach had been doing backflips for the last hour as they prepared to leave. Now the time had arrived to cram into that metal box that would drop them from space to the planet below.

"Come on, Pauli, let's go," called out one of his friends excitedly as he trotted toward the ramp that led into the dropship.

Pauli pushed aside his nerves and concerns and slapped a big grin on his face. They'd trained for years to do a mission like this. They were the Big Red One, the 1st Orbital Assault Battalion, a unit that traced its lineage all the way back to the 1st Army Division of old.

Boarding the dropship, the Republic Army soldiers settled into their seats and fastened their straps. A few minutes later, their lieutenant boarded and sat down in the chair next to the platoon sergeant.

The outer door to the ship closed, and there was a slight hissing noise as the lander sealed. A minute later, the drop arm that was attached to their lander extended, separating them from the rest of the orbital transport. Once they stopped moving, they sat for a few minutes just hanging there, waiting to be released.

*Clink.* The transport had released them.

Pauli felt a slight tap against his leg. He turned to see his friend Tom sitting next to him in the jump seat. They'd been friends since basic training.

"This is it, Pauli. We're on our way," Tom said, a grim look on his face.

Pauli just nodded; he'd had the same thought. *This is it. We're really on our way to an alien planet to go fight real aliens. How crazy is this...*

The dropcraft buffeted a bit as they left orbit, beginning its descent into the upper atmosphere.

"Remember your training, and you will make it out of this alive!" the lieutenant bellowed as they continued their descent.

Pauli snickered to himself at their lieutenant's pep talk. *Does he really believe that?* he asked himself. *If it's your time to die, it's your time to die. Ain't nothin' changing that...*

The dropcraft shook a bit more as it veered from right to left like the pilot was trying to avoid something.

A loud voice came over the intercom. "We're receiving ground fire from the DZ. This is going to be a hot landing," the pilot called out, to the angst of everyone strapped in.

The ship lurched swiftly to the right, rattling the soldiers inside so intensely that it felt like the entire lander was going to fall apart. They slid through the air. "We've been hit!" shouted the pilot. "We're going in hard; everyone get out once we land!"

*Oh God, please let me live!* Pauli silently prayed.

Seconds later, they crashed on the ground with a thud. The sounds of metal crunching, sparks crackling, yelling and screaming all echoed inside the cramped lander. A sliver of light then appeared on either side of the shuttle as the doors opened. Everyone snapped their harnesses off and bolted for the exits.

As he left the damaged dropship, Pauli observed chaos everywhere. Large and small blue blaster bolts fired at the dropships bringing the infantry down to the surface and at the grunts already on the ground.

Pauli turned to his right to call out to a couple of his buddies, only to see them get cut down by rapid enemy blaster fire. One of their heads exploded right in front of him, her headless corpse dropping to the ground like a sack of cement.

Turning toward where the blaster fire was coming from, Pauli brought his M85 to his shoulder and fired several times at what he thought was a machine-gun position. A tall figure stood behind a large blaster that fired relentlessly at the landing craft that were still descending.

Pauli ran for cover, then caught his first good look at the enemy. Two Zodarks clad in body armor, grasping wicked-looking weapons in each of their four hands, charged toward his comrades. The two beasts jumped right into the middle of a cluster of soldiers who had just exited one of the dropships.

Pauli was transfixed by what he saw. One of the Zodarks slashed at the soldiers, cutting several of them up before they even had a chance to react.

Pauli snapped himself out of it. Raising his rifle, he fired several times at the giant beast. He hit the Zodark, killing it—but not before it had killed or maimed several of his comrades. It was horrifying.

"Take that position out!" someone yelled.

"Flank right!" bellowed someone else.

"Medic! Help! Medic!" cried another.

"Frag out!"

*Crumpf...BOOM...*

"Pauli! There you are. Come on, man, let's go," called out one of the corporals, his fireteam leader.

Pauli looked at the guy, who couldn't be older than twenty-two. He saw fear in his eyes, but also a determination to live. Nodding, Pauli followed his fireteam forward. They covered each other as they ran to catch up to several soldiers assaulting one of the machine-gun blaster.

Pauli threw his body against a massive tree trunk just as a group of blaster shots hit the other side of the tree. Dropping down to the ground, he saw the next couple of blaster shots rip right through the tree where he had just been. Bringing his own rifle to bear, he sighted in on a Zodark that was shooting at him. He depressed the trigger a couple of times, and one of his magrail slugs exploded the alien's head.

*Got you, you bastard.*

"Let's move!" called out his fireteam leader.

Jumping to his feet, Pauli ran forward to the next covered position, a cluster of large rocks next to some more trees. When the four other soldiers in his fireteam joined him, they all heard some hideous-sounding shriek. "What the hell is that?" one of them asked.

"It's those damn Zodarks. It's a yell they do in battle or when they're preparing to charge," the corporal said as he stuck his head around the corner of the rocks to see what was happening.

"Oh, crap! Here they come," he shouted, firing his rifle several times at something charging toward them.

Pauli popped up from behind the rocks and fired a handful of rounds at the cluster of Zodarks running in their general direction. He hit one of them, then shot him several more times until he dropped to the ground, dead.

Moving to the next Zodark, Pauli fired a couple more times. The guys in his fireteam added their own fire. One of the privates opened up with his M90 SAW, cutting half a dozen of them down with a barrage of blaster shots. In short order, their magrails had made quick work of the charging enemy soldiers.

"You see that?" asked Pauli. "Unless those Zodarks use a blaster, they need to get in close to kill us. We just need to keep them at arm's length with our magrails. We got this."

Pauli then ran around the rock formation he'd been hiding behind and charged forward. For whatever reason, he didn't feel scared anymore. It was like a switch had just flipped in his brain.

*******

An hour later, the fighting had died down until it petered out altogether. The Earthers had captured the position, and with it, control of the area. It had been a fiercely fought battle. The RASs had assaulted the place with three battalions of orbital assault troops. They'd sustained one hundred and forty-six killed and another two hundred and eighty-one injured during the assault. However, they counted a total of four hundred and thirty Zodarks killed, twenty-four captured.

With the enemy position under human control, the soldiers went to work rebuilding the defensive positions and turning the place into a new combat outpost or COP. In time, their engineers would set up planetary defensive weapons of their own. Until that time, the RASs would turn the place into a defensive fortress, ready to repel any further Zodark attacks.

# Chapter Six
## Occupation

**RNS *Voyager***
**New Eden**

Admiral Abigail Halsey looked at the latest report from New Eden. The ground operations were well underway. In the last twenty-four hours, they had landed twelve of their thirty-two battalions of RASs on the ground. The Army had thus far managed to capture or disable ten of the fourteen Zodark bases they had identified on the planet. In the next twelve hours, the last four bases would be assaulted and captured.

Halsey shook her head briefly as she read the casualty report. It was high, but not as high as she had expected. The orbital bombardment they'd carried out prior to attacking the positions with ground forces was a strategy that was paying off.

They needed to keep offloading the rest of their soldiers and get the mining operations going as soon as possible. With the system clear of Zodark ships and New Eden almost freed from Zodark control, they *had* to get these minerals mined and shipped back to Earth. She wasn't sure how much time they'd have before the Zodarks returned in force, but she wanted to make sure they were ready for them when they did.

A chiming noise sounded, letting Halsey know someone was waiting outside the door to her office.

"Come in," she called out. The ship's computer recognized her voice and opened the door.

She smiled when she saw her friend. "Miles, it's good to see you again. I'm so glad you weren't hurt. How are you doing?" she asked as she got up and walked around her desk. She gave him a quick hug, and they exchanged pleasantries and sat down on the couches in her office.

"Thank you for rescuing my crew, Admiral," Hunt said. Then he leaned forward. In a quieter voice, he asked, "What do you want us to do now? Without a ship, we're a bit out of sorts."

"That's a good question, Captain," she said with a nod. "It was something I wanted to ask you about. I didn't want to make any personnel moves without consulting with you first. As you know, our ship took some damage in the final fight to take the planetary defensive systems down. We have a few openings from some casualties we sustained. Would you be open to any of your crewmen or officers volunteering to fill in for them?"

Hunt smiled. "I think many of them would jump at the chance. Not having a ship right now means we're either going to be filling admin billets back on Earth, or God forbid, stuck in a training billet," he said with a chuckle. "Speaking of Earth, when's the next transport heading back? Could the remainder of my crew hitch a ride? I think we should report back to Admiral Bailey what's happened. I'm sure I can pick up another command of one of the new warships being built."

"That's what I like about you, Miles, you don't dwell on the past. You just jump right back into the fight without missing a beat," said Halsey. "To answer your question, yes. I'll make sure the remainder of your crew that doesn't want to stay here catches a ride back on the transports. It's probably going to be at least a week after we get the mining operations going, though. I was going over the resource needs for those Trimarian reactors, and I want to make sure I'm sending you guys back with enough minerals to produce at least six of them. The next transport will hang around until it has reached its full capacity, enough for twenty more reactors. I'm hopeful I'll be able to keep the gravy train moving back to Earth every four or five days once we get things up and running."

"Look at you, Admiral," Hunt replied, snickering. "They've made a quartermaster out of you."

They both chuckled. It was good to laugh; it broke up the tension they had been feeling. Halsey knew the loss of Hunt's ship and a lot of his crew had been tough on him, but it had been tough on her as well. She'd lost nearly four thousand people under her command in the last five days—that was more than any military commander had lost since the end of the Great War over fifty years ago.

Halsey turned serious. "When you return to Earth, Miles, you need to make sure the politicians and the brass back home understand how deadly it is out here. These Zodarks are playing for keeps, and they've been a spacefaring nation far longer than us. We have no idea how big their empire is or how many ships they have."

Hunt nodded. "I know. I'm confident that case has been made. Our com drones with the footage of our attack should have made it back to them by now. I'm sure they've seen what happened and know about the loss of the *Xi* and the *Rook*."

Halsey sighed, then turned to look out the window in her office. She'd ordered the blast door retracted since they didn't appear to be in any more danger. The window showed her a view of the planet below, and a couple of ships nearby.

"The *Columbus* will start construction of the space elevator later tonight," Halsey informed him. "They tell me it'll be operational in thirty days."

"That's good. It'll speed up the transfer of resources from the surface and of our equipment from orbit," Hunt replied as he too looked out at the planet and the ships nearby. It was still awesome to see, even if they had seen it a million times before. Something about being in space and looking down on a planet from a starship produced an awe that was beyond words.

Captain Hunt leaned forward in his seat. "Admiral, about the Zodark ship we captured—I understand a few of our Sumerian allies have some experience with them. Have they been able to help us understand their navigation system or how the ship in general works?" he asked. "Is there a way we can salvage anything from it or ship it back to Earth?"

Halsey reached for her tablet, opened a folder and searched for a file. When she found it, she opened it up, and an image immediately displayed through the small holographic display unit in the center of the small table between the two couches.

Hunt furrowed his brow. "What am I looking at?" he inquired.

"The biggest intelligence discovery we've made thus far," she replied.

Hunt reached one of his fingers out and touched a small hexagon that said, "Rhea system." A line immediately connected to another system some hundred plus light-years away. His eyes went a little wide as he realized this was a navigational network.

"If you deselect our system, you'll see the other one it connects to," Halsey explained.

"I'm not sure I fully get this," Hunt said with a grunt. "I can see that each of these systems is somehow connected because of these lines. But what are they connected by? A wormhole of some sort? Is this what the Sumerians were telling us about?"

Halsey took a deep breath in and let it out. "I'm afraid we don't fully know yet. They could be wormholes that connect one system to another, or they could be stargates. Remember when we first met the Sumerians a few years ago? There was a Sumerian named Hosni. That guy who said he'd been a slave to a Zodark NOS. He mentioned something about their ships traveling through these great stargate contraptions. This is probably what he was talking about."

"Do we have any idea where these portals are or how one uses them?" Hunt asked next. She could see more questions were starting to form in his eyes as he looked back at the star map.

She shrugged. "I honestly don't know, Miles. I've been reviewing Hosni's information. He said a star system would usually have one and possibly two gates. He did say some systems had as many as four, but he wasn't sure if any had more than that. From what we've been able to learn from the Zodark prisoners, their ships essentially travel up to the gate, and then it's like it goes through a wormhole and gets deposited on the other side. They couldn't tell us how long it took to travel between gates, other than to say that some gates are farther apart from each other, and those jumps tended to take longer."

Shaking his head in amazement, Hunt sat back on the couch, looking at the information in a whole new light. "This is incredible, Admiral. Do you realize how many star systems are navigable? There appear to be hundreds of them on this map."

"Actually, there are five hundred and eighty-seven star systems connected via these stargates, at least according to this star map," Halsey clarified. "What the map doesn't tell us is how many planets are in those systems, but it has to be in the thousands."

"I don't mean to be cliché or repetitive when I say this, Admiral, but this changes everything. If we could get the Sumerians to help us understand what systems the Zodarks are in or where all these stargates are located, we could navigate them. We need to send out scouting vessels to locate and tag as many of these stargates as possible." Hunt spoke excitedly about the new possibilities.

Halsey smiled and let him talk for a few minutes. This was exciting, indeed. She was thrilled to share this discovery with a friend and confidant. The two of them spoke for a bit longer as they developed a plan for what should happen next, now that they had a better picture of what was going on around them.

They also plotted out some topics Captain Hunt should bring up and suggestions he should make during his meeting with Admiral Bailey and the others back on Earth. It was imperative that they get this system secured. They needed to find the stargate connecting this system and fortify it. Once they had a working idea of where they were and where the Zodark-controlled systems were, then they could build the system up and liberate the other human worlds out there from the Zodarks.

# Chapter Seven
## The Belt Grows

**Gaelic Outpost in the Belt**
**Non-Aligned Space**

Liam Patrick stood in the hangar bay with his partner and station manager, Sara Alma, as they waited for the Republic destroyer to finish docking. This entire visit had come out of the blue. No one had expected the governments of Earth to give them any sort of recognition, let alone legitimacy. They were Belters, pirates, nonconformists to the central government. Yet here they were, in charge of a station with one hundred and fifty thousand residents, and the fleet admiral was paying them an official visit.

The minutes continued to tick by until the outer door opened with a slight hissing noise. A handful of military members got off the ship and fanned out. They weren't acting in a threatening manner—they weren't armed—but they were observant of what was waiting for them and going on around them. Then three senior officers strolled down the walkway and headed for Liam and Sara.

As they approached, Liam immediately recognized Fleet Admiral Chester Bailey. The two other individuals, he didn't know. They stopped a few feet from them, extending their hands and offering a greeting.

"Mr. Patrick, Ms. Alma, it is a pleasure to finally make your acquaintance. I've looked forward to talking with you both for quite some time," Admiral Bailey said. Liam looked at Sara; she was clearly in the same state of shock he felt like he was in.

In his thick Irish accent, Liam replied, "It's a pleasure to meet you in person as well. Please, if you will, we'd like to give you a short tour of our station and then we can talk in a private setting at our residence. It's quite secure, and it's quiet."

The Republic delegation followed as Liam and Sara led them through the station, giving them a full tour of the facility. It had taken them more than fifteen years to build it and turn it into what it was—a floating home, nestled far away from the rest of the Earthers.

Liam and Sara already had their eyes set on two other massive asteroids they planned on turning into floating stations like this one, although this wasn't information they planned to share today. They also had dreams to build a larger structure that would eventually connect all of these asteroids together and essentially combine them all into one interconnected city.

An hour into the tour, Liam could tell Admiral Bailey was getting a little anxious. He was obviously interested in what they had built and asked a lot of excellent questions, but Liam sensed the man was very concerned about what he wanted to talk with them about next.

Liam eventually led them up to his and Sara's penthouse suite so they could have their private conversation. It was, after all, why Admiral Bailey had traveled out to visit them.

Once the door had finally closed, the group of five took a seat at the main table in the living room. Liam opened the conversation. "Admiral, I am pleased that someone of your stature has come to visit our station; it truly means a lot to the people who call this place home. During our tour, I could sense something was troubling you. I suspect it has something to do with why you're here. So please, let's dispense with the niceties and get down to business. What has brought you out here to talk with us?"

Smiling at the bluntness, Admiral Bailey replied, "I heard you were direct and to the point—I like that. It saves us a lot of political double talk that just wastes everyone's time. So, right to it, then—I'm here because I need your help, and I'd like to make you an offer if you're willing."

*I knew it! They want a favor...*, Liam thought. He fought to keep his facial expression as neutral as possible.

Sara spoke before Liam had a chance to. "Admiral, while we appreciate the thought that we could somehow help a great power like the Republic or the TPA, we are but a small station tucked away in the Belt. What could we possibly offer that would be of value to you?"

"Sara, is it?" asked the admiral, seemingly trying to make the conversation more familiar by using her first name. "I understand you are the engineer and station manager that is largely responsible for this facility, is that right?" he asked.

Sara nodded.

"Then you also understand the technical challenges involved in building something massive. I'm here to ask you a favor. We need your help. Rather, Earth needs your help. This isn't for the Republic or the TPA—this is for humanity."

"Whoa, hold up there, Admiral," Liam interrupted. "Before you go any further, we built this station and welcomed anyone to it because we've sought to create a refuge away from the powers of Earth—not become entwined in its politics or conflicts."

The admiral held his tongue as he let Liam finish. "I understand your point, Mr. Patrick, but I don't think you understand mine," he countered. "For better or worse, we have encountered the Zodarks. These are horrific alien creatures that, unbeknownst to us, have enslaved more than one world of humans, which may somehow be descendants of humans from Earth. Anyway, regardless of how humans came to be on these other planets, the Zodarks have enslaved them. And now that they've learned of our existence, they have set their sights on us. These beasts pose a threat not just to Earth, but to all of Sol. As humans, we need to unite for the common good to defend our species from this new enemy."

"What exactly is it you want from us, Admiral?" Sara demanded.

Admiral Bailey smiled. "We want you to help establish a shipyard out here—another location far away from our main yards in case the Zodarks eventually find our system and attack it. We need to make sure a single attack can't destroy our ability to defend ourselves or result in the enslavement of humanity."

Liam and Sara stared silently at the Earther for a few seconds before Liam ventured to speak. "OK, suppose we go along with this request. What's in it for us?"

Admiral Bailey leaned forward as he replied, "Full recognition from the Republic and TPA as a separate people, country, and government. To sweeten the pot, we'll also allow every tenth warship built at the new yard to be designated for use by your government. That'll enable you to build a navy at absolutely no financial cost to you. We'll even train your crew through our own training program if you'd like."

Liam was about to jump at the deal when his better half replied, "We're going to need more than just recognition and a ship from time to time, Admiral; we want technology. We want an agreement for long-term, continued trade anywhere in Sol and elsewhere. As you can see, we can only fabricate in our station with the resources we're able to mine and procure in the Belt. We need to be able to import equipment and components we can't create here."

The admiral nodded as he moved his hand up to his chin. He made it look like he had to think about this deal for a moment, but when Sara had laid out these other demands, Liam could tell the admiral had expected them.

Admiral Bailey looked Liam in the eye, then Sara. "Agreed," he said.

Liam turned to Sara, who gave him a sheepish smile. She should be excited—this was a massive opportunity for them and their people.

Sara then leaned forward in her chair as she asked, "Admiral, the Zodarks...how bad of a threat are they? I can't imagine you cutting a deal like this with us if things were going well. What's transpired out there that's caused you to reach out to us?"

Now the admiral squirmed a bit in his chair as if unsure if he should tell them the truth and, if he did, how much he should share. He motioned for one of his aides to hand him the case he was carrying with him, then opened it up and placed a holographic projector on the center of the table. He made a few taps on his tablet, and then an image was projected over the center of the table.

"What I'm about to show you needs to stay between us for now. Although, it won't do you any good to share it around the system; it's going to be widely shared in the coming days. Two weeks ago, we got a com drone back from our fleet in the Rhea system. I'm going to play for you a time-compressed battle that took place," Bailey explained, and then the group watched the battle unfold.

Liam watched in amazement at the real, honest-to-goodness space battle taking place. This was not one of the little shooting affairs he'd participated in as a pirate in the Belt—it was a real fight between massive warships slugging it out. When some of the smaller destroyer-class ships were blown apart, Sara covered her mouth with her hand.

The large Republic ship spearheading the attack was aggressive—far more aggressive than Liam thought it should have been, but then he saw the ship's weapons open fire. It was almost like watching one of those old black-and-white vids from the Second World War more than a hundred years ago. The Republic warship unloaded on the Zodark ship with the largest magrail guns Liam had ever seen. He watched those massive projectiles reach out and plow right into the Zodark ship. He found himself rooting for the Republic ship despite them having been his adversary most of his life.

Then the large enemy ship spat out wave after wave of smaller ships.

"Fighters," one of Bailey's aides commented. As they got closer, the Republic warship erupted in smaller anti-spacecraft fire. It was something Liam hadn't expected to see. He had no idea they had integrated something like this into their warships. It was incredible how fast the ship could spit out slugs at the incoming enemy fighters. Vast swaths of them were wiped out. Then they took evasive maneuvers.

Soon, he saw little projectiles fire from the fighters. They sailed toward the Republic warship like a swarm of angry bees. Liam figured they'd get destroyed by the anti-spacecraft fire, and they mostly did, but some of them converted into something he had never seen.

"What the hell is that?" he finally asked.

Sternly, Admiral Bailey responded, "That, Mr. Patrick, is a plasma torpedo. The Republic ship you're looking at is the *Rook*. They took two hits from them, nearly destroying the ship. Had those destroyers and the *Voyager* and *Xi* not intervened when they did, chances are the *Rook* would have been destroyed. It was a close battle: one we nearly lost."

At this point, Bailey turned the video off. "We're releasing this to the public in a few days. We want them to understand what we're facing. We need everyone to put aside our past animosities and work together, or we're all doomed. We can't fight these creatures on our own. That's why I'm here. I know we all have a past and I know we haven't always been friends. But I want us to bury the hatchet, so to speak, and find some common ground.

"At the end of the day, Mr. Patrick, you are responsible for these people now. They're going to look to you for leadership, for protection. None of us, including your people, are going to have a future if the Zodarks invade. That is why I need to know if we can count on you to help us out by allowing us to set up a shipyard here and leverage your people to help build the warships needed to defeat this new enemy."

Liam sat back in his chair as he shared a nervous glance with Sara. She had a look of fear on her face, something he seldom saw. He knew if she was scared, he needed to take action. He couldn't piss away this opportunity.

Nodding, Liam at last looked at the admiral, the man who had once been an enemy. Liam stuck his hand out. "OK, Admiral, for humanity's sake, I'll agree to allow you guys to build a shipyard out here. But you need to recognize our own sovereignty over this area," he said, leaning forward, emphasizing the point to make sure the admiral *really* understood the terms. "We'll work with you, we'll build you your ships, but we want to remain independent. When this whole conflict with these Zodarks is over with, we might even want the ability to populate our own world out there in the vastness of space. Is any of that going to be a problem?"

Admiral Bailey smiled as he extended his hand. "We have a deal, Mr. Patrick, we have a deal."

\*\*\*\*\*\*\*

**Rhea System**
**In Orbit near New Eden**

Halsey turned to find Captain Erin Johnson, her XO, "Captain Johnson, please send a message to Hadad and tell him to report to the bridge. I'd like to speak to him."

Moments later, the Sumerian came up to the bridge. Upon entering the nerve center of the ship, he made his way over to Admiral Halsey, bowing slightly when he reached her. "Admiral, you requested my assistance?" he asked respectfully.

Halsey smiled as she returned the slight bow. She was really starting to love their customs—the Sumerians were actually a very respectful culture. They were also brilliant, far ahead of Earth technologically in many ways.

"Thank you, Hadad. Please, just call me Abigail."

She then held her arm out, gesturing where they should go. "Let's go to my office and talk. We made a discovery, and I'd like to get your take on it."

As Abigail guided them off the bridge, she signaled for Captain Johnson to join her. She wanted her XO involved in this discussion as well.

When they entered her office, the three of them took a seat.

"You look concerned, Abigail. What's wrong? What can I help you with?" Hadad asked gently.

"You always are perceptive," Halsey replied. "We received a message from one of our other ships. They believe they found a stargate, and they're moving to investigate it now. What can you tell us about the stargates, Hadad?"

Hadad sat back in his chair momentarily; he didn't answer right away. He thought for a moment before he finally cautioned, "You need to be careful with the stargate, Abigail. None of us know what is on the other end."

Halsey held a hand up to stop him. "Actually, Hadad, we do." She reached for her tablet. Moments later, a holographic map floated in the center of the coffee table near them. She pointed to the Rhea system. "This is us. According to this star map, the stargate here connects us with a region of space the Zodarks call Ratan. This stargate leads to a system called SN9S-N. From there, it looks like it branches out into a host of other systems—"

"Abigail, are you saying you have a functional Zodark navigational star map?" Hadad interjected, clearly surprised.

Abigail smiled and nodded. "That Zodark ship we captured had a working star map. We've been trying to study it, but there's still some parts of the language that we don't fully understand. Maybe you could help us with the translation."

"May I?" asked Hadad as he reached out a hand to the holographic image.

Halsey nodded. She and Johnson watched as Hadad navigated through several layers of the star map. He eventually pulled up a system and somehow linked that system with the one they were in.

"This is my home system. The Zodarks call it YV-FDG; my people call it Lagash after our sun. It's a yellow dwarf, just like your own." Hadad then highlighted several other systems that traveled down what looked like a chain until it dead-ended. "Our system, Lagash, connects to a string of other star systems. I personally have never left our system except as a servant to the Zodark NOS. However, hundreds of years ago, before the Zodarks restricted our travel, we had an expedition that explored the chain. They were gone for several years, and when they returned, they reported that each system had at least one habitable planet," Hadad explained, getting more and more excited as he spoke.

"Our people were incredibly optimistic about what we had found." He paused, becoming somber. "This was right around the same time we made the discovery that we could travel through space using the folding of space and time to transport ourselves from one star system to another without the use of the stargates. We were just about to test the theory when the Zodarks learned of what we were doing and stopped us. It was during this period that they also restricted us from leaving our system and colonizing these other planets or exploring them further. They gave us free rein in Lagash, but we could not leave."

Halsey leaned forward. "Hadad, why did the Zodarks allow your people to explore space and then suddenly, out of the blue, decide they needed to rein you in? Were the Zodarks not present that often in your system?"

Hadad reached for a glass from Halsey's desk and filled it with water from her pitcher. He took a drink as he thought over what she'd said for a moment. "Abigail, there is much I do not know about the Zodarks, but I will do my best. Our history tells us we first encountered the Zodarks somewhere around two thousand years ago. Before then, it was rumored that a different alien species had been involved with our people, but we do not have very much evidence or information about them other than some prehistoric drawings on cave walls and stone tablets.

"When the Zodarks came, they set up a small city on the planet. They taught us industrial farming, medical science, and many other things. Society on our planet leaped forward. They ended wars and conflicts between various nations and groups and forced everyone to get along. Their presence in our world was viewed by most as a good thing. And then the tributes started.

"When the Zodarks began the tributes, they told our people this was the price to be paid for their benevolence and the advances in technology they were providing. I cannot say what the initial response was, but over thousands of years, our society came to accept them and found ways to deal with them. As you know, many believe the Zodarks eat the people given in tribute, and others believe the Zodarks are using those taken to act as slaves or perform some other function on other worlds the Zodarks control. To be honest, Abigail, we don't know for certain what they are doing with those who are taken.

"As you saw when you liberated us from the mining camp, some of those at the camp were prisoners who broke the Zodark rules. Some were people who had been taken as part of the yearly tribute. Now that you have freed me, I hope to learn one day what they are doing with all the people they are taking with their annual tribute."

Halsey leaned forward, balancing her chin on her hand. "But were the Zodarks not that involved in your planet prior to your people making that discovery in space travel?" she asked.

"I believe the Zodarks were distracted elsewhere. The Zodarks have been involved in a galactic war against some other species." Hadad held a hand up to forestall her from asking a question. "Before you ask me about that, there is little I can say. I have never been to any of their other worlds. I do not know much about their war other than that I know they have been involved in one, and it's been going on for hundreds of years. Hosni might be able to tell you more about it than I can, but that is why I believe the Zodarks didn't know we had left our star system or about this new space travel technology we had invented until we were about to use it."

"Do you believe these other planets in these systems are populated by people who were taken for tribute?" Halsey asked. "Is it possible the Zodarks have more planets like Sumer they are managing?"

Hadad nodded. "It's very likely that that is exactly what they are doing. I think the bigger question to ask is why are the Zodarks interested in growing the human population on other worlds? What are they ultimately using humans for?"

"Hadad, when we talked with Hosni, *he* told us the Zodarks don't cull the humans for food like many have been led to believe. He says they transport these humans to another system, where they are bred and trained to fight in their army," Halsey explained. She wanted to see what more Hadad could add to Hosni's claims.

Hadad shrugged. "Hosni said he was a slave to a Zodark NOS, and that he grew up on their home world. If all that is true, then he probably would know more than me about this."

"You sound like you don't believe him," Abigail countered, lifting an eyebrow in surprise.

Hadad opened his mouth to say something, then stopped. "I cannot say for certain if he is lying or telling the truth. There have been some rumors that the cullings are just that, a way for them to take our people and populate more worlds. Personally, I find it hard to believe that they would allow humans to fight alongside them as Hosni says. They would not allow *us* to fight alongside them, so I find it hard to believe that they'd allow other groups of humans to do so."

Abigail leaned forward as she fixed him with her steely gaze. "Hadad, is it possible that what Hosni has told us is true? Is it possible that the Zodarks have used an elaborate ruse to deceive your people?"

Hadad sighed as his body slumped back in the chair. "Abigail, I, I just don't know. I mean, maybe. Your world isn't controlled by the Zodarks, and your own scientists say our DNA is a perfect match, and our language is a language that used to be spoken on your own planet. It could be possible; I just don't know. But there are definitely other alien species out there besides just the Zodarks. Of that I am certain."

Feeling like she'd pressed him for as much as he knew about this subject, Abigail changed tracks to the real reason she'd called him up to her office. "Hadad, with a working star map, can you show us where the Zodark home worlds are and the territory they control?"

He nodded and highlighted six systems—it was becoming very useful to have a Sumerian who'd lived with a Zodark NOS. Inside those six systems, there were a total of ten planets. "These are their core worlds. I can't tell you how many people live on them. What I can tell you about the Zodarks is while they do live a long time, somewhere around four hundred of your years, they are very slow to reproduce. Zodark females may only have two or three offspring in their lifetime. Whereas on my planet, our women tend to have between six and ten children. So we procreate substantially faster and have grown our populations. Even with the tributes, we still produce more offspring than are chosen."

Halsey shook her head. She was still having a hard time accepting this practice by the Zodarks. She knew the Sumerians had no choice in the matter. Part of her hoped Hosni's tale of them being repopulated on other planets was true. If so, then maybe they could be liberated from these beasts.

"If I ordered our other ship to proceed through the stargate, do you know what would be waiting for them in that system…um…SN9S-N?" asked Halsey.

Hadad shrugged. "I can't say for certain, Abigail. What I can tell you is it took roughly three of your months to travel from my home system to here. I'm not sure how far the Zodark home systems are from New Eden—all I know is they are further away than my home world."

This caused Abigail to pause. She couldn't shake the feeling that a Zodark fleet must be headed toward them.

Seeing the puzzled, anxious look on her face, Hadad inquired, "What is troubling you, Abigail?"

She let out a soft sigh. "I find it hard to believe, Hadad, that the Zodarks would send only two warships to New Eden. And when those ships didn't report back, they didn't dispatch more ships to find out what happened. Surely they know we are here by now?"

Hadad thought for a moment. He eventually nodded in agreement. "You're probably right, Abigail. They will most likely send another set of ships to investigate what happened. But please keep something in mind—Clovis, or by your name New Eden, is at the extreme end of their known systems. This is a very remote place for them. They are probably more concerned with what is happening in another region called Intrepid, where they are at war.

"We Sumerians don't know much about who this other species is, what they are called, or what they look like. We only know little bits and pieces overheard in passing. The only reason I know anything is because I heard a couple of the camp guards talking about the war, and not in very pleasant terms."

"Hadad, why am I only just now hearing about this other species and a Zodark war?" she asked. "This is pretty important information to know."

He blushed. "Abigail, I apologize if I kept this from you. I honestly hadn't thought about it until you showed me the star map. Had I known you had a working copy of one, I could have shown you a lot more. I don't fully understand the Zodarks' written language, but I do understand enough of it to navigate their software. As a scientist on my own planet, I used this star map extensively at one point in my career."

Halsey leaned forward. "Here is what I need you to do, Hadad. I need you to sit down with some of our scientists and help us understand what all these symbols mean. Next, I want you to tell us everything you know about each of these stargates connecting New Eden to your home system and the Zodarks. I need as much tactical information as possible on what they have in each of these systems: what kind of industry they have, the number of ships they might have, etcetera."

Hadad nodded.

"We need a better understanding of the Zodark threat than I think you or your people have provided up to this point," Halsey pressed. "If you want to *stay* free, and you want our help in liberating your home world, then I need to better understand what I'm facing. Understood?"

The Sumerian agreed to help any way he could. He also offered to talk with the nine other Sumerians on the ship with him and see if any of them had additional information they could provide.
*******

## Sol
## John Glenn Orbital Station

As the destroyer approached the John Glenn Orbital Station, Admiral Bailey stood on the edge of the bridge, not wanting to get in the way of the captain and his crew. He observed the men and women as they did their duties. They were competent, professional, and ready for whatever might come. He felt good about that. It made him beam with pride that the intensive training programs he'd instituted were paying off.

When he'd taken over as the admiral in charge of fleet operations many years ago, Bailey had instituted a revamp of both the officer and enlisted training programs. He had drilled into them esprit de corps, discipline, and empathy. The latter had earned him a few laughs. However, Admiral Bailey felt it essential for leaders not just to be hard-charging men and women who adhered to strict rules and orders but also to have the ability to empathize and understand what their subordinates were going through. He empowered his entire crew to find their individual strengths and leverage them for the good of the mission and the ship. Each officer and enlisted person had faults, but their shortcomings didn't need to define them.

Bailey looked at the monitor in front of the bridge; he had a good view of the station. He spotted a transport he hadn't expected to see and walked up to the ship captain. "Ryker, is that the *Wahoo* in port?" he asked, pointing at the ship on the far side of the station.

Captain Ryker called out to one of his officers to zoom in on the ship at the end of the dock. Sure enough, it was, in fact, the *Wahoo*, a large FTL-equipped freighter the TPA had sent on the Rhea mission with Admiral Halsey. It was a massive freighter, and it also wasn't due in port for at least three months. Being one of the larger freighters, it was supposed to be one of the last ships to head back to Earth because it was supposed to be bringing a full cargo hold of the precious minerals they needed for their ships.

When they eventually docked, Admiral Bailey said he wanted a full brief on why the *Wahoo* was back in port. As he disembarked the ship, he became connected to the station's internal communications system. His neurolink synced up, and he received an inundation of information. He was also told a group of individuals was waiting to speak with him in his office at the station.

Admiral Bailey didn't work at his office on the John Glenn very often—typically only a couple of times a month at most. His time was spent mainly at Space Command headquarters and in the nation's capital, arguing over funding requests.

It took Bailey half an hour to navigate through the station to get to the military side. His security detachment escorted him past the sentries as they led him to his office. When Bailey walked into his assistant's office in front of his own, he heard a lot of talking coming from inside his office. A minute later, he walked in, and someone called the room to attention.

Bailey stood there for a second, looking at everyone who was in his office. He immediately spotted Captain Miles Hunt and then recognized several of Hunt's senior officers from the *Rook*.

"As you were, everyone," Bailey said. "Oh, by the way, welcome back to Earth, and it's damn good to see you all alive." He shook hands as he walked through the crowd until he made his way up to his protégé.

He looked Hunt in the eye and lowered his voice. "I'm glad you made it, Miles. My heart sank when I saw your ship fall into the planet. For a couple of days, I thought we had lost you."

Grimacing at the mention of his lost ship, Hunt said, "Thank you, Admiral—it *was* a tough day for us. We lost a lot of good people that day."

Before Admiral Bailey could say anything else, Captain Hunt turned to the soldier standing next to him. He was the only person in the room in Delta fatigues and not the uniform of the Fleeters. "Admiral Bailey, this is Master Sergeant Brian Royce, now Lieutenant Royce. He's the Delta who led the assault on the Zodark carrier we captured. It was also his company that saved my crew members on the planet when the Zodarks attacked us. Had their unit not arrived when it did, I'm honestly not sure any of my surviving crew would have made it out of there alive."

Bailey nodded as he surveyed the Special Forces operator, then extended his hand. "It is a true pleasure to meet you, Lieutenant. I watched the video of your assault, and I must say, I was in awe of your courage and bravery."

The lieutenant stood a bit taller. "I was just doing my job, sir—leading by example, as every NCO and officer should."

"Well, I'm not sure if Captain Hunt or anyone else has informed you, but we requested you to travel back to Earth because you're being presented the Medal of Honor in a few days at the White House," Admiral Bailey said, to the complete surprise of Lieutenant Royce. "As a matter of fact, the video of your heroics is going to be broadcast across the entire system in a few days."

"I, um…I'm not sure what to say, sir. Is that a wise idea?" The Delta suddenly had a look of horror etched across his face as he realized what he had just said to the fleet admiral, questioning his wisdom and judgment.

Bailey just smiled at the man and chuckled. He pulled the Delta aside from the others for a moment. "You and I are actually going to talk privately tomorrow. I need some straight answers from someone on the ground, and I won't get that from ship captains. I need a soldier's perspective; I need *your* perspective, OK?"

Royce nodded, clearly not sure what else he could say or do in this situation.

Bailey went on to add, "Look, son. You and I know this is going to be a tough war we now find ourselves in. In any war, they need heroes, people to believe in. Right now, that hero, that person to believe in, is you. You've seen the elephant and survived. Hell, you've survived more than one engagement with these beasts. People need to know they can be defeated, that we can win this war, and you represent that. So I'm going to need you to play your part once this award ceremony is done with, OK?"

The Delta nodded as he realized the depth of what was being foisted upon him.

For the next half hour, the officers and enlisted people in Bailey's office talked for a bit more, catching each other up on what had gone on in New Eden and back here on Earth. A lot had changed in the few months they had been gone. A lot more was about to change.
*******

A day after Captain Hunt and his remaining crew members arrived at the station, Admiral Bailey was still trying to digest all the information they had brought back with them. He felt immense information overload. At the same time, he needed to have a better understanding of it all in order to be prepared to meet with the President tomorrow for Lieutenant Royce's medal ceremony. She was going to ask some tough questions, and he owed it to her to have some answers.

*This star map changes everything…but how do we best exploit this? How can we stand against these beasts when we don't know how big their empire is, how many ships they have, or where their home systems are?*

A knock at the door snapped him out of his thoughts. Looking up, Admiral Bailey saw Captain Hunt outside waiting to speak with him. At that exact moment, the PA function in his neurolink reminded him, *Time for your meeting with Captain Miles Hunt, 0900 hours.*

He made a mental note to set his meeting reminders for twenty minutes before upcoming meetings instead of the time they started. Though he was the fleet admiral, he was quite possibly the least adept at using this new NL technology. It might have had something to do with the fact that he had been a bit older when he'd received the implant.

Admiral Bailey waved Hunt in and told his aide he wanted to be left alone for the time being. The two of them walked over to a pair of chairs and took a seat. Bailey made sure the electronic jamming equipment was turned on before he finally spoke.

"Miles, thank you for meeting with me," Bailey began. "I truly wish we were meeting under better circumstances. No one likes to lose a ship in combat, but I doubt you'll be the last ship captain to experience this. I've read over the notes from Admiral Halsey. I think she's right about us needing to launch a series of exploration missions throughout the Rhea system to find this stargate.

"However, I'll be frank, Miles, I don't know how we can do it right now. We're stretched thin," Admiral Bailey said bluntly. He'd known Hunt now for twenty years, so he felt he could be straight with the man even if he was a ship captain. The two had decades of history together.

Hunt leaned forward. "Admiral—"

"It's just the two of us, Miles," Bailey interrupted. "Call me Chester."

Hunt nodded. "Chester, I've been gone for a few months. It seems like each time I leave Earth and return, something major has happened while I was gone. I can't keep up with everything going on in Sol. I'm focused on what's going on in the frontier. Right now, we need ships, sir, no way around it."

Sitting back in his chair, Admiral Bailey let out an audible sigh of frustration. "This isn't how I thought things would turn out, Miles. When we first sent you to the Rhea system, I truly thought we'd found a new Earth—a new home for our country. Now...I feel like we've opened Pandora's box, and something hideous has crawled out of it and I don't know what to do."

Hunt seemed rather surprised to hear him admit this. *Now he finally sees that I'm just as unsure about things as he is*, Admiral Bailey thought. He'd been under a great deal of stress for some time, and he didn't have a lot of people he could talk to about it—at least not honestly.

"Chester, we've been friends for a long time," Hunt said. "You've got a tough job, but I can't think of anyone more suited to lead our people right now than you." He spoke with genuine respect.

Admiral Bailey smiled at his confidence in him. "Well, the President is the *real* leader. I just guide her where to go, but she ultimately makes the decisions."

He paused for a second before adding, "I envy you, Miles. You get to travel the stars. Hell, you've set foot on a whole new planet. I've been stuck wading through more political red tape than I care to think about. Things are changing and shifting so fast around here it would make your head spin if it wasn't attached to you."

Leaning forward, Hunt prodded, "What's going on, Chester? I don't think I've ever seen you this concerned or out of your depth."

Bailey chuckled. "Where to even begin, Miles? OK, here's one for you. The TPA isn't sure if they want to get more involved in this fight. There are some rumors that they're abandoning Earth for Alpha Centauri—going to leave Sol altogether and the entire defense of it to us—"

"What? They can't do that!" Hunt interrupted angrily. "We need their help to defeat the Zodarks. We need their shipyards, their industrial capability, their soldiers and sailors to help us defend Sol. Are you sure this isn't some sort of disinformation or rumor mill crap?"

Bailey shook his head. "I *wish* it were a bad rumor. About a week ago, we approached the Chairman in Beijing about the idea of forming a unity government here on Earth: a unified government and military to fight the Zodarks. I honestly thought they'd jump at the opportunity, especially since the Chairman would effectively become the new head of the government while the President would become the Defense Minister. He'd focus on unifying the world and the global economy while she worked with me on defending Sol and building the tools of war needed to win this fight."

"So, what happened? They didn't go for it?" Hunt asked, with a look of concern on his face.

Bailey nodded. "That's exactly what they did. They rejected it," he confirmed. "Despite his rejection, the Chairman reiterated their support for the war. However, after the meeting, my TPA counterpart told me members within the government were secretly making alternate plans. They were moving forward with their campaign to relocate their government to Alpha Centauri."

Hunt had a dumbfounded look on his face, and he didn't say anything for a minute.

Bailey went on to add, "Admiral Zheng assures me their shipyards are still going to produce warships for our joint fleet, but twenty-five percent of the new ships being built are going to be relocated to the Centaurus system. They're going to build a new base and home world there in case things don't turn out all right here on Earth."

Hunt shook his head in disbelief, then suddenly seemed to have an idea. "Chester, this might actually present us with an opportunity, then."

Bailey furrowed his brow. "How so? What are you thinking, Miles?"

"If the TPA government really is going to abandon Earth, then it may allow us to seize complete control of things *here*," Hunt insisted. "We can then place the entire world on a war footing to meet the demands to build the ships and fleet we need. If we can convince those left behind that they should join us and abandon the government that's abandoning them, we might be able to make this work."

Admiral Bailey sat back and ran some of the scenarios over in his head, trying to figure out if and how they could make it all work. Finally, he responded. "Miles, this is an interesting idea, and I'm not saying I'm completely against it. It very well might be the path we pursue, but we're probably years away from pulling something like that off. The TPA is still more than a few years away from having a decent fleet built to protect Alpha Centauri. Right now, they can only transport a million or so people a month to the new world, so it's going to take them time to get the needed industries built on Alpha to make it a fully self-sufficient place before they can abandon Earth. I fear the battle for Sol and New Eden will have already been decided by the time the TPA opts to abandon Earth if they fully choose to do so."

"Then we need to win this war and convince them to stay and fight with us, Chester," Hunt insisted. "We can't let them abandon Sol or even think that's a possibility."

"Believe me, no one is giving up the fight just yet," Bailey replied, placing a hand on his friend's shoulder. "Admiral Zheng does not strike me as the kind of man who will cut and run. The Chairman might, but not Admiral Zheng. He'll do what he can to keep the TPA in the fight."

Hunt thought about that for a moment, then nodded in acceptance. "OK, I trust you, sir. So, when do I get another ship?"

Bailey just grinned.

# Chapter Eight
## Full Mobilization

**John Glenn Orbital Station**
**Musk Industries**

"How fast is this new ship going to be?" Captain Hunt asked the lead engineer as he swiped past a couple of pages on the tablet containing more specifics on the ship.

The Musk Industries rep replied, "Three times the speed of the *Rook* and the *Voyager*. It's a fast little bastard—perfect for either reconnaissance or hit-and-run operations against the Zodarks, just as Space Command requested."

"What's its armament like?" Hunt asked, continuing to survey the newest warship the shipbuilders had come up with.

Smiling, the man brought up a schematic of the ship on the holographic display for them to look at more closely. "We took apart the few dozen working plasma torpedoes you brought back and reverse engineered them with the help of the Sumerians. Now that we have a steady supply of Morean, we're building them ourselves now. Apparently, the Morean is a key component in the conversion process from a regular torpedo to a superheated plasma weapon."

The rep continued, "We took the liberty of outfitting the new raider ships with them for some added punch. The ships are still small, so they can only carry twenty-four of them. They'll be fired from one of six forward torpedo tubes and two aft tubes, giving the ship three shots from each tube. Now, we've also equipped the ship with ten forward-facing Havoc missile launchers. Each launcher has a rotating three-missile magazine, so the ship will only be able to fire off a total of thirty missiles. The missiles can either be equipped with conventional HE warheads or variable-yield nuclear warheads, depending on the missile. The missiles will be operating on a rotary-style magazine, so they can be swapped out fairly easily to meet the mission requirements at the time of engagement. I think this gives the ship a lot of versatility and punching power well above its size."

Hunt let out a soft whistle as the engineer went over the weapons complement. He was impressed with what they'd been able to pack into this little ship.

"What about magrails?" Hunt asked. "We know those are the most effective weapons we have against the Zodarks, but I don't see any on here."

The engineer nodded. "We thought about that, Captain. We really did. However, the raider ship can't support any large-caliber magrails, not like what you had on the *Rook* or the *Voyager*. First, the recoil of the weapon is too much for this size of a ship to handle. Second, we just don't have the room for them. We gave the raider ships a single twin-barrel, five-inch magrail turret, but this is really meant for taking on smaller warships or in support of defending a larger warship against fighters. The five-inch shells can easily be configured with proximity fuses to help deal with those Zodark fighters. We also added six CIWS systems for close-in point defense weapons. The raider ships don't have a lot of armor on them because their primary mission is reconnaissance, but you could conceivably use them as picket ships for some of the larger warships if it came down to it."

"You bring up a good point about the need for picket ships," Hunt acknowledged. "Having fought against those enemy fighters, we're going to need some kind of ship like that for the larger warships. I'm not sure if it's possible, but if we can create another variant of this ship or maybe a larger version of it that's more heavily armored and equipped with two or three times the number of CIWS systems and five-inch guns, then we may be able to intercept more of those fighters and plasma torpedoes before they have a chance to hit our capital ships. We would need to place these ships further away from the *Voyager* and some of the larger warships."

The engineering rep nodded and scribbled down some notes on his tablet. "That's a good idea, Captain. Let me work with my team and see what we can come up with. If you like our initial specs, then we can flesh out more of the details to see if Space Command would like us to move forward with it."

Hunt nodded in approval. "That sounds good; I know we'd be very interested in looking at them. But back to this ship, I must say, I'm impressed with what your team came up with. I think we have to keep in mind that this raider ship wasn't designed to be the battlewagons we need. This ship is supposed to be the eyes and ears of the fleet, much like a submarine was during the last century." He crossed his arms and smiled. "So, my next question is, how fast can you start cranking them out?"

The engineers nodded and smiled at this question. "Well, this warship is a lot less complicated than the ones we've been building. It's also much smaller, for a crew of only fifty-two. If Space Command is ready to move forward with these specs, then we can start work on them right away. From start to finish, the ship should take no more than six weeks to complete."

Hunt shook his head in disbelief. "Six weeks? How the heck are you able to build them so fast?"

Now it was the engineer's turn to smile. "Let's just say our Sumerian allies have shared a lot of new technology and starship-building methods. As a matter of fact, they've helped us speed up our entire ship production by as much as three hundred percent. Plus, with the steady supplies of Trimar and Morean from New Eden, we're starting to become flush with the resources we need."

Captain Hunt took a deep breath in for a moment before letting it out. Since his return from New Eden two months ago, Admiral Bailey had made him the point man for Space Command's new ship procurement and design program. Hunt was still working under another admiral, but Hunt was the one with the experience fighting the Zodarks, so what he said would work or wouldn't work was usually implemented in any ship designs with the admiral's full support and blessing—at least, until his own warship was completed and he transferred out to take command of it.

"OK, gentlemen, the *Viper*-class frigates are approved. We need one hundred and ten of these raider ships built as soon as possible," Hunt finally said.

The jaws of the engineers practically hit the floor when he told them how many Space Command was requesting.

Hunt ignored the looks of surprise. "Can you give me a timeline for when you'll be able to have them completed?" he asked.

The two engineers looked at each other and then talked for a few minutes before turning back to him. "Eight to twelve months for the entire lot; we need at least that much time."

Hunt nodded, then took the tablet from them. He wrote a few things down on it and then signed it. "Done. Now, please hurry, gentlemen, and get them built. You have no idea how important these ships are going to be."

With his immediate business for the morning done, Hunt made his way through the promenade of the John Glenn Orbital Station to the main walkway. Looking around, he eventually found the person he was looking for.

Hunt walked up to the beautiful woman who had her back to him, reached his arms around her and gave her a quick squeeze as he leaned in and whispered in her ear, "Hello, my love. How are you doing today?"

Lilly, his wife, turned around and gave him a quick kiss. "Much better now that my Prince Charming is here. Are you ready for some lunch?"

Since Hunt was without a ship, he was finally able to see his wife every day. He'd been gone so much these last few years, and he'd nearly died several times. He wanted to soak up as much time with his bride as he could.

"I sure am, I'm famished," Hunt replied good-naturedly. The two of them walked over to the Spacers Lounge and got a seat.

"Are Ethan and Piper going to be able to make it for Christmas?" Hunt asked, hoping he'd get a chance to see his two kids in person soon. His son had just completed his basic officer course and was preparing to receive his first assignment with Space Command while his daughter was in her junior year at the naval academy.

Lilly's eyes lit up at the mention of their children.

*They aren't so little anymore, but I think they will always be little in her eyes*, thought Hunt.

"As a matter of fact, yes," Lilly replied. "Ethan was able to get a few days of leave while he awaits his next assignment. Piper also managed to get permission to leave Earth to come see you here. Apparently, having a famous ship captain for a father has its perks." Lilly winked.

Hunt had been awarded the Medal of Honor the same day as Brian Royce. The PR department was promoting him and the Delta operator as the faces of victory against the Zodarks. He understood the need for heroes, but he sure didn't *feel* like one. He'd lost hundreds of people and his ship.

Lilly squeezed Hunt's hand when she saw him staring off blankly at the mention of his newfound fame. "I think this is going to be the first time in three or four years we'll all be together for Christmas. I'm so excited, Miles—a real family Christmas."

Their waiter came and took their orders and then left them alone to talk for a bit. He brought them some waters and then disappeared while their food was prepared.

"You know, Ethan won't ask you this, but he really wants to be stationed with you," Lilly said. "He wants an assignment on your new ship."

Hunt smiled. *Of course he does.* Hunt was going to be taking command of Earth's largest, most powerful warship soon. Every officer and enlisted person in the fleet wanted an assignment on this ship.

"Ethan *does* know my ship is going to see combat, right?" asked Hunt.

Lilly looked a bit worried at his response. "He does—I think that's why he wants it. He wants to be with you, where the action is."

Hunt saw this wasn't sitting well with her, though. "You don't want him to be with me, do you?" he pressed.

His wife didn't say anything for a moment. Instead, she reached for her glass of water and drank some of it down, buying time. She finally looked him in the eyes. "Miles, I've nearly lost you twice in the last couple of years. Both of your trips to Rhea saw fierce combat. I know Ethan wants to be in the thick of the action; however, as his mother, if I'm being honest, I just want him safe. Isn't there a safe duty you could get him assigned to? Maybe Chester could get him assigned to his staff or something."

Lilly was practically pleading with her husband to do what he could to protect their son from possible danger. It hurt him to see his wife asking this of him. He wanted to help; he desperately wanted to keep his son safe. What father wouldn't? He also knew that while he could work some connections and pull some strings to get his son a safe assignment, Ethan would never forgive him for it, and it might also hurt his career.

Looking at his wife, Hunt opened his mouth to say something, anything, but he stopped. He knew anything he said was going to be the wrong answer in her eyes. Sighing softly, he nodded. "I know this is hard, Lilly. I'll see what I can do, but I can't make any guarantees. We've got a lot of ships coming online these next few months. A lot of newly graduated officers are going to be getting assignments to them."

Lilly reached across the table and grabbed his hand as she looked him in the eyes. "Please, Miles. If you can't get him assigned to Chester's staff or some other safe assignment, then please try to get him assigned to your ship. At least there, you'll be able to look out for him."

Hunt knew the chances of them serving together were close to nil. It was inappropriate for a son to serve on the same ship his father captained—nepotism and all. Lilly didn't care. She'd badger him until he got their son a safe assignment.

Squeezing her hand, Hunt replied, "I'll do what I can, Lilly. Now, let's enjoy our lunch and the fact that we can dine together."
*******

**Vale, Colorado**
**Walburg Industries**
**Residential Retreat**

It was snowing outside as Dr. Alan Walburg looked out the window to his office. Sometimes he caught himself staring at the snow as it fell. Ever since he was a child, he'd enjoyed watching the snowfall. Something about these fluffy white cotton balls of love falling from the sky just mesmerized him. No two snowflakes were alike—just like humans. Each was unique, different in its own way.

Returning his gaze to the computer terminal in front of him, Dr. Walburg recognized that his creations of the past were nothing like snowflakes. There was nothing unique or different about the synthetics—they were all the same.

*But not these Synths. These will be different...*

Like a genetically engineered crop, this set of code he was writing for this new breed of Synths was going to be drastically different from everything he'd created in the past. He still wasn't comfortable with what he was doing. If humanity weren't facing the real possibility of extinction at the hands of a brutal alien species, he wouldn't even consider building these new combat synthetics.

The video he'd seen of the Zodark attack on the *Voyager* had pretty much sealed the deal for him. A second video he'd watched a month ago had given him all the energy he'd needed to finish this work. Like everyone else on Earth, he'd watched the video of the Delta soldier that had been awarded the Medal of Honor. The viciousness and brutality of this new alien threat had horrified him. The Zodarks had torn through the human soldiers assaulting the planet like they were rag dolls to be tossed about by an angry child. Dr. Walburg knew if he didn't come to the aid of his species, he might not have a humanity left to defend in a few years.

No one knew when or if the Zodarks would attack Sol. What everyone *did* know was that if they attacked now, there was little the governments of Earth could do to stop them.

A soft knock at the door to his private office broke Dr. Walburg from his train of thought. He turned around and saw his wife standing there with a cup of hot tea and a plate with his favorite sandwich on it— pastrami on rye bread with all the trimmings. She'd even given him a bag of potato chips. He smiled at the sight. He and his wife had been married forty-six years—thanks to the invention of medical nanites, they'd probably be married for another thirty or forty more, Lord willing.

"Are you sure you don't want to come down and eat dinner in the dining room?" his wife asked with concern in her voice. She was always telling him he worked too much and way too hard for his age.

For the last month, Dr. Walburg had secluded himself in his mountain retreat in Vale. When he needed to work on a sensitive project like this, he tended to avoid people. One of the best ways to do that was to sequester himself away in his mountain villa. Being the richest man on Earth did have its benefits, like being able to purchase a hundred-acre plot of land on the side of a mountain and build his dream home on it, which was exactly what he had done nearly thirty years ago. Now he used the place as a private retreat for top-secret projects like this or his own little side ventures he was known to work on.

Dr. Walburg smiled warmly at his wife. "Thanks, honey. I appreciate the gesture. But I need to finish this last bit of code."

She nodded and placed the tray with the sandwich and drink on the side of his desk and kissed him on the forehead. "I'll leave you be, then," she said before leaving his office and closing the door on the way out.

Dr. Walburg stared at the tea as if for answers; he hoped he was doing the right thing. He was essentially done with the code—the only thing left to do was make sure the safeguards were firmly in place, so that they couldn't be overridden by some outside force. For all Dr. Walburg knew, the Zodarks could attempt to hack into the operating system of the machines he was building to try to change them—a repeat of what had happened during the last war. That was a nightmare scenario he desperately wanted to avoid. It was why his company had never used its considerable wealth to fight the ban on autonomous AI or its use in the synthetic marketplace.

Several hours later, the sun finally descended below the mountain, casting long, ominous shadows across the valley. Soon it would be pitch black, and it was only 4:50 in the afternoon.

As he finished tapping away at the keys on his tablet, Dr. Walburg nodded in satisfaction. *It's done. I've completed it…now it's time to test it.*

*******

The following morning, Dr. Walburg sent a message to his contact at Space Command that he had finished the coding for the combat synthetics. He was going to head back to his facility in New Mexico to begin testing. Once that was completed and the government certified they were happy with the product, his factory would start producing tens of thousands of them.

The only question Dr. Walburg had that Space Command still hadn't elaborated on was how they were going to transport the new synthetics into combat or wherever they would be used. He knew the Zodarks had other worlds in systems spread across the galaxy, and he suspected Space Command would probably find a way to insert them into some of those planets to cause some chaos and problems for the enemy.

Dr. Walburg made a mental note to make sure there were no markings or other ways to track his machines back to Earth. The last thing he wanted to do was leave a calling card for the enemy to read: "Hey, this machine was built by Walburg Technologies on Earth."

When he made it back to his facility in Alamogordo, Dr. Walburg saw the first combat Synth was waiting for him, ready to start the test.

The first thing they did to the machine was hook it up to his computer. Dr. Walburg then began the process of loading the programming code to the OS and thus giving it life. This part didn't take as long as one might think, especially since he had a quantum computer and a specially designed cable that transferred terabytes of data per second.

A few minutes later, the download was complete. A few of the engineers, unique individuals that Dr. Walburg trusted with this kind of technology, began conducting various system tests. They went over the

Synths' protocols for what to do when a human was threatened, how to treat humans, when it was acceptable and not acceptable to wound or kill a human and how it would decide when wounding or killing a person was both appropriate and acceptable. Next they went through a series of questions about the Zodarks: when to attack, when to hold back, how to handle surrendering Zodarks, and when not to accept surrender. They had even included parameters to help the Synths know if the Zodarks were playing a trick, like what had happened on the Zodark carrier, where the Delta battalion commander and a group of their unsuspecting comrade had been killed by a surrendering NOS. The scenarios they needed to teach the new machine were far-reaching.

The model number for the Synth was C100—C for combat, and 100 was its serial designation. Dr. Walburg hadn't necessarily like the idea of naming the Synth, but he also didn't like thinking of it as property with a serial or model number either. As he thought about the name for this child he'd just created, he decided to call the first C100 "Adam." It felt fitting that the first sentient machine created should have this name. His engineers came up with their own nickname, AA, for "Alan's Adam."

For the next several weeks, Dr. Walburg's engineers went over thousands of scenarios with Adam about when he could and couldn't use his capabilities to kill. They relentlessly tested his safety protocols until they felt confident he could not deviate from them.

In a way, Adam was much like a young child. He asked a lot of questions, as he should. But he also had an immense amount of knowledge. The challenge was teaching Adam how to use that knowledge to make better-informed decisions. They spent weeks going over Adam's primary mission, to serve and protect the Republic and humanity. They made sure he fully understood that he was a soldier first and foremost.

After months of instruction, Dr. Walburg felt Adam was ready to start getting acquainted with his equipment and learning the specifics of his job. Adam was introduced to his military trainers, who worked twenty-four-seven, teaching him everything they knew about soldiering, weapons, tactics, first aid, and combat. They gave Adam enough knowledge to also act as a field surgeon or doctor to aid injured soldiers on the battlefield. This helped to make sure Adam was much more than just a killing machine; he could also be used to save lives.

Another critical part of Adam's training was having him analyze thousands of hours of combat footage between the Zodarks and humans. Adam needed to fully understand how the human soldiers he'd be fighting alongside fought and how his enemy attacked. When they were deployed to fight for real, this training would give the C100s a real chance of making a difference. In a matter of weeks, Adam was as fluent in the ways of soldiering as his instructors.

When the military felt he was ready, they transitioned Adam to his equipment. He was taught how to use all manner of military equipment and what its limits were. The Republic Army soldiers and Delta soldiers made sure Adam knew not only how to use every weapon system the Earthers had but also how to fly and operate every piece of military equipment—everything from one of their infantry mechs to tanks, to their vertical assault craft or VACs and dropships. As they trained Adam, his knowledge was passed down to all the new combat Synths; the C100s were also being taught to function and operate as an independent military unit, able to deploy and carry out combat operations wherever their human masters ordered them.

The process of getting Adam and the Synth battalions ready for war was a daunting one. It was also scary, because if this technology was ever unleashed on Earth, it could wipe out humanity. These were the terminators of the twenty-second century, and Lord willing, they'd be the saviors of man in their greatest hour of need.
*******

A few weeks into the final testing of the new combat Synths, Fleet Admiral Chester Bailey, Captain Miles Hunt, and Lieutenant Brian Royce from Special Forces arrived for one of the demonstration events. This was Dr. Walburg's chance to show off his newest creation and get final approval before moving the C100s into full production.

Admiral Bailey extended his hand as he introduced his two other guests. Dr. Walburg already knew who they were, of course. Lieutenant Royce was a war hero, the man who'd stood against the Zodarks and prevailed. Dr. Walburg was in a little bit of awe at meeting the man who had so courageously charged into the enemy and survived. It was his actions that had inspired Dr. Walburg to create some of the features he'd incorporated into the final combat Synth.

Captain Hunt was another man Dr. Walburg had great respect for—he'd fought the Zodarks several times in space and lived to tell about it. Hunt was also the man behind the newest designs in the warships being built. The visual appeal and complexity of Earth's warships had seen a radical change for the better in the last four and a half years. They were larger and deadlier, and they actually looked like real honest-to-goodness warships.

Admiral Bailey took his seat near the demonstration quad. "Dr. Walburg, I want to commend you on a job well done," he said. "I know you and your team have been working tirelessly on this project for years."

Dr. Walburg just nodded. "I...hope they can serve their intended purpose and will ultimately save lives," he stammered, then cleared his throat and refocused, speaking with more confidence. "What you are about to see is what we're calling the C100. We personally named this one Adam. Everything we've taught Adam will be transferred to all the subsequent production models. This means each model coming off the assembly line will have his shared knowledge and experiences built into them on day one."

A minute later, the doors to a nearby room opened up, and two of Dr. Walburg's engineers escorted Adam out for them to see. This was the first time anyone outside of his small team had seen the final product. Until now, they had only seen the test Synths they'd been using.

Admiral Bailey let out a soft whistle when he saw the combat Synth. Adam moved toward them. Lieutenant Royce stood up as he surveyed the beast of a machine.

Adam stood eight feet tall, had broad shoulders, and looked scary as hell. Adam didn't have synthetic skin covering his metal frame as a standard Synth had. Instead, most of his exoskeleton was either exposed metal or armor-plated. His metallic frame or skin was also unique in that it could mimic its surroundings; in a wooded environment, his outer shell would morph into those color schemes to match what was around it. Likewise, in an arctic environment, his metallic skin would morph into a color scheme to match. His sleek and fierce design was both extraordinarily beautiful and uniquely terrifying at the same time.

Adam's face was also unusual. While it had a human-looking feel to it, its eyes were a one-inch band that wrapped around the front of the face from ear to ear. This gave Adam a full 180-degree view of everything going on in front of him. In order for an observer to know he was turned on and not in a passive or recharge mode, he had a single blue light that tracked from right to left.

Adam made his way over to Dr. Walburg and his visitors, stopping a couple of feet in front of them. "Hello, Father. How may I be of assistance today?" Adam asked in an all-too-human voice. The voice projected calm, despite the killing machine's intimidating features.

Admiral Bailey chuckled. "You have Adam calling you 'Father,' eh, Alan?" he asked with a grin.

Dr. Walburg shrugged. "I *am* his creator," he replied casually. "He knows me as Father or Dr. Alan Walburg."

He turned back to face his creation. "Adam, I want to introduce you to three very important people. This," Dr. Walburg said, gesturing to Admiral Bailey, "is Fleet Admiral Chester Bailey. He is the supreme commander of the Republic's military. He is your overall commander."

Adam extended his hand, as he had been taught to do, and shook Admiral Bailey's with just enough pressure to show respect and strength without crushing his hand.

"This is Captain Miles Hunt," Dr. Walburg continued. "He's a ship captain. His ship fought our enemy, the Zodarks, in space on several occasions, and brought us many victories. He is also one of your superiors."

Adam extended his hand to Captain Hunt as well. The C100 machine then intuitively turned to look at Brian Royce. Dr. Walburg knew that Adam immediately recognized the difference in military uniforms. He also knew that Royce, unlike the other two people Adam had just met, was an enhanced, augmented human soldier.

"This is Lieutenant Brian Royce, a Delta soldier in the Republic Army Special Forces," Dr. Walburg confirmed. "He fought the Zodarks in hand-to-hand combat; you may recognize him from the combat footage we had you study."

Adam also extended his hand to Royce and commented, "You are the great warrior I was built to assist. Father has shown me the videos of your combat. You fought with great courage—fearless, but reckless in many of your battles. Did you not care if you died?"

Dr. Walburg blushed at the question. "Sorry about that, Lieutenant," he said, trying to intervene. "Adam here is still learning how to properly interact with people. Right now, he has the emotional characteristics of a young child."

Royce just laughed. He looked at the machine as he replied, "Adam, you're right. I did fight with reckless abandonment. In those moments of combat, I knew if I hesitated in the least, the Zodarks would most likely kill me and my teammates. If I wanted to survive, then I had to be willing to die. In throwing away that desire to preserve my own life, I was able to save it, as well as the lives of the men and women who fought with me. Does that make sense?"

The machine stared at Royce for a moment, processing what he had just been told. "Yes, it makes sense, Lieutenant. I believe I have much to learn from you."

Hunt then added, "My men and I will be able to teach you a lot, Adam, but the most important thing you will need to learn is how to adjust to change. When I was growing up, my dad told me an old saying: 'Everyone has a plan until they get punched in the face.' It was said a very long time ago by a famous boxer at the time. You will see when you go into combat that no plan survives first contact. When the blaster bolts start to fly, the only thing that matters is killing the enemy as quickly and efficiently as possible to accomplish the mission and keep your people alive."

The machine didn't nod or say anything in response to what Hunt had just said, at least not right away. His soft blue light continued to move from right to left across where human eyes would normally be. Finally, Adam asked, "Will I be accompanying you personally into combat?"

Before anyone else could respond, Royce explained, "That depends, Adam, on how long it will take to get you ready for combat and how we're going to integrate the C100s into our military units. Personally, I hope I'm able to take you into combat with me; there's a lot I want to teach you in hopes that what knowledge I pass down to you will be passed along to the other C100s."

Dr. Walburg had a broad smile on his face as he saw the interaction between his creation and the soldier he had been built to help. It made him feel exceptionally fulfilled to see Adam really taking on a life of his own.

"Adam, in the coming weeks, you will learn much from Lieutenant Royce and other soldiers like him," Dr. Walburg explained. "Right now, while we have the admiral here with us, I'd like you to demonstrate some of your skills for us. Can you begin by showing everyone some of your combat skills?"

For the next hour, Adam ran through a series of drills, demonstrating what he could do. What everyone seemed to find most interesting, though, was Adam's ability to ask questions and hold a conversation. For the military men, this was important. The Zodarks were a unique enemy, one that would learn over time how to fight them and eventually win. If the combat Synths were going to be effective, then they needed to have that same ability to learn and adapt to the changes in the way the Zodarks fought.

When the demonstrations inside the building had been completed, they prepared to head out to the range. The Deltas had helped Walburg's engineers build a shoot house and urban tactical course, and it was time to test Adam's skills.

*******

### Range 5 – Shoot House

Lieutenant Brian Royce finished attaching the rest of his equipment on his exoskeleton combat suit and then did a quick double-check of the sim rifle. The sim rifles were exact replicas of their M85 advanced infantry assault rifles, with the exception that they didn't fire lethal rounds. Since the op-four or opposition force was going to consist of a company of regular army soldiers, they needed to use the sim rifles.

The platoon of soldiers suiting up with Royce looked skeptically at Adam. This was the first time any of them had worked with a C100. To say they were a little anxious about working with an automated killing machine was an understatement, given what had happened during the last Great War.

Royce saw their hesitation. "Listen up, guys. Adam here," Royce said, pointing to him, "will be accompanying us on this exercise to prove androids can function as a bona fide member of a Delta team. I want you guys to treat Adam just like a regular team member. This exercise will test his ability to work as one of us and not just a single situation operator. This is also a chance for us to show off our skills and ability directly to Admiral Bailey, so don't screw it up or Captain Hopper will have us cleaning toilets on our trip back to New Eden."

Some of the soldiers laughed while a few others grumbled. They got the not so subtle message—don't make Royce or the captain look bad in front of the brass.

"Second squad, you're going to HALO into the village at this location. As you descend, you need to be zapping guards on the roof and anywhere else you can find them before you land on the ground. Once down, reform and move to the building holding the hostages."

The squad leader and his fireteam leaders nodded in acknowledgment.

"Third squad, you'll be doing the exact same thing as second squad, except you'll be on the opposite side of the village, here." Royce used a pointer to highlight the section on the map the squad would be hitting. "Once you guys are on the ground, clear this section of the village from any possible hostile. Once second squad has the hostages, you're going to need to help cover their exfil from the village."

Royce turned to fourth squad, which was traditionally his heavy weapons squad, mortars, and anti-armor weapons. For this mission, they were suiting up to be extra shooters. "Fourth squad is going to assault the main compound with Adam and first squad to take out the enemy commander. This is going to be a tough position to assault because you can bet those RA guys are going to have it locked down tight. They'll be itching to prove to the brass watching in the stands that they are just as good as us. Well, let's show them why they aren't."

That last comment got a lot of laughs and snide comments from the Special Forces guys. The rivalry between the two factions was alive and well.

With their mission brief over, the operators filed out of the team room and made their way over to the hangars with the Ospreys. While they could pack the platoon into a single bird, they were saddling up in four different ones so they could hit their objective from multiple vantage points.

Forty minutes later, the craft carrying Lieutenant Royce and first squad made a tight left turn and suddenly dropped altitude rapidly. The pilot came on over their HUDs telling them what was going on. "We're circling in on the objective. Intelligence says this will be a hot insertion, so expect resistance immediately."

The operators grinned and fist bumped each other. They loved a good fight, and this was gearing up to be just that. While his human counterparts psyched themselves up for what was about to happen, Adam just sat there, his blue light sliding from right to left.

The Osprey made another tight turn. This time the chin gun opened fire on some unseen targets, firing their own simulator stun rounds. The pilot came on over their HUDs again. "We're almost to the drop zone. You need to get ready to jump, because I'm not sticking around."

Royce stood up, his magnetic boots helping hold him to the floor as he walked towards the rear of the craft. The crew chief was lowering the ramp so they could jump. As Royce neared the edge, he could see the small town that constituted the range, where two hundred and twenty RA soldiers were hunkered down, ready to carry out their roleplay for this combat training scenario.

The Osprey slowed its descent a bit and leveled out. The jump light turned from red to green, telling them it was time to jump. Without any hesitation, Royce ran forward and jumped out the back of the ramp. His HUD told him he was roughly a hundred feet above the ground. The automated targeting reticle was already identifying hostiles for him to engage as his body fell toward the earth below.

Out of his peripheral vision, Royce saw Adam hit the ground before him. The combat Synth had his rifle up and was engaging targets at an astounding rate. He wasn't firing wantonly either; he was hitting hostiles with the accurate precision only a machine could or highly trained individual could achieve.

In seconds, Adam was off at a trot as he moved to a covered position, his rifle tucked in his shoulder, firing the entire time. Steadily, he took defender after defender out.

As Royce continued his fall to earth, he brought his rifle up to engage the hostile targets. The green targeting reticle danced across his HUD until he managed to synch it up to the red one denoting a hostile. Royce squeezed the trigger several times, sending stun rounds flying toward the RA soldiers.

Several of the rounds slammed into one man's body, who clutched at his chest as the electricity coursed through his body, causing him to collapse to the ground, spasming. The stun rounds wouldn't kill him, but they sure did sting.

By the time Royce had hit the ground, he and the rest of his squad were moving rapidly to catch up with Adam as he trailblazed a path ahead of him. Royce saw an RA soldier with a heavy blaster try to lay into Adam. Dozens of blaster bolts set to stun flew toward the combat Synth. To Royce's amazement, Adam demonstrated his incredible agility as he deftly dodged the string of shots, moving at incredible speeds. Adam's large but agile frame then rolled to one side while still firing his rifle as he slid into a new covered position.

Royce and another one of his squadmates locked eyes for a second and shook their heads in amazement. They'd never seen anything like it.

Suddenly, a platoon of RA soldiers appeared from a couple of alleyways and windows of some buildings from further away. Their appearance caught Royce and his squad by surprise.

*I thought we'd just cleared that area*, Royce thought, trying to remain calm. They were only a hundred meters from the building where the high-value targets were hidden.

"I'm hit!" screamed one of Royce's guys as he went down hard on the ground, convulsing from the stun rounds.

Looking to his right, Royce saw two more of his guys go down. *Damn, that's three we've lost.*

He switched over to the platoon net. "Fourth squad, I need you to shift fire over to sector K and assist first squad. We're pinned down by what appears to be a platoon element in the buildings opposite our position. Second squad, I need a SITREP on the hostage recovery."

Royce could see from the blue force tracker that second and third squad had just entered the building with the hostages. They appeared to have a wide perimeter set up around the place, so they'd cleared the area of hostiles.

"Lieutenant, we've recovered the hostages. Second squad is working to exfil them now to the extraction site. Do you want me to send third squad your direction to help you guys out?" asked Royce's platoon sergeant, who was overseeing that part of the mission. Third squad had a second C100 with them. They wanted to test the synths ability to function in a hostage rescue role as well as the direct-action role where Adam was playing his part. Hostage rescue required a lot more fire discipline, so one of the hostages wouldn't mistakenly get killed.

"Yes, that'd be a good idea," Royce answered. "I want them to try and gain entry to the building from sector L. We'll continue to draw the enemy's fire over here—that should give you guys the opportunity you need to make it happen on your end. Out."

Royce and his squad continued to lay down covering fire while third squad lined up against the building to breech it. Adam's aim was incredibly accurate—his covering fire did more than just keep the enemy's heads down—he took out defender after defender.

*Smash! Bang!*

Royce heard the door being smashed in, followed by the flashbang. Third squad would clear one room at a time until they found the high-value target and eliminated them.

*Zip.* A stun round narrowly missed Adam. He always seemed to move in the last fraction of a second. Royce was actually starting to feel a bit jealous.

Moments later, the whole exercise was over. The HVI had been taken down, and the building had been cleared of RA soldiers.

The feeds from the drones must have impressed the higher-ups. "Good job, guys," Admiral Bailey told them over their platoon net. "Beers and burgers are on me tonight."

Royce and the rest of his squad cheered. Everyone liked free grub and drinks.

When everyone had recovered from their celebration, all the Deltas were interviewed on how they thought the C100 performed. The engineers wanted to know everything. From how did the android function as a team member to an individual shooter. They would review the footage of every soldier involved in the training exercise to the two C100s, but nothing beat an honest assessment from the soldiers who would be fighting with them.

The Republic Army soldiers thought the C100s were terrifying—they were hard to kill and they could fire back at them so rapidly that they lost a lot of their numbers very quickly. The Deltas loved them because they operated like a 20-year Delta veteran with how fast and smooth they moved. The human soldiers provided their own insights into what could make them operate better, but in general, they loved the combat tool.

The brass was convinced. Now it would just be a matter of drilling them some more with their military counterparts and putting them into full production. "I think we just found our new ace in the hold to fight the Zodarks with if the war ever becomes a ground battle," said Admiral Bailey.

\*\*\*\*\*\*\*\*

**Earth, Sol**
**John Glenn Station**

"It feels strange spending Christmas in orbit like this," Hunt's son, Ethan, commented to everyone as they sat in the family room of Hunt's quarters.

"Yeah, I suppose it is. I wish we could have celebrated Christmas down at our home in Florida," Hunt replied wistfully. Going to the beach on Christmas and New Year's Day had become a Hunt family tradition over the many years they'd lived in the tropical climate.

"Why are you and Mom staying up here?" Ethan pressed. "Aren't you still waiting on your ship to be completed?"

Hunt admired the small Christmas tree in the family room. He breathed in deeply as if he could breathe in Christmas and hold this family time in his heart like a time capsule. He turned back to his son. "Most of the work Admiral Bailey has me doing these days is taking place up here, at least until my new ship is completed," he explained.

His son fell silent for a moment as he looked down at his feet. Hunt's wife gave him a prodding look, which he knew to mean that he should say something about his son's next assignment. Ethan was going to finish his last round of training in a few weeks. Most of his classmates were starting to get assignments, but Ethan hadn't received one yet.

Hunt groaned, more to himself than anyone else. Then, speaking just loud enough for his son to hear him, he said, "Ethan, follow me back to my office. Let's talk."

Hunt got up and made his way to the working office he spent a lot of his time in these days. His son followed him in and they both took a seat in the chairs in front of his desk. It felt awkward, like that obligatory talk a father and son have about the birds and the bees, but it needed to happen anyway.

Looking at his son, Hunt asked, "What do you want to do with your career in Space Command?"

Ethan sized him up before he responded, "Ultimately, I want to be a ship captain like you."

111

Hunt smiled proudly at the idea of his son following in his footsteps. At the same time, he felt obligated to warn his son of the road ahead. "You know, it took me nearly twenty-six years before I commanded my first warship," he said. "And I lost that warship along with more than half of its crew after only having it for a few years."

Ethan squirmed in his seat. "I know, Dad. I mean, long-term, that's what I want—I want to command my own starship like you. I know I'll have to work through the ranks and all, and I'm willing to do that. I just want a chance."

Hunt got up and walked over to his desk. He opened one of the drawers and pulled out a couple of tumblers and a bottle of fine Scottish whiskey. Hunt poured the two of them a drink and placed them on the desk in front of their chairs. Then he sat back down.

"Before you give me a speech, Dad, I know Mom has probably asked you to try to pull some strings to get me a safe desk job here in Sol, or worse, in Alpha Centauri. But that's not what I want," Ethan insisted. "I don't want any favoritism. I want to be treated just like the others in my graduating class. I'll take a regular assignment to whatever ship requires a new officer." Ethan had a defiant look in his eye.

Hunt sighed, reached for his shot glass and downed it. He winced slightly as the alcohol burned its way down to his belly. "Look, Ethan, I can't get you assigned to my new ship. There's no way Space Command will go for it. A father and son can't serve on the same ship, especially when the father is the ship's commander. So, that leaves us with a couple of options: I can get you assigned to Admiral Bailey's staff, which would give you some incredible staff experience most officers would kill to get, or I can get you an assignment to a starship. A starship is going to place you in harm's way with the coming battles. We're going to be fighting the Zodarks again, and I have no idea if or how we'll survive the coming battles. Which would you prefer?"

Hunt wanted to offer his son some options, not just a take-it-or-leave-it choice.

"If I wanted to serve on a starship, could I get an assignment to one of the new battleships being built?" Ethan asked eagerly.

Hunt sat back in his chair and thought about that for a moment. The last thing he wanted was for his son to be stationed on one of the fleet's new battleships. They were destined for combat, and many of them were probably not going to survive. Then an idea formed in his head.

Leaning forward, Hunt asked, "What if I could get you assigned to something better than a battleship?"

Now Ethan looked intrigued. "What could possibly be better than being assigned to a battleship?"

Hunt smiled as he reached for his tablet. "You're an officer now with a security clearance. I want to show you something; it's classified, but soon everyone will know about it."

He then turned the holographic display unit on, and an image of the new class of frigates appeared. It was small, nimble, and sleek. Ethan smiled when he saw it, and Hunt knew he had found a safe way for his son to still serve and not be in direct combat.

"What is that? I haven't seen or even heard of this new ship," Ethan commented as he looked on at the floating image in front of them. He then thumbed through some of the ship specs to the right of the image and read through them.

"This, Ethan, is going to be one of the most important ships for the future of humanity. We're calling them *Vipers*. They're going to be our eyes and ears for the fleet. They're our newest reconnaissance ship. I'm going to tell you something you can't repeat to anyone else, got it?" Hunt asked as his eyes narrowed. He was giving his son that look that said he'd be a lot of trouble if he didn't listen to him.

"I understand, Dad. I've got a security clearance now; I know I can't talk about certain things," Ethan responded.

"During our last major battle with the Zodarks, we captured a working star map of the Zodark empire and the systems they've explored up to this point. The *Vipers* are being tasked with surveying as many of them as possible. We're going to have them conduct deep space recons to help us identify where the Zodark planets, starbases, and other strategic facilities are located. Their goal is not to engage in a fight but to find the enemy and report their positions back to the fleet. It's a dangerous and incredibly important job, Ethan," Hunt explained.

Ethan looked at him with excitement. "You can get me assigned to one of them?"

Hunt shrugged. "I think so. Probably. But if you want this assignment, you'll have to go through a few more training courses. The first ships aren't going to be completed for at least eight months."

"I know their primary mission is reconnaissance, but will they see combat?"

"Ethan, if this ship sees combat, chances are it'll get destroyed. It's thinly armored. While we've given it some offensive weapons to carry out hit-and-run missions if needed, if it gets hit, it's a goner. I know you're itching to get into the fight, Ethan, but a posting on a ship like this would allow you to see more of the galaxy than I ever could."

Hunt really hoped his son would go for this assignment. "It's also a small ship, Ethan," he added. "That means it has a smaller crew, which will give you more opportunities to grow as an officer and think on your own. If you get an assignment to a battleship, you'll be one officer out of three or four hundred. On this ship, you'd be one of just six. If you want command of a starship one day, then this will probably facilitate that a lot faster than going down the track of the big battlewagons."

Ethan didn't say anything for a second. He looked at the image of the ship in front of him, then reached over and grabbed the shot of whiskey still sitting on the desk. Like his dad, he drank it down in one gulp.

Finally, he asked, "You really think I should take this assignment, Dad?"

Without hesitation, Hunt replied, "I do, and this isn't me trying to protect you. You'll be in a lot of danger away from the fleet and largely on your own nearly all the time, but it's an incredible opportunity. These new frigates are going to be like the submarine service was to the Navy back in the twentieth century—the eyes and ears of the fleet, operating alone and deep behind enemy lines."

A smile finally spread across Ethan's face, and he nodded. "I'll do it. If you can make it happen, Dad, I'll do it. You're right; this is an incredible opportunity. I shouldn't balk at it. Man, my friends are going to be jealous when they hear about this."

Hunt let out a sigh of relief. He was happy his son had agreed and relieved his wife wouldn't hate him for not insisting that Ethan accept an assignment on Admiral Bailey's staff. This really was a good alternative. It'd spare his son from any pending combat in the next twelve months, and it'd place him on a ship that wasn't looking for a fight.

The rest of Christmas Day went by with everyone happy. The Hunt family enjoyed their time, alone and together. God only knew what the future would bring them, or when they'd all be able to celebrate another Christmas together. They decided to make the most of it and enjoy the time they had.

# Chapter Nine
## Stargates

**The Rhea System**
**RNS** *Voyager*

Admiral Abigail Halsey paced in front of her chair on the bridge as she waited to hear from her ground commander. They had disembarked their Republic Army contingent nearly four months ago, and still they hadn't finished mopping up the remaining Zodarks left on the planet. They were still finding small pockets of resistance that continued to harass their operations on the surface.

She turned to her operations officer. "Has the general's shuttle arrived yet?" she asked.

Her Ops officer looked down at her station to check on the status of the shuttle. She smiled. "Yes, Admiral. It just finished docking."

"Very well, Lieutenant. Please inform him he's to report to my office immediately," Halsey said and then left the bridge to head to her private office.

Halsey found herself spending more and more time either in her office or in the ship's wardroom, sitting through various briefings and daily reports. Between the scientific team, the ground operations, and the mining operations, she was inundated with the managerial duties of running a small empire out here on the far edges of the frontier.

New ships arrived from Sol every five days, bringing with them more soldiers, more military equipment, and other supplies needed to fortify the system. With each arrival, she sent back enormous amounts of Trimar and Morean to Earth, along with a steady count of body bags. RA soldiers were still dying in combat on the surface, and that was a problem. Her force was supposed to have completed combat operations on the planet a few months ago, yet here they were, still fighting a guerilla war against the remaining Zodarks.

Brigadier General Ross McGinnis knocked on her door and waited to be recognized. "Enter," she said loud enough for him to hear. The AI automatically opened the door after she authorized him to enter.

The soldier in charge of the ground forces walked in with a couple of officers in tow. McGinnis was a short man, a hot-tempered, hard-charging soldier who seldom took no for an answer. But he was also known for aggressively going to bat for his subordinates and taking care of his people. From all the reports she'd read and the informal conversations she'd had about him, she'd learned his men were fiercely loyal to him and would charge the gates of hell if he ordered them to do so. She knew she needed that kind of general in charge of the ground war.

McGinnis stood at attention in front of her desk, as did the other two colonels that were with him. She gave them a hard stare for just a moment before she relented. "At ease, General. Please, take a seat. We have a lot to discuss."

"Yes, ma'am," General McGinnis replied in a tone that conveyed that he was obviously annoyed at being taken away from his duties on the surface.

She almost chuckled at the hidden attitude in his voice. *He probably thinks that having a face-to-face with me, a "fleeter," about ground combat is a waste of his time*, she mused.

"General McGinnis, I called you up here to meet in person because I want to understand what the problem is down on the surface. Why are we still suffering hit-and-run attacks against our people down there?" she demanded. "It's a little hard to build a base and a colony on the surface when we still have bands of Zodark soldiers running around." Halsey didn't try to hide her irritation. She was annoyed that his people still hadn't fully secured the surface.

McGinnis cleared his throat. "With all due respect, Admiral, things are a bit more complicated on the ground than they may appear from up here in orbit."

*Condescending bastard.*

"Really? Please, do tell me why I keep sending dozens and sometimes hundreds of body bags back to Sol every five days," she countered, sarcasm dripping from her voice.

"Admiral, the Zodarks know the terrain better than we do," McGinnis explained, undeterred. "It's taking time for our people to adjust to this new environment. Plus, there's magnetic interference near the mountains and the areas around the mines. This interference is making it incredibly hard for our sensors to detect and track them from the air or with our drones. We're placing a variety of ground sensors around our sensitive sites to help us detect them as they approach our facilities—in the last three days, these sensors helped us identify and deter two attacks before they could get started. I believe this is going to help us turn the tide."

"Huh," Admiral Halsey replied, crossing her arms. "OK, then what are you going to do about eliminating the remaining ground forces still running loose?" she asked, not letting him off the hook just yet.

"Admiral, we're mounting more and more patrols both around our facilities and in some of the locations where we believe the remaining Zodarks are operating. It's rough, rugged terrain, so what we've done is break it down into grid boxes or sections. As more engineering units arrive, we're building firebases and patrol bases inside those grid boxes to deny the enemy the ability to freely operate there.

"As these bases are completed, we're positioning a battalion of soldiers there to carry out round-the-clock patrols of the area. Right now, nine battalions of soldiers are on near-constant patrols. We're taking losses, and the body bags are piling up because we're actively looking to engage the Zodarks."

He sat up even straighter, which seemed impossible to Admiral Halsey. "As much as I don't want to lose any of my soldiers, this is just part of the job," he insisted. "If we find and then fight them—when we do, we're going to lose people. I'm confident our current strategy is working, and we'll finish them off in the coming months."

General McGinnis had been skating on thin ice with Admiral Halsey before this meeting, and they were both acutely aware of the tension. His ground forces had been requesting a lot of orbital strikes from the *Voyager*, and while she'd happily provided them, it had only reinforced her opinion that his command was not winning the ground war.

Halsey leaned forward in her chair and stared daggers at him. "Listen, General, my ship can't stay in orbit forever. We still need to finish our survey operations of the nearby moons, and we need to keep an eye out for any additional Zodark ships. I need to know that you have things under control. We need the mining operations to continue and the space elevator to stay protected."

"Are you leaving any ships in orbit?" he pushed.

"Do you need me to?" she asked skeptically.

McGinnis sighed. "Admiral, I understand you're a fleeter, and you may not fully understand the intricacies of the ground operations. Right now, the high ground for the kind of war we're fighting is orbit. A starship sitting up here can send a railgun slug down on a hard target or provide direct fire support beyond what our VACs can.

"This is important to our mission. As long as we're hitting the Zodarks with orbital strikes, they'll know we have ships in orbit. When that stops, they'll know help isn't coming and that we aren't getting reinforced. We must keep reminding the enemy that we're not abandoned out here. If possible, I'd like it if you could keep at least one of the fleet ships in orbit over our positions."

Halsey sat back in her chair. She hated to admit it, but she knew he was right. Maybe she'd misjudged the man. If leaving one of the ships in orbit meant it could save a few soldiers' lives and help end the fighting on the ground sooner, then she'd do it.

After a pause, she nodded. "OK, General, you've made your point. I'll leave the *Wanju* in orbit. They'll provide you with any further orbital strikes. Now, when I return in a couple of months, I expect to hear that you have the planet secured and our operations on the ground are running at full speed. Understand?"

It was more of an order than a request. General McGinnis nodded. "I'll do my best," he replied.

The ground soldiers got up and left her office. She felt a lot more informed and comfortable about what was going on down on the surface. She probably could have handled this talking-to through the holographic communicator, but she wanted them to have to trek up to her turf. She needed to remind them who was in charge, which for the time being was her, until an officer with more stars than her showed up to relieve her.
*******

A day later, she ordered her ship out of orbit and set a course for the closest moon, Tigris. They were finally starting their geological survey of it after months of delay. The moon itself was fascinating. Unlike the farther moon, Pishon, Tigris could not support or sustain life. It had an atmosphere, albeit thin, but it had one. However, Tigris had a lot of volcanic activity. It spewed forth far too much toxic mess into the atmosphere to ever make it livable. But that wasn't what drew her scientific team to the moon. It was the composition of the moon. It was incredibly rich in heavy metals, resources that would be in high demand if they were going to turn this system into a real forward operating base.

The other moon, Pishon, could support life—well, not human life as the atmosphere wasn't compatible with humans outside of EVA suits, but Halsey's scientific team had already discovered that Pishon could support plants and other life-forms. On Earth, some microbes, insects and plant life survived in places with an altered atmosphere, but they still didn't know for sure what life-forms existed on Pishon, or what exactly they would find there.

As the *Voyager* settled into orbit over Tigris, her science teams deployed several satellites to orbit the moon and continue the geological survey. Next, they dropped a handful of drones into the atmosphere and a ground lander. These would focus on finding a suitable location to establish a biodome habitat for a mining colony to start their activities.

In a few months, a ship equipped with the necessary equipment to construct a space elevator would arrive from Earth. Once completed, it would help transport the mined minerals from the surface to orbit and bring people and resources from orbit down to the surface.

It was a complicated process to establish multiple colonies in a new system far from the support of your home system. For Admiral Halsey, it represented one of the most tedious and challenging parts of her job.

She wanted to be out searching for Zodarks. She also knew a stargate was somewhere nearby, and her force just hadn't found it yet. She had her lone destroyer and two of the three TPA ships out searching for it while she kept the *Voyager* and one of the TPA cruisers near New Eden in case the Zodarks somehow slipped past her.

*When is the new fleet from Earth going to arrive?* she asked herself. *We're sitting ducks out here with what we have...*

Publicly, she was the stoic image of a fearless commander. In the quietness of her own mind, though, she was nervous. If the Zodarks returned before she had reinforcements from Sol, she wasn't sure she could stop them.

*I miss Hunt*, she realized. *He knew how to fight his ship and win... he was fearless...*

Losing the *Rook* at the outset of this campaign had really hurt. It was a deep gut blow to morale too. She had some of the crewmen from the *Rook* on her ship now. Their presence only reminded her of that tragic loss. She often chided herself over losing the *Rook* and so many of its crew. Her ship was just as armored as the *Rook*, yet she had ordered them into a position that would place them in harm's way while protecting her ship. She told herself she should have kept the *Voyager* in the lead position and not Hunt's. His ship was already badly damaged, and they couldn't afford to take any more hits.

Halsey knew her hesitation in that last battle had cost her the *Rook* and a lot of dead sailors; she couldn't make that kind of mistake again. In a way, she hoped Admiral Bailey would send a more senior admiral out here to take charge of the situation—someone who could make the tough decisions for her, who would tell her what to do and bear that responsibility and not her.

"Admiral, we're receiving a message from the *Boston*. Shall I go ahead and play it?" asked her coms officer.

Halsey nodded.

"Admiral Halsey, this is Captain Shale. I believe our long-range sensors have found the stargate we've been looking for. Attached to our message is our current location and the location of the stargate. We're going to move forward and investigate. I'll send another message when we arrive, along with a video image of the stargate. Captain Shale out." The message ended, leaving everyone both excited and anxious over the news. This was precisely what they had been waiting on. They had found the stargate.

"Lieutenant, how long ago did Captain Shale send us this message?" Halsey asked, trying to gauge how far away they were.

The lieutenant looked down at her screen, searching for the time stamp. "Um, five hours ago, ma'am. They're far out. At FTL speeds, they're close to a half day's travel."

"OK. Thank you, Lieutenant. Keep me apprised of any other messages. Load this newest piece of intel into one of our emergency com drones in case we need to send a warning back to Earth," Halsey ordered. It wasn't that she was worried about her ship being destroyed in the next few hours or anything; however, it was critical that Sol was alerted that they had found the stargate.

## Chapter Ten
## Reinforcements

**New Eden**
**RNS** *Viper*

"Captain, we're coming out of FTL in five seconds," called out Ensign Ethan Hunt from his navigation terminal.

"Excellent. Once we're out of warp, let's spin up our electronic sensors and conduct a full sweep of the area. We need to make sure the place is still in our control," Commander Amy Dobbs ordered.

Dobbs was the first captain of the very first *Viper*-class frigate. It was a great honor to be chosen to take command of a ship like this. While it was a small ship, it was fast and incredibly agile. Her only gripe was that she didn't have a more experienced crew—although, she also realized her own real experience in this new war thus far consisted only of her two-year tour on the *Rook* before it had been blown apart. She didn't fault Captain Hunt for the loss of the ship, but she did harbor some bitterness toward Admiral Halsey for placing them in the situation that had led to their demise. Then again, if the *Rook* hadn't been destroyed, she probably never would have been promoted and given command of the *Viper*.

A few seconds later, their ship came out of FTL, and they found themselves immersed in the blackness of space once again. Dobbs liked traveling inside an FTL bubble. She found it mesmerizing and beautiful. She loved all the swirling lights and the flashes of stars in the distance whipping past them.

"Activating sensor suite now," called out Lieutenant Reynolds, her weapons and tactical officer.

The downside to a smaller ship like the *Viper* was it meant everyone wore many hats. They all had to take on a lot more duties that would generally be split among different sections on the larger warships. The upside of that was that all the officers and enlisted on the *Viper* were going to become familiar with a lot more of a ship's functions than they might on a larger vessel.

The sensors pulsed out their signals, blanketing the system. They detected the electronic signatures of several ships and satellites. Moments later, they determined that the electronic signatures were from either Space Command or TPA vessels. The two ships in orbit of New Eden sent her a challenge code, which her XO immediately authenticated.

"Helm, bring us to a new heading," Commander Dobbs ordered Ensign Hunt. "Take us closer to the *Voyager* and send them a greeting. Inform them we are the vanguard of the rest of the fleet that'll be arriving in the system later today and tomorrow."

"Aye-aye, Captain. Sending the message now," Hunt replied.

Dobbs knew Ensign Hunt was the son of her former commander. It didn't bother her that he'd been assigned to her ship. She liked and respected his father. When they'd spoken a few months back, he didn't make any mention of his son being assigned to her ship. She hadn't received any special orders regarding Ensign Hunt, not that she'd expected any. She knew the senior Hunt was very much a by-the-book kind of guy. He was an exceptional ship captain, and he wouldn't want his son to receive any special treatment.

An hour later, a message from the *Voyager* arrived. It was encrypted and read "Eyes Only," for the captain. She knew it must be important if she was receiving it after being in the system for only a couple of hours. Her ship was still at least two hours away from reaching the *Voyager* and New Eden.

Dobbs pulled her terminal screen up so only she could see it. She then activated her captain's code and unlocked the encrypted message. It was short and sweet, directing *Viper* to make the best possible speed to a new set of coordinates, where they'd find one of the stargates the Zodarks used to connect this system to their other networks.

*Holy crap*, Dobbs thought. Admiral Halsey wanted them to go through this stargate and start exploring what lay beyond it.

Continuing to read her FRAGO, she saw her ship was supposed to make a short stop at the *Voyager*, then pause at the newly built space elevator on New Eden to pick up a couple of passengers.

*Great, more mouths to feed*, she grumbled to herself. *Don't they know this is a small ship compared to every other one out here?*

The next three hours flew by. The *Viper* made good speed as it approached the *Voyager*. Compared to past ships and even others currently being built, the *Viper*-class frigates were incredibly fast. Where her previous ship, the *Rook,* could cover the twelve-light-year distance between Sol and the Rhea system in twelve days, her ship could do it in three. Their MPD thrusters could produce speeds five times as fast as the thrusters on the larger warships. This made the *Vipers* an excellent choice for deep space reconnaissance and exploration. It also meant that in a fleet battle, they could quickly zoom in and out to deliver a deadly barrage of plasma torpedoes or Havoc missiles. Of course, their thin armor and limited defensive systems also meant they could be blotted from the stars, so it would be risky.

"Captain, we're approaching the *Voyager*," announced Ensign Hunt. "They're asking if you'd like them to send a shuttle over to pick you up."

"Tell them yes, that would be nice," Dobbs replied. Her ship wasn't large enough to warrant a shuttle, let alone a whole shuttle bay.

Looking at the *Voyager* on the main screen, Commander Dobbs saw some of the scars and scorch marks on its armor—battle damage that had been repaired in the system. As they approached, the size difference between her ship and the *Voyager* became almost comical. The *Viper* was a mere one hundred thirty meters in length, forty meters in height, and thirty meters in width. The vessel also had two twelve-meter wings on either side where the Havoc missile pods were located. It was a packed ship—not a lot of room for nonessential items.
\*\*\*\*\*\*\*

An hour later, Commander Dobbs ducked her head as she exited the shuttlecraft and entered the cavernous area that constituted the flight bay of the *Voyager*. Dobbs always marveled at how massive the ship was— it was a few hundred meters longer than the *Rook*. *Voyager* carried a contingent of RA soldiers and a squadron of Ospreys and orbital assault ships—it didn't pack the same firepower as her old ship, but right now, it was the most powerful warship the Earthers had.

"If you'll follow me, Commander, I'll take you up to the admiral's office," a lieutenant said as he motioned for her to follow him. "She's looking forward to meeting with you."

The two of them walked through several winding corridors and eventually came to an elevator. Her *Viper* didn't have an elevator, just several stairwells that connected the two decks. Technically, her ship was probably big enough to have three or even four decks, but it didn't. Those areas were packed to the gills with supplies to sustain them for their long patrols.

When they arrived at the admiral's door, the lieutenant knocked twice. A moment later, the door opened, and he motioned for her to come in. His job of escorting her completed, he turned on his heel and headed back to his post.

Commander Dobbs walked up to Admiral Halsey's desk and snapped off a crisp salute. "Commander Amy Dobbs, captain of the *Viper*, reporting as ordered, ma'am."

From behind her desk, Admiral Halsey returned the salute. "At ease, Commander. No need to be formal. Please, join me over here. I'd like to catch you up and briefly go over your new set of orders, but more importantly, I'd like to get a rundown of what's going on back on Earth. I've been away from the rest of the fleet for a while now—what's going on back home?"

Dobbs smiled and followed the admiral over to a pair of couches and a single chair. Just then, a couple of Halsey's other officers walked in along with the ship's master chief. Commander Dobbs took her seat at the far end of the couch, and the others sat down. Halsey doled out coffee to those who wanted a cup.

For the next twenty minutes, Admiral Halsey brought Dobbs up to speed on what had transpired in the system since she had left fifteen months ago. It had taken longer than the admiral had wanted, but the RASs had finally secured the planet. The space elevator was now fully operational, and mining operations were now running at full speed. They'd even established mining colonies on Tigris and Pishon, the two moons in orbit of New Eden. Halsey said they were still waiting on the space elevators for those two moons to be completed, though.

When she finished giving the updates on the Rhea system, Admiral Halsey smiled and said, "I guess it's time to tell you about the new assignment I'm giving the *Viper*."

Halsey pulled up a video of the stargate. "Honestly, we have no idea how it works or what powers it," she admitted. "However, we do know that if a ship approaches it, it activates. Our scientists think it creates a wormhole to the stargate on the other side."

She cleared her throat. "We want the *Viper* to travel through the stargate and assess what's in the system on the other side and beyond."

All eyes turned to Dobbs, who agreed to the assignment without hesitation.

"So, your turn," Halsey said. "What's going on back in Sol?"

Commander Dobbs gave them the quick and dirty of Earth's goings-on. Halsey and the other officers grilled her for over half an hour.

Judging by the questions they were asking, Dobbs suspected they were grilling every ship captain and crew that entered the system. She didn't blame them—they were clearly starved for news, and the com drones only provided so much information. They'd been deployed from Sol now for fifteen months. That was a long time to be gone from home, and a lot of things were changing.

"When is the rest of the fleet going to arrive in the system and reinforce us?" probed Admiral Halsey, urgency in her voice.

She wrinkled her eyebrows at the question. *Just read the orders, ma'am*, Dobbs thought, but she didn't say that out loud.

"Admiral, I…um, two more *Vipers* are arriving in the system in the next twelve hours. Tomorrow around this same time, four TPA cruisers will arrive, escorting two *Arks* and about two dozen TPA and Republic freighters. Five more *Vipers* will arrive with them as well—"

Before Dobbs could go on, Admiral Halsey interrupted. "Whoa, what is Space Command shipping us? I wasn't aware of any additional RASs being sent here. And what other warships are supposed to join us out here? Nothing personal, Commander, but the *Vipers* aren't exactly armored battlewagons that'll be able to slug it out with a Zodark fleet."

Dobbs grimaced at the explanation of the inadequacy of her ship. "I can't really speak to what's being transported, Admiral. I'm sure it's in the order packet we transmitted to you. As to additional warships, Admiral Hunt will arrive in the system with his new warship and fleet in ten days. I was also told Fleet Admiral Bailey, along with President Luca, will be traveling with him to see New Eden in person."

"What?" asked Halsey, shocked. "I wish I had been told sooner I was going to have a group of VIPs visiting—hang on a second, Commander. Did you say 'Admiral Hunt'?" Halsey exclaimed.

*Geez, did she not read her new set of orders herself? We transmitted them several hours ago…*

"Yes, Admiral. Captain Miles Hunt was just promoted to rear admiral the day before my ship left for Rhea," Dobbs informed them. "His new ship, the *George Washington*, is traveling with four additional *Vipers*, four of the new battleships, and ten orbital assault ships."

The officers in the room all let out a soft whistle as she told them about the new fleet.

Admiral Halsey stood up but signaled for everyone else to stay seated. "I'm going to have the galley bring up some sandwiches and fresh coffee. Please, you all continue talking amongst yourselves. I'm going to sit over by my desk and review the order packet you sent. I apologize for not having gone through it before our meeting. I suspect most of my questions would have been answered if I had, Commander. We've had a lot going on the last couple of days. To be honest, I wasn't expecting you to arrive for a few more weeks."

Dobbs smiled. "It's not a problem, Admiral. I understand you are a very busy person out here. I believe Space Command is sending you a lot of help over the next few days—I'm sure it'll lighten your load once they get in the system."

Master Chief Riggs, the senior enlisted man in the fleet, spoke up. "Commander, mail call has not exactly been a big priority out here. Do you know what may be the holdup? I have a lot of angry TPA sailors and ground pounders complaining that they're not receiving mail from back home."

All Dobbs could do was shrug. The TPA was doing all they could to evacuate as many people from their territory as they could to their colony on Alpha Centauri. Establishing a regular shipping channel between Sol and Rhea wasn't exactly high on *their* priority list.

"Chief, when the TPA ships arrive in the coming days, they might have a better explanation than I can give. As to our people, I would have thought mail would have been traveling with the supply ships. Hasn't it?" Dobbs asked, curious if something else was going on.

"Commander, as you know, supply ships don't visit the Rhea system on a regular basis. It can be a month or more before we receive a new ship," Chief Riggs explained. "It's been a tough slog down on the ground for our soldiers, and mail from home is a big morale booster. That's all."

For the next thirty minutes, the rest of the officers continued to pepper her with questions about Earth. Dobbs did her best to share what she knew. She told them about how the whole planet was practically shaking in their shoes when they saw some videos of the fleet battles and of the RASs fighting the Zodarks. Everyone out here was being hailed as heroes back home. The number of people who wanted to join the TPA and Space Command was skyrocketing. People wanted a piece of the action, and they wanted to keep the Zodarks away from Earth.

She went on to explain the new deal that had been worked out with the Belters, and the new colony they had established under the nose of everyone. That piece of news caught a few of them by surprise. The Belters had mainly been known to be pirates, at least the ones that weren't running mining operations and shipping raw ore back to the shipyards. Before the discovery of the Zodarks, piracy was the biggest concern for Space Command. A lot had changed since then.

After eating a sandwich and gulping down a cup of coffee, which Dobbs had to admit was terrible, Admiral Halsey joined them again.

"Commander, I think I have a better understanding of what's going on and what's happening next," Halsey said. "This does change my own orders to you a bit. What I'd like you to do is skip docking at the space elevator and head directly to the stargate. I need you to make the best possible speed to the system called YV-FDG. This is apparently the Sumerian home world system, which they call Lagash. Your job is to recon the entire path to this region and gain an understanding of what the system looks like.

"How many Zodark ships or outposts are there? Are there any possible threats that may impede our liberation of Sumer? Once you have that information, you're to return and report what you've seen. You are not to engage the Zodarks or anyone else. Do not attempt to contact anyone. We need you to slip in and slip out once you have some intelligence on the area. Is that understood, Commander?"

*Finally, a real mission,* Dobbs thought. She nodded. "Yes, ma'am. We'll be in and out before they know we were even in the system."

With nothing more to be said, the meeting broke up, and Commander Dobbs was brought back to the shuttle bay. In the next hour, her ship would make the best possible speed to the stargate and venture further than any Earther had ever traveled, nearly two hundred light-years from Earth.
*******


**Star System 33-JRO**
**RNS *Viper***

"Have they detected us yet?" Commander Dobbs asked anxiously.

Lieutenant Reynolds shook his head. "Unknown, Captain. But they are definitely heading this direction."

"Helm, get us through the gate *now*," Dobbs ordered.

"Jumping," Ensign Hunt announced as he gave the ship some power. In seconds, they slipped through the stargate and started their journey down the rabbit hole.

Traveling through the stargate was an exciting experience. Once the ship crossed into it, it was like the ship was stretched like a piece of Play-Doh until it suddenly appeared on the other end of the gate. Oddly enough, the jump didn't take long. They crossed dozens, and in some cases hundreds, of light-years in a matter of minutes. On the other hand, some of those jaunts between gates could take as long as a few weeks or a month.

"Exiting the gate," Hunt announced nervously.

As soon as she had a read on the system they'd just entered, Commander Dobbs realized there was no place to hide.

"Helm, accelerate us to maximum speed, and bring us to a position directly behind the gate," Dobbs ordered confidently. "I want us twenty thousand kilometers above and behind the gate. We need to set up an ambush."

The ship accelerated swiftly as Ensign Hunt pulled the *Viper* into a tight turn. It took them a few minutes to get into position, but once they had reached the navigation point Dobbs had ordered, Ensign Hunt pulled the ship into a slow-moving circle. He kept the engines running at fifteen percent power, but they were ready to move to one hundred percent in an instant when the enemy fleet eventually jumped through.

Commander Dobbs stood up and connected her neurolink to the ship-wide 1MC, addressing the crew. "We're going to sit on the rear side of the gate and wait for the enemy fleet to jump through," she informed them. "Once the Zodarks arrive, our ship is going to fire a full spread of plasma torpedoes and Havoc missile magazines. Then we'll FTL jump away to the stargate on the other end of this system before the Zodark ships have a chance to lock onto us."

Dobbs had always been a bit of a renegade. She'd heard Admiral Halsey's orders not to engage the enemy, but she wasn't about to leave a large group of Zodark ships unscathed if she had the power to do something about it. She'd learned that sometimes it was better to ask for forgiveness than for permission—she could always play it off as self-defense if she had to.

For the next eight hours, they sat there, moving in a slow circle around their position as they waited for the enemy fleet to arrive. Commander Dobbs knew having the crew at battle stations for so long was hard on them, and they could only stay sharp and alert for so long.

She would need to stand them down if the enemy didn't show up soon. Then again, she needed to keep them close to their battle stations in case the enemy did show up. Once the Zodark fleet arrived, they wouldn't have very long to carry out their hit-and-run attack. The enemy's sensors would detect them in short order. A single shot from a Zodark vessel and they were toast. She knew it, and so did the crew.

Lieutenant Reynolds got up from his station and walked over to Commander Dobbs. "Captain, I know you ruled out using the nukes, but I've been running through some calculations on the gate. If we were to swap out the HE warheads for nukes, we could deploy the missiles now. We could position them around the gate here, here, and here," he explained, pointing to the locations on her station's map. "It'd keep the gate outside the blast radius, but it'd put the nukes right in the middle of the enemy fleet. Once they jump into the system, either we can detonate the missiles in place, or we can activate the missiles to do a quick burn and hit them or get closer before we light them off."

Reynolds had advocated for the use of their limited supply of nuclear warheads before. They didn't have a lot of firepower on the ship, but the six atomic warheads they carried could cause some considerable damage.

Dobbs shook her head. "I just don't know, Reynolds. We don't know what the gate is made of or how it could end up reacting to a nuclear detonation happening nearby. I'm concerned it could cause some unintended consequences. I do agree with you that we should use the nukes, but let's find another spot where we can carry out an ambush from and hit them with the nukes from there. Maybe an asteroid group or the dark side of a moon or something...thoughts?"

Reynolds looked disappointed but nodded in compliance. "OK, Captain. I'll start looking for another possible location we can carry out an ambush from once we jump."

Just as Reynolds sat back down at his station, the gate activated. The first Zodark ship jumped through. It was one of the battleships they'd spotted.

"Helm! Increase thrusters to full speed and angle us towards the Zodark ship," called out Commander Dobbs urgently.

"More ships are jumping through, Captain!" Reynolds shouted. Alarm bells alerted them to the new danger.

Dobbs looked at the display and saw three enemy battleships had just emerged. Then one of the enemy carriers jumped through. She smiled. It was a big, fat, juicy target.

"Lock onto that carrier and unload everything we have on it. Then get us the hell out of here before they have a chance to shoot at us," Commander Dobbs ordered, shouting to be heard over the alarm bells. They had officially been detected by the Zodarks. At least one of their ships was already trying to lock onto them.

As her weapons officer started releasing their ordnance on the enemy carrier, Dobbs activated the electronic countermeasures or ECM suite and hoped like hell it'd scramble the enemy's ability to lock onto them just long enough for them to get away.

"Weapons away!" the weapons officers yelled.

"Turning to initiate FTL," announced Ensign Hunt as he steered the ship to a new trajectory. As the *Viper* pulled away, the MPD thrusters cut out, and the FTL coils extended as the ship prepared to jump.

"They're firing!" shouted Reynolds anxiously as they waited for the FTL bubble to form.

Commander Dobbs's eyes went wide as one of the battleships' pulse beams fired. She braced herself for the hit, knowing that it was most likely going to destroy them. Just as the laser should have hit them, the ship shot like a flash of light through space as they entered warp.

"Holy crap that was close!" exclaimed Lieutenant Reynolds, clearly shocked that they had made it out alive.

"Nice flying, Ensign. Damn good job, Hunt," Dobbs said excitedly, sweat running down her cheeks.

She used her neurolink to tie into the 1MC. "We successfully jumped away from the Zodark ships and fired off our weapons," she announced.

It would be several hours before they learned if their attack had succeeded. Before the engagement, they left a communication drone behind to record the attack and transmit that data back to the rest of the Earth fleet in Rhea. They had also dropped another com drone a few days earlier along their route, so they could daisy-chain the signals together.

As long as they weren't traveling in an FTL bubble or going through a star gate, they could send and receive data, albeit with a slight delay.

"OK, people. It's time for us to get ready for the next ambush. Reload torpedo tubes and missile launchers. Then I want everyone to grab some food and hit the rack for the next eight hours. Based on the AI's analysis of the enemy fleet's travel times, they should cross our current position in fifteen hours. I want everyone rested up for this next battle," Commander Dobbs announced to the crew.

She felt they had all earned their pay today. Now it was time to rest up while they waited to see how their attack had turned out.
*******

Sitting in the mess deck, Dobbs used her knife to cut up her sirloin steak. It was something she had watched her dad do on their Wyoming ranch—he'd cut his entire steak up before he'd dig in and eat. Thinking about that moment brought her back to some happier times. She loved living in Wyoming. When she was growing up, she wanted to be a rancher, just like her dad. But that dream had fallen apart when she was a teenager and her dad had died of a sudden heart attack. Her mom and brothers had tried, but they'd been unable to maintain the family ranch, and eventually they'd had to sell it and move to Billings.

Her mom had gotten a job working for an advertising company. It was a tough time for her family. Then, in her senior year of high school, a recruiter from Space Command had come to her school. The recruiter had told her about the Space Academy in Colorado Springs. She hadn't thought she had a chance of getting in, but she'd applied anyway. Then she'd gotten a phone call from that same recruiter, who'd told her she'd been accepted. She'd left for the Academy, and the rest was history, as they say.

Ensign Hunt set his plate down across from her. "Mind if I join you, Captain?" he asked.

She looked up, her mind snapping back to the here and now. She smiled and nodded as he took a seat.

He cut his steak up, just like she did, all at once before he dug in. The ship's mess room was actually kind of small—they were only able to seat roughly twenty people at a time. With a crew of fifty-six people, they seldom had more than ten or fifteen people in the room at one time.

Looking up at her most junior officer, Dobbs asked, "So, Ethan, what did you think of your first real combat action?"

Ethan was about to shovel in another forkful of steak and potatoes into his mouth, but he held his fork in his hand for a second. "It went by faster than I thought it would," he said before scarfing down the next bite.

She laughed at the comment. "Yeah, that's what I said my first time."

Ethan chuckled. "You know what my dad would say to my mom? *That's what she said.*"

Dobbs practically spat her water out as she laughed at the crude joke. "Yeah, I could see your dad saying that. He's a pretty funny guy when he's not being serious."

"How long did you serve with my dad?" Ethan asked. He continued to eat his food like he was in a race against a clock.

Dobbs laughed again. "You know, Ethan, you can slow down and taste your food. We have some time until we receive the battle report from the drone and even more time until the enemy travels past this area."

Ethan seemed to slow down a bit after that and enjoy the rare steak dinner the cooks had prepared for them. They were, after all, celebrating their first engagement with the enemy as a crew.

Looking at Ethan, Dobbs replied to his earlier question. "I've been fortunate to have served with your dad twice during my career. Once on the *Rook* for nearly three years until our ship was destroyed, and another two-year stint when I was assigned to Space Command headquarters. Your dad is a good man. He's very devoted to his career, but I also got the sense that he was just as devoted to his family. When he wasn't talking shop with us junior officers, he bragged about his two kids and his wife all the time."

Ethan smiled at the mention of his family. He was now an officer in his own right, making his own way in the galaxy. "Dad certainly is dedicated to the job. I mean, he was there for us when he could be, but the job did take him away a lot. I think my best memories of him were during our time living on Mars. It was the one period of my childhood where he wasn't gone constantly. We got to do a lot of things together as a family during our time on the Red Planet."

"Oh yeah; I forgot you guys had spent nearly a decade on Mars. It must have been an interesting experience living there back then—back before the big population boom and FTL travel," Dobbs commented before taking another bite of her own food.

Ethan nodded. "It was a lot sparser back then than it is now, that's for sure. But in a way, it was nicer. We spent a lot of time together, playing games and talking. I miss those times," he said as his voice trailed off. He finished his last bite. "But, enough of the past," he said. "Do you think we should continue to attack this Zodark fleet or head back to Rhea to join the rest of our fleet for the next battle?"

"That's a good question, Ethan. I need to wait until I see the results of our last attack," Dobbs explained. "Once I know how well it went, then I'll be able to make a better decision. My hope is we can bloody them up a bit before they get to Rhea."

Just then, one of the senior enlisted sailors came into the mess deck and walked up to her. "Captain, we've just received a message from the com drone."

She nodded, and the petty officer left to head back to his station. She turned back to Ethan. "I guess we'll find out how well our attack went in a few minutes," she said with a wink.

The two of them got up, dropped their empty food trays off and headed to the bridge.

When they arrived, several of the officers and enlisted sailors were standing around Lieutenant Reynolds's station, looking at something. Commander Amy Dobbs walked up to them, clearing her throat as she approached. "What's going on, Reynolds?" she demanded.

The others who hadn't noticed her approaching snapped their heads around and then quickly dispersed to their stations. The bridge wasn't a very big place for people to hide or disappear.

Reynolds perked his head up, a smile on his face. "Good news, Captain. We scored some hits on that Zodark carrier."

She furrowed her brow. Judging by the facial expressions of the others on the bridge, she would have thought it hadn't turned out that well. "Why do I get the feeling that there's a *but* to this good news?" she asked.

Reynolds shrugged. "I'm trying to focus on the positive. Here, take a look for yourself." He replayed the video of the attack. "The six plasma torpedoes went right for the carrier. It looks like one of the battleships,

134

the one that tried to fire on us, managed to intercept three of the six torpedoes, but the other three slammed into the ship, as you can see."

They watched as the three plasma torpedoes tore a deep gash in three different sections of the ship. That was followed by a couple of secondary explosions as the ship started burning atmosphere.

"The ten Havoc missiles didn't fare so well, Captain," Reynolds continued. "That same battleship was able to intercept seven of them. The remaining three hit the ship, but as you can see, they didn't have the same effect as the plasma torpedoes. The Havocs impacted against the armored hull. Near as we can tell, they did minimal damage to the ship. I don't think the missiles were able to penetrate through the armor, or if they did, they didn't get very deep inside the ship before the warheads went off." Reynolds showed her several closeup images of the impact points.

Ten or twenty seconds later, the video ended. "The com drone was taken out by the Zodarks," Reynolds explained.

She mulled over what she'd just seen. *So, the plasma torpedoes were able to burn through the armor, but the Havocs couldn't.* Then there was the timing. She realized that the carrier couldn't get its own defenses up and running fast enough to defend itself. *That could certainly prove to be useful information...*

"Reynolds, is it me, or did you notice how the only ship that could respond to our attack was that battleship that jumped through first?" she asked. "Let's rewind that video and look at the timestamp from when it jumped through to when it was able to get a lock on us and engage our missiles and torpedoes. I think there may be a short window of opportunity when their ships are unable to defend themselves. *If* that's true, that might be the key to taking their fleet out."

For the next twenty minutes, they went over the video multiple times, determining exactly how long both the battleship and the other ships had been in the new system before it appeared they could activate their defensive systems. Once they had concluded that a Zodark ship took roughly sixty seconds from the time it jumped through a gate to when it could defend itself, Commander Dobbs ordered them to make the best possible speed for stargate Z-MO29. That gate connected them to one more stargate that led directly to the Rhea system and their home fleet. She wanted to report their findings and see if maybe they could use this information to pulverize the enemy fleet before they could get themselves organized.

## Chapter Eleven
## The Grand Fleet

**BlueOrigin Shipyard – Earth**
**RNS** *George Washington*

The inspection craft was just finishing its fifth hour hovering over the exterior of the largest, most powerful warship ever built by Earth. Adrian Rogers, the lead engineer for BlueOrigin, and a couple of his assistants sat at a couple of workstations, carefully watching their video monitors. They were examining their specific parts of the ship, inspecting them for any problems or deficiencies before they certified it as complete.

This was the critical final inspection. After they signed off on it and the new ship commander, Rear Admiral Hunt, signed off, the ship would officially be handed over to Space Command.

Turning to look at the admiral sitting next to him, Rogers asked, "What do you think of the ship, sir?"

Admiral Hunt peeled his gaze away from the video display of the point defense weapons. "I love it," he replied. "It's a beautiful ship, and it's massive. My only concern is getting it ready for combat. There are a lot of new weapon systems and platforms on the *GW*, many of which have never been tested or fielded before."

"You're talking about the drone fighters?" asked Rogers. He was a little skeptical about them as well. Space Command didn't exactly have a space fighter program—at least not yet. They were still in the process of training up a group of manned fighter craft. Heck, BlueOrigin was still prototyping the fighters.

Hunt nodded. "Yeah, Adrian. I don't like the idea of drones. I'm not sure they'll be nearly as responsive as a manned spacecraft would be, but we obviously don't have any of those ready, let alone pilots to even fly them."

Hunt shook his head and leaned in. In a hushed tone, he said, "To be frank, Adrian, I think we're rushing the entire deployment of this ship. We need a proper shakedown cruise and time to get the crew trained up. Nearly two-thirds of my crew is fresh from training. This will be their first assignment on a ship."

"Yeah, I heard about that, Admiral. Do you know what your assignment will be once you've signed off on the ship?" Rogers inquired. Like any other civilian, he was curious as to what was going on in the war.

Hunt sighed. "I'll be picking up my crew over the next four days. We'll be shoving off the day after they're all aboard to head to New Eden. We'll continue our shakedown cruise and training there. Until the Zodarks arrive, or we find out more information on where their home systems are, we'll continue to train and work out any kinks in the ship. Speaking of which, has your company identified who all from your group is going to be coming with us?"

Rogers grimaced at the thought of going with them—the last thing he wanted to do was go anywhere near those Zodark beasts. He wanted to stay in Sol and continue living the good life on the massive amount of money his company was paying him. But no, they said he'd be in charge of the three hundred engineers and workers that would be traveling on the ship to continue carrying out tests and fixing bugs and problems the crew found.

He fixed his facial expression and sat up straighter. "As a matter of fact, Admiral, I'll be the lead man for the company coming with you," he explained. "I'll have a crew of three hundred folks joining me as well."

"I take it you aren't happy about this?" Hunt countered.

Rogers shrugged. "I'd rather stay here, away from the Zodarks—but at least the company is compensating us for our troubles."

Hunt chuckled. "Well, at least they'll be giving you extra pay. Space Command says it's part of our mission to go and find new aliens to kill, so we don't get an extra pay bump. However, if it's possible, I'll do my best to see if your people can go dirtside and spend some time on New Eden. It's the least I can do to show my thanks for your help."

"Oh wow," Rogers replied, genuinely thrilled at the opportunity to set foot on a new planet. "That would be great, Admiral. Thank you."

The next hour wasn't too bad. They continued to examine the remainder of the ship. Once Hunt was satisfied with what he saw, he signed off. The inspection ship returned to the dock, and they all got off.

That evening, Hunt had a nice dinner with his wife on the John Glenn Orbital Station before returning to his private quarters. This would be his last night with his wife, Lilly. Starting tomorrow, he'd take command of *George Washington* in an official ceremony. From then on, he'd be staying on the ship as they got her ready to leave. He had five days to get all of the crew members and supplies brought on board before they shoved off. The rest of the fleet would be leaving over the next couple of days—his portion of the fleet would leave last.

*******

The following morning, a large crowd of several thousand sailors and RA soldiers stood at attention on the flight deck of the *George Washington*. A crowd of dignitaries, officers, and some family members sat in chairs near the front of the group as one person after another gave a short speech. The christening and change of command for the new warship was a big deal.

During the last two months, more than eighty new warships had entered active service. Many of them were the smaller frigates, the *Vipers* that would lead the fleets. A handful were the newer battleships. But this was the one and only dreadnought-class ship, the RNS *George Washington*.

As Admiral Miles Hunt stood at attention, the President read off a short speech. Her words were meant to inspire, offer hope, and provide the people of Earth reassurance against the Zodark threat. The RNS *George Washington* was the culmination of nearly three and a half years of round-the-clock work by more than thirty thousand synthetics and an army of twenty-five thousand human workers. In all, more than four hundred thousand workers on Earth and on the shipyard had worked to provide materials and equipment used in the final assembly of the *GW*. It was an enormous global effort to build this ship.

At four thousand, two hundred meters in length, four hundred and thirty meters in height, and eight hundred and sixty meters wide, the ship was enormous. And the entire thing was encased in forty meters of armor. Its weakest point, the retractable flight decks on either side of the ship, had twenty-six meters of armor. The ship was a massive flying tank, built to absorb a tremendous amount of enemy fire and survive. It had also been outfitted with a formidable armament of weapons.

Its special-purpose weapon was a single-barreled four-meter-wide plasma cannon. The barrel was fifty meters in length and could fire a single plasma projectile at speeds of sixty megameters per hour. Strung along both sides of the ship were the *GW*'s main guns: twenty-four twin-barreled sixty-inch magrails turrets anchored on the top and bottom of the ship gave it an immense field of fire.

Intermixed with the main guns along both sides of the ship were twenty-four twin-barreled sixteen-inch magrail turrets. The *GW* was also equipped with twelve pulse beam lasers. These new lasers had had a lot of input from the Sumerians, and they were modeled on the captured Zodark ship's weapon system. The lasers were actually a last-minute addition to the *GW*, one the shipbuilders hoped would add value.

Aside from its kinetic weapons, the ship was also equipped with ten forward and ten aft reloadable plasma torpedo launchers. They also carried four separate Havoc missile battery pods. Each missile pod consisted of two hundred single-shot missiles, giving the *GW* a complement of eight hundred missiles. Two hundred of the missiles were equipped with variable-yield nuclear warheads. They ranged from 250-kiloton to 100-megaton warheads, giving the ship a versatile capability.

Once the missile pods were expended, they could be swapped out and replaced with full pods by a replenishment ship. This meant the *GW* didn't need to carry the necessary equipment to fabricate additional missiles or a reloading system, thus freeing up an enormous amount of space that would be dedicated to supporting the ship's aviation wings, which, in time, would become a larger part of the *GW*.

For the time being, the aviation wings consisted of ten squadrons of twenty-four fighter drones. They also had a single squadron of twenty-four heavy-lift shuttlecraft to transfer cargo and personnel from the ship. The fighters, however, would be flown by pilots operating the drones from specially designed pilot pods on the ship. Until manned fighters were built and pilots had been trained to fly them, the *GW* would operate disposable drones that could be quickly fabricated on board the ship to replace their losses.

Hunt suddenly stopped spacing out, thinking about the ship's capabilities when his attention was drawn to Admiral Chester Bailey. "Admiral Hunt, it is with pride that I assign you to be the first commander of the *George Washington*. We are entrusting you with the lives of four thousand, three hundred sailors and RA soldiers. You are hereby ordered to assume command of the *George Washington* and its personnel."

The crowd cheered and Rear Admiral Hunt saluted before he shook hands with Admiral Bailey.

"Your first order as commander of this new warship is to lead your fleet to the Rhea system and establish a permanent military presence and base there. Your second order as commander is to find and destroy the Zodark ships threatening that system and Sol. Your third and final order as the second fleet commander is to find and then liberate the Sumerian planet of Sumer. Integrate their planet and people into our war effort and defeat the Zodarks' military force by any and all means necessary."

Admiral Bailey then turned and received the new guidon for *George Washington* and presented it to Admiral Hunt. Accepting it, Hunt did an about-face and waited for his senior enlisted NCO to walk up and receive the guidon from him. When that part of the military tradition was completed, Hunt, wearing his dress uniform and his medals, walked up to the podium Admiral Bailey had just used. He reached in his pocket and pulled out a small piece of paper that held his notes on it.

Hunt almost snickered at how old-school he was using a piece of paper to write some notes down. No one did that anymore. Most wrote whatever they wanted to say on their digital PA and then had their notes shown to them as they gave the speech—not Hunt.

He surveyed the crowd before him. "People of Earth, Madam President, Fleet Admiral Bailey, I graciously accept command of the *George Washington*, and I thank you for entrusting me with this ship and its crew. Tomorrow, this ship will leave for the Rhea system and our new colony, New Eden, to assert Earth's dominance in space and protect our people and our way of life from a hideous and dangerous enemy. I have fought the Zodarks now on three separate occasions and been victorious. Not once did I run from danger, nor did I place my ship in more danger than what was necessary to achieve victory.

"I cannot promise or guarantee victory against the Zodarks every time we meet them in battle. But what I can tell you is that we will never run from a fight. We will never surrender, and we will fight to our last breath to ensure the safety and security of our people. We will bring the fight to the enemy, and in doing so, we will hope to achieve some semblance of peace that will allow our people to thrive and colonize new worlds.

"This ship, the *George Washington,* will be the vanguard of humanity. It will lead our people into the stars and be a beacon of hope wherever it travels. I want to thank everyone for being here today, and to the families of the loved ones who will serve under my command, thank you for raising some of the best young men and women our country has ever known. Thank you to the spouses for being there for your man or woman as they embark upon this grand journey. Thank you to all who have supported our people, and thank you to the hundreds of thousands who helped to build this grand warship that will bring security and peace to Sol and the Rhea system."

Hunt then took a step back, and the ceremony concluded. The sailors and soldiers on the flight deck dispersed. The individuals who had family were given eight hours to leave the ship and spend some final time with their families on the station; those who were single were given the same eight hours to do what they wanted, but they were confined to the ship. All the holophones and means to communicate were made available, and a special surf and turf dinner was being prepared for them by a catering company hired for this momentous occasion. Unlike the Navy and military of old, Space Command allowed people to drink alcohol on the ship, but only at MWR facilities and with a strict drink limit policy.

Hunt walked up to the President and Admiral Bailey and thanked them privately for the opportunity to command such a ship as this and the grand fleet they had built to support it. The VIPs that would be traveling with them to New Eden were then escorted to their quarters for the evening. They'd be shoving off promptly at 0900 hours the following morning.

As the VIPs were escorted to their rooms, Hunt found his wife standing next to their daughter, looking fabulous in a form fitting dress. With that dress and her makeup, she looked twenty years younger and hot as hell in his eyes. He hugged his daughter, who was there with her boyfriend, and said a few final words to her.

"My all-grown-up princess," he finally said. Then he gave her one last hug before she left the ship with the others who would not be staying.

Hunt winked mischievously at his wife as he led her up to his admiral's quarters and office, which were conveniently placed right next to each other. The two of them spent several hours alone together, saying their goodbyes and making love one last time. Neither of them knew when he'd be back or *if* he'd be back. This next mission could have him gone for many years.

When he escorted his wife off the ship, it was nearly time for dinner. Hunt was scheduled to have dinner with Admiral Bailey, President Luca, and a couple of his senior staff. They were still docked to the station, so this was a very exclusive meal being prepared by the White House chefs themselves using the ship's own kitchen. Unlike the military traditions of old, the officers, chiefs, and enlisted did not eat in separate dining facilities anymore or have different quality levels of food. Everyone ate at the same dining facilities scattered throughout the ship and enjoyed the same food.

The only thing Hunt didn't like about this current deployment to Rhea was how his fleet was getting there. They'd be departing to the new system in waves instead of going all at once. They had already sent ahead several squadrons of *Vipers* nearly two weeks ago, then a convoy of cruisers and heavy transports had gone ahead. His convoy would be the final wave, consisting of the *GW*, six battleships, and a slew of orbital assault ships. It represented roughly eighty percent of the combined fleet's firepower.

When they arrived in New Eden, the President and Admiral Bailey would be pinning Admiral Halsey with her third star, promoting her to vice admiral. She was going to be made the military commander for all expeditionary forces outside of Sol.

In addition to all the military members arriving in the Rhea system, an army of nearly ten thousand civilians and two thousand government workers would also be accompanying them on the large transports. They would assist Admiral Halsey in establishing the colonies and mining facilities on the planet and the two moons. They still had a second full planet in the system where they hadn't even established a presence yet, so that was also something they were looking to exploit next.

President Luca was also appointing a governor, David Crawley, to be the new civilian leader of New Eden and the Rhea system. He'd take over the administrative details from Admiral Halsey and free her up to focus on the military needs of securing the planet and the system.

During the next couple of years, there was going to be a major push to establish a large shipyard and a couple of starbases in the system. While the TPA as an alliance was focusing its efforts on evacuating their people and government to Alpha Centauri, the Republic was going all-in on the Rhea system. Come hell or high water, the Republic was determined to take and hold this system.

\*\*\*\*\*\*\*

Standing on the bridge of this magnificent warship, Rear Admiral Miles Hunt looked at the massive twenty-meter-wide wraparound display in the front of the bridge. It showed the six battleships traveling with his warship in formation, three on either flank of his ship. It also gave him an impressive view of the front third of the *GW* and the massive plasma cannon that anchored the centerline of the forward section of the ship. It was a beautiful sight, something he'd not soon forget.

"Are we ready to leave, Admiral?" inquired the President as she stood next to him. She was going to be seated in the chair next to his. Fleet Admiral Bailey sat on the opposite side of Hunt. It wasn't lost on him that he was flanked and by the two most powerful people in his country.

Turning to look at President Luca, Hunt could see she was a bit nervous. She'd been on a starship before, but never one that traveled via FTL, and she'd also never left Sol. Neither had Admiral Bailey for that matter, so this was an entirely new experience for them both.

Admiral Hunt smiled. "Yes, ma'am," he answered. "We're about to transition from our MPD thrusters to our FTL system. Once we jump, it'll take us roughly four days to reach our destination."

President Luca nodded, a little too quickly. She looked more than just a little anxious.

Admiral Bailey got up and walked over to him. "When you first left for Rhea, it took you what—six and a half months to travel there?" he asked.

Hunt chuckled at the memory. "Yes, Admiral, your memory is correct. When we went back the second time, it had been cut down to six weeks. Now, with the new modifications we've made and the Zodark and Sumerian technology we've incorporated into our FTL and MPD systems, we've cut it down to four days. If you remember, the *Viper*-class frigates can actually make the jump in three days. That's how you both will travel back to Earth once you're ready."

The three of them talked for a little bit longer before the helmsman informed them they were ready to initiate the FTL jump. Everyone then took their seats and strapped in. A call went out across the ship's 1MC, alerting everyone that the ship was preparing to jump. They had three minutes to secure what they were doing and strap into a jump seat. The jumps were typically nonevents, but occasionally there was a bit of turbulence.

"Once the FTL bubble forms, the ship squeezes through time and space toward its destination," Hunt reminded Bailey and President Luca. "It's kind of like squeezing the last bit of toothpaste out of a tube."

It was standard procedure to be strapped in when the ship jumped. If there was a mishap with the FTL system, it would probably happen in the first seconds. It could lead to a rough, uncontrolled exit from the bubble if things went awry. After the first sixty seconds, they could unstrap themselves and go about their regular duties until they were told they were leaving FTL. Then everyone would strap back in for the exit.

Once Hunt confirmed that the President was strapped in and so was Admiral Bailey, Hunt nodded to his helmsman, who initiated the FTL jump. A bright flash of light occurred, and the ship flew through space at an incredible rate of speed. The look on the President's face said it all. Her eyes went wide first with fear, then with awe as she looked at the bubble around the ship. The *GW* flew through the stars like a car driving at night in a snowstorm passes through a cloud of snowflakes. It was an incredible thing to see. Even for Hunt, this never got old.

Leaning in toward him, Admiral Bailey whispered, "Miles, this is incredible. Thank you for insisting that I take the President and head out here. I...don't know what to say."

Admiral Hunt smiled at his friend. "I'm just glad you agreed, sir," he said. "I think it's important that you see what we're fighting for firsthand. It'll be great for the troops and sailors to see their president and commander in person so far away from home."

Hunt cleared his throat. "I'm telling you, sir, if we can fully wrestle this place away from the Zodarks, this new world will be better than Earth. It's five percent larger, its air and environment are so clean and pure, and it's got more open land than you can shake a stick at. A full seventy percent of the planet is open land—no more fear of overpopulation or a polluted world. This place is paradise."

While he was talking, President Luca had unbuckled herself and walked over near them. She heard him talking and joined in. "I'm excited about seeing this place too. I heard when the Chairman returned to China after visiting Alpha Centauri, it completely changed his perspective on Earth. He really set into motion a bold plan to transplant as much of the TPA as possible to Alpha."

Hunt laughed. "I think the Chairman did that out of fear of the Zodarks more than anything else. They are a terrifying enemy, Madam

President. I've seen them firsthand. Terrifying might even be a soft term."

The next four days sped by. Admiral Hunt had the crew run through numerous general quarters drills, which annoyed the President at first, but she came to understand the need for them and, in time, actually enjoyed watching the crew perform them. By the end of the fourth day, she was gladly observing some of the different sections go through the drills and what they were supposed to do.

The President and Admiral Bailey made a point of visiting as many of the soldiers and sailors on the ship as possible. They ate at different times and in various mess halls, so they'd see the different crews. They spent time in every section of the ship, from the laundry room to the kitchen, the machine shop, Engineering, weapons, and flight operations. They spent nearly all of their time touring the ship and getting to know the men and women operating the *GW*.

When the fleet finally arrived in the Rhea system, President Luca suddenly seemed concerned. "This jump point is so dark and devoid of life," she commented.

After a moment, Hunt ascertained that she had thought they were going to land near a planet. He had to spend a couple of minutes explaining that a ship actually had to jump to an open space in a system, so it didn't accidentally slam into a moon or a planet or get entangled in a planet's gravity well.

The first two or three minutes after a jump was the most vulnerable window for a ship. This was the time it took the ship to transition from FTL travel to its MPD thrusters. The ship had to retract the FTL pods into their armored covers and then spin up the plasma drives. All of that took some time to accomplish, even for a well-practiced crew.

While the engineering department was getting the ship ready for regular travel, the sophisticated array of electronic sensors went to work. The *GW* had the newest, most advanced sensor suite ever built by Earth. They had been able to reverse engineer some of the Zodark systems from the captured enemy ship and had integrated much of that ship's technology into the *GW*. As the sensor data returned to the *GW*, it painted a big picture of what was going on in the system.

Admiral Hunt marveled at the speed and clarity of this new system—it was truly incredible. Unlike his previous ship, the *Rook*, it didn't take hours for him to start receiving new data. It was almost instantaneous, and it was detailed. He saw the *Voyager* near New Eden, the space elevator, the makeshift station they had above the planet, and the space elevator currently under construction over Tigris, one of the planet's primary moons. Hunt also saw the massive armada of ships that comprised his fleet.

"Helm, plot a course toward the *Voyager*," Hunt ordered. "Inform the rest of the fleet that we have arrived. Tell Admiral Halsey that once we settle into a position near them, she's to take a shuttle over to the *GW* to meet with Admiral Bailey and President Luca." He wanted to get things rolling now that his fleet was fully formed.

"Yes, Admiral," replied his helmsman and coms officers.

For the next six hours, not much happened as the *GW* and her battleship escorts moved closer to New Eden and the rest of their fleet. A few of the frigates zoomed out to the location of the stargate, their own orders in hand. They'd join the *Viper* that had crossed over a few days prior as they set up a multisystem tripwire to warn them of a pending Zodark fleet.

Hunt also ordered one of their transports to immediately head toward the stargate. They'd designed a series of stationary weapon platforms they were going to anchor near the gate, including a collection of plasma torpedo turrets and magrail turrets. The goal was to establish a series of defensive weapon platforms around the gate to gain control of who entered it.

Shortly after the *George Washington* settled into a position near the *Voyager*, Admiral Halsey came over in one of her shuttlecraft. When she arrived in the starboard flight deck of the ship, Admiral Hunt and Admiral Bailey were there to greet her. They welcomed her aboard the Republic's newest warship and then proceeded to guide her up to the large boardroom near the bridge to meet with the President.

Once they were all in the same room, President Luca shook Admiral Halsey's hand. "Thank you, Admiral, for your hard work and efforts in the Rhea system," she said. Then she presented Admiral Halsey with a small box. Opening it, Halsey saw a set of three stars for her collar, to replace the set of two stars she currently wore. The President also awarded her the second-highest military award, the Navy Cross, for her gallantry in the face of the enemy during the battle to take New Eden from the Zodarks.

As the formalities of her award and promotion ceremony concluded, the senior officers of Space Command and the civilian leadership took their seats to have a long-awaited meeting of the minds and strategy discussion about the future.

President Luca led off the conversation. "Admiral Halsey, you've been in this system now for more than a year. What do you feel you need to get a working shipyard going that will handle the necessary repairs? And what about a series of defensive bases built to protect the system?"

Admiral Halsey leaned forward. "Resources, Madam President. We need people, and we need resources to get this all done." Halsey paused for a second as she looked off in the distance before returning her gaze to the President. "As you can see firsthand, Madam President, space is a big place. Trying to build an orbital station for our space elevator is proving to be challenging as it is. Building a colony on the planet, building a planetary defensive system around New Eden and the two neighboring moons—these are very resource-intensive activities. We need hundreds of construction tugs, tens of thousands of 3-D printers, an army of synthetics, agriculture, food stocks, and farm animals. I mean, the list is practically endless, Madam President."

President Luca shared a nervous look with Admiral Bailey. The two of them had known Admiral Halsey's fleet was stretched pretty thin, but they clearly hadn't fully understood the gravity of the situation.

President Luca turned to Governor Crawley. "David, it looks like you're going to have your work cut out for you," she remarked.

Not missing a beat, the up-and-coming young politician replied, "I look forward to the challenge, Madam President. What Admiral Halsey has done up to this point is nothing short of incredible, and it really speaks to her leadership abilities."

Crawley turned to Halsey. "Admiral, I'm here to help you. I'll be taking many of the administrative duties off your shoulders and will largely handle the civilian development of the planet and the system. We've heard your requests for help, and it has arrived."

Admiral Halsey smiled, and she let out a deep sigh of relief. "I look forward to working with you, Governor. This place has enormous potential, but I won't lie—it's going to be tough getting this place built up. We need an enormous amount of supplies brought to us from Sol, and I don't mean one or two *Ark* transports. I mean we need a continual gravy train of supplies and people if we're to get this place up and running."

The President turned to her military chief. "Admiral Bailey, is there any way we can speed up the transportation of supplies to assist Admiral Halsey and Governor Crawley?"

The fleet admiral scratched his head for a moment. "Not right away, Madam President," he replied with a sigh. "We're in a bit of a bind when it comes to our logistics and ship production right now. With the Zodark threat, we've gone all-in on warships. We had originally planned on building six *Ark*-class transports, but we only completed two of them. A third *Ark* was converted to become the *George Washington*, another shell has been slated to build another dreadnought, and the other two shells are still in the shipyard, incomplete. Our smaller transports were put on hold in favor of constructing a much larger fleet of frigates, battleships, and orbital assault ships. It's just going to take time to build up the navy we need."

President Luca blew some air out of her lips. She clearly wasn't exactly happy with that answer. She turned to her newly minted admiral and posed the same question.

Hunt didn't want to contradict his boss, but he was hoping he could thread the needle. "Madam President, we have limited transport capability; no one is going to sugarcoat or deny that. While we can't correct that problem right away, we can leverage what we have more efficiently.

"The *Arks* are massive. They can comfortably transport up to thirty thousand people for long distances. What we can do is have one of these transports focus on bringing materials, livestock, and necessary equipment from Sol directly to New Eden. As they offload their supplies, they can be loaded with materials to bring back to Sol. The trick to making the transports we have more efficient is going to be our ability to load and offload them swiftly in both Sol and here in New Eden. If we can solve that part of the equation, we'll be able to move twice as many goods and people in the same amount of time."

As the group continued their discussions, a lieutenant walked in with an urgent message for Admiral Hunt. He leaned over and spoke softly in his ear, and Hunt's eyebrows rose.

"We'll be up there momentarily," he responded.

"What is it, Hunt?" Bailey asked, a bit unnerved by the sudden interruption.

Hunt looked at Luca and Bailey as he explained, "One of our first scout ships, a Viper, detected a convoy of Zodark ships headed toward the stargates that lead to our system. They sent a com drone back through the gate, letting us know the size and composition of the enemy fleet before they swooped in to engage them with their plasma torpedoes."

President Luca's eyes went wide as saucers at the mention of the Zodarks. "They're headed here? When? How soon will they arrive?" she demanded.

Hunt held up a hand to stop her from asking more questions. "We need to go to the bridge, Madam President. I'll know more once we get up there. But before we do, I need to ask that you please remain calm and steady. I suspect we'll have several days before the enemy is here, so there's no need to panic. We're not under direct threat as of right now."

Bailey nodded as he made eye contact with the President, and the two of them got up to follow him out to the bridge. When they entered the massive command center, they saw officers and enlisted personnel working quietly and smoothly, running through their standard procedures and routines like nothing was out of the ordinary.

President Luca seemed to calm down at the sight. Perhaps she realized that if these professionals were not alarmed, then she shouldn't be either.

Upon entering the bridge, Hunt walked over to the tactical officer. "What's the situation with that Viper? What do we know so far?"

When the officer manning the tactical station turned around and saw the admiral followed by the fleet admiral and the President right behind him, he clearly felt a bit awkward. "Sir, um...we just received a com drone message fifteen minutes ago," he stammered. "It popped through the stargate and started transmitting. Commander Dobbs, the captain, said they had spotted a convoy of Zodark ships heading toward the stargate that would lead them to the system next door to us."

*That's my son's ship*, Hunt thought nervously. He did his best to conceal his emotions, but he knew the *Viper* was a recon ship that wasn't meant for battle against the Zodarks.

"So they're at least two stargate jumps away from reaching Rhea?" Hunt clarified.

The tactical officer nodded. "Exactly, sir. At currently estimated speeds, it places them around three or four days away from us."

"OK, this is good information to know. What's the ship composition?" Hunt asked next, trying to drill down into exactly what they were facing.

"We're still a little sketchy on their ship types, but what we do know is at least two of them appear to be just like that carrier we captured," the tactical officer explained, reading through the contents of the message again. "Four others looked like the battleship that had been escorting the carrier. Three other ships resemble the smaller type of Zodark vessel you first encountered. And there appear to be six ships that are likely transport ships. We're guessing those are probably troop transports."

Admiral Halsey let out a soft whistle. "That's a lot of ships heading our way."

Hunt chuckled. "It is, but I'm confident we can handle them," he countered. "As a matter of fact, I think this may work to our benefit."

"How so?" she replied skeptically.

"We know they're coming, and we know they'll have to jump through a specific stargate. We can move our ships over to that location and be camped out, waiting for them to arrive. When they jump through, then we spring our trap and pulverize their fleet before they even know what happened."

"Do you think your fleet is strong enough to take them on?" Admiral Bailey pressed.

Hunt nodded confidently. "I do," he said. "It looks like they have eight warships. I've got the *George Washington*, six battleships, eight TPA cruisers, and eighteen frigates. The volume of firepower we'll be able to unleash when they jump into the system will wipe them out. Once we've defeated their fleet, then we'll be in a position to launch our invasion of their space and move to liberate the Sumerian home world."

Admiral Halsey smiled. "I like this plan, Hunt. It's our turn to get some payback."

"Sir, we're receiving another message from the *Viper*," announced the coms officer a couple of stations over.

"What's it say?" Hunt asked.

"Commander Dobbs says she's retreating to Rhea to join us," the coms officer explained. "She's attached a video and some initial analysis her crew ran. It looks like they ambushed the Zodarks at one of the gates and scored a few hits. I'm sending the message and video over to the CIC to have them look it over."

Nodding in approval, Hunt pulled up the message on the command tablet he always kept on him. He briefly looked at the video and the initial notes that came along with it. The first thing he noticed was how the Zodark ships that had just jumped through the gate were virtually helpless for about sixty seconds. It confirmed his suspicions. The Zodark ships took some time after a jump to recalibrate their sensors before they could defend themselves or attack anyone. It supported his plan to gate camp the enemy fleet and destroy them as they jumped through.

He turned to Admiral Bailey. "Admiral, I'm going to move my fleet to the gate and prepare our ambush. You are more than welcome to stay on the *GW* and observe firsthand if you'd like, but I can't guarantee we won't take any hits during this battle. I think it's highly unlikely they'll destroy the *GW*, but I need to make you aware that it could happen."

"Thank you, Admiral Hunt. I think it may be best if President Luca and I transfer over to the *Voyager* and monitor the battle from a distance," Admiral Bailey announced. The President was visibly relieved by this decision.

Over the next couple of hours, the two Republic leaders hurriedly packed their belongings and transferred on a shuttlecraft to the *Voyager* nearby. Governor Crawley and his people were transported down to the main RA base on New Eden. They'd hunker down with the Army while they began the process of getting the first colony up and running and dealing with all the other civilian functions they'd been sent to handle. Meanwhile, the rest of Admiral Hunt's fleet got ready to jump to the stargate.

## Chapter Twelve
## Emerald City

**New Eden**
**Victory Base Complex**

The Osprey flew over Victory Base Complex, what the soldiers called the VBC, as President Luca looked out the window and saw the alien planet, New Eden, for the first time. It was beautiful beyond anything she had imagined. The videos and pictures she'd seen over the years couldn't compare to seeing it firsthand. She now understood what everyone meant when they described the planet's unmatched beauty.

The sprawling military bases below appeared to be scattered across several large hills and ridges. Part of one of the bases looked like it had seen better days.

"That used to be a Zodark military base before the invasion," one of the crew chiefs explained. "It's actually a conglomeration of several military bases all strung together for added protection. Each base had its own separate function."

Along one of the flat areas was a series of runways and parking ramps chock-full of Ospreys, VACs for the infantry, and several other transport craft. "The base we're headed to handles the air operations and transportation for the bases," said the crew chief.

President Luca spotted another facility being built along the ridge that seemed to be protecting the airport-spaceport facility. It was ringed with artillery pieces, fortifications, and other facilities whose functions she had no idea of. What amazed her most was how quickly all of this had been built. In fifteen months, the Army had built this massive base that was home to some fifty-two thousand soldiers.

She'd already been told by one of the generals that the army had three such facilities built in strategic locations around the planet. They had a smattering of forty-two smaller firebases in other strategic positions as well, which were more closely linked to the mining operations.

As they approached the airstrip, a massive plot of land a dozen miles from the base caught her eye. It connected directly to the ocean, and it was gorgeous. She wagered this was the location where they'd build the first human city.

"It's quite a view, isn't it, Madam President?" asked Governor David Crawley as they both looked out the window.

She smiled, turning her head slightly. "I'm envious of you, David. You get to stay and build a city from scratch on a new planet."

Crawley nodded. "I'm eternally grateful that you selected me to be the governor, Madam President. We're going to build an incredible city for our people, one that will stand the test of time."

One of the crew chiefs walked over to them. "I'm going to need you both to strap in," he interjected. "We're coming in on final approach."

President Luca reattached her harness. The time to gawk out the windows at this new world was done for the time being.

The Osprey flew over the airstrip and settled down near one of the large hangars. As its engines wound down, a large group of soldiers and a marching band moved into position outside the Osprey doors to welcome the President.

While that was happening, the crew chiefs and pilot came over to welcome Luca to New Eden and the base. They then opened the rear hatch, the warm air rushing in to greet them.

When President Luca walked near the rear ramp, she held her hand up to shield her eyes from the sunlight. They had told her it was a bit brighter on the surface of New Eden than Earth, and they were right. The Rhea system did, after all, have three suns.

The first sound she heard, aside from that of engines from various military vehicles, was a band starting up. She realized they were playing "Hail to the Chief" as she walked off the Osprey.

Several military officers stepped forward to greet her. "Hello, Madam President, I'm Major General Ross McGinnis. It's a real pleasure to see you here," the ground commander of the Republic Forces said as they shook hands.

President Luca smiled. "Thank you, General, for the warm reception," she replied. Her hand swept to her left. "This is Governor David Crawley, the new governor of New Eden and the head of the civilian government. He and his people will help alleviate a lot of the challenges you've been facing here."

"Thank you, Madam President, and it's a pleasure to make your acquaintance, Governor Crawley. We're incredibly glad you are here and for the staff you've brought with you. If you'd like to follow me, I'll take you on a short tour of some of the areas before we head back to my headquarters building."

The three of them walked past several rows of soldiers standing in formation, their M85 rifles held at attention. President Luca stopped a couple of times to say something to one of the soldiers and then continued on. When they neared the front of the hangar, there was an armored vehicle waiting for them.

The group climbed in, and a couple of her Secret Service agents settled in near the rear hatches. The vehicle drove away from the hangar, and they began their tour.

For the next hour, General McGinnis told President Luca and Governor Crawley about each of the bases and what their functions were. He informed them about life on the bases, and what the soldiers did to pass the time, and some of the things they had learned and discovered about New Eden. It was a lot of information to take in, but Luca was glad she had opted to come down to the planet and see this place for herself, even if it was only going to be a short trip.

The vehicle eventually came to a halt in front of a heavily fortified building. "We're here," said McGinnis. "If you'll follow me, we'll head inside. You can meet a few more soldiers before we go into the bunker to give you a more thorough briefing."

Luca was impressed with how rapidly things had been built up here on the surface. This military base was less than two years old, and it already looked like it had been here for decades. Sometimes she had wondered where all the money being spent on defense was going—now she knew.

When they entered the bunker, Luca and Crawley were led over to a large conference room with a massive table. Everyone took their seats. Refreshments were brought in as the briefers prepared to share their information.

For the next two hours, they went over the details of New Eden and some of the major finds they'd made thus far. They also gave a good overview of their military operations to finish rooting out the remaining Zodark soldiers on the planet. According to their best intelligence, there weren't many left at this point—however, the ones that were still around continued to cause enough problems that it was forcing General McGinnis to keep a large number of units out on daily and nightly patrols.

General McGinnis then made his pitch to have half a million more soldiers sent to New Eden, along with a slew of additional military equipment. At first, Luca balked at the idea. But as he laid out the reason for the large force, it began to make sense. The general wanted to get the units acclimated to being on New Eden, then have them train on the planet as well as on the two moons in orbit. The whole goal was to get the invasion force that would be liberating Sumer ready to operate on any alien planet.

At the end of the military portion of the briefing, Luca agreed to his request and said she'd speak to General Pilsner when she returned to Earth. She also said she was going to promote McGinnis up a grade so he could stay in command of the expeditionary force.

Next, they transitioned to the civilian projects. A dozen sites had been identified by the engineers and surveyors as locations for new cities. One of the proposals was to build in a circular spoke pattern with the capital city at the center. This would allow for mass transit connecting all of the megacities the civil engineers were planning to build with each other while still allowing for a lot of growth and green space between them.

President Luca interrupted them. "When I flew into the camp, I saw a lot of land along the water not far from here. Are we planning on building any cities there at all?" She had grown up in San Diego and loved the water. It only seemed natural.

The civil engineers didn't say anything at first. One of them, a guy named George, finally shrugged as he replied, "We hadn't given it a lot of thought, ma'am. These five cities on the spoke are very close to our mining operations. It made sense to build a large city near where the mines are, given how much work and industry is going to happen there." He pointed at the proposed map. "These two cities would be near the mountains, while these three would be in the plains, which is great agricultural land for farming. I suppose we could have a single city along the water connected into the spoke."

Another engineer added, "George, we could just build a string of cities along the coastal areas and then integrate them into our original spoke design with the hyperloop. That way, we wouldn't have to change any of our existing plans too much."

Luca smiled as she saw a couple of them work to solve the problem. They'd obviously spent a lot of time and effort surveying and designing these cities, and now she was throwing a wrench into the plan.

Luca cleared her throat. "I have another question. If we move along with your original plan, how long will it take to start construction on these new cities, and how many people will they be able to hold?"

The lead civil engineer took the center of the room. "With the governor's permission, we'd begin operations immediately using the fabricators and Synths that just arrived. We'd like to start with building the infrastructure first: hyperloops, tubes, stations, water, septic, and underground utilities. We'll start with the capital city and then build out the other spokes in the wheel as each phase of the construction is completed. So phase one would be the infrastructure—that's a hell of a lot easier to build when there are no homes, roads, or businesses in the way, so we'll knock that all out first.

"Then phase two would consist of building out both the housing units and the public works needed to support them: schools, police, hospitals, things like that. Phase three will consist of expanding the industrial needs of each city and then the planet as a whole. With our current resources, we anticipate having a city able to house a hundred thousand colonists in roughly two years. That number would increase dramatically once we get more workers and fabricators built. All told, we're hoping to have enough housing capacity for ten million people within a decade. From there, it'll grow exponentially as we build more of these planned city designs."

Luca smiled at the news, but she was always one to go bold. "Gentlemen, this is an exceptional plan. However, you need to think larger," she insisted. "This is one city complex you've shown me. We need to have ten or twenty of them going, and preferably at the same time. We cannot wait a decade to have ten million people living here. We need to build New Eden into an industrial powerhouse able to support and sustain our growing military presence in the system. That means we'll need a massive shipyard with the ability to build and repair our warships—that requires resources, workers, and more resources.

"We have billions of people on Earth. Despite the dangers of the Zodarks, tens of millions of people are lining up to travel here. I want to challenge you to move forward with this plan, but expand it at least tenfold. You're going to have an army of workers, people, and supplies headed your way in the coming year, so be prepared and act now."

The meeting ended shortly after her comments, and they traveled back to the airfield. When they reached that large hangar close to the Osprey that would take them back to the ship, there was a formation of soldiers waiting for President Luca to personally promote and award valor medals to them. She didn't have as much time on New Eden as she wanted, not with the Zodark fleet bearing down on them, but this was important. The soldiers here were far away from home, away from their families and loved ones. They'd fought a long and tough campaign to capture an alien world from a hostile force. She felt she owed it to them to spend some time with them and present them with their medals and promotions in person. She was, after all, their commander in chief.

It took her two hours to go through the rows of soldiers, pinning their medals on them and awarding them their new ranks, but it was worth it. She got to see the esprit de corps of the various units and the pride in the eyes of these brave warriors that served in them. After spending the day on the planet, she felt a new sense of urgency and vigor to make sure these men and women had anything and everything they needed to win this war. She was more determined than ever to see this conflict through to total victory, no matter the cost.

## Chapter Thirteen
## Battle at the Gate

**Rhea Gate**
**RNS *George Washington***

"We're approaching the stargate now," the helmsman called out as the ship finally came into sight of the massive floating structure.

No one knew who had created these stargates, or technically how they even worked. All the Earthers really knew was that the Zodarks used them to traverse the galaxy. Maybe they had been created by an ancient race that had once colonized the stars. Who knew? But right now, it didn't matter. What mattered was that a Zodark fleet was heading toward them, and they didn't have a lot of time to prepare.

"Something's coming through," shouted the tactical officer.

"Spin up our targeting computers. I want whatever's coming through locked up and blown apart if it's not one of ours," barked Captain Fran McKee, Hunt's XO.

When Hunt had been promoted to rear admiral and given command of Earth's most powerful warship, he'd pulled some strings to have Fran promoted to O-6, Captain, and made his official XO on the *George Washington*. He probably could have gotten her command of one of the battleships, but he really needed and wanted her help fighting on the *GW*. It was a beast of a ship, and he ultimately knew if she did a tour as the XO on this ship, the next dreadnought-class ship built would most likely be commanded by her.

Looking at the main display in front of the bridge, Hunt ordered, "Enhance that image. I want to see what's jumping through."

A second later, the display zoomed in and showed the stargate much clearer. It shimmered briefly, and then a ship shot through it. It didn't move very quickly immediately after being ejected from the gate, but it was working on increasing its speed. As soon as the Earthers had a second to respond to the visual, everyone on the bridge seemed to breathe a collective sigh of relief.

"It's the *Viper*. Stand down, everyone," ordered Captain McKee.

"Sir, we're being hailed by them," Lieutenant Molly Branson announced.

Like McKee, Branson had transferred over to the *GW* with Hunt. Hunt had done his best to have as many of his bridge crew from the *Rook* carried over to the *GW* as he could. He knew them, and they knew how to fight a warship. He wanted that knowledge and experience anchoring the most powerful warship in the fleet.

"Patch them through," Hunt ordered as he sat a little straighter in his chair.

A second later, the image of Commander Dobbs appeared. "Admiral, it's good to see you. For a second there, I thought we were goners until we realized it was you guys here when we jumped through the gate." He thought he saw a few beads of sweat on her forehead.

Hunt smiled. "We got your message a couple of days ago about the gate camping idea. I went ahead and moved the fleet into position. How far away is the Zodark fleet, Commander?"

She furrowed her brow. "That's hard to say, Admiral. We're still not one hundred percent certain on their actual travel speeds, so it's hard to know exactly far away they are right now. Our best guess is they're probably about a day and a half behind us. Now that we're back in the system, sir, would you like our ship to support your fleet?"

"Commander, how much of your ordnance did you expend?" Hunt asked.

"We used a single barrage of plasma torpedoes and Havoc missiles. I've got two more loads of both aboard," Dobbs replied. "I'm actually shorter on food than I am anything else."

"OK, Commander, make your best speed back to New Eden and restock your food stores, then head back here," Hunt ordered. "I've left our replenishment ships back near New Eden with the *Voyager*. Make sure you're back here in thirty-two hours. I want your ship here for this coming battle."

As the *Viper* headed off to resupply, Hunt ordered a couple more of his frigates to jump through the stargate and keep an eye out for the Zodark fleet. The rest of the day was primarily spent reexamining the footage of Commander Dobbs's attack on the enemy fleet. Hunt's people were looking for any and all means they could use to catch the Zodarks by surprise and hopefully crush their fleet.

The lone transport Hunt had sent a couple days ago had already made progress in unloading two of the plasma torpedo platforms. They still had one more to deploy before they could start deploying the three magrail turrets. Hunt wasn't sure if they'd get them all deployed and brought online before the Zodarks showed up, but he was hoping they could. The floating turrets would add to the mayhem and carnage they'd be able to inflict on the enemy.

Earth had spent the last few years building up a navy to defend Sol and take Rhea. If they were able to crush the enemy fleet here, then they'd be able to travel, hopefully unopposed, to the Sumerian home planet and liberate them. Then Hunt's people would work to integrate them into their military alliance and together they could liberate and free additional human worlds as they found them. The burning questions Hunt still couldn't answer were how many other human worlds were out there, how they came to be scattered across the stars, and how big the Zodarks' empire was. While he didn't have answers to those questions yet, he was going to try to find them.

Hunt checked the time log on his neurolink; it had been nearly two days since the *Viper* had jumped through the gate. That had proved to be a good thing, since it had given the transport enough time to deploy the gate guns. Hunt would have liked to place a lot more—maybe even some anti-ship mines, but he was glad to have something set up.

The two scout ships on the other side of the stargate hadn't jumped back to warn them of any approaching Zodark ships. Admiral Hunt was starting to wonder what to do.

*I guess I'll grab a shower and some food while we wait*, Hunt thought as he stretched in his commander's chair on the bridge.

He turned to Captain McKee. "XO, you have the bridge. I'm going to freshen up and grab some food. You want me to bring you anything from the mess deck?" Hunt asked as he stood up.

Captain McKee smiled but said she was OK.

Walking into his quarters, Hunt had to admit, he really enjoyed this perk of command. The admiral's quarters were spacious compared to previous ships he'd served on. Heck, the captain's quarters he had McKee staying in were amazing compared to previous commands he'd held. They'd designed this ship with the idea of a fleet admiral being stationed aboard. It had a section of quarters for such a staff, beyond the normal command staff.

The admiral quarters were divided into two sections. The first was his office, which had a large mahogany desk that also had an extension for his aide to work from. Hunt thought about how his aide rarely ever left the office—then again, it was her job to facilitate all communications and administrative duties for Hunt. She was a lifesaver.

At the opposite end of the office was a sitting area with two couches and two chairs for informal meetings, and then a ten-person wardroom table to accommodate private briefings or meals. At the rear end of the office was a door that led to his sleeping quarters. His smaller sleeping quarters were still twice as large as anything he'd previously had on the *Rook* or any other starship he'd served on. Instead of a twin bed, he had a queen-size bed to stretch out on. He also loved the comfortable leather La-Z-Boy rocking recliner and small entertainment center to watch holograph movies or listen to music. All in all, this was a very comfortable home away from home. His shower was even large enough for him to actually bend over and scrub himself. It was quite luxurious compared to what he'd grown accustomed to as a naval officer.

Stripping off his couple-day-old clothes, Hunt placed them in the bin for his aide to deliver to the ship's laundry department. He laid out a clean uniform on his bed and then hopped in the shower. He turned the water temp up pretty high before stepping in. He was steadily feeling every bit of his fifty-four years of age. Hunt was still lean, but not nearly as muscular or cut as he had been. Command was taking its toll on him physically. He found himself spending more and more time in meetings or strategy discussions and less time in the gym working out.

After squeezing some foamy soap onto his hand, Hunt turned the hot water off for a moment as he proceeded to lather up nice and good. Once he was sufficiently soapy, he turned the water back on and let it wash away the soap, grime, and stress of the last couple days.

Just then, he heard the familiar sound of the 1MC blaring its klaxon noise, alerting the crew to man their battle stations.

*Sorry to interrupt, Admiral, but the stargate is activating. Something is about to jump through*, Captain McKee said through the command's neurolink.

*Man, it's always when I'm indisposed that the battle station alarms blare*, Hunt thought.

*Thank you, Captain, I'll be up there momentarily. If it's a Zodark ship, you know what to do*, he replied as he turned the water off. He rushed to the bed to grab his clothes. He didn't have time to properly dry off, so his fresh uniform would just have to absorb the water for him.

As soon as he exited the door to his office and quarters, Hunt broke into a run, racing to get to the bridge. He was hoping it wasn't the Zodarks, not right away. Hunt wanted to be on the bridge when the first several critical decisions needed to be made. He trusted McKee to do the right thing, but he was the man in charge of not just this ship but the entire fleet. Fifteen thousand lives depended on him making the right call at the right time.

He arrived on the bridge just as two ships emerged from the stargate; he was relieved to see they were Republic frigates and not a Zodark fleet.

"Hail them, get an update and find out if they've spotted the enemy fleet yet," Captain McKee ordered the coms officer.

Hunt walked up to McKee. "Did you send a message out to the rest of the fleet to go to general quarters yet?" he asked.

"It just went out as you entered the bridge," she replied.

"Admiral, a message from the *Blackjack*," announced Lieutenant Branson. "They said the Zodark fleet had just arrived at the other side of the gate. That's why they jumped through."

Taking charge of the situation, Hunt bellowed out loud enough for everyone to hear him, "OK, people, this is it—the battle we've been waiting for. The enemy is on the other side of that stargate. They may jump across in a few minutes or a few hours. What we *do* know is they're going to be jumping across to try to retake this system. Let's be ready to give them a good old-fashioned Earth greeting when they do."

Hunt turned to look at his tactical officer. "Commander, send a message down to flight ops to begin preparations to deploy our fighters. Let's also spin up the plasma cannon. That damn thing takes a while to get ready, so let's start the process now."

Captain McKee walked closer to him and leaned in. "Admiral, when the battle starts, do you want me to handle fighting the ship while you focus on managing the fleet?"

Looking at his XO, Hunt smiled; this was why he wanted her as his XO. She was intuitive and knew how to anticipate his needs before he vocalized them. "Yes, XO, that'll work out great. I'll stay in control of the plasma cannon, but yes, please fight and manage the ship while I work with the other ship captains. This is going to get chaotic. Don't forget to stay on top of damage control once we start taking some hits. We have a lot of new and untested systems on this ship. We're bound to have some hiccups during our first engagement."

McKee nodded approvingly. She then turned to start barking more orders to various sections throughout the bridge.

Taking his seat at his terminal, Hunt had just gotten his screen brought up with an overview of the fleet when the stargate activated. Looking up at the massive display screen at the front of the bridge, he watched the stargate field shimmering a bit as whatever was on the other side traveled through it. Moments later, the first ship emerged.

"That looks to be a Zodark battleship," called out one of the crewmen in the tactical section.

"Start jamming that ship now! Weps, lock onto it with our main guns and engage them," ordered Captain McKee excitedly.

The others on the bridge all went to work on their own functions, specifically designed to make the ship work as a single unit. The electronic warfare group started their jamming protocols, Engineering ramped up power from the reactors, and the helm got the ship moving slowly, ready to accelerate or maneuver should the order be given.

Next, the tactical and weapons groups assigned targets to the primary and secondary gun batteries, while damage control parties stood by, ready to start repairing the inevitable damage that would occur from a battle. This was what days and weeks of hard drilling looked like, and it often made the difference between a ship surviving a fight or being blown apart.

Hunt sent a message to the battleships in his fleet to all lock onto the single contact. His strategy was to have his battlewagons focus their efforts on one ship at a time. If they could overwhelm the enemy ships, then maybe they could systematically take them down faster.

"More ships are jumping through…five new contacts," called out the tactical officer.

Looking at the forward display, Hunt saw a total of six ships. The lone battleship was trying to lock on the *GW*. They looked to be in too close for the *GW*'s jamming to work effectively. Seconds later, the first volley of magrail slugs fired from the group of batteries on the *GW* toward the Zodark ship. The other RNS battleships opened up as well.

By the time the other five Zodark ships could start to move and had their own targeting sensors up and running, the first Zodark ship was being pummeled with hundreds of slugs by the *GW* and the six other battleships. The enemy vessel was already in trouble; dozens of fires appeared across its armored shell.

Hunt then watched as the first string of plasma torpedoes slammed into the Zodark battleship. Eight of the fourteen that had been fired at them scored hits. Moments later, the Zodark ship erupted into a ball of flames, and the ship was ripped apart.

When the Earth fleet had scored their first victory of the battle, Hunt sent a message to the battleships to shift focus to another one of the enemy vessels. He instructed those ship captains to continue to focus their concerted effort on the same ship. Hunt wanted all the fleet's fire to stay concentrated on a single ship rather than devolving into a circus of small battles between ships.

Hunt had placed three of his six battleships on the starboard side of the gate and the other three on the opposite side. The ships would run in slow-moving figure eight patterns at various degrees and positions around the gate. This allowed the ships room to maneuver while also ensuring his fleet could thoroughly saturate the area with magrail slugs and plasma torpedoes without fear of hitting their own ships. He had created a kill box—a massive kill box.

Looking at the overview of the battle unfolding around the *GW*, Hunt saw that the plasma torpedo and magrail turrets they had anchored around the gate were randomly engaging the closest ship to them. He couldn't directly control these weapons—they were running autonomously using their own AI.

Sitting in his command chair, Hunt felt the slight vibration from the massive magrail guns firing. It wasn't one turret or a set of guns firing that caused the ship to vibrate—it was the culmination of nearly sixty primary and secondary magrail turrets firing slugs at the enemy.

As he watched the battle on a three-dimensional display, Hunt saw his tactic was having the desired effect. The second enemy battleship they engaged was succumbing to their relentless fire. The Zodark ships were in too close to jump out of the way of the Earthers' magrail slugs. They just had to sit there and take a beating while they tried to get their thrusters up to speed so they could maneuver out of the kill box.

"More ships are jumping through," the tactical officer called out.

Hunt looked up. Sure enough, eight new warships appeared. It looked like two of them were those Zodark carriers they had been warned about.

Suddenly, the *GW* shook hard. Hunt saw they were now taking some hits from the enemy. A dozen pulse beams hit them, trying to cut through their thick armor. While they hadn't been able to burn a hole through yet, the hits were shaking the ship.

"Commander Ross!" Hunt called out. The man turned to look at him, a pensive look on his face like he'd been waiting all day for Hunt to call on him. "Lock your weapon onto that first carrier's rear section and fire. Let's see if we can neutralize them quickly," Hunt directed.

Commander Ross relayed some commands to the crew operating the plasma cannon. The massive single barrel traversed slowly as it aimed at the Zodark carrier. Hunt tapped into the turret controls and watched as Commander Ross used the gun optical sight system to zoom in on the section he had mentioned. At last, the targeting reticle was locked onto the rear section of the massive Zodark vessel. The enemy ship had to be close to three and a half kilometers long—not quite as long as the *GW*, but far larger than any other human warship.

Ross looked over at Hunt. "We're ready to fire."

"Fire!" Hunt ordered.

Hunt heard a loud cracking noise throughout the ship as the massive gun fired its discharge at the enemy vessel. The sheer size of the release and its recoil shook the *GW* harder than all its other weapon systems combined.

Hunt watched the computer display to see if he could spot the plasma round. The screen whited out, and the display refocused fractions of a second later to reveal a massive gaping hole in the rear section of the enemy vessel.

"Holy crap! Did you see that?" the weapons officer said to no one in particular.

There were a few loud whoops of joy and excitement when they saw the damage the plasma cannon had done to the enemy ship.

Captain McKee looked at Hunt, an expression of shock on her face. The Sumerians had spent more than two years telling the Republic how to build and employ a plasma cannon, but this was the first time any of them had seen the new high-tech weapon used on an enemy warship in combat. It was awesome.

Hunt smiled in satisfaction at the carnage the *George Washington* had just inflicted on the enemy capital ship. "Commander Ross, hit 'em again near the same spot," he ordered, hoping to finish ripping the ship apart.

As he watched the gaping hole in the ship on his display, Hunt saw chunks of the vessel and debris blown clear out the other end of the warship. There was a line in space that looked like it stretched from where the plasma cannon and the *GW* had just been all the way to the now-massive hole in the rear section of the Zodark warship. The enemy vessel seemed to be adrift now, its rear thrusters having gone dark. Parts of the ship still appeared to have power—Hunt attributed that to backup generators or some other power source.

"We've got a problem," called out one of the officers at the tactical station.

Turning to see what was going on, Hunt watched one of the Zodark battleships move to position itself between the *GW* and the stricken carrier. The other carrier began spitting out dozens upon dozens of their version of fighter spacecraft. The volume of fire in the melee also began to shift. It was all now being concentrated at the *GW*. The enemy was trying in earnest to take out the ship equipped with this new superweapon before it could blast more of them to kingdom come.

Captain McKee had the primary and secondary magrail turrets shift fire to the battleship that had just positioned itself in front of the stricken carrier, and Hunt sent new targeting orders over to the other battleships in the fleet, directing them to focus their fire on the remaining carrier that was still operational. The damn thing was spitting out fighters at a prodigious rate.

Hunt walked over to Commander Ross's station and leaned in. "Are we ready to fire again?" he asked.

Ross didn't take his eyes away from his terminal. "Twenty more seconds, Admiral, and we'll be powered up and ready to go. Do you still want us to hit the carrier again?"

Looking at the targeting monitor, Hunt saw the enemy battleship was really doing its best to block them from scoring another hit on it. "I'd sure as hell like to, but are you able to get a decent shot in on them? I mean, can you hit anything of value on the carrier?"

Ross's forehead scrunched up as he seemed to be making calculations based on what parts of the enemy carrier were still exposed. Then he shook his head.

"If the damn gun didn't take five minutes to charge between shots, I don't think it'd matter. We could just pound away. But to be honest, sir, we'd be better off repositioning the gun to hit the other carrier, and if we can't do that, then one of the battleships."

As Ross was speaking to Hunt, the ship continued to shake relentlessly from the pounding it was taking. Hunt really wanted that first carrier destroyed. That damn Zodark ship was blocking him, and it really ticked him off, but Ross was right—they should go for the other carrier.

Looking at the second carrier, Hunt saw it was taking an absolute beating right now from the six RNS battleships. *No, that ship isn't going to last much longer*, he thought. *We need to take another ship out. There...that one will do nicely...*

"That ship right there," Hunt said as he pointed to one of the elongated ships that were doing its best to hide behind a couple of larger cruisers.

Ross smiled devilishly. "A transport. Good idea, sir. We might even nail it with a single shot."

Commander Ross traversed the massive plasma cannon to aim at the group of transports. As he was getting ready to fire their superweapon, alarm bells rang on the bridge. An automated voice called out, informing them of a hull breach on one of the decks.

"Launch our fighters!" Captain McKee ordered. She barked orders to her engineering group to get the hull breach secured and to stay on top of the repairs.

While it wasn't chaos on the bridge just yet, it was starting to get really loud. "Take that ship out, Commander," Hunt shouted over all the activity taking place on the bridge.

"Firing!" Ross announced loudly.

The ship vibrated slightly as they all heard the loud cracking noise from the gun firing and felt its massive recoil. The plasma round shot out in a brilliant flash of light that caused the bridge monitors to momentarily white out again before returning to normal.

As the monitors came back to life, several of the bridge crew let out a gasp; then cheers broke out. The transport ship they had fired upon had been ripped in half. The rear half of the vessel was moving in one direction, while the front half spun slowly in space. Near the sheared-off section of the ship, they could see sparks flying and wreckage being blown out into the vacuum of space.

"Zoom in on that debris," Admiral Hunt ordered.

Seconds later, they saw the massive cluster was actually thousands of Zodark bodies—soldiers presumably on their way to secure New Eden. Now they were just floating in the darkness of space, their transport nothing more than a wreck.

Turning to Commander Ross, Hunt ordered, "Take those other transports out. We can't let them land more troops on the planet."

While the battle continued to rage, the group of remaining transports, along with three cruisers, looked to be making a break for it. They were moving at full speed to put as much distance as possible between themselves and the battle.

"Shift the primaries to the transports and the cruisers!" Hunt shouted over the growing noise on the bridge. "They're positioning to jump to New Eden!"

"You heard the admiral," Captain McKee barked. "All weapons shift to take those bastards out. Target our Havoc missiles at them as well." McKee clearly also recognized what was happening with that group of ships. The Zodarks had probably figured they were going to lose this battle. Now they wanted to do what they could to get their troops delivered to the planet before their fleet was pulverized.

"Ross, can you get another shot off before they jump?" demanded Hunt earnestly.

"Firing now, Admiral," Ross finally said seconds later.

*Boom...*

The plasma cannon roared one more time, whiting out their screen once again for a fraction of a second. When the visuals returned, another transport ship had blown apart. This time, the ship didn't separate, it just exploded from the impact.

"They're jumping!" shouted the tactical officer a few stations away.

In the blink of an eye, the four remaining transports and two cruisers jumped. The last cruiser and two transports failed to jump; their ships had already been rocked by explosions from the volume of firepower being thrown at them. They wouldn't last much longer.

Hunt turned to his coms officer. "Send a message to the *Voyager* and any warships in orbit around New Eden. We have two Zodark cruisers inbound and four troopships. Tell them they need to take those transports out first before they attack those cruisers. We can't let them land more troops on the surface."

Captain McKee then ordered the ship's primary and secondary weapons systems to focus their fire on the remaining Zodark carriers and battleships still at the gate.

"We have enemy fighters inbound," one of the weapons officers announced.

"Activating point defenses now," countered another officer operating those systems.

Hunt walked back over to his command chair, feeling the weight of enemy fire continuing to pound his ship's armor. Looking back at his command monitor, he had a good overview of the battle taking place around them. Two pairs of frigates were swooping in from one of the flanks like a pair of dive bombers. When the ships leveled out from their maneuver, they were lined up on the wounded carrier they had disabled at the start of the battle.

Each RNS ship fired a barrage of six plasma torpedoes along with ten Havoc anti-ship missiles. The frigates then picked up speed to get out of range of the Zodark ship's weapons. One of the enemy vessels that had been trying to protect the stricken ship fired one of its pulse beam lasers at one of the frigates, and it was swiftly ripped in half by the enemy laser. The other frigate did a couple of fancy maneuvers but ultimately got blown apart by another pulse beam from a different battleship.

The last pair of frigates unloaded their torpedoes and Havoc missiles at the second carrier. Both of those frigates managed to escape and pulled out of the battle to reload their primary weapons before they could circle back to jump into another attack run.

Hunt watched the twelve torpedoes continue toward the crippled Zodark carrier. Two of the torpedoes were taken out by one of the Zodark battleships, but the remaining ten slammed into the carrier. A series of massive explosives rippled across the ship's armored hull, and several torpedoes managed to rip through the armor of the ship, causing considerable damage to its guts.

Hunt shook his head and sighed. He was ticked that most of the Havoc missiles had been zapped before they could impact. The two that did manage to hit the ship's armor didn't appear to make it through the thick belt on the ship. He was going to have to note that in the after-action report so they could get the weapon R&D guys working on a stronger warhead.

Watching the second carrier, Hunt angrily shook his head as he saw it maneuver out of the way of half the torpedoes. It looked like its point defense weapons had taken out the Havoc missiles and two of the four torpedoes. The four that scored hits, however, did considerable damage.

While the slugfest between the large Zodark and human ships continued, Hunt checked the time on his neurolink. Twenty minutes had gone by since the transports had jumped away. He hoped like hell that Admiral Halsey and her small group of ships near New Eden would be able to stop them. He had no idea how many Zodark soldiers were on each of those ships, but he'd seen firsthand what a Zodark soldier could do to humans. It was terrifying, and he wanted to do his best to make sure no enemy soldiers ever got a chance to set foot on a planet that humans controlled.

*******

**New Eden**
**RNS** *Voyager*

*I wish we had more real-time data on how the battle is going,* Admiral Abigail Halsey thought. *I hope Miles is doing OK, and the* GW *comes out of this in one piece.* She looked down at her hand and realized she was drumming her fingers on the side of her chair. She was anxious, she realized.

"How do you suppose the battle is going?" asked President Luca, looking as nervous as Admiral Halsey felt.

Trying to portray a sense of calm confidence, Halsey replied, "Admiral Miles Hunt is the most competent commander I know. I'm sure he's leading our fleet to a great victory, Madam President."

The two talked for a couple of minutes, then her coms officer, Lieutenant George Adams, interrupted their conversation. "Admiral, we're receiving a priority message from Admiral Hunt. It says four Zodark troop transports and two cruisers broke through their kill box and warped out of the battle. He believes they're headed here!"

The President's hand rose to cover her mouth as she gasped at the news. "Those things are headed here, for us?" was all she managed to say, her voice shaking.

"What else did the message say?" Halsey demanded.

"He says we should focus our efforts on taking out the troop transports so they can't land their ground force on the planet," Adams replied.

Halsey turned to her tactical officer. "Sound general quarters. When those enemy ships are in range, focus our weapons on taking out those transports."

The tactical officer nodded. He sent orders down to the primary and secondary weapon systems department chiefs to get their people ready.

"Helm, bring our engines up to full speed and head toward New Eden. I want us as close to the planet as possible before the Zodarks get here. When they do show up, keep our ship positioned between them and the planet. Is that understood?" Halsey ordered.

"Yes, ma'am."

Just then, Fleet Admiral Chester Bailey walked onto the bridge and approached Halsey. "What's going on, Admiral?"

Halsey filled him in on the message they'd received from Admiral Hunt and what was headed their way. Bailey looked over at President Luca, who was now nervously walking back and forth, wringing her hands.

*Politicians*, Halsey thought, although she couldn't blame her too much. She hadn't served in the military, so this whole experience of fighting was foreign to her.

Bailey seemed to read her mind. "I'll take President Luca to the briefing room," he said. "I'll tune one of the displays so we can monitor the battle. We'll do our best to stay out of your hair, Admiral. Do what you have to, but please keep in mind you have the President on board, as well as myself."

Admiral Halsey smiled and thanked Admiral Bailey for helping to handle the President. He was right; she needed to think clearly. Having either of them on the bridge with her during the coming battle would be distracting. Things were going to get hairy enough as it was without her having to deal with politicians, even if it was the President.

After her two VIPs had left the bridge, she turned to her Ops officer, Lieutenant Moore. "Tell the frigates in the area to form on us as we move toward New Eden. Tell the two TPA cruisers to head toward the space elevator and do whatever it takes to protect it from being captured or blown up."

While her Ops officer was handling the ship orders, she turned to her coms officer next. "Lieutenant Adams, please send a message down to General McGinnis. Inform him we have four enemy transports inbound to the planet. We're moving to intercept to prevent them from landing any forces dirtside, but he should get his people ready to repel an orbital landing in case we don't succeed."

The next few minutes were tense as the bridge crew waited for what would happen next. With the *Voyager* intensely focused on defending New Eden, they weren't watching Pishon—and the Zodark fleet dropped out of warp behind the moon, unnoticed at first. While the moon was rich in minerals, they had yet to establish the mining colony there.

Suddenly, her tactical officer called out, "Admiral, we've spotted the enemy fleet!"

"What? Where?" she blurted out. Everyone was studying the screens in front of them, trying to figure out how the enemy fleet had swooped in around New Eden and they hadn't seen it.

"Oh, hell. They popped out near Pishon—the moon that just went around to the far side of the planet," her tactical officer explained.

"Damn it! Order the fleet to maneuver around the planet now. We need to go after those transports. We don't know if they're going to drop soldiers down on the backside of New Eden or on the moon," ordered Halsey angrily. She could kick herself for not thinking about positioning at least one of her frigates or cruisers on the far side of the planet. Halsey mentally noted the error for her AAR.

The *Voyager* picked up speed as it used the gravity of the planet to slingshot them around at a higher speed than their standard thrusters could give them. At this point, speed was life, and Halsey intended to use all tactics at her disposal to get her ship in range of those enemy ships as swiftly as possible.

As they rounded the curvature of the planet, their sensors gave them a better readout of the enemy fleet. Two of the transports and one of the cruisers appeared to be in orbit around Pishon. The transports were offloading their dropships, presumably with a ground force and supplies. The second set of transports and a single cruiser had just entered New Eden's orbit. They hadn't started dropping their ground forces yet, but it was only a matter of time.

"Fire on those transports in orbit now, before they can start disgorging their troops!" ordered Halsey, hoping she wasn't too late.

The forward magrail guns fired volley after volley. Then the Havoc missile launchers joined the fray, sending anti-ship missiles at the transports. It took a few minutes for the magnetic railgun projectiles to travel the distance between the two groups of ships. While her slugs were closing the gap, one of the frigates, the *Viper*, swooped in at a high rate of speed toward one of the transports. It cut loose a string of three plasma torpedoes at each of them and then fired ten Havoc missiles at the lone cruiser.

The *Viper* started pulling up when it was struck by a pulse beam from the Zodark cruiser. The ship lost its portside MPD thruster and slid sideways in space. It took another hit to its midsection, causing more damage. When Halsey saw fire, she knew it meant the ship was leaking atmosphere. A couple seconds later, several small pods appeared around the ship. The *Viper* captain had ordered the crew to abandon ship.

Halsey watched one of the Zodark transports release a couple dozen smaller dropships toward New Eden. The enemy was clearly trying to get ground forces on the surface before their vessel was taken out. Seconds after the Zodarks unloaded their ground force, two of the three plasma torpedoes tore into the transport. It exploded in a brilliant shower of light and flame before the wreckage scattered, falling into the atmosphere of the planet.

The second Zodark transport managed to release maybe four or five of their dropships before the ship blew apart when all three plasma torpedoes nailed it. The lone cruiser managed to take out six of the ten anti-ship missiles. The Havocs scored a couple of decent hits against the thinner-skinned cruisers, but nothing that would ultimately destroy the ship.

"Target those troop landers. We need to take them out!" Halsey ordered. She wasn't sure if their weapons could target something that small and mobile, but she had to try.

While her ship attacked the dropships, the rest of the fleet attempted to take the lone cruiser out. Once they finished that ship off, they'd go after the other three ships near Pishon, not too far away. However, the enemy cruiser had already broken orbit and was speeding to the other Zodark ships nearby. The Zodark cruiser near the moon broke off from the transports and charged the human fleet. Then to Halsey's astonishment, the two other transports, which had apparently offloaded their soldiers, turned and charged her fleet.

She had a sickening feeling growing in her gut. The cruiser that *Voyager* had been attacking turned around to face them rather than trying to flee. Halsey suddenly thought she had figured out what they were doing.

She turned to her coms officer. "Relay order! Fleet to disperse. Zodark ships are going to try to ram us. Don't let them get too close. All ships, focus weapons on the wounded cruiser, the one closest to us. Take that ship out first! Then focus fire on the next cruiser. After the cruisers are taken out, we'll clean up the transports."

For the next five minutes, they watched the Zodark ships pick up speed and try desperately to aim for a ship in the RNS fleet. They weren't seeking the *Voyager*—she was out of harm's way—but they sure were aiming for two of her TPA cruisers. Her tactical officers continued to have their primary and secondary weapons lay into the enemy warships. The remaining frigates swooped in at their faster speeds and unloaded swarms of their unguided plasma torpedoes at the enemy. The Zodark transports were quickly taken out—due to their slower maneuverability and thinner armor, the transports couldn't stand up to the torpedoes or the anti-ship missiles fired at them.

At the last minute, one of the Zodark cruisers finally gave up the fight. A series of magrail slugs managed to pound enough holes in the ship that something important finally blew up. The entire vessel blew apart into several large chunks. Then the last Zodark ship started streaking flames like a fiery arrow flying through the night sky as it plowed into one of the TPA ships unable to get out of the way. The two ships slammed into each other and broke apart under the enormous strain of the impact.

The *Voyager* crew on the bridge watched the scene unfold as if in slow motion; the huge explosion lit up the black space like a surreal Walt Disney World fireworks finale as both ships ripped each other apart. Chunks of TPA and Zodark ships were flung out into space from the sudden impact and high velocity when they collided.

"Holy crap. Did you just see that Zodark ship kamikaze that TPA cruiser?" one of the officers nearby said to no one in particular.

*Damn, now they're suicidal?* Halsey thought as she watched the wreckage continue to spread out into a large debris field. *What's next with these Zodark animals?*

"Are there any more enemy ships nearby?" asked Halsey. "Did we get them all?"

It took a moment for one of her officers to reply. "We've taken them all out, ma'am. All we detect at this point are the life pods from the wrecks of the TPA and Zodark ships."

"Order our shuttles to start recovery operations. I want our people from the *Viper* and the other frigate recovered and brought aboard the *Voyager*," Halsey ordered.

She hesitated as she thought about the Zodarks floating out there in their own life pods. She sighed. Part of her wanted to use their CIWS systems on the life pods, but she knew that was morally wrong to do.

"Let's get together some of the RASs with our shuttles to collect the Zodark life pods," Halsey finally ordered. "We'll take them prisoner. If they go along nicely, fine. Otherwise, they will have to be killed."

*If we get lucky, maybe we'll get a few that will be willing to talk*, she realized. Maybe they'd be able to find out what the Zodarks knew about them, what their plans were, or other pertinent information that might help them understand this new enemy.

When the battle had been won, Fleet Admiral Bailey, along with President Luca, came back up to the bridge. The two of them walked over to her. "Admiral Halsey, it would appear we won the battle," Admiral Bailey said, shaking her hand. "What kind of damage did your ship sustain, and how is the rest of the fleet?"

"The *Voyager* only took a few hits," Halsey responded. "We didn't sustain any real damage to our systems. The enemy cruisers didn't focus their weapons on us. As to the rest of our fleet, we lost a TPA cruiser and two frigates. Another TPA cruiser took some damage, but nothing that'll knock them out of the fight. We succeeded in taking out the six enemy ships, but not before the troopships managed to offload most of their ground forces. It appears both transports were able to disgorge their troops on Pishon. One transport and about a quarter of another one were able to deploy their ground troops to the surface of New Eden."

"Oh, man. Where did those Zodarks land?" Bailey pressed. "Are they near any of our new installations?" He clearly recognized immediately the threat this posed.

Halsey shook her head. "No, they landed on the opposite side of the planet from where most of our forces and facilities are located. However, it's going to be pretty darn tough to track them down on that side of the planet. Since they aren't close to any of our forces or logistical bases, we're going to have to move several battalions to that side of the planet."

Admiral Bailey leaned in closer to Admiral Halsey. "Actually, Admiral, I think we have another tool we can try out on the Zodarks on that side of the planet."

Her left eyebrow rose; she wasn't sure what he meant by that. Halsey still hadn't been fully brought up to speed on what all they had brought with them from Sol.

Seeing her confused look, President Luca whispered just loud enough for Halsey to hear. "He means the new combat Synthetics, Admiral. We brought a small army of them with us on one of the transports."

Halsey's eyes went wide at this new revelation. "I...um, I didn't realize we had created something like that. Aren't they illegal?" she stammered.

Admiral Bailey shrugged. "When facing annihilation, a lot of things that used to be illegal suddenly find themselves legal to use again. You've been gone a while, Admiral. In the last few years, we spent a considerable amount of time coding and creating them. This was when we thought Earth might be invaded by the Zodarks.

"Now that it appears we have a fleet strong enough to prevent that from happening, we brought some of them with us to New Eden. We planned on testing them on a Zodark-controlled planet, but this sudden appearance of Zodark troops on the far side of the planet might actually be a better testing ground."

Halsey's XO, Captain Erin Johnson, broke into the conversation. "Admiral, now that we've defeated the Zodarks here, would you like me to send a message to Admiral Hunt's fleet and let them know the threat has been neutralized?"

Halsey turned to her XO and nodded. "Yes, please let them know what's transpired. Ask for a SITREP as well. I want to know how their battle is going, and if the admiral would like us to assist them."

"Do you think it wise for us to head over to the battle at the gate?" asked the President, a nervous look on her face.

"Wise? No. But if our collection of ships is what turns the tide of the battle in our favor, then it would be worth us joining them," replied Halsey.

Admiral Bailey nodded in agreement. "Admiral, when you get those frigate crews recovered, I'd like to speak with them. I watched the battle unfold, and I must say, I don't think I've ever seen anything more heroic than what I saw the commander of the *Viper* do. Her frigate swooped in so fast, practically out of nowhere, to deliver that volley of plasma torpedoes and missiles. It was impressive, to say the least. I was saddened when I saw her ship destroyed, but relieved to see so many life pods emerge before it blew apart."

"Will do, Admiral. It'll be an hour or more until we get all the life pods, including the Zodark pods, collected and brought back on board. I'll make sure the crew knows you want to meet with them personally. We'll also have a handful of Zodark prisoners. Would you like to see them in person?"

Bailey and President Luca exchanged nervous glances before the President stepped forward. "I would," she replied, possibly frightened but also very resolved. "I would like to see our enemy face-to-face. If I'm to continue to order our people to fight against them and die, then I would like to see these alien creatures with my own eyes."

Admiral Halsey nodded but didn't say anything. With their conversation over, she returned to the duties of running her fleet and warship.

*******

### RNS *George Washington*

The battle had been raging at the stargate for nearly three hours. The massive Zodark and human ships pummeled each other with high-energy lasers, magnetic railgun slugs, anti-ship missiles, and the humans' new plasma cannons.

"Admiral Hunt, we're receiving a status report from Admiral Halsey's fleet," his coms officer relayed. "They've neutralized the enemy fleet there. However, the transports landed some of their ground forces. Most were dropped on Pishon—only a small contingent made it to the surface of New Eden. They lost a TPA cruiser and two frigates."

Hunt just nodded at the information, then returned his attention to the remaining enemy ships. The one Zodark carrier they had disabled at the start of the battle was still floating helplessly in space, adrift without propulsion. The other carrier had finally blown up thirty minutes ago. It had taken more than two hours of pounding on her armor before the human ships finally landed a death blow against it.

At this point in the battle, only two Zodark battleships and a single cruiser were still fighting back. All three of them were taking a terrible beating. Three of Hunt's six battleships had been destroyed. Four of the five TPA cruisers, along with eight of his twelve frigates, had also been taken offline.

The *GW* had taken a beating but was still operational. They'd lost the use of their plasma cannon a little more than two hours ago, and close to half of the ship's primary turrets were down after hours of intense combat. Three-quarters of their fighter drones had also been shot down. The battle was proving to be a costly bloodbath for both sides.

Seeing McKee talking to Branson, his coms officer, in a whisper, Hunt suspected something was wrong. He walked over to check. They both stopped talking when he approached them.

Lifting an eyebrow at the sudden shift in their conversation, Hunt asked, "What's going on, ladies? We still have a battle to fight, you know."

McKee looked up at him, a look of sorrow and concern on her face. "Can we talk in your office, Admiral? I think it'd be best if we talk privately for a moment."

Now Hunt knew something was wrong. Had the President or Admiral Bailey been killed?

"OK, let's walk to my office," he replied.

As soon as he entered his office, Hunt whipped around. "What's going on, Fran?" he demanded. "Why do we need to talk privately?"

"I…I don't know how to say this, sir, so I'm just going to say it. The *Viper* was destroyed during the fight over New Eden."

In that instant, Hunt felt like he had been punched in the gut. He almost staggered backward at the news. Fran moved forward to help steady him. She guided him over to a chair, where he sat for a moment, not saying anything. A tear started running down his cheek before he could try to stop it. Even Fran had to wipe away a tear.

Hunt finally calmed himself enough to ask, "Did they have a chance to get to their life pods? Is there a possibility that he lived?"

"I don't know yet," Fran replied. "I sent a message to the *Voyager* to find out. Well, I asked for a list of survivors from the ships that were destroyed. That way, it doesn't come across as us trying to find out specifically about your son, sir."

Hunt shook his head, then took a couple of slow deep breaths as he tried to calm himself. If his son was dead, there would be time to mourn his loss, but right now was not that time. *We still have enemy ships to finish off*, he realized.

Steeling his nerves, Hunt's turned on the fleet commander role. "Thank you, Captain, for keeping me in the loop. Please let me know when you've received a reply to your inquiry. In the meantime, we have a battle to win. We can mourn our losses once we've secured our victory."

With that, Admiral Hunt got up from his chair, straightened his uniform, and returned to the bridge.

"Admiral, the last two Zodark battleships just blew up," his tactical officer announced. "The cruiser is the only ship left." Hunt hadn't been gone very long and was surprised they had taken out the last two battleships in his absence.

*Ah heck, why not give it a try?* he thought.

Hunt turned to find his XO standing not too far from him. "Captain McKee, send a message to the Zodark cruiser. Tell them their situation is hopeless. Ask them if they will surrender and save the lives of their crewmen. If we can end this battle now, then I'd like to. If they don't surrender, then all ships are to reposition for another attack run on the cruiser and finish it off."

Several minutes went by as they hailed the enemy ship. Eventually, the Zodarks responded with the equivalent of "Get bent." The ship's captain must have initiated their self-destruct operation because a couple of minutes later, the entire ship blew apart.

Shaking his head, Hunt turned to Captain McKee. "XO, conduct a full sensor sweep of the entire area. I want to know if we have human or Zodark life pods floating among the battle wreckage. If we do, then I want them recovered. The battle may be over, but the recovery efforts need to start in earnest now. They won't have much oxygen left at this point."

"You heard the admiral," McKee bellowed. "Lieutenant Commander Arnold, please send a message down to flight ops to launch their recovery craft. Let's get our folks pulled in as quickly as we can. Also, send a message to the *Lakeland* and the *Mobile*. Tell them to jump through the gate and monitor what's happening on the other side. If another enemy fleet is in the system, I want to know about it before they arrive."

The RNS crews spent the next two hours collecting thousands of life pods from the wrecked starships strewn about the area. It took a while to recover them with all the blown-apart ships spread across such a massive area around the gate. While the recovery operations were underway, the damage control parties were hard at work getting the *George Washington* repaired and ready for another battle.

"Admiral Hunt, do you have a moment?" Captain McKee asked as she walked away from the communications terminal.

Hunt nodded and walked with her to the back of the bridge. Judging by the look on her face and the fact that she wasn't insisting on talking in his office, he suddenly felt optimistic.

"What is it, Fran?"

"Sir, we got the report from Admiral Halsey's fleet. Your son is safe; his ship lost twenty-three people, but most of them made it out. Your son only suffered a broken arm and some lacerations—nothing too serious."

Hunt let out a sigh of relief. He looked up at Fran, wiping a tear from his eye before anyone else could see. "Thank you, Fran. I appreciate it."

She smiled. "It's the least I could do, Admiral. I'm just glad he's safe. Let me get back to a few of my duties. I'll be around if you want to talk privately or anything. Don't hesitate to ask."

Hunt took a deep breath in and held it for a second before letting it out. He wanted to make sure he had his emotions in check before he went back to his station. As the fleet commander, he needed to be strong for his crew and those looking up to him.

Hunt watched his people hard at work around the bridge, trying to get the ship ready for the next battle. Many of them had been awake for more than twenty-four hours, yet they were showing no signs of slowing down. They were hyped. They had just fought the greatest fleet battle in human history against a foe that had enslaved humanity, and they had won.

His crew was running on adrenaline, fueled by that feeling one has when scoring a great victory. Despite the adrenaline coursing through their veins, Hunt knew he needed to start cycling his people through some crew rest. He was reasonably sure this attack was the only immediate Zodark threat they'd have to deal with, but he knew it wouldn't be their last. He needed his people rested and sharp.

The crew spent the next three hours primarily collecting the life pods of his fleet and more than four hundred Zodark life pods. He now had hundreds of new prisoners to interrogate. This meant new and valuable information that could help them understand their enemy better. It was an opportunity he was determined to make sure his intelligence group fully exploited.

Once he was reasonably confident they had collected all the life pods in the area, Hunt ordered two of his frigates to stay at the gate. Their job was to work with the frigates on the other side of the gate and continue to monitor for any sign another Zodark ship or fleet was inbound. Hunt then ordered the remainder of his fleet back to New Eden. They were in need of a shipyard, and while they didn't have a full-scale shipyard operational in New Eden yet, they did have a lot of repair drones and Synths they could leverage. His main goal right now was to get his primary magrail turrets operational again and, if possible, their lone plasma cannon.

Down on the flight deck, the flight ops group was hard at work fabricating new fighter drones. It'd take a few weeks, but they'd get their squadrons back up to strength again. Hunt felt fortunate that his fighter wing consisted of drones and not human-crewed spacecraft. He'd lost nearly eighty-six percent of his fighters, but not a single pilot. Pilots took time to train, and time was something the human forces didn't have on their side—not with an enemy like the Zodarks.
*******


**RNS *Voyager***

"Commander Amy Dobbs, reporting as ordered," she said in her most professional tone. It was the best she could muster, considering she'd just lost her ship.

Fleet Admiral Bailey stood in the boardroom with the President and a couple of other officers. Dobbs had no idea why she'd been summoned here, so she stood there not saying anything further until she knew what they wanted.

"At ease, Commander," Admiral Bailey said as he pointed to an empty chair.

The group of officers sat down and waited to say something until one of the cooks, who had brought some sandwiches and coffee for them, had left the room.

"Commander, I called you up here because the President and I don't often get a chance to meet or talk with our forces battling the Zodarks," Admiral Bailey began. "We watched the battle over New Eden, and we saw what your ship did. That was some impressive flying. The way your ship swooped in like it did, using the *Voyager* to hide behind until the very last minute and then unloading your missiles and torpedoes—you guys took that enemy transport out before it was able to offload even half of its troops. That was an incredible feat."

Now that she knew why she'd been called up here, Dobbs relaxed a bit. "Thank you for the praise, sir. The flying was my ensign. You can thank him. For a new officer, he's a superb pilot. But I still lost my ship, sir. I had only been in command of it for a few months."

Brushing off her concern, President Luca commented, "Commander, we can build more ships. We can't readily replace commanders and crews like yours. You did a great job taking those ships out. I read your AAR from your attack on the Zodark fleet a few days ago. I'd say your ship and crew have done more than most. You also gave us the heads-up, allowing us the needed time to get ourselves organized and ready to meet them at the gate. You and your crew are a big reason why we just crushed that Zodark fleet, Commander."

Blushing at the praise, Dobbs countered, "We're military officers, ma'am. We all have a part to play in this war. We just played our part a bit better than the enemy, that's all."

Admiral Bailey laughed at the reply. "Well, I agree, Commander. We all have a part to play in this war. So, I want to talk with you about yours. The *Viper*-class frigate has performed exceptionally well in its role as a scout ship, but this battle identified some pretty crucial weak points that need to get fixed. I don't mean to rub salt in a wound, but you are without a ship until we get a new one built for you. I'd like you to come work on my staff and help our engineers improve the *Viper* design. Either we find a way to improve the *Viper*'s armor so it can take more than a single hit or we design a stronger ship that can still perform its primary mission of being a recon bird and raider, but take a few hits and still survive. This may turn into a long war, Commander. We need our ships to survive multiple engagements. We can't keep replacing ships at the kind of loss rate we saw today. It's not sustainable."

Dobbs took all of about two seconds to think about the offer before she responded, "I'd love to, Admiral. Having some firsthand combat experience on both the *Rook* and now the *Viper*, I think I could help us gin up the perfect warship for this kind of fight."

"Excellent. When the President and I return to Sol in a few days, I'll have you travel back with us," Bailey explained. "We'll keep your crew out here and reassign them to fill in any losses Admiral Hunt's fleet suffered. We just got a report from him. They're on their way back here now. They won, but it wasn't an easy fight. We lost a little more than half our ships in the final battle."

The President then interjected, "We lost a lot of good people today, Commander. But let's not lose sight of the fact that we scored a huge victory in this war. We defeated what just two years ago would have been a superior force. According to your own ship's reconnaissance of the area, this was probably the only enemy fleet standing between us and the Sumerian home world. We're going to repair our ships, and then we're going to liberate Sumer."

"I like the sound of that, Madam President," Dobbs replied. Then she turned to the admiral. "Sir, I still have some injured crewmen I'd like to go check on. Do you need me for anything else?"

"I'll come with you," Bailey said. "I don't often get a chance to award Purple Hearts in person. Oh, before I forget, and before we leave the system, I'm putting you in for the Navy Cross. I want you to pick five crewmen you think earned a Silver Star today or during the last few weeks. I'm going to award the rest of the crew a Bronze Star with V device. You and your crew earned it, and we need to show our people back on Earth what real heroes look like."

Dobbs wasn't sure what to say. She was a bit taken aback by the gesture. "I'll get you a few names by the end of the day," she finally managed to respond. The two names she knew off the top of her head were Lieutenant Reynolds, her tactical and weapons officer, and Ensign Hunt, her helmsman and navigator. They'd both done an exceptional job. She felt they'd earned the third-highest award the nation could give.

## Chapter Fourteen
## Terminators

**RNS** *George Washington*
**New Eden**

The flight deck of the *GW* was humming with activity. It was one section of the ship that hadn't suffered a lot of damage during the battle from a few days back. The rest of the ship was crawling with synthetic workers and repair bots, welding new armor plating across some areas while sealing and repairing tears in the hull in others. Most of the repair activity was taking place around the massive magrail turrets and the plasma cannon. Those weapons had proved to be decisive in defeating the Zodark ships.

Standing with his hands on his hips, Lieutenant Brian Royce looked at the shuttlecraft that just arrived from one of the nearby transports. A number of his Deltas stood there with him, looking at the rear of the shuttle as they prepared to lower the ramp. When it finally opened and settled on the flight deck, what everyone saw took their breath away.

Inside the darkened rear of the shuttle, a series of red glowing lights turned on. Then in unison, four columns of combat synthetics marched out of the shuttle toward the Deltas.

*Is that Adam?* Royce thought as he saw one of the new combat Synths walking toward him. It had a gold patch on its armor, distinguishing itself from the others. It was also the only Synth that fell out of formation.

The C100 walked up to him. "Lieutenant Brian Royce, it is a pleasure to see you again," he said. *It is Adam*, he realized.

Royce's platoon members looked back and forth between him and the machine standing in front of them. They weren't sure what to make of this mechanical killing machine just yet.

Smiling, Royce replied, "It's a pleasure to see you again, Adam. I hope your trip was OK?"

"Our trip was spent studying everything we could about the Zodarks and the environment of New Eden and her two moons. My command stands ready to assist," Adam replied, devoid of emotion.

Just then, a Delta colonel named Charlie Hackworth walked up to Royce. "Ah, Lieutenant. I see you've met Adam."

"Yes, sir. I actually met him several months ago with Admiral Hunt," Royce replied. "I wasn't aware we'd be deploying with them so soon."

Colonel Hackworth grinned. "That's right—I forgot you'd been given an exclusive tour with Admiral Hunt. Well, we hadn't planned on deploying them so soon, but old Walburg was able to throw together a battalion of them for this trip. They're going to deploy with our units and get some experience. It'll help us work out their kinks before we start deploying C100 battalions."

Before Royce could say anything else, the colonel turned to look at the rest of the Deltas eyeing the machines as they formed up not far from them. "This, ladies and gentlemen, is the future of modern warfare in the twenty-second century." Hackworth had a serious look on his face, a stern look that left no evidence of his opinion as to what he'd just said. The soldiers eyed the machines nervously. They'd all seen movies and videos of the human surrogate drones that went rogue in the last war, and no one wanted a repeat of that. These machines looked a lot fiercer than the surrogates of the previous war.

Adam turned and headed over to his company of combat Synths, standing in front of them like a company commander would. The machines were oblivious to the stares of the soldiers and sailors around them. They remained standing there like the sentinel warriors they were, waiting for their next set of orders.

One of Royce's soldiers stepped forward and asked the question they were all thinking, "What do we call these things, Colonel?"

Hackworth laughed. "Well, son, that's a good question. Walburg Industries calls them C100s. Space Command calls them combat Synths. Me? I call them terminators."

A nerdy-looking soldier, aptly assigned as Royce's coms and drone operator guy, lifted his hand. "I remember watching a movie from like a hundred years ago about machines that would take control of the world and try to kill all the humans. They called them terminators too."

A smirk spread across the old colonel's leathery face. He walked up to the soldier who'd just spoken. "You mean like the surrogates from the last great war? Those terminators, or some made-up crap Hollywood cooked up? 'Cause I remember fighting those bastards in the last Great War, and let me tell you, they nearly wiped us out—killed millions of people."

Colonel Hackworth paused for a moment as he surveyed the Deltas standing in front of him. "I call these hunks of metal terminators for one simple reason, Deltas. They're killing machines; they've been specifically built to kill, nothing more. They're equipped with an armored exoskeleton frame and an enhanced super-AI that is a million times smarter, faster, and more adaptable to a situation than you Special Forces grunts ever could be. These are terminators, plain and simple. Now, we're going to unleash these bastards on the Zodarks, and you Deltas are going to observe them in action from a distance. Your job is to watch them, see how they learn and, most importantly, observe how the Zodarks respond to them.

"If this experiment proves successful, we may well drop a few thousand of them on some Zodark-controlled worlds and let them go crazy. Now, in six hours, we're all going to load up into our Ospreys and head down to the surface of Pishon. This moon is not habitable for us humans. You'll need to keep your helmet on at all times. *If* your helmet loses its seal or your suit gets damaged, you'll have exactly two minutes before you'll become unconscious. In five minutes, you'll be dead. When we land on the surface, I'm going to make sure we have some medical support. However, let's not try to test their skills, OK?"

The Deltas gave the colonel a loud "Hooah," which was the official battle cry of the Republic Army to just about anything you wanted it to be. It dated back to the old days, before the consolidation of the Department of Defense from six separate military departments to just two. The Fleet had largely absorbed the US Air Force, Navy, and Space Command to form the backbone of the US Space Command naval force. Then the US Army, Marines, reserve components and National Guards had merged to form the Republic Army soldiers or RAS battalions, which had become the ground component of the Fleet. There had been a lot of grumbling for a few decades after the consolidation efforts. Some specialized groups continued to live on, like the Deltas, which traced their lineage back to 1st Special Forces Group, the 75th Rangers, and Marine Force Recon. These groups all fell under a unified Special Forces Command, performing unique military operations outside the scope of the RAS.

The old Special Forces colonel walked up to Lieutenant Royce and got right up in his face. Speaking in a whisper so no one else could hear him talking, Hackworth said sternly, "Listen up, Lieutenant. I don't trust these toasters any more than I can throw them, which, considering the fact that these bastards weigh nearly two thousand pounds, isn't very far. I want your men to keep a real close eye on them. Specifically, monitor their interactions with each other, all verbal and nonverbal communications. They've been programmed to use vocal communications for the time being so we can know what they're saying, thinking, and doing.

"Don't underestimate them, Lieutenant. If they deviate from their programming one bit, you and your platoon sergeant will be carrying a kill switch that'll allow you to deactivate them all should you need to. If that happens, your platoon needs to be ready to finish their job and take these Zodarks out. I read your file, and I know your history; killing Zodarks shouldn't be a problem for you if it comes down to it." Hackworth then patted Royce on the shoulder and turned to head toward the briefing room just outside the flight deck.

Turning to face his platoon, Royce barked, "OK, listen up, Deltas. Our mission is to observe these...terminators. So, that's what we're going to do. Pack your gear for a five-day mission. Bring enough stim packs and food pouches for ten days in case these Fleet bastards forget to pick us up. I want everyone in the briefing room in three hours. We'll go over the mission parameters, and then we'll board up with our new friends. Dismissed."

Three hours later, the Deltas of Second Platoon, Bravo Company, 2nd Battalion, filtered into the briefing room next to the flight deck. This room was generally used as a training room for the fighter drone pilots, so it was decked out with holographic map tables, three-dimensional monitors, and a few other features the newest warships were now incorporating.

As he walked into the room, Royce felt comfortable, like he belonged on the *GW*. Even if it was a short stay on board, he really enjoyed how new and clean the ship looked. Most of the walls in the corridor were an off-white color with a gray floor, which created the impression that the space was much larger. It was also exceptionally well lit, which helped with stabilizing a person's moods when they were stuck on a long cruise.

Colonel Hackworth was already inside, waiting at the front of the classroom. When Royce walked in, Hackworth motioned for him to come to the front of the room. The two talked for a few minutes, and then Royce took a seat with the rest of his platoon.

The group sat in the briefing room for close to an hour as one of the Fleet scientists gave them a rundown of the moon and what they were likely to encounter on its surface. The moon did have an atmosphere; it just wasn't breathable for humans. Apparently, the gas composition posed no problems for the Zodarks, however.

The scientist showed them several different videos of the surface on Pishon so they wouldn't be caught off guard. It wasn't quite like New Eden, but it was close. Parts of the moon had thick tree cover, while other parts were flat, wide-open plains. The moon also had two large bodies of water, mini oceans.

Once the scientist finished telling them about the moon, another fleeter came up and showed them drone surveillance footage of the area where the Zodarks had landed. Unlike New Eden, they weren't having any problems seeing through the trees or any other underbrush, so they could clearly see where most of the Zodarks were.

The Zodarks had already gone to work on setting up defensive positions. They had wisely dispersed so they wouldn't make an easy target for an orbital strike, and they appeared to be digging in for a protracted fight.

Royce wondered if these Zodark soldiers realized their fleet had been destroyed. They had to know they were alone, that no help was on the way. Then again, maybe all they had to do was hold out for a few months until reinforcements arrived from their home systems.

Once the death by PowerPoint and briefings were done, the old colonel walked back up to the front of the room. Hackworth cleared his throat to make sure he had everyone's attention. "We're done with the boring stuff," he announced gruffly. "Now it's time to earn our pay and properly babysit our military's newest toy. Everyone grab your gear and load up in the transports. Remember, each squad is being assigned to monitor a company of these new toys. Stay on top of them, observe them, but allow them to do the brunt of the killing. We're here to make sure they're working properly.

"If you run into any issues, send a message and let us know. We've got a few dozen programmers from Walburg Industries on board. They'll analyze any problems and make whatever corrections need to be made.

Got it?" It wasn't a question so much as a statement. The colonel was waiting to hear the obligatory "Hooah," which he did.

Twenty minutes later, the operators had boarded the Ospreys that would transport them down to the surface. Each Osprey had a squad of Deltas and a platoon of terminators. It would take thirty minutes to get them to the surface. The fleet wasn't going to drop them on top of the Zodarks, but they would land them within about ten kilometers. The ground pounders would hoof it the rest of the distance, hunting the Zodarks until they found them.

Once the Osprey had dropped out of orbit and entered the atmosphere of the moon, the pilots continued their downward descent until they were a few thousand meters above the ground. One of the crew chiefs opened the rear ramp of the bird, allowing everyone inside to catch their first glimpse of the place. Like New Eden, the moon had its own flying birds or creatures, a large canopy of trees covering the ground and all sorts of new underbrush, flowers, and critters they'd never seen.

Royce had to keep reminding himself he was here on a mission, not a sightseeing tour. It was just so new and exotic. He sent a quick message to his guys using the NL: *Don't get distracted by your surroundings. We have a job to do.*

Returning his gaze to the ramp, Royce noticed the pilot had just leveled them out around thirty meters above the ground. The terminators, which were plugged into the navigation computer of the Osprey, recognized they were nearing the drop zone. They all stood up at the same time and turned to face the ramp.

The pilots turned the jump light on, signaling to everyone to get ready. A few minutes later, the jump light changed from red to green. In that instant, the terminators moved forward, jumping out the rear of the Osprey without a second thought. Royce signaled for his guys to hurry up and follow them out the craft. They needed to keep up with their charges.

It was a relatively short free fall, but for that few seconds that he raced toward the ground, Royce felt acutely alive. The exoskeleton combat suit absorbed most of the shock of the jump. Once on the ground, Royce and his squad got their weapons ready. They set out after the terminators, which were already moving at a good clip toward the last known location of the Zodarks.

*Damn, those toasters move quick*, Royce thought. Instead of *Terminator*, the pop culture reference that came to his mind was *Battlestar Galactica*. He hoped that Adam and these other machines wouldn't turn on them like they had in that series.

Royce used the neurolink to send a message to the coms/drone operator, the nerdy guy who had asked a lot of questions back on the *GW*: *Make sure we have our surveillance drones deployed. I want to keep an eye on our terminators at all times.*

The squad of Deltas hauled butt through some pretty tough terrain as they tried to keep up with the mechanical killing machines. Those things apparently never got tired and also never got distracted by the new and exotic terrain of a foreign planet or moon like a human soldier did. Keeping an eye on these toasters was proving to be tougher than Royce had thought.

"Lieutenant, my drone feed says the terminators are nearly on top of a cluster of Zodarks," called out Royce's drone operator. "They should make contact with them in a few minutes."

Royce patched himself into the C100's com network. "Adam, this is Lieutenant Royce. Have your platoon hold up and wait a few minutes for my squad to get in position before you launch your attack. How copy?"

A split second later, Adam called back, acknowledging the order.

"Corporal, are the C100s holding their position?" asked Royce, wanting to double-check that Adam was in control of his platoon.

On top of keeping up with the toasters, his drone operator had the additional task of monitoring what the drones were seeing. To be honest, without their own cybernetic enhancements or physical augmentations, Royce didn't think they'd be able to accomplish half of the missions they were asked to do.

"They are, Lieutenant," the corporal replied. "They've formed up a firing line and appear to be waiting for an order to attack."

"Thanks, Corporal. Make sure the drones have a good angle to record the attack when it starts. Oh, and make sure they're synced with the command element back on the *GW*," Royce ordered as he scrambled over a pile of fallen logs.

Checking his HUD as he continued to move, Royce saw he was a kilometer and a half behind the toasters. Picking up the pace, he was practically in an all-out sprint, hurtling over fallen trees or other obstacles.

The rest of his squad was doing the same, moving swiftly through the woods. In a way, with the toasters out front, they could run and make a lot more noise than they otherwise would because the C100s were clearing a path for them.

"Lieutenant Royce, your squad appears to be approaching our position," said Adam over the coms. "Requesting permission to have my platoon attack the enemy."

"Adam, your platoon is cleared to attack the Zodark position. If you require assistance, ask," Royce replied. He could see the C100s. It was time to get them going.

"Attacking now!" replied Adam over the squad net.

"Was that one of the terminators?" asked Royce's platoon sergeant.

Before Royce could respond, he heard the familiar sound of human blaster rifles, followed quickly by the ruckus of magrails. A couple of fragmentation grenades also entered the mix.

*The battle's on. Time to earn our pay*, Royce thought as his squad charged forward.

*Remember, we're here to observe the battle, not join in*, Royce barked over the NL to his squadmates. *Keep your distance and observe how the toasters do, OK?* It was difficult not to charge right in there. After all the Zodarks had done to them over the last few months, Royce wanted some serious payback.

Rushing forward, Royce stopped against the side of a tree a few hundred meters from the Zodarks. He then used the enhanced optics on his HUD to zoom in and watch the toasters assault a fixed Zodark position.

At first, several of the machines charged forward, disregarding their own safety. The Zodarks fired their blasters right into the toasters and took out three of them before they had a chance to react. It was brutal to watch.

A couple of the C100s tossed some fragmentation grenades at the enemy positions and then charged forward. They used the cover and confusion caused by the grenades to cover half the distance to the enemy position. This group of toasters appeared to be using standard infantry tactics. When their first couple of comrades went down, they adjusted to the enemy. One group would lay down covering fire while the other group would toss some grenades and charge.

As the C100s got in close to the Zodarks, Royce saw something unlike anything he'd ever seen before. A group of five Zodarks tossed a couple of objects in the direction of the toasters and charged. When the devices blew up, there was a bright flash, and then some electrical sparks emanated from a couple of the combat Synths. Royce zoomed in on the three toasters near the explosion—two of them were down, inoperable or something. The single remaining toaster fired away at the charging enemy. However, it looked like its system wasn't working correctly as it was firing wildly and inaccurately.

When the Zodarks got within a few meters of the C100s' position, they used two of their four hands to draw a shortsword or blade of some kind. Whatever it was, it looked nasty.

Two of the Zodarks jumped right on top of the disabled toasters and attempted to drive their swords into them. Another Zodark dove on top of the remaining toaster that was still fighting. The machine aptly deflected the Zodark's forward momentum and was able to toss it several meters in the air and over its shoulder.

Seeing that it was now in a hand-to-hand combat situation, the C100 let its blaster hang by its single-point sling and withdrew two eight-inch knives—one in each hand. Then it attacked the next charging Zodark. One of the enemy's blades slashed the toaster's chest area, but its chest rig absorbed most of the brute force of the hit. The C100 deflected the second blade the Zodark tried to stab it with and thrust its own knife into the chest of the beast. It then used its mechanical power to pull the knife up several inches through the Zodark's chest, causing the alien creature to let out a horrible howl of pain.

Another Zodark attacked the toaster from the rear, driving both of its blades right through the back of the machine. Then Royce observed something terrifying—the shortsword the Zodarks were using suddenly changed color, turning a bright red. When the Zodark ripped both its blades in opposite directions, it sliced the toaster into pieces. The fragments of the torn-apart terminator collapsed haphazardly to the ground.

The three Zodarks that had survived the encounter so far then turned to find the next toaster to attack and ran toward them.

Royce and his squad watched the battle rage on for another ten minutes as the platoon of forty-six terminators fought probably four times that number of Zodarks. For a few minutes, Royce thought the C100s were done for. Then the Zodarks started falling back rather than pressing home their attack. At that point, the terminators shouted out orders to each other to pursue the enemy.

Not wanting his force of terminators to be wiped out in their first battle, Royce overrode their orders and told them to stand down. Less than a minute later, the remaining toasters took up defensive positions and continued to snipe at the remaining Zodarks with their magrails.

Once the Zodarks fled the area, Lieutenant Royce walked toward the terminator that was designated to be the platoon leader, essentially Royce's equivalent.

"Adam, acknowledge me," Royce said aloud in a commanding voice.

Adam turned and looked down at Royce with his eye band of moving lights. "Lieutenant Brian Royce, how may I be of assistance?"

"Adam, how would you assess the results of this battle?" Royce asked the C100 in a harsh tone.

The toaster didn't say anything right away, like it was trying to figure that out itself. Finally, Adam spoke. "It did not go according to plan. My platoon sustained unacceptable losses."

Royce nodded in agreement. "That's correct, Adam. What caught you by surprise during the battle?" Royce wanted to see how adept the terminators were at assessing their own performance and then correcting the deficiencies in it.

"The Zodarks fought more ferociously than I thought they would," Adam explained. "The video archive files I have of past battles appeared to show a different type of Zodark soldier and weapons used. These enemy soldiers appeared to have better training and equipment, and they were fearless in their attack against us."

"Adam, what would you do differently in your next attack?" Royce asked.

"Lieutenant Royce, I would have had my platoon approach the enemy more cautiously. Instead of charging right into their positions, I would make use of our superior rifles and do our best to engage them from a great distance. Once we had sufficiently thinned their ranks, then

I would order my platoon to advance under better cover and maneuvering fire," Adam explained.

The machine paused for a moment and then tilted his head to one side. "Lieutenant Royce, I have seen extensive videos of your battles with the Zodarks. How would you have attacked this group of enemy soldiers?"

Royce smiled. *These little bastards really can think for themselves, can't they?*

Lieutenant Royce spent the next twenty minutes going over the battle with Adam in detail. He showed him video footage of the fight and went over what they did right, what they did wrong, and what they could have done better. Royce was impressed with whoever had programmed these machines. They knew how to ask good questions, and they appeared to understand the data given to them. The question Royce was asking himself now was if they could they implement the new information he'd just provided them.

*******

That evening, Royce had his squad settle in for the night. They'd go Zodark hunting again when the sun was up. In the meantime, he wanted to go over individual and group tactics with Adam. Royce knew that everything he taught Adam was passed on to the rest of the toasters—it was like a hive.

Shortly before dawn, Royce got an alert from the *GW*; they had spotted a cluster of enemy soldiers moving toward their position. Sitting up, Royce shook off the sleepiness and woke the rest of his team up. He also passed the information over to Adam, who immediately requested permission to attack the enemy.

"Stand down," Royce ordered. He wanted to get more information on their attackers first before releasing the terminators on them.

The drone footage showed they had five or six hundred enemy soldiers heading toward them. That was a good-sized force. Royce placed a call to the *GW* to see if they could lend some help by hitting them with a few orbital strikes before they got too close.

Unfortunately, an orbital strike was out of the question. The enemy was too close to them for the *GW* to risk something like that. The magrail projectiles flying down from orbit would slam into the enemy force with power equivalent to or greater than that of a one-hundred-kiloton warhead—they needed some distance between friendly forces and that impact to avoid casualties.

Royce sighed at the realization that he and his men would have to handle the Zodarks on their own and called his team over. "OK, guys. Here's what we're going to do. Adam, you're going to break your force down into two segments. They're going to move to these points here and here," he said, using the NL to highlight locations on their shared map. "Once they're in position, wait for the order to attack. Keep four of your C100s here with my men, two of them on each flank, ready to assist and defend my squad. Is that understood?"

The machine looked at Royce. "It will be done."

"Adam, when the enemy attacks, have your two groups attack their flanks along these positions here and here. You need to let the enemy commit their force to attack the front of our positions first. We need their focus to be on us, not your units attacking their flanks. Once your groups do attack, you need to hit them hard and fast. We have a few hundred of them heading towards us. This is going to be a tough fight. I'm going to work on getting us some air support from the fleet to help us out as well."

Royce paused for a moment as he used his PA function to check the time, then examined the map of the enemy soldiers heading toward them one more time. He figured they had around fifty minutes until the Zodarks would be in a position to attack them.

Royce talked to his other squads to find out what they were facing and get some air support from the fleet organized. One of his teams hadn't made contact with the enemy yet. Royce found that almost hard to believe. When he looked at the squad's map, he could see the Zodarks that were in their vicinity had shifted to attack the fourth squad. Knowing he could use the added firepower, Royce got a couple of Ospreys from the *GW* to come down, pick that squad up and reposition them with his force.

The added platoon of toasters and a Delta squad would seriously beef up his position. Air support also began to arrive. The higher-ups on the *GW* had maneuvered two more platoons of toasters that hadn't seen combat yet over to help Royce out.

As the minutes ticked down, the Zodarks moved closer and closer to their position. When they were within a couple of kilometers, the Deltas could hear the hooting and howling of those nasty beasts. They were whipping themselves up into a fighting frenzy. For the life of him,

Royce couldn't understand why the enemy liked to give away their positions like this—they'd be more effective if they stayed silent and tried to sneak up on them.

When the Zodarks looked to be about a kilometer from their positions, Royce turned to his squad leader. "Deploy the Guardians," he ordered. Their newest platoon weapons were small suicide drones about the size of a fist. A single soldier would program in what the Guardians should attack and then release them into the air via a launch tube. Each launch tube contained ten drones, so they didn't need to blow their entire complement of Guardians when they only needed a handful.

The Guardians were nasty little buggers. They used a sophisticated facial recognition software to identify their prey and then zoom in to attack them. When the suicide drones hit a meter away from their intended target, they would either shoot a single projectile into the enemy's head or detonate a small explosive device, spattering the target with shrapnel. With several hundred Zodarks preparing to assault their position, Royce ordered all sixty of their Guardians launched. He wanted them in place for the coming battle.

Royce heard the familiar sound of a transport craft landing and turned to look behind him. Exiting the rear ramp were eight of the Republic Army mech fighters. Special Forces seldom ever fought with these big clunky beasts. They were meant for large pitched battles. Come to think of it, this was shaping up to be a very heavy fight, so maybe it was a good thing the higher-ups had sent some down to help him.

A platoon of regular RA soldiers joined the eight mechanical beasts. Their platoon leader trudged up to him. "Sir, I was ordered to report to you. Where would you like my men and our mechs to deploy?"

Nodding in acknowledgment, Royce told the lieutenant where to deploy his mechs and where to have his soldiers filter in to support his own positions.

Moments after the reinforcements arrived, Royce's platoon sergeant shouted, "Here they come! They must have completed their war dance, or whatever it was they've been doing for the last ten minutes."

In the distance, Royce saw the mob of Zodarks sprinting out of the tree line, full of bloodlust and rushing toward Royce's hurriedly prepared positions. The horde was three hundred meters to their front with only a smattering of trees, bushes, and other underbrush between the two opposing forces. It wasn't a lot of cover for the enemy to hide behind.

Still, the Zodarks weren't exactly known for using cover to assist them in their charges. They seemed to just bum rush an opponent and hope their howling and screaming would scare the defenders into making mistakes.

Had this been the first time Royce and his operators had fought a Zodark, their reckless charge and horrendous screams just might have caused them to break ranks and run, but this was now the seventh time they'd fought these beasts, so he was becoming adept at dealing with their tactics.

On the digital map on his HUD, Royce watched the enemy continue to close the distance. They were now using their blasters, sending brilliant streaks of light at his ranks. Some of the shots would hit a tree and blow a chunk off or hit a stone and shatter it. Some of the shots unfortunately met their mark on one of the RA soldiers, often killing them.

Royce's forces started firing, sending their magrail rounds back at the enemy. "A little closer, a little closer," Royce mumbled to himself.

Royce linked himself with Adam and sent the message. The toasters needed to launch their attack now. He monitored the map on his HUD as the two flanking groups of toasters rose to begin their assault. They closed the distance rapidly, cutting off the Zodarks' path of retreat.

Returning his gaze to what was going on in front of him, Royce realized he probably hadn't watched what was going on as carefully as he should have. The first rank of Zodarks was now less than thirty meters from his position. His men and the toasters were doing their best to cut them down, but they weren't thinning their ranks fast enough.

Lifting his rifle to his shoulder, Royce fired several aimed shots at the Zodark nearest him. He hit the beast several times in the chest, causing him to stumble and fall to the ground, dead in his tracks.

To his right, Royce heard more screaming. He turned to see what was going on and saw four Zodarks jump into the fighting position two of his Deltas had dug. One of the Zodarks plunged one of its two shortswords into one of the Delta's guts and slashed him wide open. The man's bowels spilled out of his ripped-open abdomen. With the second blade, the Zodark severed the man's head.

It then turned and looked right at Royce, hatred and savagery in its eyes. It screamed that telltale horrible shriek and charged right for him, blood still dripping from its shortswords.

Royce swung his rifle to the right and fired two quick shots, hitting the Zodark once in the chest and a second time in the face. The beast went down, hard. But his remaining friends were still in the fight.

Another Delta in that fighting position killed the Zodark he was grappling with and then took a blade to the side of the third Zodark's rib cage. Royce fired a single shot from his rifle and nailed the beast right in the head, ripping his skull clean off his body.

"Look out, Lieutenant!" yelled one of Royce's soldiers.

Instinctively falling to one knee as he turned to his left, Royce saw a Zodark charging right at him, two menacing-looking shortswords in his hands. Anchoring his right foot and lowering his left shoulder, Royce braced for the impact that was fractions of a second away.

As the Zodark's massive ten-foot body slammed into Royce's, he used the forward momentum of the big beast and his exoskeleton combat suit's added strength and lifted the Zodark up and over his shoulders. Royce threw the beast a few feet through the air and then swirled around to meet him head-on.

The enemy was now in too close to keep using the magrail on his rifle. Royce reached for his four-inch knife and charged the Zodark as he was clambering to his feet. Hitting the beast hard with his shoulder, Royce lunged his knife into the creature's midsection and then twisted it as he pulled up with all the strength he could muster.

The Zodark howled in agonizing pain as one of his four arms swung down hard, hitting Royce across his right shoulder with a force Royce didn't think was possible. He heard an audible crack, and a fiery string of pain flooded his brain. He knew the beast had either broken his collarbone or shoulder. In either case, Royce was in trouble.

Using his neurolink, Royce told his combat suit to inject him with a nerve block, a shot of adrenaline, and a shot of nanites to stop any internal bleeding. In fractions of a second, the pain completely disappeared. The adrenaline gave him the energy needed to thrust his knife right back into the Zodark's chest. This time he twisted it first to the right, then to the left to kill the big blue beast. The Zodark grunted and then collapsed to the ground.

Covered in bluish gore, Royce turned to see a wounded Delta a few feet away, resting against the side of a tree. Moving towards the man, Royce reached for the first aid pouch on the side of the Delta's chest rig.

He grabbed it and pulled out the first nanite auto-injector. "This might hurt," he told the wounded man.

The Delta was losing a lot of blood from the wound to his side. Royce jabbed him with the nanite injector, sending ten times the number of nanites into his body as the regular implants in their combat suits.

While Royce waited for the tiny medical devices to do their trick, he reached for his rifle that was still hanging from the side of his suit and looked for a target.

Over to his right, Royce saw one of the RA's mech units tearing the Zodarks apart. The fifty-caliber magrail gun was like a scythe. Every time the soldier inside would sweep it right or left, it cut down a vast swath of enemy soldiers as they advanced. Then to his horror, two Zodarks managed to flank the killing machine and pounced on the mech's back. One of the Zodarks used two of its four hands to pound on the glass front of the machine the operator used to see out. The beast couldn't break through the bulletproof glass. The operator inside was trying to toss the beast off, but this also meant it wasn't using its primary weapons to keep attacking the enemy that was on the verge of overwhelming them.

One of the Zodarks placed an explosive device in the rear of the mech, and then they both jumped off. Seconds later, the mech blew apart, killing the operator inside. A swarm of Zodarks rushed forward now that the one obstacle between them and their human prey had been eliminated.

*GW, if you have some air support for us, now would be a good time for it,* Royce said over his neurolink to their command element back on the ship.

Grabbing for his rifle again, Royce saw a pair of Zodarks ripping one of the toasters apart. He took aim and fired several shots, hitting them both. The terminator was done, though; both of its mechanical arms had been sheared off by the Zodarks shortswords. They were still glowing red as they sat there on the ground.

Royce wanted to look at his HUD and figure out how the overall battle was doing, but he couldn't spare even a few seconds. The enemy was in their ranks. The Zodarks were all over the place, and it was now a life-or-death fight.

Then he heard the very welcome sound of one of their VTOL ground attack craft or Reapers. The Reaper swooped in and unleashed a torrent of anti-personnel rockets into the center of the Zodarks, exploding amongst them. Zodark bodies were tossed about by the series of explosions ripping through their ranks.

The armored bird then flew in low and slow over Royce's men as its nose gun and two side gunners opened up on the enemy. The roaring sound of propellent-fired weapons was something Royce never got tired of hearing.

The Reapers were a cross between twenty-first-century American V-22 Ospreys and Apache attack helicopters. They had a single tiltrotor on each side sheathed in an armored ring for protection. They boasted a 20mm chin gun and two-door gunners who operated the M134 miniguns. Unlike the older twenty-first-century weapons, these used a liquid propellant, which allowed the aircraft to carry a lot more ammo on board.

The Reapers also packed two rocket pods on either side of the body, each carrying thirty-six 60mm anti-materiel rockets. In case they ran into any air or armored threats, they carried twelve dual-use missiles. The missiles could be used against aircraft or tanks and had a range of twenty kilometers. They could also carry eight passengers behind the door gunners.

"Woohoo!" shouted several RASs and Deltas—not one but four Reapers now swooped in overtop of their positions.

The attack aircraft spat out rockets and machine-gun fire on the remaining Zodarks, breaking up their attacks before they could overrun them.

A handful of Zodarks fired their blasters at the Reapers. A couple of their shots bounced off the Reapers' armor. Then a couple of the incoming blasts hit one of the Reapers' side rotors. A few more rounds hit that section of the VTOL and caused the entire sheathed rotor section to blow up. With half its wing and fifty percent of its lift capability gone, the Reaper spun out of control and tumbled to the ground. The aircraft landed with a hard thud, sending a plume of black smoke into the sky.

Seeing the aircraft go down reminded Royce that this adversary wouldn't give up; they'd fight on even when they should throw in the towel. Just a few seconds ago, their air support had been slaughtering them. That had changed in the blink of an eye when the Zodarks had turned their blasters and anti-air missiles on them. The remaining Reapers accelerated quickly and rose in altitude to get out of range. From a much higher position, they circled and fired down into the enemy positions.

That lasted for all of a minute before the Zodarks fired off a missile at one of the VTOLs. The aircraft being targeted spat out flares and dove for cover to try to throw the missile off. The Zodark missile whipped past the countermeasures and slammed right into the Reaper, blowing it completely apart. Wreckage fell to the ground, still smoking and burning.

The last two Reapers zoomed away to return to the *GW*.

Looking at the battle in front of him. Royce watched the toasters he'd been skeptical of earlier throw themselves right into the middle of the Zodark positions. The two platoons' worth of terminators were locked in hand-to-hand combat.

*Those killing machines are relentless; that's for damn sure*, Royce thought as he raised his rifle to his shoulder and did his best to snipe at a few of the Zodarks.

Royce knew he needed to get back to managing the battle. He was, after all, the ground commander. But part of him was drawn to be in the thick of the fight. To be locked in mortal combat with the enemy was an adrenaline rush and thrill nothing could replace.

Royce's left shoulder still wasn't fully functioning, despite the nanite injection. He had limited use of it. It was mostly his combat suit that was enabling him to use it at all.

Once Royce had made sure his immediate surroundings were as safe as they were going to get, he pulled up the HUD in his helmet and looked at the overall situation. On his right flank, the Zodarks were being wiped out. That reinforcement of toasters just before the battle started had saved their bacon. The left flank was still iffy; the toasters were still fighting, but they'd lost more than half their numbers. Now the center—that was the section of the line that concerned Royce the most. Five of his ten Deltas displayed as KIA, while the other five, including himself were all injured.

The platoon of RA soldiers had also taken a beating, with nearly half their platoon wiped out. All four of the mechs the RA had brought were dead. The Zodarks had made taking them out a real priority once the battle had started. Royce knew they couldn't keep fighting unless they got reinforcements, and reinforcements from the *GW* weren't an option—at least not in time to make a difference.

*Adam, order your squad attacking the Zodark rear position to leave and reinforce the left flank. How copy?* Royce ordered over their neurolink.

*Lieutenant Royce, if I do that, the Zodarks will escape to fight another day. We should keep them trapped and finish them off right here,* Adam in responded.

*Adam, this is an order. You are to pull your squad blocking the Zodarks' retreat. Acknowledge.*

*Acknowledging order. Withdrawing the second squad now.*

When the toasters broke ranks and ran to the left flank, the Zodarks seized the opportunity to extricate themselves from the battle. They filed out of the fight and retreated deeper into the woods, away from the human forces. In five minutes, the last of the Zodarks had withdrawn.

When they were gone, Royce had the toasters fall back to his position. He then called for a medical transport to pick up his wounded and dead. He wanted to get them off the moon and back to the ship ASAP.

When the first medical shuttle arrived, it offloaded another platoon of RA soldiers and two more mechs. The soldiers looked all gung-ho and ready to fight until they saw the ground littered with dead Zodarks and the bodies of their comrades.

Then a larger transport landed, bringing with it additional reinforcements. It offloaded eighty additional C100s, fresh from the mothership in orbit. Once they linked up with Adam, the toaster in charge would share their collective knowledge of the last couple of days of battle. The newly arrived toasters would absorb the information and work it into their programming to benefit from the experience of the previous batch.

One of the men who got off the transport walked up to Lieutenant Royce. It was Colonel Hackworth.

Nodding as he approached, Royce asked, "Sir, how can I help you?"

Hackworth smirked as he surveyed the carnage all around them. "I'm here to relieve you, Lieutenant. Hell of a job—you fought well. Actually, you fought better than I thought your group could have, but you, along with everyone in your squad, are injured. Your squad is relieved and will head back to the *GW* to get fixed up. I'll stay down here with a couple of toaster platoons and a platoon of RA pukes to clean things up and finish the job. You've earned your pay. Go get patched up." The colonel motioned with his head for Royce to get on the shuttle.

Since he was wincing at any slight movement, Royce knew his shoulder needed a permanent fix, not a short-term patch. "Thank you, sir. Good hunting."

Royce ordered the rest of his squad to get on board. Their fight was over. Now it was time to get fixed up and say a few words about their comrades that had died on Pishon.

\*\*\*\*\*\*\*

Lying on the bed in the medical bay of the *George Washington*, Lieutenant Brian Royce was glad he was getting his shoulder fixed. The doctor said a couple more days and the nanites should have his collarbone fully healed along with the torn tendons and muscles. He'd be back to normal in no time flat.

The downtime in the medbay gave Royce some much-needed time to catch up on paperwork. God knew the military would collapse if it didn't have its i's dotted and its t's crossed. With sadness, Royce looked over the roster of soldiers needing enlisted performance reports or EPRs, physical fitness tests, or other mandated appointments. Nearly a quarter of the names on the lists were no longer with them. They had died on Pishon.

*We've lost so many people since we first discovered New Eden*, he thought, feeling a heaviness in his chest. *Half of my buddies have died in this bloody war...*

Royce tried his best to maintain a strong façade. He was an officer now, in charge of a platoon of Special Forces soldiers. It was his job to fight the enemy and keep as many of his people alive as possible. He missed being a sergeant. Back then, his job had revolved around killing the enemy. Giving orders that he knew would likely get some of his people killed unnerved him. For the life of him, Royce couldn't understand how a general—or a ship captain, for that matter—could make so many decisions that could lead to the deaths of their subordinates or even the loss of their ship.

*Maybe I'm not cut out for a command position*, he thought.

Snapping himself out of those dark thoughts, Lieutenant Royce resumed his paperwork. He opened up the EPR for his platoon sergeant, Master Sergeant Joe Tanner. Tanner was an outstanding NCO, a true leader. Royce wrote up the bullet points that would help him make his next promotion.

He looked over Tanner's service jacket, scanning the military schools he'd attended, the continuing education the sergeant had pursued, and the awards and recommendations he'd received over his time. Like many pre-war soldiers, Tanner didn't have a lot of medals— mostly achievement and commendation medals—awards you got when you transitioned from one assignment to another or did something above and beyond your regular duties. This deployment was Tanner's first combat deployment. Up until today, he'd been lucky—he hadn't gotten injured during any of their previous assaults. Today a Zodark blaster had hit him, but so far, he was doing OK. He was resting a few beds down from Royce.

Sergeant Tanner had fought exceptionally well on New Eden and Pishon. Royce wrote a decoration for a Bronze Star with V device for the assault to capture New Eden. He then wrote up a separate award for the same medal for this recent assault on Pishon as well as a Purple Heart. Joe had earned those awards, and Royce was glad to be in a position to provide his men with the medals and commendations they deserved. He hated when he saw other officers award medals more on interpersonal politicking than actual performance. He vowed not to be like those fake brownnosers.

Three hours into his administrative duties, a figure appeared at the foot of his bed. Royce put his tablet down and smiled as he looked up. "It's good to see you… Major? They promoted you again?"

A broad smile spread across Major Jayden Hopper's face as he shrugged. "It's not by choice if that makes you feel any better. I'd much rather still be down at the company level. At least as a company commander, I could still be involved in the actual fighting. How's the shoulder doing? I heard you had a pretty bad break."

"It'll heal. I'm glad we have these nanites," Royce replied. "The doctor told me if we were still using the same medical technology and procedures from the last Great War, this might have been a career-ending injury. As it is, I'm only going to be down for a couple of weeks. It's pretty amazing how far battlefield medicine has come. I think half my injured guys are going to make it and keep serving because of these nanite injectors in our first aid pouches."

Royce knew the newly promoted major was busy. "I appreciate the visit, sir, but I get the sense that you're here for more than a welfare check," he said with a chuckle. "What can I do for you from the medbay?"

Hopper smiled. "Always direct and to the point, Brian. In private, you can call me Jayden. No 'major' stuff when it's just us officers, OK? So, here's the deal, Brian. Our battalion's been on this deployment for five months. In that time, we've sustained a forty-two percent KIA ratio. Add in that nearly everyone in the battalion has been injured at least once, and we've sustained a lot of casualties. We've seen so much action during this deployment, and I can't say that it's going to slow down anytime soon."

Royce furrowed his brow. "I heard we finished wiping out the Zodarks on Pishon and the RAS and Delta company had cleaned up New Eden. Has another group of Zodarks entered the system?"

Hopper shook his head. "No, no more Zodarks. The brass is cooking up a plan to liberate the Sumerian home world, Sumer. Our battalion is splitting to form a new Delta battalion. I've been selected to lead this new unit, hence the promotion. We're officially forming up the new 1st Battalion, 3rd Deltas. This new Delta group is going to be based out of New Eden. We're going to be the first battalion of the new group...I'd like to know if you'd like to be one of my new company commanders."

Royce laid his head back on the pillow for a second. *A company commander...I've barely had time to get used to being an officer in charge of a platoon.*

Seeing the conflicted look on his lieutenant's face, Hopper interjected, "I know this is a lot, Brian, asking you to take over a company. We've sustained a lot of losses, but we need good officers in charge who have combat experience and know how to lead. We don't have a lot of officers or enlisted that have the skills you and I have.

"Collectively, our original company that left for New Eden six years ago has more combat experience than all of Space Command Special Forces. We, meaning the command, need to get our combat veterans spread out in leadership positions with these new units. We need to build a new nucleus from which to grow these units. I need you, Brian. Will join my battalion and help me turn it into the best Delta battalion in the new group?"

Looking his friend in the eye, Royce asked, "Do we even have enough Deltas to constitute a company, let alone a new battalion?"

Hopper's hand stroked the twelve-hour stubble on his chin as he thought about that for a moment. "To be honest, Brian, no. However, the C100s have proven to be pretty adept at fighting as part of a human team. Heck, your own battle on the moon was a great case study on how to integrate the new combat Synths into human units. Based on how well things worked out, command wants to incorporate the C100s."

"Actually, Jayden, we tend to call them toasters or terminators, not C100s or combat Synths," Royce corrected with a chuckle. "Except for Adam, their leader, of course."

Hopper snickered at the derogatory nicknames the soldiers had given the C100s. "Ah, yes. The *toasters* have proven they can work and operate with a human squad. As I was saying, Command has decided that until our training program back on Earth can fill our vacant slots, we're filling them with C100s." Hopper held a hand up to forestall any comments from Royce. "Look, Brian. I know the troops all have nicknames for them, and yes, I know that crotchety old Delta colonel calls them toasters and terminators too, but we need to call them by their actual names. So, please, if you can, around the brass or anyone in authority, call them C100s if you don't want to use the term combat Synths. OK?"

Royce nodded, his cheeks reddening a bit. He knew Hopper was right. This was one of the differences between an officer and an NCO. An officer had to be professional at all times; an NCO, well, they could get away with things an officer couldn't.

"By the way, Colonel Hackworth is our new group commander," Hopper remarked. "Your new company will consist of twenty-five percent human soldiers and the rest C100s. This percentage will change as new replacements arrive, but until they do, we will be heavy with combat Synths. Of course, you'll need to figure out how you want to integrate your C100s with your human soldiers and how you'll want to operate your platoons. I'm sure you'll come up with some unique tactics using the simulators. So, Brian, may I offer you these and have you cross over to join my battalion?" Hopper asked as he held out a small box with two sets of captain's bars in it.

Royce shook his head as he smiled; he couldn't let his friend down. They'd been together since they'd left Sol more than six years ago. Of course he was going to accept the promotion. Officers like Jayden Hopper didn't come along very often. If the brass was seeing fit to promote him through the ranks, then Royce would do his best to ride his coattails and see where he ended up.

"I'll do it, sir, but you need to let me spend a couple weeks working with the Synths and my human soldiers to figure out some new tactics to make this work better," Royce replied. "Our battle down on the moon was some seriously thrown-together crap that just so happened to work. I wouldn't want to wing it like that with future battles. If this is how we're going to fight going forward, we need to develop particular tactics and plans to utilize the unique set of skills the C100s bring to augment our human shortcomings. Fair?"

Hopper extended his hand to shake Royce's. "Sounds good, Brian. I can't tell you how relieved I am to have you on my team. Oh, before I officially leave our company, get me your award packages and all your other platoon paperwork. I'm still the company CO for another twenty-four hours—I want to close out my company duties before the next guy takes over."

"Jayden, before you leave, if you don't mind me asking, how are we going to fill all these officer and NCO positions?" Royce asked.

Hopper smiled. "Pretty simple, actually. We keep promoting those who outlived everyone above or parallel to them. If this war drags on for a while longer, you and I will probably be colonels. It's just the way things work, Brian. When an army grows rapidly and the officer and NCO ranks get devastated by combat losses, a lot of people find themselves getting promoted very swiftly."

With that, the newly minted major left the box with the captain's bars on Brian's bed and made his way over to talk with a few other wounded soldiers in the medbay. Reaching down to grab the box, Brian looked at the captain's bars. Never in a million years had he thought he'd be an officer, let alone a company commander. Before the war, his goal had been to make sergeant major.

*Who knows? At the rate this war is chewing through soldiers, I could end up being a general.*

# Chapter Fifteen
## Shipbuilding

### John Glenn Orbital Station
### RNS *George Washington*

Rear Admiral Miles Hunt let out a deep sigh once his ship had finally connected to the massive station. The *GW* was going to be in port for twenty-four days. Then they'd ship out to the Rhea system to lead a new expedition, an invasion of Zodark-controlled space. That meant he had twenty-four days to get his ship repaired and his crew some modicum of R&R before the next major campaign started.

Hunt turned to his XO. "Captain McKee, please release the nonessential crew for two weeks of R&R. Make sure the remaining crew cycles through at least ten days of leave either on the station or Earth. It's time we let our people have some downtime and take a short break."

"Aye-aye, Admiral," McKee replied excitedly. She had the first ten days of leave in port. Then she'd swap out with the admiral while he took ten days himself.

The maiden voyage for the *GW* had been a brutal five months, during which they'd sustained an enormous amount of damage to the flagship of the RNS fleet and lost a lot of friends along the way. This wasn't how a maiden voyage was supposed to start, but they were at war, after all.

Following the climactic battle at the stargate, the *GW* had returned to New Eden. While they were able to get a lot of their damage repaired in orbit, some things required a more advanced shipyard to repair. It was risky having the *GW* leave Rhea, but this was the only way to get their superweapon fixed for the coming battle.

Before the *GW* had left the Rhea system, one of the engineers at BlueOrigin came up with the brilliant idea of weaponizing the stargates, which was how they'd been able to make this trip home. While they couldn't control the stargates or even understand how they worked, they sure could fortify the hell out of them.

After seeing how the limited gun batteries they had placed at the gate worked, they had gone full bore, creating a host of weapon platforms to surround the gate at Rhea. They had built a series of plasma torpedo launcher pods and more magrail turrets. These were fixed platforms anchored around the gate. They were also heavily armored with roughly forty meters of armor. If an unknown ship jumped through, they'd be blasted. It would also alert the Earther forces in the system that an intruder had entered the system.

*******


An hour after the ship had docked, the shipyard workers came aboard to start their repairs. The lead engineer for BlueOrigin, Adrian Rogers, walked onto the bridge and spotted Admiral Hunt right away, sitting at his captain's chair with a tablet in hand.

Hunt looked up, saw the familiar face and smiled. He got up and made his way over to his friend. "Hey, look what the cat dragged in. How are you doing, Adrian?" The two men shook hands.

"Ah, Miles—I mean, Admiral. It's good to see you as well," Rogers said.

Hunt brushed off the comment about his rank. "Call me Miles, Adrian. We've known each other too long for titles or ranks. You know, it's too bad you weren't able to come out with us on our maiden voyage. What happened that caused you to have to leave at the last minute? I never did get a good answer."

"It was a personal matter," Rogers replied, his voice becoming sad. "My mother had a massive heart attack and passed away the day before you left. I hated ducking out on the deployment, but I couldn't leave my dad like that. Did Eric handle everything in my absence?"

Hunt nodded. "He did fine, Adrian. I just wanted to make sure things were OK on your end. How is the family doing now?"

"My dad is still struggling with it. You know, despite all the medical wonders we can do these days, we still can't predict when a massive heart attack that'll kill you will happen. My parents were married for eighty-two years, if you can believe that. It was really hard on my dad, losing Mom like that, but I'm glad I was able to be there for him when he needed me."

Hunt thought about that for a moment. *Eighty-two years of marriage.* It warmed his heart that medical technology had advanced to such a level that people could live into their early to mid-hundreds, and people could stay married that long. He and Lilly had just passed the thirty-seven-year mark themselves.

*How time flies...*

Rogers continued, "My wife is doing well, though. The kids...they're all grown. Actually, we're empty nesters now."

Rogers looked like he wanted to say something but hesitated.

"Hey, what's wrong, Adrian?" Hunt prodded. "Something else going on I should know about?"

Rogers looked a little embarrassed. "Uh, since you brought it up, my daughter, Tina, got drafted six months ago."

A few months before Hunt and his fleet had shipped out, President Luca had announced a massive conscription effort across the Republic. The TPA was likewise raising a large military force.

"Huh, I didn't know that, Adrian. Do you know where she's being assigned or what her job is going to be?" Hunt asked. He motioned for the two of them to take a seat near his captain's chair. A small army of contractors was filing onto the bridge to run some diagnostics and figure out what were priority repairs versus things that could wait.

Rogers blushed. "Actually, she's been assigned to your ship, the *George Washington*. She said she's supposed to report to the weapons department. She was assigned to be a gunner's mate."

Rogers looked concerned. He would have known from the damage report the *GW* had sent ahead of their arrival that the ship had sustained a lot of damage to its magrail turrets—a group of weapons where the junior GMs would typically serve.

Hunt felt for the man. He'd worked with Rogers on the designs for the *GW* and had gotten to know him pretty well over the years.

"I thought Tina was going to college," Hunt said. "Didn't they offer deferments for those going to university?" He'd been deployed so long, he was clueless as to what had been going on back on Earth.

Rogers just shook his head. "No, they aren't offering deferments to anyone. If your number comes up, you have to report. I couldn't try to pull any strings and get her out of her service—that wouldn't be right. While the father in me wanted to do that, my daughter was having none of it."

Hunt nodded in approval. "Tell you what, Adrian—I'll see if I can get her assigned to one of the CIWS systems. They didn't see a lot of action, and they weren't heavily attacked during the battles. It's about the best I can do for her."

Rogers seemed at ease with his answer. He smiled and thanked him. "I appreciate it, Miles. Well, I suppose we should talk about the critical repairs. I saw the list you sent over, but what do you believe are the most important things to get fixed?"

Reaching over to grab his tablet, Hunt highlighted a couple of items and then handed the tablet over to Rogers. "I've outlined what I think are the most critical repairs. Aside from the plasma cannon, our most crucial item to get repaired is our 3-D printers. The starboard-side primary and secondary magrail turrets took a beating. A few laser shots burned through our armor and managed to hit our fabricator section. That was one area we couldn't fix on our own. Without those fabricators, there's a lot we can't do.

"Also, the armor. We used a lot of that nanite paste to patch things up, but I'm not confident it'll hold up against those Zodark pulse beams. We encountered a new, larger battleship, and those carriers hit hard, much harder than the previous ships we've encountered," Hunt explained.

"Yeah, I read about that in the AAR you sent forward with Admiral Bailey. I'm frankly surprised, but glad that you were able to hold up against them. I still can't believe they tore through our new battleships as they did. It was a herculean effort to get those six battleships built for your last campaign. Losing three of them in a single battle and the damage the remaining three took, I mean, wow." He leaned forward and practically whispered, "If they can keep throwing ships like that at us, Miles, how are we going to win this war?"

Hunt also leaned in so no one else heard him. "We beat them, Adrian, by outsmarting them," he countered. "We beat them by being able to adapt to the changing situations and integrating this new alien technology as quickly as we can."

Then Admiral Hunt sat back up and spoke in a normal voice again. "Now, I've been gone for five months—tell me you all have made some improvements to our tech since the last time our ship was in port?"

Rogers smiled devilishly. "Well, now that you mention it, our R&D team worked with our Sumerian allies and did a thorough examination of the Zodark carrier's armor—you know, that ship you captured a few years back? We believe we've identified how they're able to modulate their armor so effectively, thus negating the effectiveness of our lasers. We're going to integrate that same technology into the new generation of warships we're building. We're taking our existing ship designs and just adding it to them. I think this is going to increase your survivability in future battles immensely."

Hunt patted Rogers on the shoulder. "See, that's what I'm talking about, Adrian," he said excitedly. "It's that kind of ingenuity that's going to lead us to victory."

Hunt's PA notified him that it was almost noon.

*Lunchtime*, he thought. His wife, Lilly, had sent him a note that she'd arrived at the station. She was waiting for him in his temporary quarters on the station. If he was able to get away for a couple of hours, he could get in both a meal and a little action with his bride.

"OK, my friend. Time for me to let you get back to work," Hunt told Rogers. "I have an appointment I need to be heading off to." He winked mischievously as he stood.

"Ah, yes, of course. I thought I saw Lilly getting off the beanstalk this morning when I walked past it," Rogers said with a chuckle. "I'll catch up with you tomorrow, then."

*******

### Jericho Station
### Republic Naval Shipyard

Commander Amy Dobbs liked Jericho Station very much. It had been designed to build large-scale warships from the ground up in a very streamlined fashion. It was laid out very much like a factory with multiple stages or sections for each production line.

There was a large drydock facility followed by multiple construction bays for everything from smaller frigate class warships to the much larger battleships or even dreadnought-class ships. About thirty percent of the facility had been completed. They were still years away from having the entire shipyard fully operational.

Blowing some air out her lips, Dobbs looked at the floating holographic representation of the ship she'd spent the last five months helping design. She wondered how it would hold up in combat. The *Viper*-class frigates the Navy had introduced more than a year ago were fine ships. They performed well, but they had their own set of flaws that hadn't become evident until they'd gone into battle. Even though the *Vipers* weren't designed for battle but rather for reconnaissance, the war with the Zodarks required all ships to be battle-ready.

Following the loss of her ship, Dobbs had been reassigned to help the ship designers come up with a new class of warship that could still handle the same missions as the *Viper*-class frigates but also survive a bit longer in a fight with the Zodarks.

This new warship Dobbs had helped design was a beast. They'd incorporated the latest in armor technology and added some powerful new weapons. The ship had a three-meter-thick hull that integrated the Zodarks' modulated armor technology. These improvements should allow them to hold up much better in a shooting match during the coming battles.

One of the ship designers for Musk Industries walked up behind her. "Have you come up with a name for this line of ships yet?" he asked.

Dobbs blushed as she turned around. "Hi, John. I have, actually. I'm not sure if Space Command will approve it, but we'll see."

"OK, the suspense is killing me, Commander. What's it going to be?" the engineer asked with a smirk on his face.

"If they approve it, I'd like to call them the *Scorpion*-class destroyers," Dobbs announced.

He nodded approvingly. "I like it. Catchy. Given this bad boy's weapon loadout, I think *Scorpion* suits it."

"John, I have to brief Admiral Bailey on the status of this project tomorrow," Dobbs said. "He's coming up to the station to meet with Admiral Hunt now that the *GW* and most of his battlegroup has returned. The admiral's going to ask me about the production timeline. How long is it going to take to build these ships?" she asked. "When will we be able to start fielding them?"

"That is an excellent question," John replied. "I can tell you how long it'll take to build, but as to how soon they'll be built and ready to deploy...that largely depends on the admiral and when he wants them."

Dobbs furrowed her brow. "What do you mean by that?"

She felt she was way out of her depth when it came to shipbuilding and procurements. This was a side of being a senior officer she had no experience with. She knew, however, that if she wanted to become an admiral one day, the experience she was gaining in this position would prove to be immensely helpful.

John walked over to the holograph image she was looking at. Using his hand to swipe away the image of the ship, he brought up the shipyards. "Commander, right now, we have four of our five Earth shipyards building warships. The Jericho Station is still only thirty percent done, so we've got many more years of construction before we'll be a fully operational shipyard. The fifth shipyard I mentioned is building large civilian transport craft for the TPA—they're still emigrating as many of their people as possible to the Centaurus system.

"The two TPA yards are building two classes of ships: their version of a battleship which is considerably smaller than ours, and cruisers. Their cruisers are solid ships and have done exceptionally well in past battles with the Zodarks. Half of those ships they're building are sent to guard Alpha Centauri as they build up that system's defense.

"Our two shipyards over Earth are building battleships and one additional dreadnought-class warship. Our yard over Mars is building orbital assault ships, and the smaller shipyard being run by the Belters is producing frigates. As you can see, we're pretty tapped out when it comes to capacity. Admiral Bailey would need to determine which ship line he wants to pause and for how long to start running off copies of these new Scorpions."

*We're fighting this whole war with superglue and duct tape*, Dobbs thought.

"John, how many Vipers are we building?" she asked.

He tapped on a folder and brought up the information. "Right now, we have twenty-two under construction. When they're done, another twenty-two will start. It's taking the Belters twelve weeks to build a Viper. Once it completes its time in the yard, it takes another three months for the guts of the ship and its weapon systems to be completed. Then it's turned over to Space Command to be issued to a crew."

Dobbs shook her head in amazement. "What about an orbital assault ship? The ones you said are built over Mars?"

John closed one folder and opened another. A second later, the information appeared in front of them, floating above the table. "We can build twelve orbital assault ships. They carry a battalion of RA soldiers and all their equipment for deployment. It takes our shipbuilders twelve months to build one, then another three to complete the guts and the weapon systems."

She squirmed in her seat, and John smiled. "Before you ask, Musk Industries is building fifteen battleships. It takes us fifteen months to complete one, then another five to finish off the guts of the ship and its weapon systems. All told, twenty months from start to finish, and that's with twenty-six thousand human and Synth workers on a twenty-four-seven production schedule. It's an incredible operation when you think about it."

Dobbs opened her mouth to speak, but John cut her off. "Oh, and before you bring up the dreadnought, that line of ships takes roughly three years to build. Another year to finish off the interior and the weapon systems. We have two of them under construction right now plus the *GW* essentially back in the yard for repairs. So back to your original question, Commander—how long will it take to start cranking out the *Scorpions*? We can probably have a ship built inside of twelve weeks, another six weeks to finish off its interior and weapon systems. *But*, and this is a big but, it means we have to stop producing something else—some other ship class that is desperately needed, especially after our losses from the battle at the stargate."

Dobbs shook her head. "Is there any way we can get the Jericho Station yard completed faster so we can pick up the slack?"

John shook his head jovially. He seemed to be holding in a laugh.

Dobbs gave him a dismissive look as she canted her head to the left. "Was that a stupid question I asked, John?"

John turned serious again. "No, Commander, it's not a stupid question, but it's not that simple either. That station the Belters built took them nearly fifteen years to build. Our yard over Mars took us close to twenty years to build up to what it is today. Admiral Bailey commissioned the Jericho Station a little more than three years ago. As you can see, we're still only thirty percent complete. These are massive structures that consume enormous amounts of resources and manpower to build.

"Every time we divert Synths or human workers to speed up a section of the Jericho yard, it means we've diverted those resources from the completion of a battleship, frigate, or orbital assault ship. Right now, it's a matter of what's more important, finishing Jericho Station, or a hundred more warships. So far, Admiral Bailey has told us it's warships."

Dobbs thought about what John had said, and she didn't like it one bit. Humanity really was in a race against time.

John got up and walked over to his computer terminal. He typed a few things on his laptop and then pulled a small data drive from the side of the terminal. He handed it over to Dobbs. "This has all the specs and technical information on the *Scorpion*. If Space Command wants to proceed with building them, send me a message and a contract, and we'll get started on them. In the meantime, Commander, if we don't see each other again, stay safe, will you? We need more officers like you around."

Dobbs took the data drive and placed it in her pocket. "Thank you, John. It's been a pleasure working with you these past few months. I'm glad we've been able to get this project completed, and with any luck, the brass will approve what we've designed, and we'll have a new kickass ship for the fleet. I'll let you know what the admiral says tomorrow and if we're a go or not. Hopefully, we'll get *Scorpion* in production sooner rather than later."

\*\*\*\*\*\*\*

## John Glenn Orbital Station
## Space Command First Fleet HQ

Admiral Chester Bailey was in a foul mood. He'd had a particularly nasty meeting with President Luca, the TPA Chairman, and his TPA military counterpart. The TPA leadership, growing concerned with the ship losses in the Rhea system, had actually asked if it might be possible to pursue a truce with the Zodarks.

Admiral Bailey reminded them several times that all attempts thus far to establish contact with the Zodarks had gone nowhere. The Zodarks wouldn't even surrender a ship when it was disabled and unable to fight. It was hard enough to get any of their soldiers to surrender—they were fanatical in their zeal to fight to the death.

Instead of supporting Admiral Halsey's fleet with ships, the TPA restricted the majority of their new warships to Sol. Bailey knew it was only a matter of time before the Zodarks would send another fleet, a more substantial fleet, since their last two expeditions hadn't returned. If Bailey didn't get more ships to Admiral Halsey's fleet, they could lose the Rhea system.

Bailey's PA reminded him it was almost time for the next meeting at 1300 hours. He sighed. Through sheer force of will, he pushed himself out of his chair and trudged toward the conference room down the hall. As he entered, someone shouted, "Attention on deck!"

Bailey waved them off and told everyone to take their seats. Then he walked over to the large circular table. He found the spot reserved for him and sat down—everyone else followed suit. They looked pensive, almost anxious. Everyone knew the situation was getting desperate. Since the battle at the stargate nearly five months ago, they'd been trying to figure out what to do next.

Surveying the room, Bailey saw Admiral Hunt, along with a couple of people from his staff with him.

"I'd like to welcome Admiral Hunt to our meeting. It's good to see you in person, Admiral," Bailey announced. "But let's get down to it. Commander Dobbs briefed me on the status of the new destroyer-class ship, the *Scorpion*. They look amazing—just what we need to fill out our fleet's capabilities. The question is, what ships do we postpone building so we can run off a line of new destroyers? Suggestions?"

Clearing his throat, Admiral Hunt was the first to speak. As the expeditionary force commander, he probably knew better than most what they could live without. "Sir, if it's a matter of what we need most versus what we can do without, then I recommend we put the orbital assaulters on hold and focus that entire yard on producing the *Scorpions*."

"You mean finish the ships currently in production and then start the new ships?" inquired another admiral.

Hunt shook his head. "No. I mean *stop* their construction and shift everything we have to crank out these new destroyers. I also recommend we double down on getting our second dreadnought and battleships done ahead of schedule." He looked at Bailey. "If you'll give me a second to explain, sir, before everyone adds their two cents," Hunt requested.

*I hope Miles knows what he's doing*, Bailey thought. He had enough headaches to deal with right now without adding some angry shipyard managers to the list.

"OK, Admiral, proceed. But understand Admiral Lewis and I are the final authority on this matter," Bailey said as he shot Hunt a pensive look that said *This had better be good.*

"Thank you, sir. We currently have eight orbital assault ships ferrying troops from Sol out to New Eden and the two moons. Right now, we don't need more than the eight we have," Hunt explained.

Admiral Lewis, the man in charge of Space Command's ship procurement program, interjected, "Admiral, what about your new campaign? If you're going to invade Zodark-controlled space and potentially liberate the planet Sumer, how are you going to do that with just eight orbital assault ships? Won't you need more ground forces for a campaign like that?"

"That's a fair question, sir," Hunt said with a nod. "If we hadn't sustained such great losses in our last battle, then yes, I would like to have a larger ground force come with us. However, the last fight changed the dynamics. We thought the *Vipers* would have solved a critical problem of the current fleet composition. Mainly, we needed a scout ship to conduct deep space reconnaissance and help screen for the fleet. While the *Viper* packs some awesome firepower, it's also paper-thin when it comes to armor. We lost half our *Vipers* in their first engagement. We can't keep cranking out ships that are being destroyed this easily. We need to switch over to the new destroyers, which we expect to fare much better."

Hunt continued, "Second, we started the last campaign with six battleships. We lost half of them, and the remaining three sustained significant damage. I would like to point out that while we did suffer serious losses in this last battle, we effectively crushed a massive Zodark fleet. They outnumbered us nearly two to one. I'm confident the next iteration of battleships will do even better. If we're going to successfully launch an invasion of Zodark space and liberate the planet Sumer, then we're going to need more battleships to do it."

Bailey saw that many of the others at the table nodding their heads. "Lastly, the *George Washington* made the difference between victory and defeat. Our superweapon, the plasma cannon, was a real game-changer. We blew right through the Zodark ships with it. The armor on this beast also played a big role. We were able to absorb an enormous amount of enemy fire. Our primary and secondary turrets were able to hit multiple Zodark warships at a time, giving us a lot of versatility. While the enemy largely focused their weapons on us, the rest of the fleet was able to lay into them.

"When we complete the second dreadnought, we can create a third fleet around it. Having two battlegroups would give us an enormous amount of flexibility in our future military operations. That's why I recommend we stop production of the *Vipers* in the Belt and switch that yard over to making *Scorpions*. We also need to halt production of the orbital assault transports to build more *Scorpions*. We can then double down on our efforts to finish the battleships and dreadnought currently under construction."

When Admiral Hunt had finished, he sat back in his chair, looking confident after arguing his point. Bailey thought it was a solid case. He certainly saw the merits in it, but what about Admiral Lewis?

The older admiral in charge of ship procurement leaned back, appearing to consider Hunt's proposal. The room fell silent as they waited for his response. Admiral Lewis stood as he finally spoke. "This war with the Zodarks has been costly. Admiral Hunt has laid out a very expensive plan to protect the citizens of Sol, Centauri, and Rhea, and to free our human brethren enslaved on other worlds."

Bailey held his breath, waiting for what he thought would be a resolute rejection.

"We have lost many great men and women in this battle. I do believe to do anything less would come at a far greater cost," Lewis said to Bailey's shock. "I approve changing the shipbuilding strategy as Hunt outlined."

## Chapter Sixteen
## New Worlds

**Lagash Star System**
**RNS *Franklin***

Lieutenant Commander Joe Reynolds was always nervous when they exited a stargate. He never knew what could be waiting for him on the other end. Frankly, he was shocked the Zodarks didn't have these gates fortified or camped out with warships. Then again, from what limited understanding he had of the stargate system, there were *thousands* of gates across the universe. It made sense that they couldn't fortify them all.

"Entering the system now," Lieutenant Junior Grade Ethan Hunt announced. The odd-looking warp tunnel that had appeared to swirl around them as they traveled through from one stargate to the next one ended. They exited into a new and utterly unknown star system—the home system of the Sumerian people.

Reynolds smiled when he saw the gate was clear. He turned to Ethan. "Excellent, Lieutenant. Get our engines up to full speed," he ordered. "Let's see if we can find an asteroid belt to hide in while we collect our data. Make sure we keep our sensors in passive mode. I want to get a lay of the system before we go active with them."

Reynolds and Ethan had previously served together on the *Viper*. When their last ship had been destroyed, it had looked like their crew was going to be reassigned to a variety of other starships. Then a new frigate had come out of the shipyard, and they'd gotten a chance to get back in the fight.

Ethan applied more power to the thrusters, and their frigate picked up speed. The passive sensors showed five planets in the system and a massive asteroid belt that bent along the edge of the system. Looking for a cluster of large rocks to hide behind, Ethan found a section and guided the ship there.

As they hurried toward the belt, Ethan, who was also dual-hatting as the electronic warfare officer or EWO, extended their electronic sensor antennas up. Even in passive mode, their advanced suite of tools could detect virtually any electronic emissions in the system—especially since they now knew what frequencies and bandwidths were used by the Zodarks and Sumerians.

The losses from the previous battle at the Rhea gate and New Eden had cost Space Command a lot of officers and enlisted personnel. Ships could be replaced, but experienced and trained people took a bit longer to replace. That was why Ethan had to fill in as the EWO in addition to being helmsman.

The next eight hours went by both quickly and painfully slow. Traveling to the asteroid belt seemed to take forever, even at full speed. However, in terms of collecting electronic data, as soon as their suite of tools came online, they were inundated with information. The second planet from the sun appeared to be the hub of electronic activity, but data also came in from the third planet and at least three moons.

More ominously, there appeared to be a lot of emissions matching Zodark signatures. So far, they'd only spotted three Zodark ships, none of which seemed to be very large; they were probably smaller warships or transports. The question now was, how long would the Earthers hang out in the asteroid belt before they withdrew to Rhea?

Turning in his pilot's chair, Lieutenant Junior Grade Ethan inquired, "Sir, do our orders allow us to make contact with the Sumerians?"

Reynolds had been wondering that himself. His orders were to scout the system, get a lay of the place for the main fleet. They didn't say he couldn't make contact, but they didn't say he could either. It was a gray area. If they hadn't spotted a couple of Zodark ships and Zodark facilities on some of the nearby planets and moons, he'd probably make contact without a second thought, but now he wasn't so sure.

"I don't think the timing's right," Reynolds said. "It looks like there's a fairly large Zodark presence in the system. We can't take that on, and frankly, I'm not sure what kind of response we'd get from the Sumerians. For all we know, they might side with the Zodarks. After all, they've been part of their empire for hundreds, maybe even thousands of years."

Ethan bit his lower lip, thinking it over. He seemed to agree with Reynolds's assessment.

"What do you want us to do now?" Ethan asked. They'd already been in the system for ten hours.

Reynolds shrugged. "I suppose we stay put for a few days, collect data, see if anything interesting happens and try to decipher what we can with our equipment. Unless we see something interesting, I'll probably have us bug out in four or five days.

"We're at least two months out from Rhea. The fleet isn't going to make a move on this system until we return with our data or our com drone does. Make sure the drone is updated hourly. If we somehow get zapped, we need to make sure the com drone can make it back to our people. They'll need our intelligence."

\*\*\*\*\*\*\*

Two days later, Ethan Hunt was sitting in the ship's mess, sipping a cup of coffee. Lieutenant Commander Joe Reynolds finished grabbing a fresh cup of black gold himself and sat down across from him.

"Penny for your thoughts?" Reynolds asked. He ripped open a creamer packet and dumped it in his coffee.

Ethan placed his coffee cup down and looked at his friend. "Is it wrong to be afraid of going back into battle again?" he asked pointedly.

Reynolds took a sip of his coffee and winced slightly at how hot it was. "No, it's not wrong to be scared, Ethan." He stared off into space for a moment before adding, "Frankly, I'd be more concerned if you *weren't* afraid. Heck, I'm just as nervous as you. I mean, this is my first command. I'm new to all of this. Before being assigned the weapons officer on our last ship, I was on patrol duty in the Belt. We were supposed to be hunting pirates. Ironically, for all the pirate activity they talked about on the news or even in our intelligence briefings, we never spotted a single pirate ship."

"I'll bet you wish you could go back to the days of pirate hunting," Ethan said whimsically.

Reynolds shrugged. "Yes and no. It was a simpler time before the Zodarks, no doubt about that. But I think if we hadn't discovered them, we humans would probably have found a reason to fight each other. I think a lot of people forget that toward the end of the SET, tensions were getting pretty high between the Asian Alliance, the GEU, and the Republic. In a way, it looks like the Zodarks helped humanity find peace and come together as a species."

A smile spread across Ethan's face. "That's what my dad said last Christmas. Still, I'm concerned we're in over our heads. We don't have a clue how big the Zodark empire is or how many other races of aliens are out there."

He downed the rest of his coffee. "Joe, weren't you scared when Commander Dobbs launched our first attack at the gate?" he pressed.

Reynolds took a deep breath before he replied. "Ethan, I was terrified. It was my job to fire the weapons, get a lock on their ships and get our weapons off, and hopefully hit them. I also had to jam their sensors at the same time."

"How'd you overcome that fear, Joe? I almost feel paralyzed by it," Ethan stammered as he looked nervously around the room to make sure no one else could hear him.

Shrugging, Joe replied, "I guess I just fell back on our training. I knew if I didn't get those torpedoes fired and jam their sensors, we were most likely going to die. I took a deep breath to focus, then I just did my job to the best of my abilities and hoped everyone else did the same thing. That's why we run so many drills and train as hard as we do. So when we're in a situation like that, we fall back on our training like second nature."

Reynolds tilted his head. "What's going on, Ethan? I haven't seen you this unsure of yourself before. Something going on I should know about?"

Ethan struggled to answer right away. He suddenly felt a wave of emotions hitting him. He grabbed for his coffee cup and saw it was empty. He stalled a moment to let his body get his emotions back under control. "I...I'm not sure. In the last few weeks, as we've traveled here, I keep having dreams and memories of that day: the alarm bells going off, the ship taking hits, smoke, people yelling, and then finally, the order to abandon ship. I mean, my life pod barely made it out of the *Viper* before it blew up. I pissed myself when the ship blew up just below my pod. I hardly made it out of there, Joe. I mean, a second or two longer...and I'd be dead."

Ethan paused for a second as he wiped a tear away. "We lost nearly half our crew, Joe. A friend of mine from the medbay, Susie, she died. She wasn't able to make it to the life pods fast enough...how do you deal with that kind of loss and still keep going, Joe?"

Reynolds took a breath in and looked off to the corner of the room. "Ethan, we keep going because we have to. We honor our friends we've lost by avenging their deaths and by living good, honest lives. We help others when we can, and we try to be the best possible officers and people we can.

"They died—we can't change that, but they died for something they believed in. They died defending their friends, their families, and, most importantly, our way of life and our freedoms. We can't forget that. They died so that we may live. That's how you keep going, Ethan. We don't forget about them, and we don't pretend it didn't happen; we remember them, we live in their honor, and we do our jobs."

Ethan thought about that, then nodded. "You're right, Joe. Thanks for framing it that way. That really helped. And it helps knowing I'm not alone in feeling this way."

"Just keep your chin up, Ethan," Reynolds said. "Know you're not alone in this struggle or with these thoughts. We all experience them, OK? Now, if you'll excuse me, I need to get back up to the bridge. My shift starts in a few minutes."

Reynolds left Ethan to finish his break. He wasn't due to come on shift for another couple of hours. Since they were still playing cloak-and-dagger, hiding in the belt, Reynolds was letting his folks rest up and enjoy some downtime. The bulk of the work being done on the ship right now was electronic intelligence, and it didn't take a lot of people to man that equipment. The AI did most of the work.

What *was* consuming a lot of time was writing up the hundreds of contact reports and summaries of what they were collecting. Some might have thought of it as busywork, but it was interesting, and it needed to get done. With a working understanding of both the Sumerian language and the Zodarks', the AI deciphered everything being transmitted, even the encrypted message traffic.

So far, they'd been able to determine that the Sumerians had a station in orbit over their planet, connected to the surface by a space elevator. They also appeared to have a colony on another planet and two of the moons in the system. Interplanetary commerce was taking place between them all, with some mining operations in another part of the asteroid belt. This was actually good news as far as Commander Reynolds was concerned.

One of their priority intelligence requirements was to ascertain the level of sophistication of the Sumerian space program. While they'd only been in the system for two days, it was clear the Sumerians could travel between planets and their colonies. The Zodarks might not have allowed them to have a space navy, but they certainly could build one. This was a crucially important piece of intelligence. If Space Command was going

to launch further operations into Zodark-controlled space, they needed to establish forward operating bases. They also needed an ally that could actively participate in the war, one that could build warships.
*******

Three days later, when Reynolds and Ethan were on duty together, Reynolds was starting to get a bit bored when Ethan suddenly announced, "Captain, I'm finally getting some sensor data from deeper in the system. It appears there is not one but three stargates in this system."

Reynold's left eyebrow rose in surprise. "Really? Why are we only just now learning about this?"

Ethan looked more closely at the data. "Um, this system is a bit larger than we initially thought, Captain. Those stargates are pretty far out. If we engaged the FTL drive, it'd take two days to reach the first one. The other gates are roughly the same distance, just in different directions."

"Let me look at something," Reynolds said as he pulled up a holographic representation of the systems they'd traveled to that connected directly back to Rhea.

If they backtracked out of the system they were in right now, the next order was H8-ZTO, which had a total of three stargates in it. One gate led back to 0ZN7-G, which led to Rhea. The other gate, HHJD-5, led deeper into the Zodark empire—at least according to the captured Zodark star map.

"If HHJD-5 leads deeper into Zodark space, and YV-FDG leads to the Sumerian home system, where do these other stargates lead?" Reynolds said, thinking aloud. "I mean, according to the star map, it leads to a dead end. Then again, there are twelve systems down this chain..."

Reynolds looked at Ethan—it was only the two of them on the bridge. The other three crew members were off. "Lieutenant, how much do you know about the Sumerians or the Zodarks and their relationship with the Sumerians?" Reynolds asked.

Ethan's face scrunched up. "I've had some time on my hands these last two cruises, so I've spent a fair bit of it reading up on what we know thus far. From my understanding, there are two current theories. One says the Sumerians are essentially cattle, a food source for the Zodarks—

not their whole diet, but definitely part of it. The other theory says the ten percent taken as tribute are slaves and may even be used in their army.

"That second theory coincides with some other sources I've heard about," Ethan continued. "There was a researcher from Istanbul who has speculated based on a single report from one of the Sumerians that the Zodarks might be using this culling as a means of integrating humans into their own army, creating a janissary force as the ancient Ottoman Empire had. Supposedly they place these culled humans on other planets to grow their numbers and integrate them into their military war machine."

Reynolds thought for a moment. The theory mostly jibed with what he had heard as well. But something else was nagging at him. "Yeah, I've heard about that alternative theory. It might be true, but I'm not sure. Hunt, if I'm not mistaken, I think there was one Sumerian who also said he had been a slave to a Zodark NOS—his pet, so to speak. Right?"

Ethan nodded. "Yes, that's correct. He's the Sumerian who told us about this other theory of the cullings. That Sumerian is now in charge of a newly formed up Sumerian RA battalion. They plan on using him to help become the nucleus of a new Sumerian military leadership once we liberate their home world."

"Yes, exactly. I know no one else was able to corroborate some of the other information he provided. If I'm not mistaken, he mentioned humans populating other planets. He said he hadn't personally been to them, but he heard his master speak of them at one time. Do you remember reading that report?" Reynolds asked.

Ethan suddenly realized where this line of questioning was going. "You think these other stargates might lead to those systems? Those planets with other humans on them?"

Reynolds smiled. "That's exactly what I'm thinking. Get us out of this asteroid belt and set for FTL. We'll set a course for the nearest gate. I'll get the rest of the crew ready while you get the ship in position."

Twenty minutes later, the crew and the ship were ready to jump. It was unknown if the Zodarks or the Sumerians could detect them activating their FTL drive, but Reynolds deemed it worth the risk. If they could explore the rest of the chain and discover other human worlds, that would be incredible. It could help them unravel the origins of human history, and answer questions like why there were humans on other planets, and why the Zodarks ruled these other planets, but not Earth.

The *Franklin* spent the next two days in warp, traveling to the first gate. If the star map was correct, this stargate would lead to the system UAAU-C, which was connected to two other star systems. It also bypassed the star system LUL-WX, in case they needed an alternate route to escape out of the chain.

They had no idea what was in any of the star systems down this chain. Still, if their hypothesis was correct, this could be an enormous discovery, and well worth the detour from their original mission. They were, after all, a deep space reconnaissance ship.

"Captain, we're approaching the stargate. Do you want me to activate the gate as soon as we emerge warp?" Hunt asked.

Reynolds was nervous but excited as well. "Yes, just as soon as we come out of FTL."

A couple of minutes later, the warp bubble around their ship collapsed, and the massive circular structure known as the stargate came into view.

Lieutenant Hunt switched them over from FTL travel to their MPD thrusters and applied power to the main engines. The ship accelerated quickly. It didn't take them long to approach the stargate threshold before the gate activated. In the blink of an eye, a shimmering wave appeared in the circle, beckoning them to enter it. In a way, it looked like a puddle of light gray liquid in a cup. When they entered it, they were transported across hundreds of light-years.

Reynolds thought traveling through the stargate was far and away the coolest thing he'd ever experienced. The tunnel they went through wasn't a straight, linear path. It snaked down, up, to the right and left, almost like they were flying in a fighter plane in the atmosphere or riding a super scary roller coaster. It didn't take long to travel through the gates, sometimes just a few minutes. The longest jump they'd experienced thus far was close to five minutes. Most of the jumps lasted around two to three minutes.

When they popped out the other end and into the star system UAAU-C, they were greeted by the blackness of space, a canvas of stars, and three suns.

"OK, Hunt. Get our engines up to full speed and start looking for a place to hide. Initiate passive sensors as well. Let's get a lay of the land," Reynolds ordered as his crew went to work.

They moved away from the stargate, heading in the direction of the three suns, in search of any planet that could potentially house humans. An hour into their journey, their passive sensors started picking up results, showing two planets in the system. One appeared to be habitable, so they headed in that direction.

Turning to Reynolds, Lieutenant Hunt announced, "I'm not showing any signs of Zodark ships in the system. Can I go active with our sensors?"

"Yeah, that's a good idea. Let's get a better lay of this star system," Reynolds replied.

Ethan's fingers danced across the keyboards as he activated their sensors. In seconds, the ship emitted high-energy waves across all spectrums and wavelengths, blanketing the entire solar system. This would last for a few hours while they waited for feedback to their ship with a good view of objects and activities in the system.

Half a day went by with the *Franklin* heading toward the one planet they believed could support human life. Eventually, the planet appeared on their sensors. It was fascinating looking—bright yellowish-orange. Their immediate sensor returns indicated it was an arid planet, but it did have an atmosphere that looked like it could support humans.

Lieutenant Commander Reynolds sat forward in his chair as he looked at a magnified view of the planet. "It looks like a desert. Any evidence of water?"

Ethan's fingers tapped away on his keyboard, bringing up some basic information they'd collected thus far. "Um, we can't see it right now, but on the far side of the planet, there is definitely a large body of water. Down at the south pole, there's another body of water, but it isn't as large as the one on the far side."

"How big is this body of water?" Reynolds asked skeptically. "I mean, the planet looks pretty arid."

"I guess we'll see in another hour when the planet rotates around," Ethan said sarcastically.

"Ah, I see. A wise guy, eh?" Reynolds joked as he broke some of the tension. "OK, yeah, we'll see in an hour. In the meantime, are we showing any signs of humans down on that planet?"

"Our sensors indicate some level of activity on the planet, but we aren't detecting a lot of electronic emissions," Ethan replied. "*If* there are people down there, it's a less advanced society than ours or the Sumerians'."

An hour later, the planet rotated to reveal a decent-sized body of water. Some flat fertile lands were near the water and extended out several hundred kilometers before they ran against a vast tall mountain range that appeared to cover a considerable percentage of the planet. It was obvious why the planet appeared to be arid. The moisture from the body of water was trapped on one side of the mountains, leaving the opposite side to become a desert.

The lush green areas looked like they had dozens of cities all linked together by road networks, maybe even trains. But there was no evidence of anything that flew.

Reynolds ordered them to settle into orbit and continue to study the planet and people for a bit longer. They decided they'd spend two days observing the planet and the life-forms there. It was hard to do that from orbit, but they did the best they could. From what they could tell, the society appeared to be about as developed as Earth was in the 1800s or early 1900s—industrial age, but not yet using electricity.
*******

Toward the end of their second day of observations, Reynolds commented to his bridge crew, "I wish we had teleportation capabilities or a shuttlecraft. It'd be great to go down to the surface to study the people down there. We could see what they look like, what kind of language they speak, what kind of religion they practice, and if the Zodarks cull their society like they do the Sumerians."

Ethan spun his chair around. "I don't know, Skipper. If we went down there, how would we know what kind of clothes they wear? I mean, maybe we could observe from a distance, but there's no way we could get close to them."

Reynolds shook his head dismissively. "Always the party pooper, Hunt. You're no fun."

The others on the bridge laughed. They joked about how they'd sneak their way into one of the cities and what it would be like to walk around a town that looked like it was a time capsule from four hundred years ago. Even the best cameras and sensors the *Franklin* had could only give them a glimpse of what the cities and people on the surface looked like.

The five of them on the bridge joked about how easy Hollywood made it look on *Star Trek* when the ship's crew would beam down to the surface and automatically be wearing whatever clothes were worn by the native people to help them blend in. In reality, it obviously didn't quite work like that, but it was fun to joke about.

A buzzing noise suddenly interrupted the jovial banter. Ethan turned back to his station. "Captain, we're getting an alert. A new ship just entered the system. I'm still waiting to see if it's a Zodark ship, but I don't see how it could be anyone else. What are your orders, sir?"

*Crap, just what we need*, thought Reynolds. He did not want to get spotted by a Zodark ship while in orbit.

"OK, set condition one, battle stations," ordered Reynolds. "Hunt, get us up to full speed and break orbit. Get us positioned on the opposite side of the planet and FTL us to the next stargate as quickly as possible. We need to get out of the system before we're noticed."

A flurry of activity transpired over the next twenty minutes as they sought to get themselves out of orbit and away from the Zodark ship. Reynolds crossed his fingers that if they stayed behind the planet, it'd prevent the Zodarks sensors from spotting them.

"We're ready to engage FTL," Ethan finally announced.

"Do we have a firm idea on whether or not that ship is a Zodark vessel?" Reynolds asked. This deep in uncharted territory, it really could be anything.

"I can't say for certain, but its electronic emissions match those of a Zodark ship," Ethan replied. "Once they entered the system, they went active with their sensors, so that's how I'm able to make an educated guess."

"They went active with their sensors?" Reynolds asked, the pitch of his voice rising in concern. "Is it possible that they already detected us before we could get positioned on the other side of the planet?"

Ethan didn't respond right away. He was crunching some numbers at his terminal. Finally, he replied, "It's possible, sir. But they don't appear to be racing toward us, which leads me to believe they don't know we're here."

Nodding at the logical assessment, Reynolds remarked, "OK, I'll buy that. In the meantime, FTL us the heck out of here."

"Copy that. I'm setting a course for the nearest gate. This one will take us to system 3PPT-9," Ethan called out as he engaged their warp drive.

The warp field formed around their ship, and then they were gone—shot like a bullet as they were squeezed between the time-space fabric around their ship.

The *Franklin* stayed in warp for roughly eight hours before emerging right in front of the next stargate. When their ship dropped out of warp, Ethan switched their engines over from FTL drive to their MPD thrusters. This was a significantly faster process on a small frigate like theirs than on the larger cruisers or battleships. Just as they were approaching the gate, an anomaly occurred in front of them.

"What the heck? I'm detecting another ship materializing near the gate!" Ethan announced in a panic. His hands raced over to the electronic warfare board.

"Battle stations! Get our weapons spun up and ready!" Reynolds barked at his weapons officer. He turned to Ethan. "Get ready to jam whatever that ship is and get us through that gate as quickly as possible."

This was the worst-case scenario a ship captain feared—jumping to a gate only to find an enemy ship waiting for them before they could get away.

A bright shimmer of light blinked, and then a ship suddenly emerged. The unknown ship was no more than eight hundred kilometers from their current position—practically on top of them.

Several people on the bridge audibly gasped. Reynolds's jaw hit the floor. This wasn't a Zodark ship. This was something vastly different. The vessel was a sheer white color, dotted with small lights all along its sides. Their sensors told them it was roughly a thousand meters in length, but looked incredibly sleek with soft, rounded, smooth curves. It was completely different from the types of starships they'd seen up to this point.

"What the hell is that?" Ethan said aloud to no one in particular. He hadn't started jamming it; his hand was frozen over the controls of their EW system.

Reynolds was the first to react. "I don't know, Ethan, but get us through that gate. Hold off on jamming them unless it appears they're trying to target us. We have no idea if they are friendly or hostile, and I'm not going to sit around and find out."

Ethan steered them further away from this unknown ship and applied maximum power to their thrusters. Then a chirping noise emanating from Ethan's station told them they were being hailed by.

Ethan turned to Reynolds. "Sir, they're trying to talk to us—what do you want me to do?"

Reynolds furrowed his brow; he wasn't sure. His first thought was to get the hell out of Dodge, but he was curious why a hostile ship would try to hail them.

"Patch it through the bridge intercom," Reynolds finally replied.

The message came through garbled and unintelligible at first. Then the AI went to work deciphering it. It quickly identified the language as Zodark, but with a different accent.

The message said, *Unidentified ship, please identify yourself.*

"What do you want me to say?" Ethan asked.

Reynolds thought it really unlikely that a hostile ship would ask them to identify themselves. *They could have just shot first and asked questions later*, he thought.

Reynolds cleared his throat. "Um…tell them that this is the Republic Navy starship *Franklin*. We are explorers. We mean you no harm. Send that message in Zodark, Sumerian, and English," Reynolds concluded. He hoped he'd said the right thing.

Their ship continued approaching the gate. *Three minutes more, that's all we need before we're close enough to jump*, thought Reynolds.

"We're receiving another message. Patching it through the AI translator," Ethan announced.

The message played over the bridge's intercom. "We mean you no harm. Please do not jump through the gate. We are a species called the Altairians. We would like to talk further. What are you called?"

Now Reynolds was confused. They were in Zodark-controlled space, heading down a dead-end system controlled by the Zodarks, or so they thought. Was this really an entirely new species?

Everyone on the bridge stared at Reynolds, asking with their eyes what to do next. Finally, Reynolds replied, "Hunt, relay this to them. We are called humans. We are from a star system very far from here. Are you allied with the Zodarks? The race that controls this system and the nearby systems?"

At this point, Ethan had slowed down their speed towards the gate, but he still kept the engines ready to accelerate if needed.

A few seconds later, the intercom relayed their response. "We are at war with the species you call Zodarks."

Reynolds grinned. He grabbed the coms handset so he could speak directly with this new ship. "My name is Commander Joe Reynolds. I am the captain of this ship. Our race is also at war with the Zodarks. Is it possible for us to talk further with you about a possible military alliance to fight against the Zodarks together? Our sensors show there is at least one Zodark ship in this system. It may not be safe for us to stay here much longer."

A second later, the alien ship replied. "Our sensors show the Zodark ship in the system is a transport ship. It is not a threat. The nearest Zodark warship is several systems away. We are safe to continue talking here. If a Zodark warship jumps into the system, our ship is more than capable of destroying it."

This was the best news Reynolds had heard in a long time. Reynolds depressed the talk button on the hand mic. "I would welcome the opportunity for us to continue talking. Are you willing to accept an electronic file? My people have put together a package of data that explains more about our race, who we are as a people, and some history about us. This is part of what we call our first contact protocol. Would you like to receive this exchange of information?"

A moment later, the Altairians replied. "Yes, please send the information. We will review it. We also have a similar package of data we can send you. In the meantime, let us continue to talk. How did you first encounter the Zodarks?"

"We first discovered the Zodarks almost seven of our years ago," Reynolds answered. "We encountered them on a planet we call New Eden in the Rhea system; the Zodarks call this planet Clovis. They had enslaved another human race called the Sumerians there. We liberated the enslaved Sumerians on the planet and have been fighting the Zodarks ever since."

For the next hour, the two ships sat at the gate, talking and exchanging information. That hour turned into six hours. Eventually, it turned into three days. The Altairians then offered to use their advanced form of travel to transport the *Franklin* back to the Rhea system. They said they would like to speak in person with the leaders of the humans and determine if an alliance could be formed.

At first, Reynolds wasn't sure what to do with this proposal. This was an incredible opportunity, but what if this new race didn't really want an alliance? What if they just wanted the location of the human forces so they could destroy them? This was a major dilemma.

*Crap, I already told them we encountered the Zodarks in the Rhea system*, Reynolds chided himself. *At least I didn't tell them about Sol.*

The Altairians agreed to transport them to the stargate in Rhea. They'd stay near the stargate until a meeting was secured. A short while later, the Altairians' ship generated a wormhole, allowing both vessels to pass through it. Moments later, they appeared a hundred thousand kilometers away from the stargate in the Rhea system, a distance that would have taken the Earthers three months to travel.

As soon as they jumped into the system, the *Franklin*'s sensors lit up like a Christmas tree—eight human ships on guard duty near the gate painted their ship, and presumably the Altairians' ship, with their targeting lasers.

Grabbing the ship's mic, Reynolds announced over an open channel, "This is Lieutenant Commander Joe Reynolds, captain of the RNS *Franklin*. Identification code Zulu-Niner-Niner-Zed-Lima-Charlie. Stand down weapons lock. This other ship is here under my protection. I am requesting to speak with Vice Admiral Halsey immediately."

A few seconds passed as the human ships near the gate all changed their lazy circling patterns around the gate to form up into two distinct attack groups.

"We're being hailed," Ethan announced. "It's the *O'Brian*."

Reynolds smiled. He knew the captain of the *O'Brian*. They had gone to officer candidate school together many years ago.

"Joe, is that really you?" asked a familiar voice.

"It's me, John. Don't blast away at us. I need to talk to Admiral Halsey," Reynolds replied.

"The *O'Brian* just sent a stand-down order to the rest of the ships," Ethan announced, clearly relieved. "They've authenticated our codes. They're sending a message back to New Eden, sir."

Jumping into a heavily militarized stargate with an unknown starship in tow wasn't exactly a smart move. Reynolds didn't know how else to do this, though.

"The *O'Brian* is asking to speak with you in private," Ethan told Reynolds. "Should I patch it through to your communicator?"

"Yeah, send it."

A second later, Lieutenant Commander John Blanch came over the radio. "Joe, what the hell is going on, and what is that unknown ship? Our sensors are showing they locked us all up as soon as it jumped in."

"Did they unlock once you stood down?" Reynolds asked.

"Yeah, they did. What's going on?"

"It's a long story, John. Let's just say we fell down the rabbit hole and came out the other end with a potential new friend," Reynolds replied cryptically.

A short pause ensued.

Reynolds looked at the main monitor and the tactical screen on the bridge. He saw his friend had redeployed his squadron in a defensive position. They weren't lining up for an attack anymore, but they were positioned to pounce on them if things went sideways or didn't pass the stink test.

"You've been gone, what, three months, Joe?"

"Yeah, something like that. Have any of the other scouts reported in yet?" Reynolds's asked.

Their ship wasn't the only frigate out doing deep space reconnaissance. Four other scouts had been sent in different directions with orders to travel for two months in one direction and then return with the information they'd discovered. Space Command was doing its best to get a better understanding of who and what was on the other end of these stargates. It was a daunting task, and a risky move considering there was virtually no help coming should their ships run into trouble.

"Not yet, Joe. You're the first one. I must say, we weren't expecting you to appear as you did. Our sensors told us a space-time hole or something like that appeared, and then these two ships suddenly popped out. What the heck is going on, Joe?" His friend pressed.

Reynolds sighed to himself, then explained what had happened when they were exploring Zodark space. He told him about the discovery of the Sumerian home world, Sumer, and the other human world. He explained how this other ship had appeared right in front of them near a stargate, and they had started talking. He and John talked privately for maybe ten more minutes before a hail finally came in from the *Voyager*, Admiral Halsey's flagship.

There was a bit of a time lag in the message, but they could still talk. "Commander Reynolds, this is Admiral Halsey. I just received a flash message from Commander Blanch that the *Franklin* and an unknown starship just appeared out of nowhere near the gate. What the hell is going on, Commander?" There was a bit of steel in her voice as she questioned him.

The only time Joe had ever met Admiral Halsey was when she had awarded him, Ethan and three others a Silver Star medal and promoted them all one grade. Even at his rank, he didn't usually talk to officers with as many stars on their collar as she had.

Reynolds explained what he had just told his friend. He also ordered Ethan to send her the data packet of information they'd both collected on their mission, and the packet they'd received from the Altairians. The time delay was killing Reynolds. There was roughly a ten-minute delay between when he'd ask a question and receive a reply.

Eventually, the delay got annoying to the admiral as well. She requested that Reynolds escort this new ship to New Eden. She'd meet with them in person.

Reynolds relayed the information to the Altairian ship, who said they'd follow the *Franklin* to the destination.

"Do you need us to send you the coordinates?" Reynolds asked.

"Our sensors have already identified the ship that the admiral is on," the Altairians replied. "We'll follow you to the location."

That information unnerved Reynolds. It meant this race was probably a *lot* more advanced than the Zodarks.

*God, I hope we found a new friend*, Reynolds thought. He didn't think the human species could survive another hostile enemy like the Zodarks.

*******

**RNS *Voyager***

"What can you tell me about this unknown ship?" Admiral Halsey asked her tactical officer. The *Franklin* and this new ship had dropped out of warp. The two of them were now approaching the *Voyager* and her meager fleet around New Eden.

They'd received some preliminary information from the guard force around the gate, but they were still trying to make heads or tails of it. All they knew thus far was the ship could travel via temporary wormholes they generated on their own. Their sensors also appeared to be more powerful than theirs or the Zodarks.

Lieutenant Adams, her coms officer, interrupted before they could discuss anything further about the alien ship. "Admiral, we're being hailed by them."

Halsey straightened her uniform blouse as she stood up. "Patch them through with video and audio," she replied.

A moment later, she was talking with them. The Altairians didn't share a video link with her, but their audio came through clearly, in English. Thanks to the information Commander Reynolds had shared with them, they had integrated the English language into their translator.

The Altairians asked if Admiral Halsey and any of her officers would like to speak with them in person on their ship. "We breathe a similar atmosphere," said their spokesperson. "If you meet on our vessel, we'll provide you with a medical device that will allow you to breathe our atmosphere without harming your human bodies."

Halsey had to think about that for a moment. This was an incredibly precarious situation. If she went over to their ship and something happened, she wouldn't be able to order her minimal fleet to respond. The *GW* hadn't returned with additional reinforcements yet. If this ship decided to attack them, she didn't have a prayer. Then again, if they had wanted to attack them, they probably would have already.

Before she agreed to go over to their ship, she ordered one of the frigates in her fleet back to Sol to take all this information about the Altairians and the info the *Franklin* had gathered to Space Command HQ, Admiral Hunt and his fleet. She had to make sure they knew what might be coming if this didn't work out.

Finally, Halsey turned to her XO. "Captain Johnson, you have the ship. You are temporarily in command of the fleet in case something happens. Inform Chief Riggs to join me."

A few minutes later, Admiral Halsey and Master Chief Riggs stood in the location where the Altairians told them to stand on their bridge. Halsey took a deep breath and then announced, "We're ready."

Some twinkling lights started swirling around them. Halsey saw the people on the bridge look on with surprise, and then they were gone. The next thing she saw was a sterile-looking white room coming into focus. Then the twinkling lights stopped, and she was on a foreign ship.

Halsey didn't move right away. She stood there for a moment, trying to get her bearings. Looking to her right, she saw four figures standing there, observing her.

The Altairians were a lot less menacing in appearance than the Zodarks. For one, they were about five and a half feet tall, so relatively short in the eyes of humans. The aliens seemed somewhat similar to a human in that they had two arms and two legs, only their hands appeared to have six fingers and a thumb. Their skin was pure white and looked tough, almost like leather. The hair on their heads was thin-looking, cut short, and pure white. Other than their heads, the rest of their body didn't appear to have any hair. What unnerved Halsey a bit was their eyes. They were cobalt black with no discernible pupils, and they didn't have eyelids, so they never blinked. It was kind of odd, and unnerving if she stared at them too long.

Turning to face them, Halsey announced, "Hello, my name is Vice Admiral Abigail Halsey. I am the commanding officer for all human forces and operations in this sector. Who are you?"

Chief Riggs looked nervously at her but kept his mouth shut. He was here to observe and offer her counsel, not speak unless asked to.

"Hello, Abigail. Abigail, I may call you?" one of the aliens asked.

Halsey nodded. "Yes, that is my first name. Halsey is my surname or family name, and Vice Admiral is my rank," she clarified.

The smallish alien only nodded. "Thank you for that brief explanation. That is what our protocol program confirmed for us. My name is Handolly. I am the protocol officer for this ship. Standing next to me is Pandolly. He is the captain of this ship. The two other individuals are medical technicians. With your permission, we would like to give you these breathing devices to use during our talk. The oxygen levels on our ship are about twenty percent less than your body needs. If you take a breath every few minutes from these devices, they will help your body handle the decreased oxygen level on our ship."

The two other aliens walked cautiously to the humans and handed them what looked like two inhalers, then explained how to use them. After Halsey used it the first time, she felt the difference; it was like she had been on top of a mountain and suddenly traveled down to sea level.

"Abigail, please take a seat over here," one of them requested, and she and Chief Riggs joined the group of four Altairians at the table.

The protocol officer, Handolly, spoke first. "Abigail, to you, I must confess something. Our race, the Altairians, have known about your species for many thousands of years. We know about your home world, Earth, and your solar system—although we had thought that the last of the Earth humans had perished in a planetwide extinction event. We have been quietly monitoring human evolutionary development and scientific discoveries for some time. However, when one of your Earther ships appeared in the system UAAU-C, we decided it was time for us to meet and introduce ourselves formally."

Abigail had to fight back the urge to look surprised or angry. She wanted to keep her face as passive as she could. But this acknowledgment by this alien creature had caught her off guard.

Before she could say something, the protocol officer continued, "Our species has made it a point of principle to allow other species to self-govern, evolve and advance on their own without interference on our part. We are very different from the Zodarks and the Orbots, which are their patrons. Both of these species look to conquer and subjugate other species as they grow their empire to serve their expansionist goals."

Halsey took a hit from the inhaler before she interjected, "Hold up a second, Handolly. You're saying the Zodarks are a lesser species or client race of another race in some grand galactic scheme?"

The Altairian didn't speak right away. Instead, it typed away on a keyboard that appeared on the table in front of him. A second later, a holographic image appeared over the center of the table between them. It then populated with data and images of this other species that caused Abigail and even Chief Riggs to gasp a bit.

The Altairians then changed the image to show the vastness of space and the numerous galaxies within it. Handolly explained, "Abigail, it might be easier for me to explain our interactions with humans and a little history of the galaxy from the beginning. The universe, as you can imagine, is a vast place with more than two hundred billion galaxies. There are thousands of species that occupy tens of thousands of habitable planets across the vastness of space. Habitable planets, however, are still scarce, which means they are often fought over to see who will retain control. I should also explain that while there are thousands of species in the universe, only a small percentage of them could be considered sentient. An even smaller percentage are spacefaring races."

Admiral Halsey and Chief Riggs both took a hit from their inhalers as they continued to absorb the information the Altairians were throwing at them. Halsey thought if she hadn't received those brain implants more than a decade ago, most of it probably would have gone over her head. As it was, her brain was wired to use a higher percentage of her potential cognitive power. This meant she was grasping much more than she otherwise would have.

Handolly continued to explain. "Your planet, Abigail, resides in what you call the Milky Way Galaxy. Our home world also resides in the same galaxy, though our planet is more than two thousand light-years from Earth. Each galaxy has some spacefaring races that fight for control of both their own galaxy and the habitable planets in it. Some races have consolidated their galaxies, and those races now wage war on other galaxies to control them as well.

"In our galaxy, we Altairians have been fighting a race called the Orbots. They are an advanced species that consist of creatures who are part biological and part machine. Their client race or proxy is the Zodarks, though they have several other client races that serve them as well."

An image of what the Orbots looked like appeared on the holograph floating in the center of the table. They were an ugly race. They had a mechanical body that consisted of four spiderlike legs and two arms with hands. The Orbots stood six feet in height, nearly half the size of the Zodarks. Half of their face looked like it was biological, while the other half looked mechanical. They looked like a mad scientist had put them together.

Handolly saw their facial expressions when he showed them what the Orbots looked like. "The Orbots are a uniquely dangerous race. They weren't always like this. There was a time when our two species actually got along. Several thousand years ago, they began to experiment with cybernetics and created a cyborg caste of warriors to fight for them. We are not sure what happened, but something caused this cyborg caste to overthrow their creators, and they turned their species into what they are now. This was when they became Orbots. I believe the term Orbots in our language translates to cyborgs in your language."

*God, I hope that doesn't happen to us with the C100s,* Halsey thought. She was personally not in favor of developing combat Synths after what had happened in the last Great War, but this was something that was still above her paygrade.

Handolly paused for a second, seemingly evaluating her body language, and then he continued. "Because they are half-machine, half-biological, they now believe they are the master race of the universe and therefore should be the only race. They maintain non-Orbot allies, like the Zodarks and others, but that is largely to use them as foot soldiers to fight their wars. They provide them with some technology and assistance to help them win wars or battles, but they also make sure to keep them dependent on them. This ensures their client species never become strong enough to challenge them. We Altairians believe that one day, the Orbots will force even their client species to assimilate into their collective hive—"

Halsey interrupted, "If they have essentially become cyborgs or half biologicals, do they still breed to grow their numbers, or is that only done through forced assimilation?"

"The Orbots still maintain a caste of society that is fully biological, used only for breeding. At a certain age, the adult biologicals are turned into the creatures you see before you. Being machines, they can share and grow their knowledge base as a collective. What one Orbots thinks or knows, the collective knows. It is how they can pass down thousands of years of knowledge and information. It's also what makes them so dangerous—"

"I'm sorry, how is any of this even possible?" Halsey pressed. "I mean, why would the Zodarks go along with something like this and not just turn on the Orbots?" She struggled to wrap her head around this whole thing.

Pandolly, the ship captain, answered. "Admiral, the Orbots are an advanced race like us. Tens of thousands of years old. The Orbots and we Altairians have been spacefaring people for thousands of years. Our two species have been able to invent incredible technologies and travel the stars. Still, the one thing neither of our species has been able to overcome is death. Some of us may die in battle, some from an accident, but many of us will, at some point, die of old age.

"The age-old question is what happens after we die. Some species believe in a deity, a god that created life and death. I am not going to have a philosophical debate on whether there is or is not a god; what I will tell you is it was this search for a god that ultimately led to the Orbots becoming what they now are. They believed they could transcend their physical bodies by becoming cyborgs.

"However, even though the vast majority of their bodies are now mechanical, their brains are still biological. It was this biology that led them to create what we now call the Hive. This is where their collective shared knowledge and identities reside. By creating this Hive, they believe they have now transcended their biological limits and become deities themselves. This is what makes them so dangerous, and why we Altairians have been fighting against them now for thousands of years— to prevent them from doing this to the rest of the galaxy."

Chief Riggs broke into the conversation. "Pandolly, if the Orbots believe they have ascended to some higher state of being, what is the purpose of their alliance with the Zodarks or any other species? Why do they need them? Can't they just produce a mechanical army of Orbots to fight for them?"

Pandolly raised both hands, in what seemed to be the equivalent of a nod. "Ian, as Handolly explained earlier, space is a vast place. There are literally millions of systems with planets in each of them. The Orbots use their allies to help them expand their empire.

"Before the Orbots discovered the Zodarks eight thousand years ago, there was another species called the Rindulu. They controlled more than fifty star systems at one time. They fought with the Orbots for many hundreds of years. They realized the Orbots were just using them and that, one day, they would be assimilated into their collective Hive, just like the other species they had helped the Orbots subjugate. By the time the Rindulu rebelled against the Orbots, it was too late. They had become too dependent on the Orbots' technology, and the Orbots were able to control their technology and use it against them. Whether the Zodarks want to acknowledge this or not, it will eventually happen to them."

Halsey interjected, "Pandolly, is it possible the Zodarks have found a way not to be controlled by the Orbots like the Rindulu?"

Handolly and Pandolly looked at each other before returning their gaze back to Abigail. "It is possible. Anything is possible," Pandolly replied. "What I think more likely is that the Orbots are content in allowing the Zodarks to build up their own fiefdom in the stars and will at some point swoop in to snatch it from them."

"Pandolly, why haven't we encountered the Orbots during any of our battles with the Zodarks?" Abigail asked.

This time, Handolly answered the question. "Abigail, even the Orbots have physical limits with their part-mechanical, part-biological bodies. This is where the Zodarks come into play. The Zodarks are 'their muscle,' as you would say in your language. They have passed down considerable technology to them, but not so much that the Zodarks could hope to challenge them. The Zodarks, in return, are allowed a large swath of space to call their own. Still, they report to the Orbots and support their military campaigns."

After taking a hit from the inhaler, Abigail held up a hand to pause again. "Handolly, this is some incredible information you've shared with us. But how do we humans fit into this equation? Why are there humans on other planets?"

Handolly didn't say anything right away. Instead, he typed something on a digital keyboard that suddenly appeared in front of him. Moments later, the lights in the room dimmed, and a holographic image of Earth or a planet similar to Earth floated in the center of the table.

The Altairian explained, "I told you earlier that our people have known about humans for some time. What I want to show you right now is how and why there are humans on other worlds than just Earth, and how that came to be.

"This is an image of your home world, Earth, twelve thousand years ago. Your world was an incredible biosphere of living creatures and humans, encased in a protective water sphere. The fact is, we discovered your planet by a complete accident. We had a ship in a nearby system monitoring a large comet that was traveling through several star systems.

"A star had gone supernova, and when that happened, it expelled a lot of material in all directions. One of the planets in that system that had been destroyed was a large ice planet. When it broke up, it formed multiple ice comets that struck out in all directions. One of the comets struck one of our colonies and destroyed it. It was a small colony—a new one we had recently established, so we did not have any early warning or defensive systems in place. In the aftermath of its destruction, we sought to monitor and, if need be, intercept these comets before they could destroy any other worlds."

Handolly paused a moment. Halsey couldn't read his facial expressions, so it was hard to tell what was going through his mind. "Habitable planets are rare in the galaxy, Abigail," he said. "Even if we cannot colonize them, they almost always have some form of life developing on them. We Altairians consider ourselves to be one of the elder races in the galaxy as we have been a spacefaring species now for tens of thousands of years. As such, we believe it is our responsibility to protect as many habitable planets as possible so new life can be cultivated on them.

"When we saw the comet was on a trajectory that would impact Earth, we tried multiple times to destroy it. We succeeded in destroying a large part of it, but there was an ice core we could not eliminate, even with our advanced technologies. When all of our attempts to save your planet failed, we identified two planets that could support and sustain your species."

"We dispatched ships to your planet to evacuate your people and transported the humans we could save to these two planets. As the comet neared Earth, we abandoned the remaining humans. When the comet hit, it broke through the water barrier that had encompassed Earth, causing all the water to rush onto the planet, and impacted in an area you now call Russia. I believe your religious people now call it the Great Flood and relate it to a religious person called Noah in your Christian Bible. When the flood happened, it absorbed all the dust from the comet's impact that would have wiped your species out. The catastrophic event also killed off all your dinosaurs due to the floodwaters and the massive atmospheric pressure difference the absence of the water sphere had created on the planet.

"Your species, Abigail, was the most resilient of them all. Humans were somehow able to adapt to the atmospheric change and survived, although the lifespan of your species dropped significantly. Your bodies were used to the higher levels of oxygen, which allowed you to live longer lives. Considering your species was supposed to have been wiped out, it is amazing any of you survived." As Handolly spoke, the holographic image floating in front of them told its own story, a visual version of what he was describing.

Chief Riggs spoke up again. "So, the Altairians moved a small number of humans to two new planets. How did the *Zodarks* acquire humans, and why are there humans on so many other planets? How did that happen?"

Handolly turned to Riggs. "The humans we saved flourished on the two planets we placed them on. Their societies grew much like Earth. A client race of ours, the Primords or Prims as we call them, first encountered the Zodarks roughly three thousand of your years ago. We provided technology to them so they could fight the Zodarks and protect a section of space they lived in. We helped them expand and secure their territory from the Zodarks."

Chief Riggs and Admiral Halsey both leaned forward as they listened to Handolly, totally mesmerized by what he was telling them.

Handolly continued, "Around two thousand of your years ago, the Orbots started to lose their war against us. It was around this time they began to give the Zodarks a lot of new technology—technology that allowed them to skip hundreds, even thousands of years of development. The Orbots equipped and trained the Zodarks to become a true fighting force that could assist them in their war against us. Shortly after that, the Orbots directed the Zodarks to attack the Primords."

Handolly showed them a giant star map of several star systems and regions of space that Admiral Halsey was not familiar with. "For a few hundred years, the Primords and the Zodarks fought each other to a standstill. While the Zodarks were fierce warriors, their starships were no match for what we had provided to the Prims. That changed when the Orbots gave them the warp drive, or what you call FTL or faster-than-light travel.

"We have another ally from a nearby galaxy called the Gallentines. They are a near-peer species to us, an elder race if you will. Our military assisted them in a campaign against one of their enemies. In exchange for our help, the Gallentines assisted us in capturing one of the Orbots' core home worlds. This was a turning point in our thousand-year war. It was a huge defeat for the Orbots and forced them to pursue a peace treaty with us.

"When a cease-fire was achieved, the Orbots knew they could not retake the two systems and five planets we had captured without the help of the Zodarks. As you can see from our stature, we are not a physically large species. Besides their significant height advantage, the Zodarks are incredible warriors when it comes to ground combat. The Orbots marshaled their fleet and helped the Zodarks crush our allies, the Prims.

"Unfortunately, we were not able to help the Prims in time. The Prims lost most of their core worlds. They managed to hold on to a few systems, but they lost more than seventy percent of their previous territory. We provided them with enough advanced technology to stop the Zodarks from wiping them out. Still, it will be a long time until we can count on the Prims to help us battle the Zodarks or the Orbots again."

Seeing a break in the explanation Handolly was giving them, Chief Riggs interjected, "Handolly, that still didn't answer my original question—how are there humans now on several planets?"

Halsey turned to look at Riggs, shooting him a look that said he should stay silent for the moment and let these new friends of theirs talk. Seeing his cheeks redden, she knew he'd received the nonverbal message.

"Ah, yes, my apologies," Handolly said. "I was giving you an overview of what had happened with these human worlds. When the Prims lost control of their space, the two planets we had placed the humans on were part of that space. The Zodarks, as you know, are meat eaters. While they do eat human flesh from time to time, they are not culling them for food as many of the Sumerians believe or may have told you."

"Whoa, what do you mean, 'as the Sumerians believe'?" asked Halsey heatedly. "We haven't told you anything about the Sumerians or what they told us."

Pandolly, the Altairian ship captain, spoke up this time. "Admiral Halsey," he said, using her formal rank, "we know everything about your encounter with the Sumerians and everything they have shared with you up to this point. You may think your computer systems are secure, but our sensors have already scanned and assimilated everything your society and people know up to this point."

Now Halsey was piping mad. She held a hand up to stop him from speaking further. "You've penetrated our systems? How dare you!" she barked.

Chief Riggs reached his hand over and placed it on her left forearm, whispering softly, "Admiral, it won't do any good to get mad at them. They are clearly a super-advanced society. You had to expect they'd have some kind of ability like this."

Halsey let out a sigh and slowly nodded. She whispered back, "You're right. I lost my cool."

"My apologies, Captain," she said to Pandolly. "I shouldn't have gotten angry at you. You are doing what you feel is best to protect your ship and people. I'd do the same thing if I were in your position."

The Altairian lowered his head in acknowledgment of what she had said.

"Abigail, we mean you and the people of Earth no harm," Handolly replied. "If we wanted to harm you, our single ship could do so. Please, let me finish explaining what has happened to your fellow humans.

"What the Sumerians have told you is religious folklore—it is not factually true. The Zodarks have created rumors, stories that they are like demigods, and that they cull a percentage of humans as a sacrifice to them, to be eaten like cattle. This is all wrong. The Zodarks have actually taken this percentage of people and brought them to a new planet deep within their space.

"The Zodarks have shared a great deal of their technology with this group of humans, and so have the Orbots. As a matter of fact, the Orbots have even allowed some of the humans to create their own humanoid versions of themselves, half-human, half-machine cyborgs just like them. The Zodarks and the Orbots have been using this process of culling these other human worlds to create an army of new soldiers to fight us. You see, the Zodarks, like the Orbots, do not procreate quickly or often. So while they have vast sprawling empires, planets, and colonies, their populations do not increase rapidly. Each major battle, whether won or lost, continues to diminish their population. It is only during the periods of peace that either species has succeeded in growing its population. Humans, however, can procreate rapidly and often, thus giving both species a near-endless supply of soldiers."

"As to your question, Chief Riggs," Pandolly said as he moved to answer his question. "The Zodarks took the humans from the two planets we had placed them on and populated many other habitable planets with them. They did this for the reasons I just stated—to allow their populations to multiply, so they could be culled and brought to other planets deeper in their territory and used to create these new soldiers to fight for them. You see, while the Zodarks are a client species of the Orbots, the Zodarks have now made the humans from these planets a client species of the Zodarks. The Orbots, of course, have caught on to this as well and have begun spawning their own colonies of humans. After all, they couldn't let the Zodarks grow too big, or one day they might overthrow them."

Shaking her head dismissively, Abigail uttered softly, "Humans are the slave caste of the galaxy."

Pandolly, the Altairian ship captain, heard her comment. "I can understand you believing that, Abigail. Our experience with humans shows them to be among the most adaptive, clever, and ferocious species in the galaxy. Just look at how your people found a way to survive the Great Flood—we had written the rest of the humans off.

"When you began fighting the Zodarks a few years ago, you certainly caught their attention after you destroyed a few of their ships. When we heard you had defeated a Zodark battlegroup, our elders ordered us to make contact with you. Our orders are to assess if your people can be cultivated into a true ally that could help us fight the Orbots and their client species."

Halsey sat a little straighter in her chair. "For the last seven years, our people have fought and defeated the Zodarks. We have successfully integrated both their technology and Sumerian technology into our own. This has given us the technological edge to defeat them. It is my firm belief that, with some assistance, we would be able to help you defeat the Zodarks and the Orbots."

Pandolly countered, "How would you begin to defeat the Zodarks? Even now, there is a second battlegroup being dispatched to deal with you."

This news of a second battlegroup caused Halsey's heart to race a bit. She knew the human fleet wasn't ready for another significant clash just yet. Admiral Hunt's fleet was still back in Sol, and many of the replacement ships they had under construction weren't ready yet.

Chief Riggs leaned over and whispered in Halsey's ear. "Admiral, may I give them an idea of what we are planning?"

She turned and looked at him briefly, then nodded her head in approval.

"Pandolly, our plan is to liberate the Sumerian home world, Sumer. With their help, we would bring that human world into the fold of our alliance. Then we would liberate the remaining human-occupied planets along the chain of systems where you encountered the *Franklin*. Our goal is to integrate these human worlds into our military and industrial base. This would allow us to grow our fleets and carve out a piece of territory while we continue to build up our forces.

"What you've just told us about how the Zodarks have been using these human worlds shines a whole new light on the situation. By removing the Sumerians from the Zodarks' control, we'll reduce their ability to use the humans there as their soldiers against us in the future."

For close to a minute, no one said anything. From Halsey and Riggs's point of view, it was hard to tell what the two Altairians were thinking. Their facial expressions were either too subtle or nonexistent.

Finally, Handolly, the protocol officer, spoke. "Admiral Halsey," he began, using her formal rank and not her given name like they had been up to this point, "I would like to speak with the leaders of Earth and the military commander Rear Admiral Miles Hunt."

Halsey furrowed her brow at the mention of Admiral Hunt. "Our military commander is a man by the name of Fleet Admiral Chester Bailey," she replied. "Rear Admiral Miles Hunt is our expeditionary commander. His fleet is currently in the shipyard undergoing repairs. Right now, I am the military commander for this sector."

This time Pandolly spoke. "Admiral, we understand your military rank structure. We've reviewed the summaries of your battles with the Zodarks. Your Admiral Miles Hunt is by far your most competent and experienced military commander. If we are to entertain a military alliance with your species, we will want only the most capable military officers to be in charge of the new warships and weapons we will be teaching you how to build.

"We also know Earth is currently ruled by two factions, your faction and another group you call the Tri-Parte Alliance. This power dynamic will also need to be resolved if we are to allow you to join our alliance. We are not going to support one faction over another. If you are amenable to this arrangement, then I would like you to send a message to your second-in-command and tell her that you will be accompanying us to Earth to introduce us to your leaders and this Admiral Hunt."

Halsey was a bit taken aback by the sudden demand, and she stumbled briefly for what to say. "Uh, normally it would take us four days to travel to Earth from here. I really can't be away from my command for that long. Especially if you say a new Zodark battlegroup is headed towards us," she replied, hoping she wasn't causing a diplomatic problem with the Altairians.

Handolly gave a slight wave of his hand as if to dismiss her concern. "Abigail," he said, slipping back into a casual form of address, "our ship can travel from here to Earth in less than a minute. You will only be gone a day. Then we will return you to your fleet. As to the Zodark fleet heading here…they are still more than two months away. We have plenty of time to help you organize a defense that will defeat them."

Halsey's eyes widened and she tried hard to keep her jaw from dropping to the floor. She knew the Altairians were fast, but she had yet to understand their full capabilities. *If the Altairians can show us how to travel with that kind of speed, then the entire galaxy just got a lot smaller*, she thought, processing the possibilities.

She gulped down her surprise and did her best to maintain an even keel. "OK, Handolly, I will send a message to my ship and relay what you just told me," she said as she touched her communicator, connecting her to Captain Johnson on the bridge of the *Voyager*.

# Chapter Seventeen
## The Elders

### John Glenn Orbital Station
### First Fleet Headquarters

Rear Admiral Miles Hunt lay in bed, looking at the ceiling as he remembered the night before. He and Lilly had gone to a great dinner party and stayed out rather late. He enjoyed being home to rekindle some relationships and friendships that had fallen by the wayside during his years of being deployed, even if it was for just ten days at a time.

His only gripe now was that, despite being home on leave, he still couldn't sleep past 0500 hours. Decades of military rigidity beaten into him seldom allowed him to sleep in.

The repairs on his ship, the *George Washington,* had been completed nearly a month ago. With no sign of the Zodarks, Space Command had kept them in station longer so additional minor repairs could continue to take place. The added time at the station gave his crew the chance to take leave and spend much-needed time with their families. They knew when they left Earth this next time around, they'd be gone for probably at least a year if not longer.

Turning over in bed, Hunt saw Lilly was still asleep, dead to the world. He stared back at the ceiling, and his thoughts drifted to his son, Ethan. He'd nearly lost him in that last battle over New Eden. By the time his ship had arrived, the battle had been over. Hunt had been powerless to help his son, and that had really affected him. He was proud of Ethan and the way he'd handled himself. He was especially proud when his commander had put him in for a Silver Star, saying it was his superb ability to fight and fly the ship at the same time that had helped them win the day.

Hunt had thought he could get his son a posting on Admiral Bailey's staff or maybe a safer job back in Sol now that he had seen some action and earned a couple of combat medals, but when the *Franklin* came out of the shipyard, his son had volunteered for it faster than he could get him a new assignment. Now Ethan's ship was on a deep space patrol, and the *Franklin* had been gone for nearly three months. A once-a-month com drone told them that they were still alive, but the *Franklin* still had another month until it was due back in Rhea.

252

Just as Hunt was about to climb out of bed and take a shower, his communicator chirped, letting him know someone was trying to reach him. Reaching for the device, he laughed privately at how that damn little thing had ruined his thirtieth wedding anniversary in Bora Bora. Depressing the talk button, he said, "Admiral Hunt. Send it."

"Admiral, this is Captain McKee. We're receiving a flash message from Admiral Halsey. You're not going to believe this, sir."

Hunt shook his head. "Calm down, Captain. I'm in my quarters. Go ahead and tell me. I want to grab a shower before I head over to the ship."

The radio squawked briefly as Captain McKee made sure no one was electronically listening in on their conversation. It might have been an encrypted communicator, but there was a lot of sophisticated military equipment hanging around this station that could crack it.

"Admiral, she says they encountered a new alien species. They're transporting her and her senior enlisted advisor to Earth to meet with President Luca, Fleet Admiral Bailey, and *you*, sir."

*Ah hell, this must be a joke*, Hunt thought. *The crew's trying to prank me before we head back out on patrol.* His blood pressure started to elevate at the thought that this was a practical joke.

A second later, his communicator emitted a loud gong sound and then an alarm that'd wake the dead. Well, the dead except his wife, who somehow managed to sleep through the general quarters alarm being blared through every Space Command communicator on the station.

*Crap, it's real*, he thought in horror, wondering whether the *GW* was about to be attacked. *I better get back to the ship ASAP.*

Hunt depressed the talk button. "I'm on my way. Bring the ship to general quarters. If you need to do an emergency separation from the station before I get there, do it."

Hunt grabbed his trousers and put them on, sliding his feet into his boots next as he reached for his blouse. He didn't even try to wake Lilly; he grabbed his cap and bolted out the door.

As he ran through the corridor, Hunt was still buttoning up his blouse. He rounded the corner out of officer country and sprinted into the main hallway leading to the ship piers. He made it just in time to hop on the tram before it took off.

When the driver saw his rank, he immediately asked, "What ship, Admiral?"

"The *GW*," Hunt ordered as he finished tying off his boots and situating his uniform.

The *GW* was on the far side of the docking pier of the station. As the tram zipped past other docking slips, some of the passengers did their best to jump off. A few went tumbling, but generally they managed to get off without hurting themselves. Those officers and enlisted ran for their own ships.

By the time Hunt made it to the *GW*, they were just getting ready to close the gate connecting the ship. When the guards saw Hunt and a couple dozen crewmen jump off the tram and start running for them, they held the door open just long enough for them to make it through.

A few minutes later, they were on the *GW*. The door behind them shut moments later, fully sealing the ship off from the station. Hunt hadn't even moved a dozen feet when he felt the warship shudder slightly.

*Fran's pushing off from the station*, he realized.

Hunt ran over to one of the shipboard trams and hopped on. The tram would zip him and the others on board over to the center part of the ship and several other trams and elevator banks. It was the fastest way to move from one end to the other end of this four-kilometer long warship.

When they reached the elevator bank, Hunt jumped in and announced to the computer, "Bridge. Now!"

The ship's AI recognized his voice and proceeded to take everyone to the bridge first. Getting him to the bridge was the priority. It would drop everyone else off on their floors later.

Running off the elevator, Hunt barged on to the bridge just in time to see an unknown ship jump into the system. It emerged out of nowhere, less than a million kilometers from the station.

*Holy crap! What the hell is that?* was all Hunt could say to himself as he made a beeline to his command chair.

"Get us away from the station and start to spin up our primary and secondary turrets. EWO! Get us a lock on that ship and prepare to start jamming them!" Hunt barked as the bridge crew went to work preparing to defend Earth and the station from this new and unknown threat.

A second later, an image appeared on the main screen. It was Admiral Halsey and Chief Riggs. They were standing next to two aliens that didn't look anything like the Zodarks.

"Admiral Hunt, I know you're in the process of getting the *GW* ready to engage this ship. I need you to stand down, Admiral. These are the Altairians. They are here under my request to speak with President Luca, Admiral Bailey, and you. Please acknowledge you've heard this message," Halsey ordered.

*What the hell is this?*

Hunt grabbed for the communicator. "Admiral Halsey, when you and I served on the Ganymede mission, why did you order us to eat all the steaks the first day we arrived in orbit?"

Captain Fran McKee and the others on the bridge all turned to look at Hunt with a quizzical look that said *What are you doing?*

Almost laughing, Admiral Halsey countered, "Good try, Miles. It was the Io mission, and our refrigerator stopped working. We didn't eat all the steaks on the first day in orbit; it was the fifth day. Did I pass your test?" She had a mischievous grin on her face.

Smiling, Hunt turned to Captain McKee. "Order the ship to stand down. It's her, she's telling the truth."

"Thank you, Miles," said Halsey. "Chief Riggs and I, along with our two new friends, are going to meet you in your wardroom in five minutes. Please be there to meet us. Halsey out."

*Five minutes—that's not nearly enough time to transfer from one ship to another*, Hunt thought. He told McKee to follow him over to the wardroom, then sent instructions down to his security detachment to send a platoon to the flight deck and the wardroom as well. He wasn't taking any chances.

Hunt and McKee had just reached the wardroom when Admiral Halsey, Chief Riggs, and their two friends suddenly materialized right in front of them. Moments later, President Luca and Fleet Admiral Bailey materialized right next to them.

"What the hell?!" was all Admiral Bailey was able to say before he recognized everyone around him. The man was still in his workout clothes.

Chairman Hong Jinping of the TPA materialized next to them, along with their fleet admiral, Zheng Lee. Both looked extraordinarily startled and bewildered at what had just transpired. One minute they were in China, the next they were in the wardroom of the *George Washington*.

President Luca let out a yelp and gasp. She'd been transported to the *GW* in her sweatpants, and she looked just as surprised as Chairman Hong.

"What the hell is going on?" demanded President Luca and Chairman Hong practically at the same time. The two world leaders were clearly ticked off at suddenly being transported to the *GW*.

"President Luca, Chairman Hong, I apologize for our method of bringing you to this meeting, but it is important that we speak with you all," one of the aliens said as he spoke for the first time.

Everyone except Halsey and Riggs's jaws fell open when they finally realized they had two unknown alien creatures standing a few feet away from them, and they had just spoken.

Admiral Halsey quickly announced, "A lot has happened in the last eight hours. I think it would be best if we all took a seat. I'll bring you up to speed and introduce you both to our new guests."

Hunt nodded in shocked agreement. "Yes, I think that'd be a good idea. Madam President, Chairman Hong, I'll have the galley bring us something to eat and some fresh coffee for everyone."

When the group sat down, Admiral Halsey and the Altairians brought the two world leaders up to speed on what had been discussed. For several hours, the TPA and Republic leaders peppered the Altairians with questions about the Zodarks, the Orbots, the Primords, and how humans had come to be scattered across the galaxy. The Altairians showed them video footage of what the Earth used to look like before the Great Flood. This was the event that had resulted in them resettling humans on other planets to save them from extinction.

After several hours of discussion, the Altairians made their offer. They'd bring the humans into their sphere of influence and under their protective umbrella, but they wanted some things in exchange—namely, for Earth to commit to helping them in their war against the Orbots and their client species, the Zodarks.

President Luca was the first to speak. "Handolly, our people have been at war with the Zodarks for seven years. By your own admission, this war you've been fighting against the Orbots and the Zodarks has been raging for many thousands of years. I'm not sure the people of Earth want to fight a war with no end. What is your solution for winning this war if we were to join your alliance?"

Turning to look at the leader of the Republic, Handolly answered, "Madam President, it is true this war has been going on for many thousands of years. Our species has been fighting the Orbots and their proxies for generations. We must if we want to survive. What should be understood about wars fought in space is that they often do not happen quickly. They take many years and sometimes decades to develop and eventually happen. Space is quite vast, so even with our superior travel speeds, it takes time to move soldiers and ships to do battle. It can take even longer when you have to search for the enemy fleet you want to destroy.

"We ask for Earth's help in fighting the Zodarks and assisting one of our other allies, the Primords, in their own fight against the Zodarks. I cannot tell you how long this war will last, but what I can tell you is this—if the Primords lose their war with the Zodarks, Earth will not last much longer. The Zodarks will either enslave your world or destroy it. We are offering your people a chance to survive and grow among the stars."

Chairman Hong from the TPA spoke next. "If I understand things correctly, Handolly, our choice is to join your alliance and fight in your never-ending war, or we can hope our military will be able to stop this Zodark fleet heading toward the Rhea system? If you ask me, this doesn't seem like a choice, but more like an ultimatum."

This time Pandolly, the military officer, countered, "Mr. Chairman, humans have spent most of your history in one war or another. What we are offering Earth is a chance to join the rest of the civilized starfaring species in an alliance of mutual assistance. We know you have made multiple attempts to contact the Zodarks. They are not interested in peace with your species. They want to subjugate your people and use you as cannon fodder in their own wars. While you may view us as wanting to use you for the same purpose, I can assure you that is not the case.

"If we did not care about sentient beings, we would not have sought to save humanity during your Great Flood some four thousand years ago. Humans are an intelligent and ingenious species—perhaps the most resilient we have ever met. There is so much potential for your species. What we are offering, Mr. Chairman, is an opportunity for your people to survive, thrive, and expand into the stars. We can show you where other habitable planets are that you can colonize. We want to cultivate more civilized species like your own, to grow our alliance with like-minded species. We cannot do that if the Orbots and the Zodarks enslave the galaxy. Will you fight with us? Will you join our cause?"

"If we join this alliance of yours, what other requirements are you going to impose on us aside from providing military support?" asked Admiral Bailey.

"Yes," President Luca said with a nod. "If the people of Earth are going to commit ourselves to this path with the Altairians, what else are you going to require of us?"

Handolly turned to look at them both as he replied, "We will provide Earth with substantial technological advancements, but we need humans to put aside your tribalism notions. If humanity is going to survive in the galaxy, you need to come together as a planet to become one people under one banner. We will need the governments of Earth to unify. We do not care which one of your factions represents Earth, but it will need to be only one. We will only provide our technology to one government, and we will require that government to support the allied war effort."

Chairman Hong cleared his throat. "Handolly, as I am sure you know, we recently started colonizing another planet, Alpha Centauri. Would you accept us having each of our planets operate as loosely governed planets but still falling under one government control?"

The Altairian military officer, Pandolly clarified, "You mean the TPA controlling Alpha Centauri and the Republic controlling Earth?"

Blushing at the bluntness of the question, Chairman Hong just nodded.

Before President Luca or anyone else could interject to say something, Handolly interceded. "Let me be clear, Mr. Chairman, we are not going to dictate how you humans govern or run your planets and colonies. If you join our alliance, we will only accept one government in control of your budding empire. We will help you colonize new worlds, but all of these worlds will subject themselves to a central government. *If* there is any deviation from this government, then your species will be in violation of your treaty with us and be removed from the alliance. If that were to happen, we would cut you off from any further technology sharing, and you would be on your own against the Orbots and their client species. Does that answer your question?"

Chairman Hong didn't say anything right away, but it was clear he had his answer.

President Luca sat up a bit straighter. "Handolly, I'm sure the Chairman and I can come to an agreement on how we will handle this transition. You have to keep in mind that we lead billions of people. These changes will not be easily received by our citizens. We will need some time to make this transition work."

For the next few hours, the Altairians showed the Earthers many technological wonders they'd share with the people of Earth if they joined their alliance. Toward the end of the meeting, they told President Luca and Chairman Hong that they would give them both forty-eight Earth hours to think about the proposal and render a decision. If they opted to join the alliance, then they would send for additional Altairian warships to help them defeat the looming Zodark fleet approaching the Rhea system.
*******

**Two Days Later**

President Alice Luca studied the latest piece of technology the Altairians had shared with them. It was a large tower device that used an organic material that absorbed high concentrations of $CO_2$ emissions and other harmful chemicals that were causing a great deal of harm to the environment. The Altairians said that over the course of two or three decades, just twenty of these devices built in strategic positions around the planet would restore the environment to an optimal level for humans. It was truly incredible. It also produced a nanocarbon byproduct the Altairians said could be used to create very strong and durable body armor for human soldiers, among other domestic uses.

Another piece of technology their new Altairian friends had provided could increase human food production and public safety—a device that could manipulate the weather. While it couldn't make it rain or snow with the flick of a switch, it could influence weather patterns to cause it to rain or snow within a day or two. It could also disrupt the formation of hurricanes, typhoons, cyclones, and tornados. They could also use it to increase the ice formations in the polar caps, reducing the growing concern over their melting.

A third, and perhaps most profound technology transfer the Altairians would give to humans to help sweeten the deal to join their alliance was a medical breakthrough to help heal and restore the human body. Humans had already made significant gains with medical nanites, but the Altairians had taken that technology to the next level. Not only did they provide the missing pieces to prevent cancer from ever occurring in a human body, they also provided long-term cures for Alzheimer's, Parkinson's, MS, and many other diseases, including aging. This massive improvement to medical nanites would mean humans could now live for hundreds of years and essentially never grow old. If anyone had doubts about humans joining forces with the Altairians, these technological advancements put an end to them.

President Luca's secured phone vibrated on her desk, letting her know someone was trying to reach her. Reaching for the device, she saw the call was coming from Chairman Hong's private number. She immediately tapped the connect button.

A second later, a small holographic image of Hong Jinping appeared on Luca's desk. Jinping smiled at her. "Good morning, Madam President," he said in a very chipper tone.

"Good evening, Mr. Chairman," President Luca said with a smile. "To what do I owe this great honor of a private call?"

"I wanted to speak with you away from our advisors and discuss this proposal the Altairians made to us." He cleared his throat. "As you know, at this point, our country has transported more than six million people to Alpha Centauri. The Altairians have said they would share the technology to travel between here and there in minutes—that means we'll be able to keep transporting large swaths of our people to the new colony in even less time. We would also be able to start colonizing the other planets and moons in that system with the technology they are going to give us."

She waited for the punchline, but he paused for a moment, collecting his thoughts. "What I'm trying to say, Alice, is I think you should take control of Earth," he finally said. "I will focus humanity's efforts on the Centauri system."

President Luca was a bit taken aback. She had been anticipating a bit of a drawn-out battle over who would ultimately control Earth and the human governments.

Leaning forward in her chair, she asked, "Why the sudden change of heart, Jinping? I honestly thought you would insist on controlling Earth."

Jinping audibly sighed before he replied, "Alice, my governing style is frankly going to work better in the Centauri system, colonizing and rapidly expanding humanity's presence beyond Earth. You, on the other hand, are going to have a hell of a fight on your hands trying to keep the Zodarks and Orbots at bay. Right this moment, your military force is far superior to ours. If humanity is to have a hope of defeating the Zodarks and these Orbots, then we need our best military force to lead that fight—that's the Republic, not the TPA. It makes sense that the Republic should then lead the Earth and the human race."

President Luca sat back in her chair; she couldn't fault his logic. She just hoped they'd be able to make it work long-term.

"Jinping, if we move forward with this proposal, we either need to put a unity government in place or something to make sure our people do not become estranged or competitors. Humanity is only going to survive this next challenge if we stay united as a race and not divided because we're in different star systems. Does that make sense?" Luca asked.

The holographic image of the TPA leader looked like he was staring off in some other direction for a moment before he returned his gaze to her. "I agree, Alice. Let's establish a senate to act as a governing body for this new republic we're going to be establishing. We can create elected governors to rule over the planets with a certain number of senators from each planet or colony. These senators will propose who should be president; then, the governors will either approve or disapprove of their selection."

A broad smile broke out across Luca's face. "Jinping, you've really put some thought into all of this, but why the sudden move toward a democratic form of government?"

He laughed at her question. "I thought you'd be ecstatic over my sudden support for your system of government."

"I am. It just seems very unexpected, that's all," Luca replied hastily.

"Last night, the Altairians brought me up to their starship to talk. We spent six hours together. They showed me so many different things. Let me tell you about one of them. They showed me how humanity would evolve if the TPA's form of government was implemented across the human-controlled worlds. In the short run, we thrived and did very well. But long-term, we eventually stifled our development and became no better than the Zodarks. Then they showed me how humanity would evolve under your form of government. Again, it thrived for a while, but ultimately it would become controlled by megacorporations and the super-wealthy.

"Then they showed me a hybrid form of government, merging the best parts of our political systems. It's the same government their allies the Primords currently have. Under this form of government, humanity not only thrives, it survives and grows for thousands of years because it's able to adapt and change as our people, technology, and situations change. They told me the best form of government was the one I outlined to you and the ones our new Primord allies currently have.

"At first, I didn't like being told by an alien species how to govern or run our planet and people. But the more I thought about it, Alice, the more I realized they were right. I know this is a lot, but I think we should reorganize our planet and government the way they suggested."

President Luca blew some air out from her lips. *This is a lot to take in*, she thought. She couldn't just agree to this proposal over a holographic talk.

"Jinping, let's meet tonight and discuss this further," she proposed. "I'd like to talk with the Altairians myself about this. In principle, I agree with what you said, but I need some more information and some time to think about it first."

The two talked for a few minutes more before they ended their call with an agreement to meet soon.
*******

Sitting aboard the Altairian starship in orbit above Earth, the human delegation looked on at the two representatives. Handolly, the protocol officer, and Pandolly, the captain of the ship, were aboard.

"Then it's agreed," Handolly said matter-of-factly. "Your people will reform your government and accept our terms to officially become members of the Galactic Empire."

The Republic and TPA leaders exchanged a quick look with each other and then nodded. "We both agree," Chairman Hong Jinping said on behalf of the TPA.

Handolly looked at President Luca. "You are in agreement? Your country will accept these terms?"

For a moment, Luca hesitated. She knew she had to agree. If humanity was to survive, there really wasn't much of a choice. They wouldn't last very long on their own against the Zodarks. They'd been lucky up to this point, but that luck could only hold out for so long. What was causing her to pause was that she'd just realized that in a few seconds, she would officially become the last president. She was actually surprised she hadn't thought about that until right this moment. How could she not have even considered that? Looking at Jinping, she realized he must have thought the same thing. He was essentially the last leader of China.

Steeling her nerves, she lifted her chin up a bit as she replied with conviction and confidence in her voice. "I am. The People of the Republic accept your offer. We welcome the Altairians and the opportunity to join the Galactic Empire."

The Altairians' facial expressions never changed; Luca wasn't sure if they could. However, the two of them did seem pleased once both sides had agreed to the terms.

"Excellent, then it is official. You will now be known as the Human Republic within the Empire. We will work with you on establishing an embassy and permanent presence in the Senate. As a new member of the alliance, you will have full voting rights and representation in the Empire immediately," Handolly explained with a bit more excitement and emotion than they had seen him show up to this point.

After they had congratulated the humans on joining the Empire, Pandolly announced, "We have a pair of Altairian battleships and four cruisers on their way to Sol. They will help shore up the human defenses against the Zodarks until the human shipyards can integrate the new technology we will be providing.

"We will give you eighteen months to have your first battlegroup ready for combat with an Empire fleet. You will now be responsible for fielding a battlegroup's worth of ships and ground forces every five years for the foreseeable future in the Empire. This is your contribution to the alliance you have just joined."

The humans were also being given dominion of thirty-two-star systems, which included the current three they occupied and one planet closer to the Altairian home world to colonize and establish as a conduit between humans and the many other species that comprised the Galactic Empire or GE as the Altairians called it. The remaining twenty-eight systems were under Zodark and Orbot control. If the humans wanted them, they'd have to fight for them.

## Chapter Eighteen
## Birth of the New Republic

**Four Months Later**
**Jacksonville, Arkansas**

The shuttle carrying Rear Admiral Miles Hunt to the surface made several slow arcs around Jacksonville and the Little Rock Spaceport. Hunt looked out the window in awe at how much the place had changed in such a short time.

Once Earth had allied with the Altairians, a new, unified human government had formed as part of the new pact. Not all the people of Earth had agreed with this proposal. A surprisingly large percentage of people had wanted to hang on to their national identities, even in the face of the pending Zodark threat. Many world leaders, including a lot of people in the Republic, and even the Tri-Parte Alliance, felt they were giving up the right to self-determination. There were some initial protests during the first few weeks of the transition, but as more technology and information was shared with the people of Earth, they died down.

The Altairians eventually showed themselves directly to the people of Earth. They gave the Earthers a simple choice: they could live as they once had without the new technologies provided to Earth, and risk annihilation by the Orbots and their proxies the Zodarks, or they could accept the alliance with the Galactic Empire. There was no middle ground, and eventually, everyone accepted the new reality, begrudgingly as that might have been.

It didn't take the people of Earth long to start coming up with some new nicknames to call their Altairian allies. The more neutral terms were Alts, ETs, or Ghosts on account of their white skin. Less flattering was White Walkers, after an old fantasy book and TV series *Game of Thrones* by George R.R. Martin, popular eighty years ago. In that series, the all-white characters brought either death or assimilation wherever they went. More than a handful of Earthers felt that was what the Altairians had brought Earth: death, or assimilation.

Hunt only had pleasant interactions with their new allies. One of their military commanders and ship captains, Pandolly, took Hunt under his wing. The weapons and capabilities of their new ally astounded him. Hunt had thought the Zodarks were an advanced society, but they paled in comparison to the power of the Alts. What concerned Hunt was that, as powerful as the Alts were, they had been unable to defeat the Orbots after being at war with them for thousands of years. It unnerved him a bit that there were alien races out there that had as much power as the Alts, or even more.

Hunt returned his gaze to the city below. He liked how Jacksonville was shaping up. Although the Alts had more or less promised to allow humans to govern themselves, they had determined that this new unified human government should have a new capital city or governing seat of power, and there was no real arguing on that point. For reasons no one on Earth could understand, the Altairians had recommended the small city of Jacksonville, Arkansas. President Luca had agreed because it was the home to the former Little Rock Air Force Base. It had been converted decades ago into a Space Command spaceport, an alternate command post should something happen to the current HQ in Florida. This would make it easier to make link the capital to Space Command systems.

When the Alts had recommended Jacksonville become the de facto capital city for humanity on Earth, the entire place had transformed overnight. Anyone who owned a home, business, or land within a twenty-mile radius of the city suddenly became a millionaire as land prices went through the roof.

Hunt wasn't sure how the new government had convinced so many people to sell their land, but the Human Republic had acquired nearly the entire town and everything around it for close to ten miles. In a herculean feat, the government had cleared the place in preparation to build some super-advanced new mega-city based on designs and suggestions from the Altairians.

Around the newly redesigned spaceport, Hunt saw a handful of transport craft had already landed. *The others must have arrived already.*

For Hunt, the last four months had been a busy time. His battlegroup had tagged along with an Altairian group during a major battle in a star system near Rhea. It was the first time Hunt had seen an Orbot ship and a Zodark star destroyer, and he could safely say that without the help of the Altairians, humanity would have been wiped out.

The Alts had lost both of their cruisers and Hunt three-quarters of his fleet in the engagement. In exchange, they had destroyed the Orbot ships and the entire Zodark fleet. The Alts said it would most likely be years before the Zodarks would try to attack the Earthers again. The

Orbots would leave this lesser fight to their proxies after the bloody nose they'd just received, and now that they knew the Altairians were allies. The fact was, Earth wasn't strategically important enough to expend more resources trying to defeat and occupy it—at least not yet.

The Altairians said humanity needed to use this period between battles to rapidly build up new warships—ships they would show their human allies how to build and operate. Hunt had been summoned dirtside for this very purpose. The Alts wanted his opinion on the new ships before they finalized their designs and handed them off to the human shipbuilders.

Hunt was a bit excited about this meeting. He was eager to see the new Altairian starship designs for their human allies and how their weapons and capabilities would differ from what they were currently using.

When the shuttle finally landed, the rear ramp opened, letting in the morning sun and a fresh breeze. Standing at the edge of the ramp, Hunt took in a deep breath of honest-to-goodness air and let it out slowly. For nearly eight years, he'd spent nearly all his time on either the John Glenn Station or a starship, so it was refreshing to breathe in the fresh air and feel the warmth of the sun on his skin.

A lieutenant and a captain walked up to greet him, snapping off a crisp salute, which he quickly returned.

"Do you have any bags you need us to take care of, sir?" asked the captain, his eyes looking behind him and into the rear of the shuttle.

Hunt shook his head. "No, I'm just down here for the day, then back up to the station."

"Very well, sir. We'll lead you to the briefing room. They have some fresh coffee and pastries inside if you'd like some fresh-cooked Earth food," the captain said with a slight smile.

Walking off the ramp of the shuttle, Hunt said, "That'd be great, Captain. Food cooked on Earth always seems to taste a bit better than the stuff they make on the station or a starship."

Three months ago, when the Earth's militaries had been reformed, Hunt had been promoted from rear admiral lower half or a one-star to a full rear admiral or two-star. He was still getting used to some of the new protocols for being a senior flag officer in the new, unified human military.

As he walked toward the main building, Hunt got a good view of all the activity on the flight line. He spotted a couple of the new ground attack VTOLs the Army was going to start fielding. They were slick-looking flying death machines, but most importantly, they could deploy from an orbital assault ship—no more transporting them down to the surface in large cargo haulers and putting them back together so they could be used in combat. These little monsters would be able to get into the fight right from the get-go.

Hunt stopped walking for a moment, which caused his minders to practically crash into him. "What is the problem, sir?" the captain asked.

"Captain, I'd like to take a moment to look at that new bird and ask one of those mechanics a quick question."

The captain tilted his head to the left, just like Hunt did every time he checked the time using his neurolink; then he grunted but nodded. "We can spare a few minutes, sir."

The three of them walked over to a group of mechanics who looked to be doing some daily maintenance on the new bird. The group looked up, startled to see a two-star admiral appear out of nowhere.

"Atten-*shun*!" barked one of the sergeants to the surprised mechanics. They all stopped what they were doing and stood ramrod straight, hands at their sides, eyes front.

"At ease, soldiers. I haven't seen one of these things in person yet and wanted to check it out. Can you tell me about it?" asked Hunt as his eyes looked over the machine.

One of the things Hunt liked about being an admiral was stopping and talking with the lower enlisted and junior officers. It helped him stay in tune with what was going on, and it also earned him a lot of respect and loyalty with his crew and those under his command.

Lifting an eyebrow at the question, the sergeant stammered, "Ah, sure thing, sir.

"This, Admiral, is the AS-100, an Army Assault Ship 100," the sergeant continued. "We like to call them Reapers, on account of that they're like the Grim Reaper when they arrive on the scene. They're the latest in ground attack support ships to assist the Army in clearing out some tough targets. They're a single-person ship that can be flown remotely if needed. They come equipped with four pulse beam lasers, two on either side of the cockpit. They also hold thirty of these new little bad boys the Alties told us how to build—they're the latest in smart

268

munitions. You can either fire them like unguided rockets or use them as smart missiles to loiter or target specific targets you tell them to." The sergeant clearly had a sense of pride about working with these new beasts.

Hunt nodded his head in approval. "That's truly incredible, Sergeant," he remarked. "I think you picked a good name for them, Reapers. The title fits. OK, well, that answers my questions. I have a meeting I need to head off to, but thank you for talking with me," Hunt said and then reached into his pocket. He pulled out one of his *George Washington* commander's coins and shook the sergeant's hand, passing him one of his coveted challenge coins.

The sergeant smiled widely, and then his troops went back to work.

The captain politely said, "If you'll follow me, sir, we need to get going to the briefing. It's supposed to start in a few minutes."

Hunt smiled and followed their lead. As they walked, he asked, "Captain, when's the last time you held a command?"

The captain turned slightly as he replied, "It's been a few years, sir. I'm an administrative officer. Most of my military service time has been spent in one headquarters group or another. Why do you ask?"

"When the sergeant was explaining how that new ship worked, you seemed pretty interested, that's all."

The captain shrugged as they walked through the door and into the building. "I find it all very interesting, sir. It's probably the closest I'll get to any action in this new war."

"Would you be interested in a combat posting?" Hunt asked, curious to see what the administrative officer would say.

The captain didn't say anything for a moment. As they approached the briefing room door, he finally said, "If the opportunity were presented to me, sure."

Hunt filed that away in his brain for the time being. As his command responsibilities grew, so did his administrative pain in the butt. He needed good officers who could handle some of these things for him. He made a note to look into the man's service record and ask a few people about him when he got back to the *GW*.

When they entered the briefing room, Hunt saw everyone had finished getting their coffee and a pastry and taken their seats. He quickly found his own seat and whispered to the lieutenant to grab him a coffee and one of those lovely-looking apple danishes.

\*\*\*\*\*\*\*

Fleet Admiral Chester Bailey saw Hunt finally enter the room and head toward his seat.

*Cutting it close, aren't you, Miles?* Chester said over their neurolink, so no one else heard them talk.

*Sorry about that, sir. I got distracted by something on the flight line. Took a moment to talk with a couple of mechanics about those new Reaper VTOLs*, Hunt replied as he sat down.

"It looks like everyone is here. Let's get started," Admiral Bailey said loud enough to get everyone's attention.

Nodding toward Admiral Hunt, Bailey said, "It's good to have Admiral Hunt here with us. He brings some fresh combat experience fighting against the Orbots and with our new allies. The Battle of Two Stars was our first joint battle. I don't have to explain that this was, by far, the costliest battle in our war with the Zodarks and this Orbot-Zodark alien alliance, called the Shadow Dominion.

"We Earthers fought bravely for the Galactic Empire, and the Altairians told me and the Chancellor that despite our losses, we fought exceptionally well. Our allies were impressed with our ability to adapt to the changing dynamics of the battle and inflict serious damage on a superior force with our crude weapon systems."

Many of the officers around the table chuckled at that. The Altairians found it hard to believe the Zodarks had suffered as many defeats against the Earthers as they had, given the human level of sophistication of space weapons. If the Earthers hadn't liberated some of the Sumerians and integrated captured enemy technology, it probably would have been a different story.

Admiral Bailey continued, "Our Altairian allies have shared a vital piece of intelligence with us. The Shadow Dominion is launching a new offensive against another Altairian ally, a group called the Tully." He held a hand up to stop them from asking questions. "I've only been informed about the Tully a few hours ago by our liaison officer, Pandolly. He will provide a briefing tomorrow morning, giving us a better understanding of the alliances in our galaxy—apparently, it's rather complicated. I told him with our simple human brains, it'd be best to show us pictures and diagrams to explain everything."

This last comment drew a few laughs. No one liked change, but so much change had happened these past eight years, especially these last four months. They all had to learn to roll with it and adapt, or it would drive them insane.

"OK, back to these Tully characters. The Orbots' decision to attack them is both good and bad news for humans. While we've never encountered the Tully as of yet, their controlled space is essentially a buffer zone between our little sliver of the galaxy, the Prims', and the Orbots'. With the Orbots' new focus on the Tully, they're ordering the Zodarks to leave us alone and assist them. That means we're going to have a short reprieve to rebuild our navy, integrate the Altairian technology and then learn how to use it."

Admiral Bailey heard several sighs of relief among the officers at the table. After this latest battle, the Earth fleet was in a bit of a shambles.

"It also means if the Tully lose their territory to the Orbots, it'll place an even more dangerous enemy at our doorstep," Bailey explained. "As such, we're going to assist the Tully in their fight as much as we can, given our technological limits. That brings us to the crux of why we are here—in a moment, one of the Altairians will join us and go over the specs of the three new ships. Then the Altairians will go over the mission we've been assigned to help the Tully."

The admiral had barely finished speaking when a transporter aura appeared not far from Admiral Bailey. A split second later, an Altairian materialized in their briefing room.

No matter how many times Bailey watched this happen, it still caught him off guard. The fact that a race of beings could transport a person from a starship in orbit down to the planet in seconds was truly incredible. If only they could do that for thousands of soldiers at a time— that would be truly incredible. As it was, even for the Altairians, it was a relatively new technology and not yet something they were willing to share, even with their closest allies.

"Hello, Admiral Chester Bailey, and military officers of Earth," the lone figure said. "My name is Trigdolly. I am an Altairian shipbuilder and engineer. I have been instructed to present you with several possible ship designs for you to ask questions and approve before I assist your shipbuilders in constructing them. May we begin?" The Altairians were all businesslike—no sense of humor and always direct and to the point.

One of the officers asked a question before Admiral Bailey could screen it. "Excuse me, Trigdolly, I have a question. Have you studied our existing capabilities to know if we can produce these ships, and if we can, would you be able to tell us how long it'll take to retrain our crews to operate this new equipment?"

A lot of the officers at the table nodded—it was a good question, though Admiral Bailey probably would have found a more diplomatic way of asking it.

The Altairian didn't seem fazed at all. "I have spent the last three months examining every known resource in the three systems you control. I have examined your rudimentary shipyards and your production capabilities. For a less-developed species, you have done remarkably well in leveraging humanoid synthetics and 3-D printing."

This was about as close to a compliment as they were going to get from an Altairian. It wasn't that they looked on humans with contempt— it was more like how a parent looks at a five- or six-year-old as they try to teach them how to ride a bike. Of course a parent wants their child to be successful, but they might also get annoyed when the child doesn't seem to understand the basic concept of pedaling and using the front wheel of the bike to help balance and steer. Try as a parent might to explain this to their five-year-old daughter, she may still not grasp the concept and fall several times. This was the kind of relationship the Altairians and the humans had at the moment.

"Sorry for the interruption, Trigdolly," Admiral Bailey said as he shot the rest of the room a dirty look that said they should hold any further questions. "Please continue."

The Altairian placed a small device on the table and turned it on. A moment later, an image of a ship appeared in the center of the table. It turned slowly, allowing everyone to see its detail from different vantage points.

"The ships I am going to show you will be built at the new Republic Navy shipyard you constructed near your moon. This facility, after some modifications by our engineers, is now your most advanced shipyard, able to build the type of ships we are proposing. To get the human fleets built up promptly and allow you to contribute effectively with our own fleets, we propose several classes of ships. Each of these ships has a specific purpose. They have strengths and weaknesses, but when integrated with a combined fleet, they form a powerful force.

"The first ship I am going to show you is a smaller ship your facilities will be able to mass-produce quickly. We call this ship the frigate class 001. What we have done is infuse the best parts of your technology with ours to create a vessel your people will be able to operate, maintain, and construct on your own once we have given you some proper training.

"It is roughly two hundred and twenty meters in length with a crew of fifty-two human operators. As you have made good use of synthetic humanoids, we recommend integrating them into many aspects of the ship's operations. In addition to the fifty-two human crew members, it will be augmented with one hundred and eighty synthetic workers."

Trigdolly then zoomed in on a couple sections of the ship. "Its armament consists of two forward phaser banks and one rear bank. We are impressed with what you have done with your magrail systems, and, frankly, we are surprised at how vulnerable both the Zodark and Orbot ships are against them. For Altairians, this is very old technology—something we have not used in thousands of years. However, it appears to be effective, because most starfaring races have moved on to phasers, masers, plasma, and particle beam weapons, which require a completely different type of armor and defensive measures to defeat. We believe the magrails are a very rudimentary weapon. That said, we are going to exploit this vulnerability while it is still present until they adjust their ship designs."

The Altairian then brought up some detailed schematics of the magrail system for them to look at as he continued to talk. "With this in mind, we have modified your magrail weapons to make them more efficient, but also more potent. Your integration of a small rudder and guidable propulsion system on the projectiles was something we had never seen or even thought of. We have obviously kept that in this new design. We believe this new magrail system is going to make your ships even more potent in battle."

Trigdolly hit a button and an image of Frigate 001 reappeared on the floating holographic image in the center of the table. "This is a frigate 001. It is the smallest fleet vessel we are proposing you build. However, it plays a critical role in overall fleet operations. It is going to be an exceptional fast-attack ship—what you call a picket ship—to operate on the edges of your territory or fleets. As you can see, the ship has only a single twin-barrel turret that will fire a twelve-inch projectile. The

273

muzzle velocity on this improved weapon is one hundred thousand kilometers per second, roughly five times the speed of your current systems."

This elicited a few whistles of excitement from the officers. Bailey was sure many of them would have loved to have had that weapon in their previous battles against the Zodarks.

"The frigates will also be equipped with twenty anti-ship missiles. The new missiles we are helping you build will have several booster phases. Like your magrail systems, we have greatly increased their potency and their speed. The missiles can now reach speeds of one hundred eighty thousand kilometers per second, so they will play a greater role in fleet battles. Aside from direct energy weapons, we have found missiles to be an effective weapon in battle, especially as we improve their stealth and electronic spoofing capabilities. I would also like to point out that in the past, your forces had not made use of atomic weapons. We are changing that. Your missile warheads will now either have conventional high-explosive warheads like what you have been using, or they will be equipped with variable-yield nuclear warheads. However, the atomic weapons we are showing you how to create are weapons designed to be used in space battles—"

One of the admirals interrupted. "Excuse me, Trigdolly—what do you mean by that? We've refrained from using atomic weapons in the past because we didn't want the Zodarks to decide they wanted to use them against our own forces or against Earth."

Trigdolly paused. "Admiral, there is much you will learn about the galactic rules of warfare. Basically, we have a set of rules that state that atomic weapons cannot be used on habitable planets. They are too rare in the galaxy to wantonly destroy them. However, that does not mean they are not used in space warfare. As Admiral Hunt will be able to attest, Orbot ships use a shielding technology in addition to their thick armored shells. The atomic weapons are incredibly effective at degrading and, eventually, defeating their shield technology. The electromagnetic pulse produced by the explosion disrupts the energy frequencies used in the shielding technology. It also absorbs large amounts of the shields' energy, which means the shields become weaker."

Another officer broke in. "If that's the case, then how are we going to effectively defend against these types of weapons?" he pressed. "We haven't encountered the Zodarks using them against us yet, but if they do, how will our ships hold out against them?"

The officers all nodded—this was something they were all concerned about. Frankly, none of them liked the idea of using nukes. They'd rather just focus on the weapon systems they knew and had already been using.

Trigdolly plowed ahead. "What I need you all to understand is that the way you have been fighting space battles is about to change dramatically. While you have not seen the use of atomic weapons by the Zodarks, that does not mean the Orbots or other allied races of theirs do not use them. We are not saying that humans need to use them extensively in your future battles or campaigns, but you need to know how they are used and how to defend against them. Is that understood?"

There was a moment of silence as everyone absorbed what had just been said. When no one objected or asked any further questions, Trigdolly brought up another image of the frigate and continued his explanation.

"We found your primitive use of what you called close-in weapon systems or CIWS to be very effective at intercepting enemy missiles and smaller starfighters. Like your other weapon systems, we have improved this as well. The frigates will now have eight of these systems on board. In addition to their deep space reconnaissance mission capability, when the frigates are placed in a carefully designed screening position, they will be able to protect the larger warships and troop transports exceptionally well."

When Trigdolly had finished going over some of the main features of the new frigates, he told them about the food replicators. Food replicators were an incredible new technology the Altairians had given the humans. In one swoop, this technology had ended hunger and solved an inordinate number of deep space problems for humans.

Previous human ships had either had to stock or grow their own food or bring along replenishment ships that did this for them. It was a huge drain on resources and created a critical vulnerability to any human-operated fleet. By eliminating this need with food replicators, the ships could now be packed with more weapons or given additional armor.

The next twenty minutes went by with Trigdolly showing them two more versions of the proposed frigate. Each version varied slightly in its aesthetics but had essentially the same armaments and number of crew, except for the 003 version. The 003 ship had room for up to sixty additional passengers. One of the officers mentioned that it could come in handy if they wanted to use the frigates to deploy Special Forces or conduct more clandestine missions with a smaller ship.

Eventually, the officers making the decision on the type of frigate the humans would produce settled on the first version, frigate 001. They also decided to produce at least twenty of the 003 version so they could use them for Special Forces missions or to transport high-value individuals. The Altairians agreed but stressed the importance of creating uniformity in their ship production for both simplicity and speed, as well as training the crew to operate them.

Next came the cruisers. Trigdolly explained that these ships would be the workhorses of the fleet and the most prolific ships to be built, next to the frigates.

"The cruisers come in only one choice," Trigdolly announced to the chagrin of everyone in the room. "I believe your Henry Ford once said, 'You can have a Model T in any color you want, so long as it's black.'"

That drew a few chuckles from the officers, and it was the first time they'd seen an Altairian try to be funny or crack a joke.

"The cruiser is your tank. It is heavily armored and packs a punch. The ship is one thousand, four hundred meters long with a crew of eleven hundred and twenty-two people. The ship has four reactors that produce more power than a dozen of the Arkanorian reactors you recently incorporated into your ships. These reactors power the six phaser banks and the twelve thirty-six-inch magrail turrets. We have also included two plasma cannons, which give the ship some serious hitting power."

One of the officers asked, "What kind of armor belt does this cruiser have?"

The Altairian didn't seem fazed by another interruption. He actually seemed to enjoy the fact that the humans asked a lot of questions. "The ship has a twelve-meter-thick armor belt, similar to what you currently use on your existing warships. We have taken the liberty of improving the armor density and its heat dissipation ability. This will allow the ship to absorb direct hits from Orbot ships without exploding in the first few seconds. The ship can also carry up to one hundred and thirty soldiers and a limited number of assault ships to support their operations on the ground. This gives each cruiser the ability to carry out specific missions on the surface of a planet or support Special Forces missions."

"Is there some way to incorporate a shield into these warships?" asked another officer.

Trigdolly turned to look at the officer before replying. "When your child first learns how to drive, do you give them an expensive sports car to learn with, or do you give them a less expensive vehicle they can effectively handle and gain some experience with first?"

No one said anything for a moment as they looked at each other, unsure if this was a rhetorical question.

"When your species has the technological know-how to understand the physics involved in creating, building, and maintaining such technology, then we will share it with you. Until then, let us see if you can handle what we are sharing with you now," Trigdolly replied.

The Altairian brought up the third class of warship. "This is a battleship. This will be the largest warship we will have you create for the time being. The battlegroups that humans will be fielding will be anchored around your battleships. We are not asking you to build many of them, but in time, you will want to build more of them as you expand your territory and hold it.

"Unlike the dreadnought ship you have, the *George Washington*, this ship is smaller but far more capable. It is approximately two thousand, six hundred meters in length. It has an armor belt of forty meters. We have incorporated eight phaser banks and twenty of your magrail turrets, ten on either side. We have also added thirty smaller magrail turrets, fifteen on either side, to give it added punching power. This is in addition to the fifty anti-ship missile tubes. It has a crew of two thousand, two hundred personnel. It can also transport up to two hundred and sixty soldiers."

Hunt leaned forward in his chair. "Trigdolly, how long will it take our shipbuilders to start cranking these warships out?"

All eyes then turned back to the Altairian. Hunt had asked the question a lot of them had been itching to ask.

"These ships are a lot more complicated than the ships you are currently building. Even with our advanced shipbuilding techniques, the frigates will take eight months to complete. The cruisers will take fifteen months, and the battleships will take two years. We have a fourth ship, but I am not sure if your people are ready for that one yet. It may be too soon to introduce this to you," Trigdolly said. His last sentence caused them all to perk up. A new ship they hadn't been told about piqued everyone's attention.

Hunt cleared his throat. "Perhaps you can tell us about this new fourth ship, and we can give you an honest answer about whether we can handle it or not."

Trigdolly briefly looked at Admiral Bailey to see if he had any objections. He nodded, and Trigdolly went on to explain. "The fourth ship is a star carrier. It is a brute of a ship, and frankly, you need to build up your other naval ships before you take on a ship like this. We also would need to spend some time training a fighter wing. You presently have no fighter pilots. No, drone pilots do not count. Nothing replaces a live operator inside a fighter."

One of the officers asked, "How large is this ship? How many fighters can it carry, and how long would it take to build?"

"So many questions about a ship you are not ready for," Trigdolly countered. "In due time, when you are prepared, we will help you build these star carriers. For the moment, we need you focused on building a suitable navy to protect your tiny area of space and become an ally the rest of the alliance can depend on."

The meeting broke up a few hours later for lunch. Many of the officers wanted to grill Admiral Hunt on how the battle had gone. They had all seen the reports and the classified videos, but they wanted to ask questions the videos didn't answer.

The discovery of so many new alien races over the last few years had turned their worlds upside down. The knowledge that humans had been transplanted from Earth to a smattering of other planets around the galaxy had come as a big shock. When they'd learned how the Zodarks were essentially farming humans to use as disposable soldiers in their galactic war, it had only further infuriated the humans on Earth.
*******


"Admiral Hunt, why did we lose so many of our ships during this last battle?" asked one of the captains. The others at the table stopped talking amongst themselves as they waited to hear his response.

Hunt felt everyone's eyes on him. He knew they wanted to know why so many of their friends had died, and yet, he'd lived. His own ship, the *GW*, had sustained near-catastrophic damage. This was the part of command he really hated, ordering the deaths of so many of his fellow

Earthers in a battle that wouldn't ultimately change the outcome of the war. It was one thing to go into a battle of survival where there wouldn't be any second chances. But while this last battle might have ultimately saved Earth, it didn't even register as monumental in this enormous galactic war.

Hunt placed his fork down on the table as he looked at the officer who'd asked the question. "When the battle started, the Orbots jumped a battleship and three cruisers through the stargate. The Altairians moved their cruisers to engage them, and two Altairian battleships joined the fray. At that point, the Altairians ordered our human fleet in to assist them, and our ships engaged the Orbot ships. Just like the Zodark ships, Orbot ships proved to be vulnerable to our magrails. We didn't score the same level of damage against them like we have against the Zodark vessels, but we were getting through their armor and causing some considerable damage."

Hunt paused for a second as he shook his head. "One of the Orbot ships fired its particle beam and hit the *Yorktown*. It…it sliced the ship in half with a single shot. The Orbot then hit it a couple more times, blowing up the remaining pieces—they didn't even have time to eject their life pods. At that point, I ordered our fleet to reposition behind the Altairian ships so we could use them as shields if needed. At the same time, we continued to snipe at the Orbot ships with our magrails."

"That's when the Zodarks showed up, right?" asked another rear admiral, a grim look on his face.

Hunt nodded. He reached for his glass of water, noticing a slight tremor in his hand. He tightened his grip on the glass so his hand wouldn't shake. Just talking about the experience was causing him to feel like a panic attack was about to happen.

"That's right," Hunt continued. "At first, it was just a couple of Zodark cruisers and then a battleship. Nothing we hadn't seen or battled before. Our fleet tore into them while the Alts continued to battle the Orbot ships. Then this massive ship jumped right in the middle of our formation. It was the first time I had ever seen a Zodark star destroyer. The ship was massive, as I'm sure you've seen from the videos. It was nearly twice as big as the *GW*, and man, did it pack a punch. I ordered our engines to full speed, and we attempted to run a circular path around the enemy fleet so our vessels could continue to use our magrails and pound them."

As Hunt continued to recount the battle, more of the officers sitting nearby stopped talking and eating to listen. "The *GW* got hit by a particle beam from that star destroyer. It ripped into the lower four decks of the ship and nearly cut through us. It took half of our secondary weapons offline with a single blow. By this point, though, we had positioned ourselves so the majority of our primary gun systems were now able to fire on them. We opened up with everything we had. We hit them with a spread of twelve plasma torpedoes, two dozen Havoc missiles, and hundreds of slugs from our primary weapons…the enemy ship just took it. We were scoring hits, we could see secondary explosions rippling across its decks, but we weren't scoring the knockout blows we needed. Meanwhile, that particle beam weapon knocked another one of our battleships out.

"Captain Zamani's ship had already been critically hit when he ordered his ship to ram the star destroyer. I don't think the Zodarks knew what he was doing, at least not right away. Once it became clear he wasn't just maneuvering for a better shot but was lining up to ram them, they turned all their weapons on the *New York*. Zamani somehow managed to get his MPD thrusters almost up to full speed when the ship was practically blown apart by an Orbot ship. They hit it with a particle beam that sliced the entire rear half of the ship off. Fortunately, for us, the forward momentum of the fore section of the ship was still headed right for the star destroyer. The front of the ship plowed into the midsection of the Zodark vessel. It continued to impale itself all the way up the rest of the ship until it had completely pulverized the command section.

"At that point, chains of explosions rippled along the star destroyer. By then, the Altairians had all but destroyed the Orbot ships, and there were only a few Zodark vessels left. With the star destroyer taken out, we were able to finish the rest of the enemy fleet off," Hunt finished explaining.

One of the captains commented, "I saw that video. I couldn't believe Captain Zamani was able to get the *New York* turned around like that and was able to hit them. That was some real heroic stuff right there."

Hunt nodded solemnly. "Yes, it was. I think he single-handedly won the battle for us. I think if he hadn't sacrificed his ship like that, the *GW* and the rest of the fleet might have been destroyed by that particle beam weapon. He and his crew died so the rest of us could live. I want to personally let you all know that I've recommended him for the Medal of Honor and valor medals for the entire crew. It's the least we can do to honor their sacrifice and loss."

Another captain asked him, "If the Altairian ships they're going to help us build are as good as they say they are, do you think we have a chance at beating the Zodarks and the Orbots? I mean, is there any hope that we can win this war, or are we just prolonging the inevitable?"

A few of the officers shot the captain a dirty look for sounding defeatist, especially in front of Admiral Hunt and the other admirals, but Hunt came to the man's defense.

"That's a good question, Captain. It's one I've struggled with as well. I think we have to believe that we can win. Otherwise, what are we doing this all for?" Hunt paused for a second. He wanted to be truthful with them, but he also needed them to know that there was hope, even if it was small. "I think there are some long, dark days ahead of us, and we are certainly in for some rough times. However, I also think that as long as we continue to adapt, overcome, and never give up, we'll make it. Remember, it was just five decades ago we developed interplanetary travel. Less than two decades ago, we developed faster-than-light travel. Eight years ago, we discovered the Zodarks and the Sumerians. Eight months ago, the Altairians made first contact with us. Humanity has come a long way in a very short time. Let's not forget that."

Hunt sat up straighter, feeling emboldened. "The Altairians have agreed to let us join their alliance, and they're helping us build a naval force to defend our territory and be an active member of their alliance. It's up to us to use that time to build up a substantial navy and find new ways to integrate their technology and advance it further. We can do this, and more importantly, we *must* do this. I couldn't be prouder of the officers and enlisted we get to serve with, and together, we are going to win this war, no matter how long it takes."

After that rousing little speech, everyone in the dining facility that heard it cheered and clapped. Humanity had been kicked in the nuts, but now humanity was recovering and was about to unleash holy hell on its enemies.
*******


When everyone had finished lunch and returned to the briefing room, Trigdolly went over the new training requirements that needed to be put in place to get the human crews ready to operate and maintain these advanced new warships. This part of the briefing, frankly, bored Hunt to death. From his point of view, it was a colossal waste of his valuable experience and time. To think his shore leave with his wife was canceled so he could sit through this part of the briefing ticked him off— he'd probably been gone from his wife more than nearly any other military officer in the last eight years. All Hunt wanted was a handful of months with nothing to do other than write his memoirs and spend time with his wife and his two grown kids.

His son, Ethan, was blossoming into a real capable officer himself. Despite only having a few years of service in the fleet, he had been promoted twice and received a Silver Star, a Bronze Star with V device, and a Purple Heart. He was well on his way to one day becoming an admiral like his father.

Admiral Bailey must have sensed Hunt's annoyance. He sent him a short note via their neurolink for him to join him in his office.

It took Hunt a few minutes to find the place. The entire headquarters building was brand-new, and this was his first time visiting the new base after all the changes. Even now, the base was crawling with Synths expanding the sprawling facility. They had already completed the command center and bunkers deep below the facility. Now they were building the aesthetically pleasing upper levels of the massive edifice.

Rounding a corner, Hunt was greeted by Admiral Bailey's assistant, an old battle-axe of a woman. She was nice to Hunt, mostly because he'd shared a lot of baby pictures with her when his kids were little and continued to share more throughout the years. She was a brute to everyone else, though.

"There you are, Miles. It's so good to see you. I heard your mini-me, Ethan, is turning into a real war hero like his dad," she said as she gave him a gentle hug.

"He sure is, Yvette. It's good to see you as well. How are you liking the new digs?" Hunt asked.

"Oh, you know me, I'm comfortable wherever I go. I do miss Florida, though," she said cheerfully. She led them down the hall and into her outer office. Everyone had to get past Yvette if they wanted to see the admiral. That used to be a challenge until the Altairians had demonstrated that teleportation was actually possible.

"The weather was much nicer there than here, but I'll make do. You can go on in; Chester's expecting you," Yvette said, motioning toward the office door.

As he walked into the room, Hunt saw Admiral Bailey sitting on one of the couches with two Altairians. The three of them stood when he entered.

"Come on in, Miles. Take a seat. We have something we'd like to talk with you about. Oh, and call me Chester, it's just the four of us," Bailey said, wanting to put Hunt at ease that this would be a casual conversation.

Hunt took his seat on the couch, unsure what to make of this impromptu meeting. It sure beat going over training requirements.

"Miles, there is much we don't know about this galaxy and military alliance we're now a part of. Handolly—you remember him, don't you, Miles?" Chester asked as he reintroduced the Altairian liaison to Earth.

"Of course I remember Handolly. It's a pleasure to meet with you again," Hunt said, giving an Altairian greeting in their native language. He was sure he was butchering it, but it was the thought that counted.

For the first time since meeting the Altairians, Hunt noticed a facial expression from Handolly. He said something in his language Hunt couldn't understand, but he nodded anyway.

"Pandolly speaks very highly of you, Miles," said Handolly. "He says you are an exceptional military commander—not afraid to take risks when needed, but not so cavalier that you would put your ship or fleet in any more danger than is absolutely necessary to win a battle. This is a hard trait to find in military commanders."

Hunt felt his cheeks reddening a bit. This was the first time he'd ever received praise from an Altairian. They were not accustomed to this human trait.

"Miles, Pandolly is not just a ship captain in our navy," Handolly continued. "He is an admiral of equivalent rank to yours. He is part of a first contact team that helps us assess and determine if a race should be allowed to join the Galactic Empire. If it is believed they can make a contribution, then he helps to integrate them into our coalition.

"Your ship, the *George Washington,* is going to need more than twelve months of repairs before it will be operational again. It is also going to take nearly two years to build your new ships, given the rudimentary size and capability of your shipyards. I have proposed to

Chester that he allow you, along with many of your leading scientists, engineers, and military officers, to accompany me back to our home world, Altus. By your units of measurement, Altus is close to three million light-years away from Earth. With our advanced travel capabilities, we can traverse that distance in several weeks."

Hunt took a deep breath in and let it out. This was a lot to take in.

"I would like to take your people on a tour of the Galactic Empire," Handolly explained. "This would be an opportunity for you to meet your new allies and gain a better understanding of what you are fighting for, who you are fighting with, and what you are fighting against. When we eventually arrive in Altus, we will spend some intensive time training and educating you on many of our ways. Your scientists and engineers will be taught many new technologies and ways to understand how the universe works. While this is taking place, your new star carrier and human flagship will be built by our shipyard. When it is completed, you and the rest of your people will return to Earth with your new star carrier. This will be a long trip if you come with us, nearly three of your years in length. Would you like to go?" Handolly asked as his eyes surveyed Hunt.

Bailey chimed in to add, "You'd be able to bring Lilly, Miles. If you wanted to bring your daughter or Ethan, I could arrange it. I'm not going to order you to go, but this is a great opportunity, Miles. Something I wish I could do but can't do myself."

Hunt smiled as he thought about it all. This was a great opportunity—the chance to see not one but multiple new planets and races along the way.

"Wow, Chester. This is an interesting proposition. Are you sure my presence here wouldn't be missed or needed?"

Bailey leaned back on the couch. "Your presence and leadership would always be missed; there's no doubt about that. But you'd be returning to Earth with an incredible new warship for us. Frankly, we need someone of your caliber to learn as much as possible about our new coalition and develop those trading and military alliances we'll need long-term. I couldn't think of a better person to represent Earth than you, Miles."

"As long as Lilly can come with me, count me in," Hunt replied. "I'll talk with Ethan and our daughter and see what they think. I certainly don't want to hurt their military careers or anything."

Pandolly stood up. "Excellent, then it is settled. Please inform your wife and the others. We will leave Earth in three days."

# Chapter Nineteen
## Task Force Intus

**Space Command HQ**
**Jacksonville, Arkansas**

"I don't like it, Admiral. It leaves my forces way too exposed on the ground," General Ross McGinnis said.

General Pilsner, the head of the Republic Army, agreed.

Shaking his head as he sighed, Admiral Bailey looked at the planet and the disposition of the enemy fleet around it.

Admiral Halsey interjected, "We could break the assault force down into two task forces. The first one swoops in to attack the enemy ships and break the blockade. During the cover of battle, we could have several of our Special Forces units conduct an orbital assault to take out the ground-based laser defense systems. Once they're taken out, and the battle around the planet is in full swing, my second task force jumps in to finish off the enemy ships. Then we can disembark the rest of the infantry to support the Special Forces already on the ground."

No one said anything for a moment as they each looked at the disposition of the troops and ships Admiral Halsey had just mentioned. They were running through the various scenarios in their heads.

"It's risky, but it just might work," General Pilsner finally said.

General McGinnis grunted at the suggestion. "If your force doesn't break up the blockade and get those reinforcements planetside quick, you'd be leaving a lot of Special Forces alone to die on that planet," he countered.

"Then my ships had best not fail," Halsey shot back, confident that they could get the job done.

"What kind of support are the Primords going to give us?" asked General McGinnis.

"You mean on the ground or in space?" clarified Admiral Halsey.

"I mean in space. My guys can handle the ground operations. I'm more concerned about us either getting trapped on the planet or not getting enough forces dirtside fast enough to make a difference," McGinnis countered.

Admiral Bailey walked up to the holographic map floating in front of them. "I've been assured by the Altairians that a fleet of twenty

Primord ships will support our operation. Once we begin the ground operations, they have some two hundred thousand soldiers they'll be dispatching to assist us in recapturing the planet."

The generals and admirals didn't say anything right away. They looked at the planet and the data at hand. This was a tall order they'd been given. It was their first real military operation with the Galactic Empire. They'd been given six months to prepare to help their new allies, the Primords, retake a planet they had lost thirty years earlier to the Zodarks.

The planet had been a Primord colony for three hundred years until the Zodarks had managed to wrestle it away from them. The leaders of Earth had hoped to have more time to build and prepare themselves to battle the Zodarks again, but the Altairians said the recapture of this planet was important in keeping the balance of power in this region of space tilted in the Galactic Empire's direction. They'd been tasked with assisting the Primords in retaking the planet with the existing ships and troops they had on hand.

Nodding in acceptance, General Ross McGinnis looked the others in the eye. "Admiral Halsey, if your task force can break that blockade business, I'm confident my Special Forces can carry out an orbital insertion to take out those ion cannons on the planet. Once they're down, though, you've got to have a path cleared and ready for the infantry. If you're certain your forces can do it, then I say we move forward with this."

Halsey paused for just a moment before she responded, and a smile crept across her face. "My forces will clear you a path, General. You take those Ion cannons out, and I'll get you that infantry."

With nothing more to be said, Operation Intus was officially a go.

## From the Authors

I hope you've enjoyed this book. If you're ready to continue the action with book three of the Rise of the Republic Series, simply visit Amazon to reserve your copy of *Into the War*.

If you would like to stay up to date on new releases and receive emails about any special pricing deals we may make available, please sign up for our email distribution list. Simply go to https://www.frontlinepublishinginc.com/ and sign up.

If you enjoy audiobooks, we have a great selection that has been created for your listening pleasure. Our entire Red Storm series and our Falling Empire series have been recorded, and several books in our Rise of the Republic series and our Monroe Doctrine series are now available. Please see below for a complete listing.

As independent authors, reviews are very important to us and make a huge difference to other prospective readers. If you enjoyed this book, we humbly ask you to write up a positive review on Amazon and Goodreads. We sincerely appreciate each person that takes the time to write one.

We have really valued connecting with our readers via social media, especially on our Facebook page https://www.facebook.com/RosoneandWatson/. Sometimes we ask for help from our readers as we write future books—we love to draw upon all your different areas of expertise. We also have a group of beta readers who get to look at the books before they are officially published and help us fine-tune last-minute adjustments. If you would like to be a part of this team, please go to our author website, and send us a message through the "Contact" tab.

You may also enjoy some of our other works. A full list can be found below:

Nonfiction:
**Iraq Memoir 2006–2007 Troop Surge**
*Interview with a Terrorist* (audiobook available)

Fiction:
### The Monroe Doctrine Series
*Volume One* (audiobook available)
*Volume Two* (audiobook available)
*Volume Three* (audiobook available)
*Volume Four* (audiobook still in production)
*Volume Five* (available for preorder)

### Rise of the Republic Series
*Into the Stars* (audiobook available)
*Into the Battle* (audiobook available)
*Into the War* (audiobook available)
*Into the Chaos* (audiobook available)
*Into the Fire* (audiobook still in production)
*Into the Calm* (available for preorder)

### Apollo's Arrows Series (co-authored with T.C. Manning)
*Cherubim's Call* (available for preorder)

### Crisis in the Desert Series (co-authored with Matt Jackson)
*Project 19* (audiobook available)
*Desert Shield*
*Desert Storm*

### Falling Empires Series
*Rigged* (audiobook available)
*Peacekeepers* (audiobook available)
*Invasion* (audiobook available)
*Vengeance* (audiobook available)
*Retribution* (audiobook available)

### Red Storm Series
*Battlefield Ukraine* (audiobook available)
*Battlefield Korea* (audiobook available)
*Battlefield Taiwan* (audiobook available)
*Battlefield Pacific* (audiobook available)
*Battlefield Russia* (audiobook available)
*Battlefield China* (audiobook available)

**Michael Stone Series**
*Traitors Within* (audiobook available)

**World War III Series**
*Prelude to World War III: The Rise of the Islamic Republic and the Rebirth of America* (audiobook available)
*Operation Red Dragon and the Unthinkable* (audiobook available)
*Operation Red Dawn and the Siege of Europe* (audiobook available)
*Cyber Warfare and the New World Order* (audiobook available)

Children's Books:
*My Daddy has PTSD*
*My Mommy has PTSD*

## Abbreviation Key

| | |
|---|---|
| 1MC | Main Circuit (shipboard public address system) |
| AAR | After-Action Review |
| BLUF | Bottom Line Up Front |
| CIC | Combat Information Center |
| CIWS | Close-In Weapons System |
| CO | Commanding Officer |
| COP | Combat Outpost |
| DG | Division Group |
| ECM | Electronic Countermeasures |
| EPR | Enlisted Performance Report |
| EW | Electronic Warfare |
| EWO | Electronics Warfare Officer |
| FTL | Faster-than-Light |
| GE | Galactic Empire |
| GEU | Greater European Union |
| GM | Gunner's Mate |
| GW | George Washington |
| HB | Heavy Blaster |
| HE | High-explosive |
| HQ | Headquarters |
| HUD | Heads-Up Display |
| HVI | High Value Individual |
| KIA | Killed in Action |
| MA | Master at Arms |
| MPD | Magnetoplasmadynamic |
| MPH | Megameters per Hour |
| MS | Multiple Sclerosis |
| MWR | Morale, Welfare and Recreation |
| NCO | Noncommissioned Officer |
| NL | Neurolink |
| NOS | Zodark admiral or senior military commander |
| PA | Personal Assistant |
| PFC | Private First Class |
| PR | Public Relations |
| R&D | Research and Development |
| R&R | Rest and Recreation |

| | |
|---|---|
| RA | Republic Army |
| RAS | Republic Army Soldier |
| RNS | Republic Navy Ship |
| SET | Space Exploration Treaty |
| SF | Special Forces |
| SITREP | Situation Report |
| SW | Sand and Water (missiles) |
| TPA | Tri-Parte Alliance |
| VAC | Vertical Assault Craft |
| VBC | Victory Base Complex |
| VIP | Very Important Person |
| VTOL | Vertical Take-off and Landing |
| XO | Commanding Officer |

Printed in the USA
CPSIA information can be obtained
at www.ICGtesting.com
LVHW012208030424
776388LV00008B/201

9 781957 634050